W.K. PHOENIX

—PRESENTS—

PECULIAR CASES OF SOMETHING DEVINE:

GRAVITY OF DEVOTION

(PART 2)

Table Of Contents

"The World Committee sends their regards to those affected by the Cloudy Curse Tragedy. Provisions have been sent to those affected in the region. We wish you an impactful healing journey."

Chapter Zero

It's another marvelous day.

"**M**e for a devil? Yeah, sure, like my wife gives me the time. If I'm home a minute after seven, no MAM for a week."

"Still watch that child's play? Get up on LCW; that's where it's at."

"Wrestling blokes in tights'll never match true martial arts masters. Maybe you should've married my wife since you share views."

"You'va knack for exaggeration. No wonder Zoa makes sure your days off are far away from the precinct. Your wife's doing you a favour. Knockout her age should be zipping through London with her best mates, seeking some flesh closer to her generation."

"Bite me. And tell your son to stay away. Or this town'll be missing another kid."

"There's the villain I know. Hell, you might've done the bloker yourself. I heard all about your family's history with blood. That damn Head Case beat you to it. And my son's a grown man."

"Twenty and pissing crooked. Hey, she's here."

"Who?"

"Cam Scrubber's guardian."

"Ah. Shithell. Think she's working for the Head Case? Cleaned up the evidence?"

"Not at all. She's one of them loony kids from last year."

"Damn. Our town is cursed indeed. Poor lassie."

The steel bars slid open to the left, bringing in a waft of nougat, garlic and a hint of marijuana. Polished brown shoes entered the frame as the last bar **clanged** into the pocket of the cell's entrance. The pair of shoes moved further into the cell. They were in impeccable shape.

Clean. Unlike me. The eyes of THE PRISONER stayed on the shoes. Her mouth opened.

"It's alright. We'll fix this. Come on." The man's voice was desert dry, but brought promise of rainbows and clouds into the dank cell.

Just like it always has. The Prisoner's mouth closed. She rose to her feet and followed the brown shoes out of the cell, keeping her eyes fixed on them as She made her way down the hallway. They passed the two detectives She had heard speaking a few moments ago, and up to the front desk, where She stood beside the man with the brown shoes.

A pair of chunky purple loafers stepped on the other side of The Prisoner.

The Prisoner slouched, walking a few paces behind her *guardian.*

The older woman turned to her with piercing blue eyes on her *irresponsible granddaughter. Huh?*

The Prisoner stared at a deep, dark red cut on her grandmother's cheek. "What happened to your face?"

"That mangy token in the basement caught me off guard. Think it's time I expelled it."

"I can help."

"I'd say your rage has fulfilled its appetite." The grandmother faced forward and pointed to something as they walked past it. "When a Devine is knocked to hell, they stand right back up."

The trunk of the crooked tree she pointed at stood up straight as though it heard her. Its blue-indigo branches expanded like wings with firm golden leaves, despite it being the windiest day of the week so far. It was the only tree of its kind amongst the rest of the greenery.

The Prisoner took her gloved right hand in her left. Squeezed it. "It's a better Devine than me."

Gma told me that after Clou... after that thing from last year... after that despicable, worthless, manipulating thing— our lives would be more susceptible to further cursed spirits who relish feeding on weary souls.

She was right.

And I can't do much about it because I've never stopped being fed on. Every day I lose a little more of myself.

If you're reading this... it was nice knowing you.

— Amy D.

BEFORE

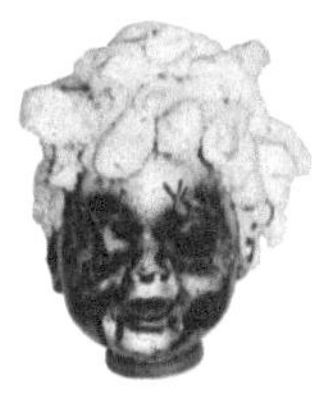

Chapter One

The Death of you / r.i.p. you

"*Eres sólo ficción para tu alma. Alma es tu Prime. Es Overbeing. Debes escucharlo. Listen.*" The patient sensation *seethed* inside her rectal cavity before it spread through her chest, then exploded out of her head, wiping everything with it. Those *trivial* attributes gripping her: creativity, individuality, purpose, and whatever else plagiarized the whole of her—gone. Falsities ripped from her unimpressive head swifter than the blade of a guillotine. Even that would be less painful. Nothing remained inside this *useless carcass.*

What use is my inner power? What use am I?

—"*Debes escucharlo. Listen.*"— The woman's words floated in the air of *my mind.* "¿Qué alimenta tu ira?" The green-haired spiritualist asked with a twinkle of pink in her eye. She sat right across from—

SHE. She picked at the loose denim straps on the knees of her black jeans. The clouds in her eyes were captivated by this moment where cannabis kept the lovely green-haired woman's questions far from her consciousness. *Her gorgeous verde updo is classic; ala Selena Quintanilla. I'm not worthy of its presence.*

"¿Qué alimenta tu deseo?" The waves of the green-haired spiritualist's voice danced around then through the earlobes of She.

She just stared at this spiritualist, *ignorant of my woes. But she came this far to help—What can I give her? The last year's been... a razor blade in the ass.* Continued to ignore her grandmother's passive-aggressive stare beside her. She chuckled at the triangular formation of her *intervention* that the three of them made in the middle of her messy bedroom. *Doesn't matter. Today could be... the day I die. Any day it's possible. Doesn't make it any less scary.*

"¿Qué alimenta tu corazón?"

Living on time that isn't mine. My time ended a year ago. Thoughts rushed. She dipped further into her chair. Her eyes landed on the back of her right hand and stayed on the scar it wore in shame from a year prior, burned in for eternity. *The ruler of* her mental captivity. She shifted her scarred hand between her thighs.

She carved away into her notebooks—the ones she loved, but her *psychotic town refused to do away with despite the rest of the World's advancement. Why?* The astronomically derelict collective minds of a people far too stuck in faded memories. She wondered *more than they ever could.* Yet her imagination was a foreign entity she longed to regain.

"They'd never understand..." She repeated at least a dozen times since *07:08* this morning. *Why should I walk outside amongst them all when they'd never accept my world in theirs?*

Chitter-irp-chit-irp. Chitterchitterchitterchitter-irp

A quick glare at her room's walls, but even her fury couldn't hold its stare. *Dread it. Run. Destiny remains sealed. What time was it now?* Morning and evening, it all blended in. Which was She at? *Might be best to disregard...*

C h i t t e r c h i t t e r - i r p - c h i t - i r p - c h i t - i r p . **Chitterchitterchitterchitterchitterchitter**

The *disgusting* smell of the critters, *like wet Brussels sprouts,* filled her nostrils. *Fucking wall infesters.* A small voice at the back of her head pleaded for the critters to never return. Despite their absence, She felt the prickly legs of the hairy baby creatures hanging off the tip of her tongue.

<u>*—She pulled out her hair—tiny insects fall out—*</u>

She gagged. *I've been sealed for a kiss of death on its way.*

Her winged companion fluttered with passion in shifts around her head throughout her days. *The madness keeps spreading.* Pages of scattered pieces of *my mind,* She hated to acknowledge. Sometimes, the doll's voice in her head growled its ambition... She once etched the name of the doll—*it wasn't a doll, it was a storybook character*—the name of the doll into her phoenix-scaled journal, but never again—*the name of the doll*—It was a swear word denounced to her—*the name of the doll*—and the fear of it crept up her legs. *I can feel his head looming over me at my worst moments. Raising the dread inside me. That damn doll...* She'd never let them see her **fear**. She'd never let it know it won... That cursed doll's name—

"Cloudy." Her astral form spoke from atop the mighty perch of her wardrobe, shaking her head as she cackled. Through a thin white veil *with 3% visibility,* her projection craned *its*/her neck to follow every move her physical form made. The translucent sheet of **their** mind's design comforted her with warmth, security... *everything She lacked.*

"Fuck!" Although her obsessive practice of this *new* technique removed months of her life, She had gotten enough control of it, gaining an invaluable getaway from the World, and the practice could prove fundamental to re-understand her *missing...* aura's depths. *Again.* Through the Astral Field, *I should be able to recontact my aura*— "Whatever." She shut her journal. *Another rubbish calculation. Only an annoying astral Me to bother my work.* Swiveled around—

To an empty room.

Breathe. Breathe. It's okay. Just your anxiety kicking up. Breathe. Black liquid arms dripped around her, decorating more of the room than her journal pages. Writings and drawings that She couldn't yet decipher. Drafts, theories, and trials of her *obsessive need* to solve the missing link of her aura. Her sketches bore a resemblance to mathematical equations. She doubted *even her ungrateful grandmother—*

"Enough!" Her astral form popped right in front of her, hands on her hips. "How much longer are you going to have us sit here wallowing in the luxury of our own shit?"

"I just need to... Fuck!" She twirled around in her seat. Seconds later, her lost eyes found the drawer before her. Grabbed it open. Left hand pulled out one of her favorite delights: a *scrumptious* lemon-flavored ZenDrop.

"Your sweet tooth is unnerving." Her astral form kicked the chair She sat on. "It's been weeks since we've gotten proper sunlight. Bad for aura, Gma 101."

"Don't you dare!" Eyebrows jumped as She held her mouth. Her bark surprised her. She was stupefied at her *less-than-helpful* astral mind's audacity to bring up *that—thing—*the thing She lost... *my aura...*

"Oh, lost what?! Nothing's lost." The astral form waved her off, mouth agape. "I think." The nearly invisible form straightened up. "Don't be a raving tosser." Danced around her owner's head and the entire room, leaving sparkles of light in her wake, creating a beautiful display of movement between her and the batty-winged loyalist. "You don't look well. Your hair's an inferno of desperation."

She studied her *calendar* map of activities hung against the wall, scanned the X's, and added the numbers—all progress notes for her madness. The first quarter of the month showed her despair, while the second quarter shat on it further. *Here we are, third quarter.*

Adds up to shit. It's November!

"Oh." She shrugged. "Alright, off you go." She shooed away

her astral form. "Creaevix, you know what to do." She turned her chair from her desk as a flat ziccographic screen materialized across the room from her, slashing her astral form from existence.

Chitterchitterchitterchitterchitterchitter-irp-chitterchitter-ch-irp.

They're not here, they're not here, they're not here anymore... "Shuffle channels, please."

On command, channels shuffled with five-second intervals in between. The latest upgrade meant Creaevix advertisements populated your digital real estate. *What more could that company manufacture? Monopolizing every craft! Entertainment, healthcare, security—to name a few.* Mindless visuals *stroking my ego's impulse,* promoting this week's pleasurable escape to distract the measles from the dirt underneath. *Oh look, another pleasure bot—mind my language— pleasure mate for the lonely. I'm of age now, a new target for funding the machine.* The Internet once harbored communities to collaborate; now reduced to one strict model: sell, sell, sell. Whether it be your soul or the souls of the ones you hold dearest. *Also, literally. Heligjars to hold the souls of your lovely departed. If only they knew what I knew...*

Once the high kicks in, it all gets better. Easier to swallow. Her eyes drooped less than four hours ago. She crawled her fingers into mid-air.

A soft white light twirled around them.

My aura's not gone. Can't be. Biologically impossible. I'd be dead. A smile crept on her mouth. It left. She went back several pages in her journal. Stopped on the one She returned to daily.

The ziccographic flatscreen flashed images on her face as She recited her lines:

Your orange's not lost
It's up in the air
Learning to fly
To save you despair

That's it. That's all I could write today.
Sad shit.

"Stop." She gestured to the channel on-screen. *News coverage. Yay.* A face in a box appeared She's seen before, in some distant past… *A former shell of me knew her.*

"—ox Institute for Mental Restoration, we have breaking news here again."

The reporter's voice cracked. Her eyes carried the volume of her voice.

"A seven-year-old boy and his twin brother were found in a sixth-floor shower room. The two were a part of the many community youths affected by the Peculiar spirit who self-identified as Saint Cloudy last year—"

It never ends. She closed her journal. Stared at the jagged scar on the dark brown skin of her right hand.

"—was found holding onto his brother's lifeless body. We're told the sibling took their own life around 0—"

I'll always be with you.
Always.
Always.
Always.

She stared at the lightning-shaped crack in her ceiling as the flatscreen lights dispersed into little white lights, a second later becoming

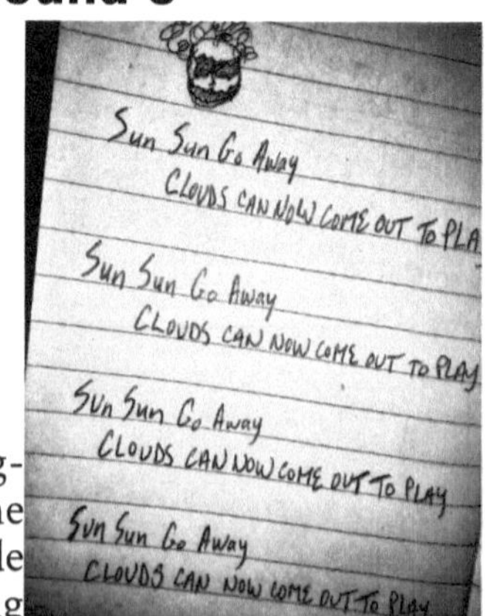

nothing. Her attention shifted, finally won by her winged companion, who sat on the edge of her left knee.

The bat lowered his head as a tear escaped his eye.

It's all been dark. No matter where I turn. Media, shops... Nothing but darkness. Humans question their existence while the kingdom of nature's most fantastic beasts turns from us in shame. World's lost its plot—What—

"Laaaa laaa, la la la. Laaaa laaa, laa..."

My head's lost the plot.

"Only if you say so." Her astral form reappeared beside her ear.

"I told you to hitch one!" She swatted a hand, and her friend disintegrated. "Lil bug." Closed her eyes. Sighed. "Language." *I'm part of the problem.*

A strange song filled her head. She rose, entranced. *That's not in my head.*

"Laaaa laaa, la la la. Laaaa laaa, laa..."

Her eardrums flushed with the sounds of angels as a repetitious incantation rode the air. She unraveled the shades whose frame She had mangled in a tantrum several weeks prior. Flinched at the stream of light that dared kiss her cheek. *Disgusting.* Peeked through the hole into the outside world.

"Laaaa laaa, la la la. Laaaa laaa, laa..."

Eyes winced, She stared down the brand new granite-infused marble streets, where a rather colorful choir pranced along their way. Their cloaks carried such importance with heavy cerulean blues outlined by reddish, almost browns. Their capes of honor fluttered as though holding a wind of their own.

"What is happening?"

Each choir member's delighted face held a book tight against their hearts while their feet bounced to the ending syllables of their chant. Their bodies swayed along with their siren song.

Those eyes. *Why is she staring at me?* A sudden rush of failure and demise swept her bowels.

The intense crystal-grey eyes of their leader never left her direction. Though dressed like her unit, her demeanor set her apart from the crowd. In her stride, without missing a single step, the old woman's gaze bounced along the way, never leaving its chosen mark.

Unsettled by the implausible knowing of the woman's stare, She shut the shades, sealing most of the sunlight. Still, the room felt colder than before.

Unevenly crafted wooden shutters over the window **click click clacked** shut, leaving her in shadow.

Her vision struggled to return to its senses pre-sunlight, with no time to recover as new intruders entered her vision. White gooey spots overpowered her peripherals *like the violent river breached those villages last month. Another tragedy. Twenty families—gone.* She rubbed her eyes, and her efforts rid her of the strange visual interference.

The crystal-grey eyes of the *leader* broke this disturbance periodically for the rest of the morning.

She knew it was time to leave the long oasis permitted to her once her birth-given name came from somewhere below.

The dread grew worse with each step down the creaky, reupholstered stairs. Reaching the bottom, her pacing grandmother met her in front of the reconstructed obsidian-molded entrance that loomed behind in grandeur. They met as rivals *on various topics*, a few feet apart, with their bodies disagreeing in their awkward stances, but neither would turn from the other.

"She rises again," the old woman said. "We'll call you the 5 o'clock shadow. Cold breakfast on the warmer, so mind your hands. Take this—"

Eyes raised at the old woman, She grabbed the book, its cover's contents blurry but slowly coming into view. Sat at the kitchen table. Jerked her hands back at the slight touch of her plate.

"Hot." The old woman pointed at the heated pad under the plate.

She fought the rolling of her eyes and just nodded at her grandmother.

Chitterchitter-irp-chit-irp. Chitterchitterchitter-irp-chit-irp-

chit-irp

She turned away from her steaming plate. Glanced at the book She was gifted.

"Getting harder to find pure literature. Everything's online." The old woman tapped the book's cover. "Beyond the labels, are you aware of his eminence? Don't get too attached to who society knew him as. He was a martial artist, philosopher, and scientist of the human form."

"And I'm starved."

Chitterchitterchitter-irp-chit-irp-chit-irp

Nevermind.

"Who is to blame except your obsessive slumber? I would pay you to stay awake if I thought it would make a difference." The woman regarded her granddaughter as though for the first time. "And ease up on the reefer."

Just once, I'd love to hear her say, 'Love you, darling! You're doing a splendid job, overcoming the burden of survival. She didn't watch the woman leave, but her *dear* grandmother's soft feet trailed away with puncture to the soul. *Ugh.* Her eyes returned to the book in her hands. *Of course, it's another lesson, within a lesson, within a lesson, within a lesson...*

"Drink water!" Gma screamed from somewhere far away.

With her half-eaten breakfast now disposed of, She stepped onto the front porch of her home, the silence broken only by the eerie presence of death. Though her concerns about the dead didn't seem as scary these days...

Who damn-well-minded opts to live on a plot of graves full of the dead? Eyes to her feet. *Me.*

As her foot crossed the barrier between her door frame and the World, a spot of sun hit the skin revealed by her pant leg. She fully exited onto the first step. A boiling stew rose from the pits of her belly. Her left hand clutched the ache in her chest. *Breathe. We can do this.* Her shallow breaths broke the confidence She managed to maintain over the last two hours, and her mind raced too fast for her to keep up with. "What is..." *Oh, no. Oh no—don't black out.* The distant ringing overtook her hearing as She fell to a knee. *Don't black out.* Her vision left her, with every nerve inside trembling, threatening to disable her further…

Anxiety's a bitch.

She was only out for a minute or two *this time.* When She woke, The memory of the warmth of a certain red-haired man's sweater over her head made her smile. She nodded. *'We conquer our fears by living them.'*

Half an hour later, She walked with her head bowed most of the way. Despite her regrets and failures, today, She had a friend at her side. She found solace in walking with a friend. It eased her mind, especially in case She collapsed in a less-than-optimal place.

"You alright there, champ?" His frisky red hair was more porcupine-like these days. His face captured boyish joy, as if wishing others to relish in empty happiness.

"'Ready to wash and dry this,' Jim." Her voice surprised her twice—*it hadn't been used for a while*—the voice She put on around everyday folk. And it was… *playful.* "Did the crime, I've gotta pay the fine." Her awkward chuckle wasn't returned. Her insides curled into themselves.

Jimmy cleared his throat. "So, uh, Demora's been asking for ya. She's excited to come home after her studies wrap up."

Least she's been contacting one of us. She smiled. *So far away… who's thinking of her?*

"Surprised Archie didn't come along," the eager man continued.

"Told him I'll bring him back the sweetest treat."

"No time to waste. Your boy needs some treats." The *kind* man smiled.

They stepped into the rare surge of activity bustling throughout the Jadesfeld Police Department HQ. They moved through the commotion, pieces of information flying about the spot.

She flared her nose and stroked her tongue in her cheeks as her friend was regarded by his colleagues as either a cowboy or a sinner. A flash of anger awoke inside her. She hugged herself, eyes down, but glanced up now and then for a fight amongst the fish who made her feel unwelcome in her home pond.

In front of this HQ's burly Jury Foreman, She passed her arm under the glass window he sat behind. Behind him, a frantic detective ran back and forth in a room made of glass walls, tripping over scattered boxes as he moved yellow ziccolit Xs on a digital map.

"It's straightforward. You sign…" the Jury Foreman went on, punching his fingers on a screen embedded into his desk's countertop. "Let me play Dalestone's advocate here a little and ask: Why'd you do it?" The man gestured around as though pointing out dozens of buzzing flies. "Scrubbing cams is a serious offense. That's common law. And with cameras everywhere? You still went on, huh?"

She shrugged.

"Live one you got here, Jim. Easier to get away with murder these days, heh-heh. Alright, well." He made some taps on his screen. "Your fine's gonna be twenty-seven hundred UDs."

She pointed at the frantic detective behind the glass, who devoured three bagels, one after the other, with haste behind a row of files. "A bagel come with that?"

The Jury Foreman peeped back at his partner, then back at her. "Remember, you've committed a Class C civil with a slight pardon; that's coming off a narrow Strike Five on the yearly. You've got a hell of an angel on your shoulders."

"Wish it felt like it." She grabbed the paper slip he handed her and turned to leave.

"No answer, huh?"

She continued her aloof walk away from his prying, turned the corner, and bumped into a man whose torso shamed his legs.

"Oop! Excuse me there, lil lady." He was twice the size of the detective who walked beside him. His cowboy hat wasn't the only sign of his foreign nature; it was the size of his boots, with spurs larger than tennis balls and a badge worn over his left breast different from any She had ever seen.

"Dam! Yall shining on these ol' systems, huh? I tell ya…" The Cowboy Detective released his grip on an angry stooge of a cuffed man, passing him off to some detectives. He moved up to the Jury Foreman's desk, stroking his chiseled chin as he signed some paperwork. "Hey, there, O'Bry!" He took the hand of a detective, tipped his hat to her, and winked at another Det. "When's that barbecue? Alright! Ay-ya, Jimbo! Long time, pal!"

Jimmy skated by to meet the Cowboy Detective's handshake. "You're far from home, Praisure," Jimmy said. He winced as he released the man's grasp.

"Bounty huntin's carried me far, friend. You've still got that real shark's eye, don'tcha? Come on down to the ranch sometime!"

Oh?

"I'll pass. I like to save a little soul before shift's end."

"Your loss." He rubbed his fingers together *with a smile that didn't lie.*

Bounty hunting always did sound a bit fun. What's this gig really like?

"All for you. Be safe out there. C'mon," Jimmy turned to her. "Let's get you home."

"Enjoy your vacation, Jimbo." Praisure tipped his hat toward them.

"Vacation?" She whispered to Jimmy.

He held the door open for her as they exited the JPD. "Yeah, remember?"

He had already told her about his luxurious three-month vacation to Myanmar, the hometown of the love of his life, Fazura. It got lost in the ramble of thoughts that frequent her existence daily. The more they talked, the more She reconnected with her humanity. Her warmth came from knowing he deserved every peaceful moment after her world's intricacies almost cost him his life. What the hell was she thinking, bringing him into it? It pained her to experience his open arms despite the detriment that associating with her brought to his life.

"Sunlight's important, champ," Jimmy said. "You've earned some. Don't let the past take it away." He stepped out from under the oak tree's shade, the sun's rays catching him off guard. "I get out here and there... been busy these days."

"Oh, yeah?!" His eyes sparkled. "Whatcha getting into?"

Kill me. "Ah, metaphysical nonsense, as usual, and training."

"Ah, Yeah." *He simmered down after hearing that one again, true as it is.* "Yeah." He looked into her eyes. "I, uh, drove past the house a few times, and… the boarded window is an interesting design choice."

She crawled into her skin and turned her attention to the nearest butterfly.

"I know you're stronger than most, but after everything… a little time working with an MHP could help you out."

For the fiftieth time— "Yeah," She smiled, with enough eye contact to make her next words appear meaningful. "I'll look into that." She had to be human. Last thing She needed was him worrying about her while he was away, living an extraordinary life of his own. No need to invest him in this any deeper than he already was. Not when the call of death grew nearer to her.

"If anything happens, call me, no matter what. Anything at all." His eyes stared with the eyes of a thousand crying souls.

"You got it, Jimmy. Thank you." She needed to add something more to ease him. "You make the day a little brighter."

"Just want to make sure you're okay, and if not, you will be."

"I know," She said, sharper than expected for both of them, as his head shot down and away, and her eyes shrunk. She found a smile to wear once more. "I know, thanks, Jimmy."

"Oh, lemme take this," he said. He tapped his wristband and wandered off course. "Yes, sir, got it all…"

She wandered away, taking in the fresh air through her nostrils, with a sense of liberation washing over her with each exhale. *This is good. Good… What the hell does that mean, anyway?* She looked back at Jimmy and *things felt easy again. I don't know what <u>good</u> is, but this feels better.*

Her eyes found the butterfly She lost some seconds ago, now watching it take its time traversing a grand oak it found favor in. She could feel the pleasant vibrations of its aura rise as it reached higher highs.

As it rose, the heat grew until scalding against her skin.

She—sliver of consciousness fading—curled her body inwards as tight as possible before accepting the full weight of the Deilva X-80 heavy truck carrying her down the road. The impact from the luggerauto was the first thing that gave her life in ages. She almost forgot the sting of pain, at least the physical kind.

Free now, her body rolled in the air, then smacked onto the bone-cracking road.

Lying in a twisted heap, sizzling flesh under an angry Sun, She *hoped for uninterrupted sleep. Nights exceed the dreams of most days.* This final thought came as all the others rushed out of her mind before one last word penetrated.

"AMY!"

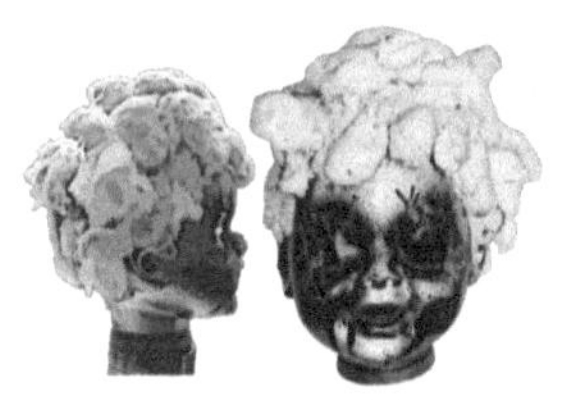

Chapter Two

The Damned

There she goes. Wheeled in like a sorrowful bird ignorant of its wings. May well have smashed our ventricular folds for eons, the scatterbrained fuck-nut.

That was harsh. I take it back. Just a little.

Hours of physicians sawing through to get our voice box's supped-up electrolarynx back to factory settings. The only specialist for our condition around these parts. Terrible. Every breath aches like a fiery blade being jammed up and down our trachea. Murderous intent fills the mind. Only to avoid boredom. I wish this useless vessel of mine would just fight. Again. And keep at it. Couldn't even beat a luggerauto.

What are you three leaving for? Doc, wait?! No time for a smoke break, ol' chap. Ugh. My head. Disastrous migraines mocking me after these quadrennial checkups. Dagenham has some stellar ice cream parlours, though. Maybe Gma can work on her appetite for pride above all else and locate a throat surgeon closer to home. No one's watching us, no one cares, Gma. Hold on... This isn't Dagenham.

Am I still asleep? Yup. This place is different. Why's your face so glum, doc? Too-somber-for-me written on his face. I don't like it.

Look at her. Sleeping like a lambyolk, unaware of its birth. My lack of training shows. I sound like Gma... speaking of which, she looks rather spicy today. Quite glum in her purple cloakress, but must say it is to die for with her matching headwrap. Woman of—wait, WHAT? Limited Schizophrenia? Two weeks? Bullocks. As if this girl I share a body with hasn't put enough on our plates... stu... silly... wha sa... sleepy...

—The green-haired spiritualist peers. The stylized makeup streaks around her eyes grows across and pulps out of her face. "¿Qué alimenta tu deseo?" —

"Ms. Devine, you're awake?" A blur of white coat and mustache flurried above.

AMY DEVINE stirred in the unknown bed, her vision clearing, but the migraine wouldn't. *Still. Might have been the best sleep I've had in ages.* She sat up on her bandaged arms, but slumped back, too weak to support herself. "I..." She clutched her throat's burn.

"Ms. Devine, please don't speak or get up," the doctor said. "You're in a special quarter of Lakewood. Incredible you're even able to pick yourself up halfway, if I'm being honest. Your two-week journey is going to be a little challenging. First, we should..." He droned on with the medical jargon that summed up *my impending sanity lapse.*

Can't Speak? Spectacular. Left alone to contemplate her new temporary reality, Amy's eyes scavenged the sparkling floors, impatient for finding a speck of dirt to confirm some imperfection within this facility. Stared at the black band on her wrist. A message in white light scrolled across it: Amy Devine - Level 8 - Head Trauma

Knock knock knock. A boy's small head poked into the room. "Hey!" Waved in by Amy, he bounced into the room with his toothiest smile. "What's a bird without its voice?" He jumped on quiet feet until he stood in hero pose in front of the bland white room's single bed.

Amy lifted her palms to the sky.

"Sorry, I was eavesdropping earlier. Call me Trinks." He bowed to read the floating ziccolit chart on her side table. "Pleasure to meet you, Amy."

She smiled and bowed her head.

"I'm schizophrenic too, but unlike you, I've got it for life. Psychotherapy twice daily and three different meds to cope with five different dysfunctions. That's normie life for ya. Aren't you lucky?" His voice lowered with the last few words, followed by hollow, infectious laughter puncturing the air. "I'm the family burden, opposite my twin. My mum's a royal mess cuz of my illness. Dad too… but he's taking us to California this year!"

"I—" She coughed, a plop of blood escaping onto the back of her right hand.

"You don't follow doctor's orders, do you? What's a bird without its voice?" Trinks laughed. "What protects your lot, anyway? What makes you special enough to avoid the pain I so easily get?"

Sparks flew from the wall across from Amy's bed. A ziccolit screen **buzzed** to life.

Trinks froze. "Oh." His demeanor lost its vibrant flavor. His hunched shoulders led him out of the room.

The ziccolit screen blared with a news report. Amy's eyes widened at it. She summoned the strength to turn away, holding her stomach *from unleashing whatever mess they fed me*, but swiveled back onto the child's image on-screen. *The boy who took his life.* The same smiling face who left her room moments ago.

"Trilbledy 'Trinks' Williams was a budding painter from age three. His parents often—"

Amy eased into the plush pink pillows. Cracked a small smile out the window at the zig-zagged patterns of the robin on the other side. *Seeing dead children again.* "I've mad gone," She whispered. "Gone mad." Dozed off.

"In other news, there are currently five possible cases

of cursed individuals, known as The Damned, in Jadesfeld. This number of affected residents has prompted the involvement of Callisto's Light to help remedy the situation."

Amy's eyes quivered. *Curses. Please, not again.*

—A silver babyhand fell on the back of her scarred right hand—

Amy jerked her hand away.

—I'll be with you always and forever—

The hospital's PA system **pinged**:

"Welcome to Lakewood Hills Medical Center, where your health is important to us. We have medical staff available for you twenty-four hours a day, seven days a week. It's your health, your currency, and your life we value here. Please note, if you are suffering symptoms of the head, direct yourself to Level Eight and await further assistance."

Days later at the end of her physical and psychotherapy, Amy signed the discharge papers. Rezna never left her side. On that final day of her hospital stay, Amy gathered her somewhat scorched clothes from the bedside drawer, shoved them in her handbag, and lugged it across her chest. Looked over the fresh fit her grandmother brought her from home.

Rezna studied her from the hospital room's corner with a raised eyebrow. "Eat. Your bones are showing."

"Anks, G," was all Amy could muster with the razor-blade itch in her throat. Her eyes rolled off the old woman.

"Don't shut me out, girl."

Swarms of dark grey clouds surrounded Amy, now in her 50% transparent astral form. The clouds moved past her in a never-ending loop that dodged around her slumped body. "Not sure doing this in the middle of Lakewood is the wisest."

Rezna's undeniable white-lit outline appeared dozens of miles away. Her small astral form walked towards her relative but disappeared behind a passing cloud.

"Not up for a game of where am I either." Astral Amy ducked a zooming cloud. Massaged her throat, amazement written in her eyes. *Hey, I can make full sentences* <u>*here*</u>.

"You need to stay sharp. Your ego is playing house with your demons." Rezna's voice echoed through the atmosphere of gloomy weather, the sound of it everywhere.

"I… I thought I saw a child. The one in the news. He was here."

A flicker of Rezna's face flashed in the grey sky above. "Your past with children makes you more susceptible to their presence. It's only fleeting images. Your lack of energy won't allow you to create a strong communicative link with the dead."

Way to put it, Gma. "We had a full conversation."

"There have been no traces of residual spiritual energy in this hospital. I've checked as per my usual precautions. Except for the parking lot. Don't get there, lots of anger."

"Well, I didn't just imagine it."

"No, but it couldn't have happened either. That auto blow would've killed any Class of being. You and I are built differently. We train for situations worse than that. So instead, you teased death. For an aura-inclined individual, the side effects will laugh at you and test your nerves. Which means your prescription calls for a specific training regimen. Perhaps more frequent sessions with Poruma are necessary."

—*The green-haired spiritualist peers. "¿Qué alimenta tu deseo?"*

Amy released her pinned tongue from between her teeth. "I don't need more sessions. I need you to—"

"Heed your words." Astral Rezna appeared mere feet away, her fingers locked in front of her. "Yes, I've gotten your message clear as day many times over the Summer. What now shall I do when you refuse mine?"

She's doing <u>*it*</u> *again. Just say what this is really about. Your disappointment in me can't wash away, no matter how hard you try.*

"You know it's not my fault, <u>right</u>?" The words left Amy's mouth before she could stop herself. *Fuck it, rip the bandaid.*

"Which part?"

You'd think she'd care about the hit-and-run. "Cloudy was an anomaly."

—A sobbing man's blurry face took over the frame of vision, filled with blood—

"So you need a warning from danger?"

—A silver spotlight shines down on the bobbing, bloody man's body—

Kill me.

"Sorry, that wasn't fair," Astral Rezna *admitted.* "But people like us don't get hit by autos that easily. One with aura, girl. You must always be one with your aura."

Hands in pockets, Astral Amy's eyes rolled away. "What would the impressive Rezna Devine do?"

"Anything."

Only the speeding clouds interrupted their staredown.

A blink later, Amy found her feet back on the hospital floor. The staring contest didn't cease, but a shuffle behind Rezna caused attention to shift to the door.

"Am I interrupting something?" Jimmy edged into the room.

"Affairs of a world beyond your understanding," Rezna said. Her squinted eyes pierced into his soul.

"Noted." Jimmy smiled, rubbing his hips as though for lost change.

Silence. His banter is finally waning. At least, I hope. Sorry Jim. I'm just not up for talking. I hate my voice, and I love yours, but it's all a lot for me at the moment. This lingering moment...

"Whatcha writing? Oh, sorry, your voice."

Amy shut her journal. "Iz fine." She cleared her throat *for the zillionth time.* "G gave a book ta-read. Left home. Jottin' notes." She swiped a slick of drool and red from her mouth and shut the door of Jimmy's *baby, the new* brown Mazuka Bx4 compact crossover SUV. *Yes, Jimmy. I heard you the first hundred times.* The eight miniature cherry lights on the side of the SUV oscillated and dimmed until they disappeared. *'See there? That's*

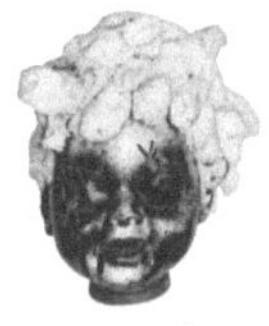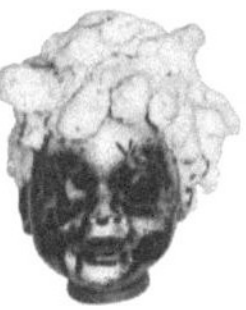

top-of-the-line ziccopower. It's one—'

" —hell of a ride." Jimmy slapped his auto's hood and took the lead. "We walk from here."

"Field trip. Jolly." Each syllable strained as Amy hugged her shivering arms. Wiped her hands on her dark navy denims. "Last one ended well, right?" She chuckled *in spite of* the pain and rolled her shoulders while scanning the plot.

"Not funny. Almost gave me a heart attack…"

There are gaping corpses staring at your soul.

Amy's peripheral caught her undead doppelganger's cheek-to-cheek smile dip behind a massive oak. Shook her head and kept her eyes forward. "Why's he being held in Enfield?"

"JPD's stacked with perps. Lots of buzz going around with The Light in town. Mayor wants the streets squeaky clean." Jimmy sighed. "A citizen getting hit by an auto is at the bottom of his priority stack. Ridiculous."

"I think I could jump high enough to kick somebody straight in the chest, he thought, wondering whether the day would come when his ego overcame his humanity." The voice went on from behind them.

Six-foot-four mosh pit of clothing strutted towards them. From top to bottom, back to front, the symbols on his jet-black coat were icons representing religious symbols from yesterday and today's World. The fabric had patches of different textures accumulating to *what looked like a coat?* with parts of the bottoms appearing to be straw material. Adorned on top of what might be his face was an all-black spiral-shaped hat with reel-like strands flapping in the wind.

"'cuse me?" Amy took a cautious step back.

"Kiaixai apologized for his disturbance to your character," the strange man said. "He sometimes forgot to switch to Internalization Mode." He twirled a beak-like covering under his hat. "See?" he answered with a less modulated voice.

Interesting. "Right."

"That's alright, pal." Jimmy stepped ahead of her. "What's with all the symbols?"

"Callisto's Light is in town! It's a marvelous time to spread awareness, my friend." He thrusted the ends of his coat into the air as he eased down into a cross-legged position on the ground in one elegant motion.

"Mm..." *Quick mover. Sick move.* She eyed the slim holster-like pouch on the side of his right leg. Two long bulges ran from it and down his leg, *some weapons concealed inside. Sword? That's illegal unless your law enforcement. Staff? Nunchucks?* "Oo's light?"

"Callisto's Light."

Oh, wait. The Callisto's Light, huh?

"Kiaixai believed that the only thing society recognized was symbols. So Kiaixai became a symbol himself."

"Symbol wit wep-ins?" Amy pushed past Jimmy, her right hand itching the side of her thigh.

"He understood where she was coming from." Kiaixai chuckled. "Kiaixai was a man of peace."

"Waz?" She inched closer.

"Was?" Jimmy inched ahead of her.

"When evil rose to the occasion, so would he. His staff was only meant for combat." He tapped his holster pouch and smacked the beak of his mask. His war-painted face peered out, an eyebrow raised at them with a half-smirk. "Say, you two wouldn't be active spars, would you?"

"Oh, no." Jimmy held his arm out and placed himself between both parties. "We are fresh out of spars, my good man. We're actually a bit late—"

"Wha style you train in?" Amy asked.

"Health and security. Style without it doesn't matter.

Kiaixai could only imagine what would happen if he forgot himself." Kiaixai scanned her head-to-toe. He pointed at Amy's scarred right hand. "So you do spar, the one known as—?"

"When life depends on it." She hid her right hand under her left. Cleared her throat. "Amy." Swallowed her *painful* stubbornness.

"You from Enfield, Kiaixai?" Jimmy asked.

"Kiaixai came such a long way for simple protest. No violence was planned whatsoever. For many years, Kiaixai lost his way. Now, he helped others find theirs. Quite an unusual scar." His eyes remained on Jimmy while he pointed at Amy's concealed, scarred hand.

Should've seen me the other day. Never thought I'd loathe my accelerated healing. Only scar left after the luggerauto accident is the one I got from Cloudy...

"We'll be on our way, Mr. Kiaixai," Jimmy said, extending a hand. "It was a pleasure meeting you."

"Likewise, Detective." Kiaixai took Jimmy's hand, holding eye contact for several moments. "You have a kind soul. Goodnight."

"Thanks." Jimmy beckoned Amy ahead, but kept his eyes on the departing man. "But it's 11 a.m. ..." His whisper trailed off as he scratched his head. "How could you protest The Light? That's like spitting on what Callisto's done for us. Couldn't find a cleaner organization."

"Clean can sin."

"Yeah, true. Their Create-A-Wish foundation says otherwise."

Amy watched the small dot that was Kiaixai move further away in the distance. "Think he'll be trouble?" She massaged her throat.

"We'll find out after whatever protest. I will <u>not</u> cancel my vacation. Can't believe The Light's in town."

The Light. Their commercials are comedy. She kept her eyes off the dozen undead eyes behind trees and boulders following her every move down the golden brown dirt trek towards city life. A glimpse of Jimmy's smiling face looking at her was all it took.

The living nightmares her mind conjured *for fun* slowed down, sluggish in their movements, outpaced by She and Jimmy. The nightmares ceased once they got closer to New Enfield.

An arousing attraction *gliding* into town caught all of Amy's attention. "Are those...?"

Jimmy's scrunched face nodded. "Looks like it, wow. Gyaads in Enfield, huh..."

The Gyaads. Their otherworldly whitish veils covered their midnight-bluish feminine forms. Their forms rumbled something utteral within Amy's gut. Only seeing them online, their presence here, live, near her hometown, felt like a profound pleasure. The flutter of their white eyelids revealed yellowish diamond eyes before the eyelids hid them from view again. *How can they see with closed eyes?* Their bodies floated in unison across New Enfield's bustling daytime routines as onlookers stopped to gawk.

Amy shivered as She followed Jimmy through town and the Enfield Detention Centre, ignoring her undead selves. They peeked at her behind random corners, tables, and desks. The last made her flinch as She entered Interrogation Hall and forced her to offer Jimmy a half-baked excuse for her behavior. Eyes dug into her back, sides, and somewhere above her head. *Eyes always on me... Living, dead, or somewhere in between, I don't know. As long as the screaming stops...*

Beside her face, her purple-faced doppelgänger bled from its forehead between bulging eyes. Its drooling mouth stretched towards the ground.

Amy shuddered at the snarl of her carcass beside her. She leaned towards the one-way interrogation window.

Inside the interrogation room, he sat there, a spectacle of marriage between tough and terrified. His knees quivered. "I wish I never heard `um," he said. "They whisper horrible things to me." He chuckled with glances over his mountainous heaps for shoulders. "Takes three Class 1 humans to do my workload, detective. So I'm usually alone on the road. I nodded off for a second, hands still on the wheel." His Irish-Scot crass provided all the details he could remember to the two detective—*jokes*—blokes interviewing him. From leaving his home to his travel to work, and finally to the bleak details of the hit and run. "Please... I need some sleep. If your lot could watch me back for an hour... or two!" He scratched at his skin, staring at the wall to his right as though it took something from him, but he was terrified to ask for it back.

"Transporting three tons of cargo requires plenty of responsibility there, mister uh, Cha—I'm not going to try. No." Detective *Number One* stroked his sea-green wristband. A string of green ziccolights blinked to life in front of him and formed green text and a map. "How long have you been out of contact with your mission squad? We checked with the contact you gave us and couldn't get a match on your luggerauto or the fleet you say you came in with."

"It's a loaner. I had a small wreck last November—"

"No wreck is small, Mr. CathalmorMac," Detective *Number Two* said, combing back his parted white locs above his squared crimson CrownEagle glasses.

The angry swarm of their voices droned in and out of Amy's ears. *Why am I even here? It's a cut-clean case.* Dreadful details led to boredom rising into anticipation, with each piece of memory regained from the trucker's story. *He's sobbing again.* Her eyes rounded and stared down at her dirt-ridden sneakers. *He's hearing voices, too. Trauma said hello to us both.*

"Bollocks! Every man is sociable until a cow invades his garden, don't you see?" The truck driver shrank in his chair, cuffed hands trembling. His cap created a shadow of dread where his face once held anger. "Those damn eyes outside the window at night..." His whispers continued off-trail.

Amy stared at her GCID on her left wrist. The screen had small cracks in every corner. The metal frame of the GCID wrapped around her wrist was bruised and dirt-ridden with chipped parts. *Fantastic. Another thing to fix.*

"You alright?" Jimmy asked.

"Yup," Amy said. "What do you make of him? He's a bit off-key, no?"

"Nods off, gets spooked, and crashes into you. He could be on something we can't detect or... something you can."

Ugh, don't give me those eager eyes, Jimmy. "No, no curse here." Was She sure? *Absolutely not.* "I'm sure." She coughed into her hand and stuffed her bloody palm into her pocket. Swallowed *the pain.* "I would've felt something." *Right?*

Two for one special kiddo.

Amy flinched at the *strange* voice.

"What about his coworker?" Jimmy pointed across the hall's spotless, overbearing steel architecture towards another interrogation room.

Inside room two sat a box-headed, droopy-eyed *bot— language*—AItiman, cuffed to the steel table, feeding incoherent whispers into it. The yellowed and weathered frame of the AItiman stood out against the room's interior. Its bulging inorganic eyes scanned up and stared through the one-way viewing window, *it couldn't see through. I hope.*

Amy backed away from the window. "Don't make um like they used to." She leaned in. *Is it distressed? Looks like your everyday poolboy but with skin of chrome. Built like a farmer though. Slap some flesh on you've got a rare Andryex.* "It seeing and hearing things like the trucker?"

"More like cursing," Jimmy said. "It's a language that an advanced artificial intelligence model made up. Forgot the name. Learned some from my uncle years ago. He used to work with a pair Andryex in his lab. It's an incantation. Well, hex more so."

"Against?"

"The Gyaads."

"Unearthly fucking broads!" A poofy-eyed, grey, and purple-haired detective gloated as he and another skimmed past. "Searching for their younger sister, the blue wenches are."

The other detective shook Jimmy's hand.

"Hey, Jimbo," the leader gawked back. "You like finding kids. Want to take over the briefings? I'm sure those sorry blokes at the JPD ain't got nothing better for you to do." He snorted and guffawed his way off. His partner, in-toe, did not join the laughter.

"Wouldn't want to—take your only bonus this year." Jimmy frowned at their backs.

"Don't play into their unwitted lark." Amy gave him a soft knock in the stomach. "You're better for it." She grabbed his arm and led him towards the exit.

"Jerk." Jimmy popped his brown trench coat's collars. "When's the last time he solved a case without pissing off the victims?" His mouth stood open. "Damn, should've said that..."

You're better than most. "Listen, those trucker blokes are severely troubled. I'm not pressing charges. Put him on public duty or something. We both know I'm more than fine. Or will be." *Public duty, yes. Now's my chance.* Amy's chin rose. "Speaking of public duty. Tell me more about that bounty-hunting gig. What's it like?"

"Why are you bringing that guy up again?" Jimmy rolled his eyes as he marched past the automatic glass doors.

"I'm not bringing him up; you are." She tugged his arm. "I mean, how's it work? Hands-on, not the brochure version."

"He doesn't even wear his star!" Jimmy put his brown deerstalker *of comfort* on his crown.

"Do you want a star, Jimmy?"

"It's not about the star!"

"No, but what's the stark difference between your detective work and his detective bounty hunting?"

Jimmy scoffed. "Oh, there's no detective work involved in his funky line of business."

"Right, but your case solved is equivalent to—" She leaned into him. "How much coin for bounty capture?"

"Coin? What are you, a Westerner? There's more to happiness, ya know."

"Currency shields the pain, Mr. Carolina."

Jimmy's clean brown shoes clicked, spun, and faced Amy. "You're not actually considering—?"

"Nooo. I'm just curious!"

"Right. Well..."

Jimmy turned around to face the Enfield Detention Center's green brick structure. "Maybe I should've applied here when I started out. Enfield Dets may be bigger pricks, but they deal with cases in outer vicinities. Could really make a difference."

Look at him. I don't deserve him. She covered her mouth and swiped the splash of blood on her jeans before he faced her again. "Don't worry, I'll always be a detective. Through and through."

He smirked. Eyebrows frowned. "Should you be talking this much? Respectfully, of course."

"Respectfully." Amy laughed *for the first time in...* "Of course."

"Detective." The syllables rang, and all friendly air of banter brushed off and away. Rezna Devine, in all her glory, stood behind them, stoic behind her fashionable black sunblockers. "Has your investigation been settled?"

"Oh, Ms. Devine! Yeah, we're all set. You heading out on some business?" Jimmy pointed out a graphite-colored tote slung across Rezna's left shoulder.

Yeah, she doesn't bring that bag out for fun.

"I'm afraid the news is rather dreary. So I won't pester your being. I'll require my granddaughter's attention on this course as well."

"Me?" Amy blurted. *What on Earth—*

"I gather you're still of the same biological framework?"

"I ask myself that question every day."

Chapter Two: The Damned

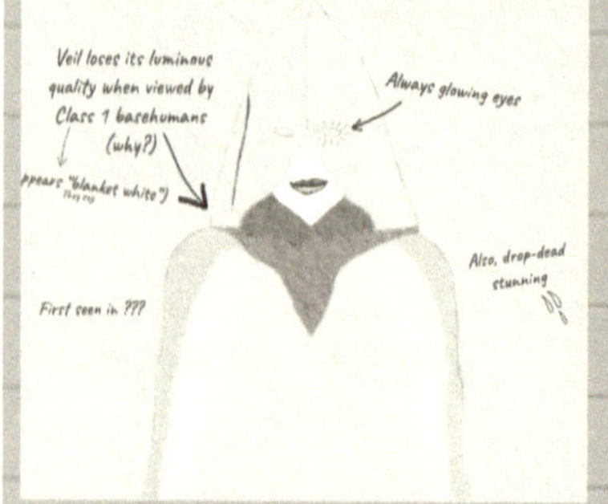

Gyaads. They appeared only a decade ago, yet they remain the most civilized species among us, in my opinion. They just have it together more than we humans. Even more than the Animalia Kingdom. No crime, violence, or even an argument is seen in their company.

I'm curious about the perspective the humutts in their society have. Why would a human allow themselves to be enslaved by the Gyaads? Is life truly better on their side of things? To the extent of becoming a pet?

Oh no. Here comes the lugger! CRASH!

Hello, I'm a snobby Det with my fancy clothes, and my simple brain can't begin to try and properly pronounce a name because I have no respect for culture. Look at me.

AJtiman: lower intelligence class of robots used by humans that serve as policebots, dronebots, guardbots

Andryex: Looks like us. Increased intelligence? Anything else??? No one knows for sure.

There's only one rule known Worldwide when dealing with lambyolk: Never disturb their slumber.

Such an impressive species.

They sleep for six months after birth

while asleep, their auras allow them to perform bodily functions such as eating, sex, bowel movements, swimming

they are able to attack predators in their sleep

they retain the scent of predators and send older sheep out to find the predator of their predator, sort of like little contract killers

If they are wounded in their sleep, they can lose a substantial amount of their aura. However, their survival instinct kicks in, and they're able to gather all their energy reserves to pinpoint remedies that will help them replenish.

All this shows how much they have such a great sense of their auras. Understanding them may help me find my true orange. I need to think like the lambyolk.

I am the lambyolk.

And I've been in slumber for far too long.

Chapter Three

Curses.

"I see them all the time. In my nightmares, my dreams. I see them in my soup. See them in my piss!" The lady smacked herself, leaving red behind on her cheek. "I… I love them, but they're not the same. They are fucking everywhere." Her face carried the warmth of a dear aunt, with yellow eyes full of baggage underneath, and mascara running past her cheeks, creating patches in her navy blue crumpled mess of a skirt, dark masses blotched from the sorrow. "They're my world. I used to love seeing their smiles." Her voice broke. "There's something else behind those smiles now. Something… dirty. Malicious. I forgot how they were before. And now my world is only them as they are now. Everywhere. They're always fucking watching. Watching me, catching me. Catching me. Catching me…"

"When did the visions start?" Rezna asked, sitting across from the woman. Her stern expression softened into pity as she watched her long-time friend crumble into herself.

"Must it be so close?" Her friend leaned back on a puffy quadplex couch with sunken pouches that declared it had seen many occupied nights. She had a cautious eye on a scarlet quill, jotting on paper in midair beside her face.

"It must feel your thoughts," Rezna reassured her. "To make sure they aren't being corrupted."

"Well, I'm not mad, Rezna. I'm—" The woman's hands squeezed together as she shook her head. "I've tried everything we know to do when these things happen. Nothing works."

"How long, old friend? I believe you're dealing with something vengeful. Tell me, how long have these visions ailed you?"

"They aren't just visions." The woman nodded to no one. Reached over to a side table, but pulled back and clasped her hands on her lap. "It's been two–" She searched the floor and windows for her words.

Amy frowned at the side table, which overflowed with books; some with the author's names scratched out, most in other languages she could not read, and all having unrecognizable symbols along their spines and covers. A bottle of pills lay beside four cups of water at various states of finish.

"Two weeks. Two months, it's all blending," the woman replied.

"Take your time, dear."

The ever-scratching quill in midair between them broke the silence during the Q&A with a looping track of itches and scratches.

"Are there any patterns in what it's telling you?"

The woman shook her head.

"And you're positively sure it's not—"

"Never! Never would they show up like this. Not my sweethearts. Not that way!"

Rezna nodded. "Our hearts can cloud our judgment. Even the slightest disagreement or dissatisfaction before death can cause a soul to stir after it departs its body. Were there any arguments before they left, or anything they were dissatisfied with?"

"Nothing!" The woman shot up on her feet, her arms trembling at her sides. Her tear-filled eyes left Rezna, found

Amy, and then fell to the floor. She sat back down. "Sorry. I know you have to ask."

"It's okay." Rezna rose halfway and scooted her cozy armchair closer to her friend. She took her hand and held it tight. "Let's visit what you see."

Amy sank into her solo couch in the room full of shifting shadows. She rubbed her hands together, her breaths now visible. The only source of warmth in the room came from within her chest. It spread to her body with every breath. The dimly lit room cast a sinister outline on everyone that betrayed the pain in their faces, mistaking it for malice.

"Stella, I need you to breathe. We'll solve this together, so concentrate with me." Her eyes closed. She outstretched her free hand.

Stella bowed her head to mirror Rezna's. Raised her arm to align with Rezna's, creating a cupped high five with inches between the palms.

The quill scribbled faster than before.

Stella's wild eyes burned a hole through it.

"The only way through this is to get through them," Rezna said. "We must get to the source of the vengeance. Concentrate."

Her quill stopped.

Ska-THUNK.

Amy's head swiveled, but She didn't find anything to explain the strange sound. She opened her mouth to ask her grandmother.

"Are they with us now?" Rezna asked, eyes still closed, but she shook her head to answer Amy.

"No." Stella kept her eyes on a particular spot outside the room in the barren, pitch-black hall and its echoes of silence.

Amy's stomach swirled in knots as the room expanded and her movements slowed down.

"Remember to breathe," Rezna whispered, but her unopened eyes focused on Amy. She thumped her chest thrice with a slow, wavy movement of her arms. "Be there with her." She nodded towards the trembling Stella.

Amy nodded. She closed her eyes, breathing in deep, then let her breath escape through pursed lips.

Rezna sat straight up, unopened eyes back on Stella. "Visualize. Show me what ails you." The skin of her eyelids jerked under her meditation.

"What's a bird without its voice?"

"Trinks." Amy opened her eyes to absolute darkness. *He's not here. He can't be here.* On her left, Rezna sat cross-legged in meditation. To her right, Stella searched through the darkness with closed eyes. The three of their astral forms were alone in the never-ending nothingness of the Aura Realm. *Can he be... here?*

"They're not here," Stella said. "But something is."

Ska-Thunk. Ska-Thunk.

"I see." Rezna's face scrunched as she groaned deep and exhaled. "Clever curse."

Amy snatched her arm away from *something* that grazed her, but her movement took *decades* to complete. She rubbed the spot on her arm that experienced the scalding touch. She bent her knees, but it *seemed to take* five minutes to do so. She put her arms at the ready and locked her eyes ahead, ready to encounter what was coming.

"Unnerve yourself, girl," Rezna said. "You can't fight memory."

How does she do it? It feels like I'm dropping into myself. Amy gasped. A rush of wind flushed against her skin.

She fell into bottomless air.

This cursed spirit is vengeful. Rezna's voice flowed through her head. ***Mask your fears.***

Amy took a shallow breath.

"Look deeper, Stella," Rezna's voice called out. Her astral form circled above. "The invader is hidden from sight, but not far. Remember your anguish. Let them come to you."

Ska-Thunk.

Amy's breath echoed, skipping as it traveled away from her. Distant rumblings transformed into the voices of *angels.*

Ska-Thunk.

Seeee-aaaaaaaaaaaaaaaaaaaaaaaaaaayayayayayayayay The voices mangled together and cut through the thickening air.

Dangle Dolly, can you feel me?

Dangle Dolly, won't you...

Amy's foot stepped into a tiny pond.

The pond's water dripped upward into the clouds.

A small red house sat across the quaint green field.

Dangle Dolly, can you feel me?

Dangle Dolly, won't you trust me?

The song grew louder.

Amy unwillingly moved within seconds— to a cliff's edge. Five children surrounded her.

Moved again— Amy stood on the face of the cliff, looking up at the sky. Behind her, thousands of meters below, was a rocky beach that bent the will of gravity. It stretched itself closer, then further away from her. She turned from the dizzying sight to face the cliff's edge.

Ska-Thunk.

Their backs to her, the children threw their heads back in laughter. No sound.

A boy with blond locks held the foot of an *equally adorable* blond girl with similar features. She hung upside down over the cliff's edge, swaying her head against the winds to the beat of the children's song.

Dangle Dolly, can you feel me?

Dangle Dolly, won't you trust me?

Dangle Dolly, keep me partially.

Dangle Dolly, fly with me.

Little shits! Amy's mouth screamed for the children to get away from the cliff's edge, but no sound was available to her. *What are they thinking? Careful!* She clutched her throat in protest.

The blond boy let go of the girl's foot.

NO— Her frustration melted into sorrow. *I can't stop this. It's already done.* She could feel the cold sweat on her face despite its absence in her astral form. *It's already done.*

The girl remained in place, suspended inches from her brother's open palm. Her body lowered itself down the cliffside, centimeters at a time. Gained speed.

A squint and a few breaths later, Amy could see it: their connected thin strands of aura. A green*ish* strand hung from the boy's palm and connected to the red strand on the girl's bottom foot.

The girl's falling body closed in on Amy. She giggled hysterically as her face passed by. Her glowing, green-pink eyes looked right through Amy's astral body as she continued her way down, arms swinging in the breeze. "Ow!" The girl rubbed her elbow vigorously. "Watch it, Cheneley! You made me nick my elbow!"

"Let's bring you up, you little crybaby!" The boy, Cheneley, shouted from above.

The girl levitated quicker than she lowered, soon passing by Amy at a nauseating speed. At the top of the cliff, the other children grabbed her limbs and pulled her onto solid ground.

"It's my turn now, Prist!" Cheneley said, peering over the cliff's edge.

"No, last time you went twice!" his sister replied, struggling to pull him back.

The other kids turned to the siblings and grumbled things unheard.

Amy held her head as her body jerked upwards and stopped on top of the cliff, right behind the group.

"Come on!" Cheneley pushed one of the other boys back.

"Mom told you no more fights!" Pristine pulled him away from the others.

The argument amongst the group grew louder.

Amy circled them, but the grumblings from the children did not become any clearer. She paused, tilting her head as she gazed at their faces; smooth slabs of flesh on a canvas, twitching with the movements of expression. On one of their faces, the skin folded over into a pouch that laughed as the kid pointed at Cheneley.

The scene diminished into darkness.

Ska-Thunk.

The argument went on somewhere in the distant void.

Amy was once again all alone. Stepped forward.

Found herself staring back up at the same cliff's face, from the same disorienting vantage point as before, except now the moon hung in the purple sky.

"Be careful!"

"Oh, just hurry it. I'm missing my *Night Stories*."

The blonde, almost twins, came into view. Cheneley held the heel of his sister's upside-down body over the cliff edge. "Night stories, night stories. All you go on about, Pristine. Bloody night..."

"Ok, lower me, Chen!" She stretched towards the rocky beach below.

An "athlete's" warm-up. What the hell are they thinking, little... Amy shook her head, not wanting to confirm her suspicions about their future.

"We have to sing the song!" Cheneley said. shifted his hip and solidified his footing.

"What a time for the bloody song!" Pristine shouted.

"I can't focus without it!"

"Grrrrrrr, FINE! Go on then!"

"Can you sing it with me?" His plea, *too sweet, to ignore.* "Please, Prist?"

Pristine sighed. "On three! Quickly!"

"Okay! One, two, three!"

"One, two, three!"

Dangle Dolly, can you feel me?

Dangle Dolly, won't you trust me?

Dangle Dolly, keep me partially.

Dangle Dolly, fly with me.

Their voices merged and circled the winds like vultures

in starving heat. The siblings kept in tune with one another, their chests bouncing at the sharpest syllables of their lullaby.

Pristine lowered towards Amy. Slow and steady, with her arms swaying in opposite directions. *Swimming in air.* The darkness of the night made the siblings' connected aura strands stand against it, *with shimmering results.* His was a yellow-green *chartreuse, and* hers was a *Rosso Corsa* red. On a synced cue, the siblings sang again.

Dangle Dolly, can you feel me?

Dangle Dolly, won't you trust me?

Dangle Dolly, keep me partially.

Dangle Dolly, fly with me.

Pristine dropped.

Amy flinched as her body flew past her quicker than it had the first time.

Slowed *its* descent.

"We're almost there!" Pristine twisted her torso to search the rocky area behind her.

"Watch it!" Cheneley's arms shook. "Do you see it yet?! Mind your head!"

"I'm on it! Almost there!" Pristine dropped at an alarming rate. "STOP!"

The boy's grunt echoed from above as he reeled himself back. "Are you alright?!"

Pristine's body jerked.

Amy blinked.

Pristine's back smacked against the wall.

The line of aura, her only other contact with the land through her brother, jumped once, then twice, before it stiffened. *They must have considerable aura control. To be able to hold the consistency of his aura that... It's incredible! At their age, I couldn't even make a solid shape with my aura.*

Pristine twirled like a ballerina. Used her hands to steady herself along the jagged surface. She grabbed several knacks on the wall and crawled to her target. "Almost... AH!"

"What?!" Her brother's head jerked left to right. "What?!

What?!"

Pristine steadied herself. Beamed back up at her brother, something shiny in her hands. "Lift me, Chen!" Her body jerked up.

"Done." He tightened his stance as his eyes focused on his line of aura.

"Can you make me an appleberry tea when we get home? You always make it just right."

"Ugh! First, you lose your bracelet. Then the night stories. And now—Watch your—"

Thunk.

"NO!"

The girl's missile of a carcass dropped straight through Astral Amy.

Cheneley's foot staggered towards the cliff's edge as he pulled on his aura strand. His cries ripped the air as he stomped his back foot for leverage.

Chunks of the earth on the cliff's edge crumbled underneath him.

A second line of aura sparked to life and coursed its way toward the falling girl. It coiled around her ankle.

Amy held her chest.

"AHHHHHHHHHHHHHHHHH!"

Another missile—_Cheneley, no!_—fell through Amy.

Amy's stuttered breaths got quieter with each passing second. Bird cries flooded her hearing, but ceased a moment after. She flew back as though punched in the stomach, with her surroundings warping around her. Her body followed the exact path of the siblings. Through her half-open eyes—

Amy's undead doppelgänger sat on an invisible perch meters away. It clapped as it watched this trail of human bodies dip into unseen depths against the mountainous backdrop.

The undead Amy smiled. Slow nod.

Amy froze in midair. "Wha—"

Her entire body— encased in CHARTREUSE AURA.

She looked at her hands—the small hands of a child.

"Pristine! NOOOOOOO!!!" Amy screamed in Cheneley's voice. Her thoughts weren't her own. *Please—no! I'm sorry, I'm so sorry, please don't let it happen. Please wake up, Prist. My spirit isn't working! WHY isn't it working? Please wake up. Please please please please please. PLEASE!* His/her body fell, arms reaching for Pristine.

His sister's body crumpled onto the beach below.

His aura flickered. Distinguished.

"No!" His tears smacked his cheeks on the way down. **"AAAAAAaaaa**aaaaaaaaah!" Cheneley's body stalled in midair.

Dropped again—

Leg first into a boulder—**CRUNCHSNAP!**

Darkness flushed the scene.

Amy **gasped** awake, clutching her right leg. The excruciating pain she felt a moment ago no longer existed. She hugged her shivering arms with her knees crunched into the sandy beach. Blood ran down a rock next to her. She stared across the ocean as the tides rippled.

Tiny footprints in the sand led away from her.

A crabsteed clicked its way along the sand using its eight alternating legs on either side of its vertically curved abdomen. **Click-click click-click click Click-click click-click click** Its two crabhammers stabbed a hole into the sand, digging away, digging away, as its feet shuffled.

It froze. Curled on its curved torso like an unoiled Androscort—*working hard for UDs, this one*—flip after flip rotations until it stopped again, facing a new direction. Clicked its way toward *an odd stone?*

It was unlike any stone She'd seen before. Furry leaves were partially obscured atop the stone. But the more She looked, the more this plant resembled dirty, crumpled blond hairs. The more She tried to tell herself it was just a stone, the more the denial ate through her esophagus and upset her stomach.

Click-click click-click click Click-click click-click click The crabsteed climbed over one of the humps of the *stone* and paused a bit out of sight behind the part it climbed over. Lifted its crabhammers high—**STRUCK** with vicious intent into the squelching mess of the odd stone; its feet excited from the conquest.

Click-squelch-click click-squelch-click click Click-squelch-click click-squelch-click click Click-squelch-click click-squelch-click click

Click-squelch-click click-squelch-click click Click-squelch-click click-squelch-click click Click-squelch-click click-squelch-click click

"Get away from her!" Cheneley's broken and bloodied hands swatted at the excited creature.

It dodged his efforts and swung back at him with its crabhammers.

"His spirit saved him," Stella's voice said.

The boy knocked the animal several feet away from the clump of hairs.

The crabsteed scuttled off towards the sea.

Cheneley stood with a boulder's assistance and shifted onto his left knee. Swung his unnaturally bent right leg to a more comfortable position in front of him. Knee down, it flailed like an airy mascot. He shifted the broken leg to meet his good leg's balance. "Ahh-ssss…" His groans turned to obnoxious yelps, but he smashed his teeth together before the sound of pain could betray him further.

He laid his scraped backhand onto his sister's cheek.

Her eyes. Amy stared into those blank, grey eyes,*formerly yellow*; their literal divide created by the gaping valley of flesh that revealed some innards of the girl's small crown.

Cheneley's first step rewarded him with a stumble, but he kept going. It took his right leg a few seconds to catch up to the left. He continued his limp walk in a semicircle. "There it is, c'mon! Stupid leg." A few full circles later, he smacked his broken leg into place. "That's enough practice."

He stooped to his sister's crumpled carcass. Cleared the beachlife around her face. Lifted her into his arms in one swoop. "I got you, sis." He walked towards Amy.

Amy watched the boy limp his way towards her, carrying the weight of his world. When close enough, She shifted out of their way as though it mattered.

A horn honked in the distance as the world around Amy faded to nothingness once again.

You just have to accept it.

Amy backed away from the voice. *Who's there?* Her head spun in every direction. *That wasn't Gma or Stella. I've been on this magic trip for too long.*

More voices echoed in the deep distance. Dozens, hundreds, thousands. **Screaming**.

Amy slapped her palms over her ears.

Ska-Thunk.

"Hey, sis." Cheneley trudged down a spacious, dusty road, Pristine's body hauled safely on his back, as the world around them filled in. "You figured it out yet?"

A bustling red aura ball zipped around his head. It flew back and hovered over Pristine's slumped noggin.

"Guess not," he said. "Come back soon, yeah? We'll get to the nearest COIC. I promise. They won't judge or ask questions. I've heard they can help kids who end up... I can fix... I can help raise you as you are now. But we can't go home." His thoughts streamed through Amy's mind: ***Our Mum doesn't need this. She's already hated because of her spiritual works. Talking to dead people wins you no friends. They'll never understand what we can do. We can't add an undead kid to her plate. A lifesnatcher is a lifesnatcher no matter the age. She's better off without us. We can't go home.***

"I wish he had come home," Stella's weeping voice said.

In the distance, bright lights illuminated the sky.

"Travelers' Hub," Cheneley said, eyes ahead. "Always wanted to visit one." He kneeled, carefully placing Pristine's body between a cluster of orange, heat-scorched boulders. "You're gonna stay here and—"

A red glint lay in the middle of Pristine's dead, grey irises.

"You've always had the best timing, haven't you?" He

smiled. "I'll be back in ten with supplies. If I'm not..." He got level with her eyesight. "Tear anyone apart that messes with you."

Several eyes in the massive lot followed Cheneley as he made his way towards the hub. Bikers, bounty hunters, and tourists of all kinds, sprinkled in and out of the lot.

Cheneley's eyes stayed on a man further from the rest near one edge of the lot. The man stacked barrels and more into the back of an Expeditioner 3k; a monster cross between brig and auto. "A pirate! No way..." Cheneley whispered. He marched around four scruffy individuals, one of whom purposely stepped in his way. He went around them, averting eye contact.

"Looks like one of them COIC kids," one of their voices called from behind him.

"Far from home," another said. "Hurt wing. Could be worth a lot to some parents wanting a kid."

"Chill, bounties scattered out here. They might get heroic."

Cheneley approached the Travelers' Hub. "Please be human." He stopped in front of the glass doors.

A robotic clerk manned the register inside.

"Shoot," Cheneley muttered under his breath. "Bloody bot'll rat me out to Dets." He surveyed the lot.

"Hey, kid!" The group of four men he passed made their way towards him.

"Shoot." Cheneley put on a cheek-to-cheek smile. "Hey, Rex!" Waved over to the pirate across the lot.

"Pirates," Stella's voice said. **"Some of the most honourable humans on this planet."**

The massive frame of the owner of the Expeditioner 3k exited the Traveler's Hub with two small navy Travelers' Hub-branded boxes. A compass swung on a chain around his neck, partially covered by his overcoat. His belt had stylized letters C and L engraved deep in the crimson square buckle. The pirate man took off his almond-brown tricorn and wiped a slick of sweat from across his forehead as he approached his vehicle. "Ha, Rex. That's a good one, kid. You're a quick thinker. I can relate.

You take me for a Rex, huh?"

"Thanks for helping me get supplies, 'Rex'." Cheneley smiled. "Super cool set-up." He pulled his prying eyes from the controls inside the brilliant vehicle and took the boxes from 'Rex'. "Creaevix, send 100 UDs."

Ching!   "Oh, nonsense! Here." *Rex* pulled a circular radar from under his jacket. Pressed the screen. **Ching!** "Sent it back. We're square, little lad. Never take from the needy." The pirate man bit doggily into a chocolate bar before waving it. "Got this with a five-finger discount."

Cheneley frowned. "Not very honourable, sir."

"Noo, but last week, old metal-face in there stiffed me on a few parcels of my regular shipments. Not to mention the bot's a bit racist."

"You can't be racist towards a pirate."

"Says who?" The pirate chuckled. "Gimme an ear's hour and I can tell ya different." He sat inside his vehicle and adjusted the controls on his interior dashboard. "Me name's actually Milard, by the way. What or who are you running from?"

Cheneley looked back at the Travelers' Hub lot and turned back to the pirate. "Say, Mr. Milard, do you know whether the next town over has a Youth Site?"

"Mmm. No COICs near. Not for many towns over, lad. I got a nice little spot if you're looking for refuge."

"No offence, but I'd rather not. Maybe a ride to the closest town if it's not too far?"

Milard smiled. "Where's that extra luggage you got?" Peered inside his Expeditioner. "Think I can carry a few more boxes."

"Not boxes." He pointed at the man's buckle. "Do you truly believe?"

The pirate looked down at his buckle. His smile faded, back straightened. "Always."

CHAPTER THREE: CURSES.

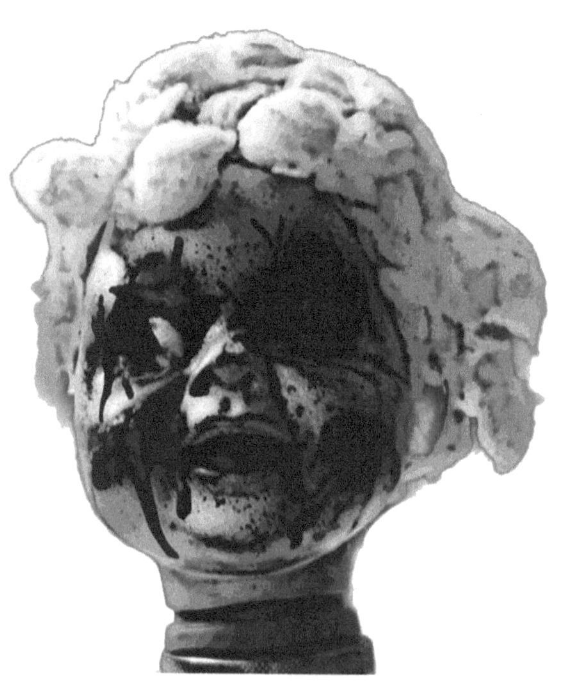

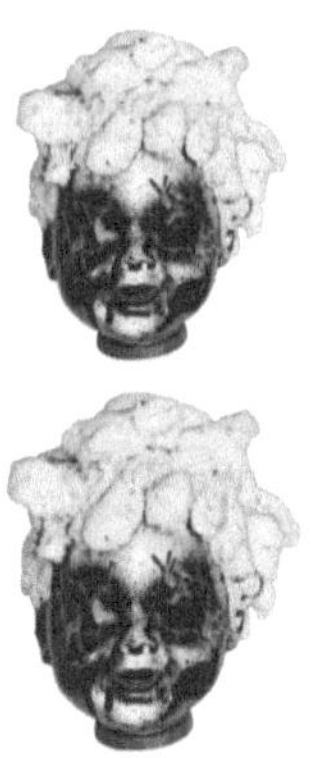

Chapter Four

The Honorable Pirate

Miles of dusty fields stretched alongside the single road, as camels raced one another through brittlebush stalks. Some raced alongside the Expeditioner 3K for a little before the excited mammals trailed off to catch one of their own.

Backseat inside the Expeditioner, Cheneley watched the wildlife. Pristine rested her head on her brother's shoulder, her slow-to-blink eyes peering ahead. Her agape mouth let go of tiny croaks with chokes in between. Greyish drool leaked from the sides of her mouth.

"They say The Light shines brightest on the undead." Milard chuckled.

Cheneley flinched.

"Relax, lad." Milard threw up a lazy hand. "I'm a believer. Your sister's a part of a greater journey now. She's part of our evolution. And she's a-coming-to, soon. Reckon she's been gone no longer than fifteen hours." His eyes in the rearview mirror met the boy's.

"How'd you know?" Cheneley brushed his sister's hair out of her face.

"In the pirate's life, you see it all. No surprises. You're a standup brother taking such good care of her. You'd make a solid pirate, mate."

"Really?!"

"Oooh, yeaaah. Top of the line heart in ya. I can see it easy."

Cheneley beamed at him. "Wow."

"You see, we pirates have a strict code. For example, that bot at the old Traveler's Hub. Showed it the utmost respect despite its wicked words towards me. One part of The Code of Pirate goes: Pay praise to every soul because one day, that soul may have the power to strike you down. But teach good manners to a lost one." His breathy smile lingered in Cheneley's eyes. "Especially if it's got a nasty mouth. Whoooa."

The vehicle stopped in the middle of the road. Two women in dirty, knee-length skirts stood in its path.

"Where'd they come from?" Cheneley scooted forward, hiding behind the passenger's seat.

The women sashayed from side to side, hands stretched out like tipsy ballerinas. Each approached the opposite sides of the vehicle. One of them leaned onto the hood and scraped her claws on it, some fingers missing.

Cheneley backed away from his window as the other undead woman pressed her chipping face against the glass. Her purplish skin showed years of scars. "Lifesnatchers," the boy said, out of breath.

"Don't call 'em that!" Milard barked. "They prefer their proper name. Angels." The Expeditioner's obnoxious engine died. Milard draped his arm across the top of the empty passenger seat. "They can patch y'all up and help your sister adjust. Go inside and wash up."

Cheneley's eyes burned into him. "I told you we're not going home with you!"

"This AIN'T my home!" Milard laughed. "It's meh hideout." He nodded to the window.

An undead woman opened the door with a blank expression that never left the children. Her hand reached up to them. A smile cracked into her face.

"Go on now," Milard said. "Survive."

Cheneley and Pristine stared ahead as water rushed down their dirty faces.

A clump of hair is SNATCHED off one of their heads.

Pristine growled, baring the razor candy corn teeth in her blackened gums.

Her *born-again helper* hissed back. Snatched her fingernail out of the top of Pristine's head wound. A squirt of blood spritzed out of it—onto the undead woman's greenish lips. She licked them clean.

Darkness flushed in.

"You have to let us see," Rezna's voice called from somewhere high in the dark. "So we can understand."

"I know. I know," Stella's voice responded. Her face appeared, grey-scale, high above Amy's tiny figure.

Amy rested on one knee, eyes on the emptiness below her. *Those kids...*

"Supper time!" Milard's gruff voice shouted from far away.

Amy brushed her hands along the walls inside a cabin. Nine helms befitting the pirate goddesses of the 2040s adorned the walls.

"**Me trophies!**" Milard, the pirate's voice said. His disembodied arm waved towards the wall of helms. "**All right, up she goes then.**"

Milard. Bloody fuckin bas—

A wooden round table appeared in front of Amy.

Followed by Cheneley in one seat.

Pristine at his side.

Milard stood in front of the fireplace.

Cheneley charged between his sister and Milard. "What are you doing?"

"Time to break her in, lad. Prep her."

Three new undead women entered the *suddenly small* room. One of them snatched Pristine to stand, the other two with their hands on the young undead's shoulders. A fourth marched her square shoulders in the doorway and grabbed Cheneley's arm, thrusting against his feeble escape attempts.

"Stop!" Cheneley thrashed for freedom. "I'll fucking kill you!"

"Bet you would." Milard barked with laughter. "Listen, lad." His hands spread matter-of-factly. "She's fresh! Ya haf to influence the brain of the deceased early in order for 'em to get the <u>right</u> program." He frowned. "After the first twenty-four, the soul syncs to brain, and the brain connects certain pieces and gives the deceased an idea of who they **were**. You install the right program at the right time—Magic!"

The two guards led Pristine towards the open bedroom door.

"NOO!!!" Cheneley kicked and punched with vigor.

"Hey," Milard's face soaked with sorrow as he got down on a knee in front of the sobbing boy. "Listen, man. Welcome to the team. You're a pirate now. Act like it!" He thumped the boy's chest. "You see, there are two unspoken yet unchallengeable rules in this pirate game. One: Like a lackey, even a Captain pays dues. And two..." A tiny smile crept from one corner of his mouth to the next. "Pirate always gets the booty."

"NOooo, Get OFF her! NO! Get th—off me—off—fuck youuuuu!"

"Oooh, might have to wash that potty mouth after." Milard rose and strolled his way into the bedroom, shutting the door behind him.

Darkness.

"I'm not reliving what my baby went through..." Stella's voice rang out. **"My blood are champions! Fighters till the bloody fucking end."**

Back inside the cabin, Cheneley kneeled, his desolate eyes fixed on the floor. Two of the undead women conversed as they held him down. The bulkier one guarded the closed bedroom door behind her.

All sound lowered until none remained.

Cheneley screamed in silence. Picked his eyes off the floor

and laid them on the bedroom door.

His eyes GLOWED GREEN.

He smashed his hands into the floor. His aura exploded around him, knocking everything away, his guards included.

He tackled the bulky undead guard, smashing them both through the bedroom door, as the sound of the scene faded back in.

"Wha—" Milard spun to the broken-down door.

Cheneley bounced up and grabbed the pirate's arm.

Milard's body smashed into the wall, Cheneley right over his groaning body.

The furious boy's hands beat into the face of the disoriented pirate, who barely got to his knees. Cheneley pulled back and shook the blood off his fingers.

"You Peculiar piece of shit!" Milard grabbed the slight gash in his neck. He swung a magnificent slap that flung Cheneley to the ground. "I don't hurt kids, and I ain't got a thing for fudge, but discipline's free. Even a lackey's gotta pay his dues." He punched down into the disoriented boy's left lumbar region twice.

Milard **screamed** into the ceiling.

Pristine's bloody mouth clamped deep into his leg. She released—sharked her teeth into another portion of the leg. Then again. And again.

Cheneley dropkicked Milard to the ground, grabbed his sister's hand, and they dashed past the slowly recovering undead guards.

Outside, several feet from the cabin, Cheneley's legs gave out.

Pristine dipped under Cheneley's chest and lifted him up and over until he was firm on her back. She took both of his hands in hers and ran.

Faster.

Faster.

Faster.

"You're incredible!" Cheneley chuckled.

"Death… brings… light." Pristine's weary voice, ragged, got out—*but her eyes had fire.*

"Get 'em!"

Behind them, an unholy abomination. Milard rode the backs of two undead warrior women clad in pirate armor, slim-fitted, looking melted to their decayed yet firm, muscular bodies. The hulking figures ran side by side on all fours, forming a perfect mad carriage for the pirate's pursuit.

"Uh…" Pristine slowed down.

"What's wrong?!" Cheneley asked.

"Tired," Pristine whispered.

A polished wooden necklace around her neck SPARKED to life with jolts of white electricity that exploded around the rest of her body.

The siblings tipped over and rolled onto the ground.

"Prist!"

Milard's chariot caught up to the fallen siblings. "I keep mine in line." He tapped his CL belt buckle and pointed at Pristine with his ring finger, showing off a large black ring with red accents and a matching ruby.

Cheneley crawled to his sister's face-down body as she shuddered. More white strips of electrical manipulation sparked around her fragile frame.

"STOP!" Cheneley hobbled to his feet.

"And I amp them up." Milard's ring pointed back to his two undead soldiers.

One after the other, each of their bodies trembled in delight as they rode out the shockwaves from white bolts around their bodies. The scarification adorning their muscular bodies released smoke into the air as their snarling, drooling faces fixated on the children.

"Callisto brought these lovely Angels to existence to right the wrongs the World has done. The World belongs to them. They are evolution, and I'm happy to be of service. Keep 'em safe until they can take it all back."

The two undead soldiers ran and skidded to either side

of the siblings with hunger in their eyes.

"Now, I'm not gonna have 'em tear you apart. Yet. If you make me wait too long, I will. They don't usually feed till midnight, so they're plenty hungry."

Cheneley's green aura burst around his body as he bore holes into Milard's eyes.

"It's a fine day," Milard said. "I'll either get to skin a Peculiar or teach him to be my ally."

The undead soldiers circled their prey.

Cheneley grabbed his sister's necklace, seething from the pain of the voltage, and yanked it on either side, snapping it.

"Hypocrite." Cheneley tossed its pieces at the pirate's feet. "What happened to Pirate's Honour?"

Pristine rose, growling at the two undead women. Her red aura burned bright around her.

Milard stepped towards them. "Before you do the worst decision of your life… that little bustle of efficiency your sis got there? Thinking she's faster than the speed of light?" His hearty laugh made both siblings jump. "Happens all the time when the soul finally tickles the brain. Be harder to train now. That'll cost ya. But these two—" He pointed to his undead trophies. "They started feisty. Broke 'em in just fine. Your sister's nothing but a seedling. She's overdone it, and she'll fall apart quicker than she can save you from being dinner."

Pristine buckled to a knee, clutching her heaving chest.

The undead women moved in close to the siblings, smiles on, baring sharp jagged teeth and arms wide, ready to embrace.

"Survive, boy." Milard slapped his chest. "Survive. I'm a survivor, too. We'll go patch y'all up again, make it right. All you have to do is—"

Pristine's fists smashed the nose of the undead henches, launching them backwards into nearby trees. She picked up her brother by the chest of his shirt.

Milard snatched Pristine by the hair.

Cheneley kicked the pirate's nose to angle. Leg retracted— SMASHED into Milard's eye.

An undead hench tackled the sibling duo into the leaf-ridden dirt.

Pristine grabbed her arm and tossed the hench into her charging teammate.

"Little fighting shits." One of his eyes hanging by a thread out of his socket, Milard's hand covered his face as he shook out his leaking nose, blood spraying. Removed his hand, nose bent almost completely to the left, and pointed at the fleeing siblings. "Get them shits!"

—Amy falls into a sea of black—
—Her face and Milard's smash into each other, becoming halves of the same whole—
—Amy's body is yanked back—
—falls upwards into Stella's mouth —
—swallowed—

Pristine chucked Cheneley onto her back and dropped to her hands.

Cheneley's good foot launched back to meet Milard's nose again. He held onto his sister's neck for dear life.

Pristine booked it on all fours.

"You got this, sis! Don't stop!"

"I won't."

Ahead of them, bits of light peeked through the abundance of trees.

Visible from between the dense thickness of the woodland, pieces of the road's edge.

Pristine jumped over boulders and a variety of mute colored but radiant plant life.

A claw of fury DUG into her back, taking some of her garment and flesh with it.

Hot on their trail, one of the two undead roared at her partner, who trailed behind. Their eyes glowed; one set purple, the other blue, as they neared the siblings.

The undead pursuers doubled in speed, closing in on their prey. They danced between either side of the siblings. Their desperate wolf's teeth for claws took turns to swipe.

Cheneley kicked back with his good leg, a loosened grip around his sister's neck.

An index nail and pinky caught onto threads of Pristine's hair.

Pristine chugged ahead with hicks in her step that she conquered, obsessive in her movements as she dodged and thrashed left and right through the denser bush, taking over the path.

Cheneley slipped off.

Pristine clung to her brother, secured him onto the middle of her back, and pressed her neck against his arms.

An undead soldier clamped onto more of her hair, causing Pristine to miss a beat or two.

Pristine tugged her head away, growling at the ripping sound that came with it. She punched forward as the sun's blinding light overtook the path ahead.

She tripped over her momentum but regained her footing in a heartbeat.

Moved faster.

The undead soldiers snarled—a fingernail's length behind.

Pristine passed the thickness of the wood onto the road. Roared into the air.

Cheneley smiled, nuzzling into her ear.

A tanker truck CLEANED the blur of Pristine and Cheneley's bodies, hurling them away before braking. Underneath the truck, its ziccothrusters ERUPTED from normal discharge as the truck took its unplanned path up to the sky before crashing in a burning rage in some trees down the way. The ziccothrusters' white lights spread out, catching nearby trees on fire.

Darkness ate the scene.

"We've always been spiritualists, out of time and place." Stella's voice called out. **"Wasn't easy keeping**

something from the World that ultimately benefits it. Wasn't easy hiding such a big part of yourself from the masses..."

Amy stood on the edge of the road. Her eyes fell to whatever her feet kicked.

Pristine's body was curled into a ball, holding the carcass of her headless brother. Her grey eyes rolled back and forth from view as she frothed, blood mixed with it. Attached to the back of her head—the undead arm of her almost captor.

The hand tugged, *trying to complete its master's last task,* though not with enough strength to make a difference.

Pristine's body twitched as she cradled what was left of her brother, *even after death.*

Ska-thunk.

Ska-THUNK.

Darkness.

Amy found herself back in Stella's sweltering living room.

Rezna's hand extended on top of her friend's. Their sweat-drenched faces stared into each other's souls.

Stella's tear-filled eyes fell. "I could have been a better mother."

"They loved you." Rezna embraced the wet puddle of a woman. "They loved you."

Stella traced the pressure sores tattooed between her fingers. "When they called me... Law be damned, I exhausted my aura running to make it to my babies. Once I heard they were... found." She broke into upset, her head flung into her receiving hands. "I watched her bleed out." She wiped her eyes and faced Rezna. "Before dying her Final Death. Hours later, her soul came out, and I kept it for a week. Saw everything she... They had been through. Then I had to let her go. His soul was never found. He must... must've got out quick." She chuckled through tears. "Always on an adventure, my Chen." She smiled at Amy. "Maybe they'll find each other out there again."

SKA-THUNK.

All three women jumped out of their seats, staring at the same corner of the room.

Pristine's upside-down down crumpled body watched them. She snickered.

Popped up and down on her bloody head towards them.

SKA-THUNK   SKA-THUNK   SKA-THUNK   SKA-THUNK

"Ma-ma ma-ma ma-ma ma-ma ma-ma ma-ma!" Pristine **ska-thunked** with glee toward her mother. The **squelch** between the top of the child's crown and the wooden floor left a mess behind it. She kept her arms open, ready for a hug.

Amy blinked.

Opened her eyes.

Amy's body leaned forward, her right arm extended in front of her, her other palm reaching toward the ceiling, with her neck and legs bent, crooked, scarecrow style.

Pristine growled onto her knees from across the room. Above her, a dent in the wall. She scratched her nails into the ground without pause, revving up for a charge.

Rezna and Stella stared at Amy with dumbfounded faces.

Off the unusual look from her grandmother, Amy's eyes snapped back to Pristine—

—who prowled towards her.

"Wha—Hey, steady now." Amy backed up, her arm still raised in defense.

"Babygirl…" Stella took cautious steps towards her daughter.

The windows behind Stella BURST—A body crashed through it, and landed perfectly on top of his mother Stella. Cheneley the Undead. He juggled his severed head as he rode his mom's torso. With a wave of his arm, he presented his head to the rest of the room.

"Are you proud of me now, Mum?!"

PECULIAR CASES OF SOMETHING DEVINE:

GRAVITY OF DEVOTION

64

Chapter Five

Maaura Shield

"They would have been about my age, yeah?" Amy asked, alongside her stiff grandmother, whose eyes hypnotically traversed the road before them every stride of the way home.

"About so, yes. Just about…" Rezna's voice trailed away.

"And the cursed soul connected to Stella masks itself as her deepest fears?"

Rezna nodded. "Stella's curse is only an imprint, I'm afraid. Left behind by the source. I've quelled her pain for now with caramel honeybee juice mixed with snailskeed. Keeps the senses in line so she can fight off the imprint haunting her. Either way, Stella's curse is tamed. Lacks a certain… presence. She'll be in top form in a month. I know her."

"If that was tame, I don't wanna see worse."

Rezna nodded. "It's a cruel affliction to be wed with a curse. But once it's clear, memories of that time of infection usually fade. The feeling of what it's like to be tortured by a curse remains forever."

"How can the curse attack us, though?"

"Love. More scientifically, desire. That's why I kept mentioning to Stella how much love existed between her and hers. At the same time, I didn't want to overdo it in fear of providing the curse more fuel."

"You mean the curse would get angry with you?"

"The curse can feel how powerful Stella's love is for her children. It fuels the curse's desires."

They need to be stopped. They ruin everything. "How did Stella's children learn to connect their auras? Didn't think that was possible."

"Flower studies. Stella told me how they loved to watch flowers through the oneity process." Rezna pointed above them. "See?"

They ducked under two crepe myrtles that stretched their branches toward one another. One of the tree's branches continued to wind around the trunk of the other.

"Those crepe myrtles are on their last year. By coming together, they can expand their lifeline by another half-decade, maybe more."

"The Plantae have got it figured more than us." Amy watched a lily pour water into the expanding ovary of another lily. "But how did Cheneley and Pristine apply the concept?"

"Acute fusion. Sometimes, to grow, we latch on to one another. It's not always healthy or in our best interests, but it creates something new. Something unstable. It can be beautiful, but not always. The path of instability is up to the hosts." Rezna intertwined her hands in front of her. "Cheneley and Pristine's auras combined to adapt to their situation of hanging over a cliff. Life or death. To protect one another, their auras became one solid link."

Lilies around them intertwined and poured water into one another.

"It's intriguing, isn't it?" Rezna said. "Watching a flower through the process of oneity master its internal evolution. Something had to scare it enough to change." Rezna stopped eyes ahead with an elevated eyebrow *and a twitch in her cheek.*

"What the fuck is this?"

They stepped between mixed patches of acacias and periwinkle lilies, all leading to the mouth of a quaint village. A row of charming wooden cottages outlined the outskirts of the bustling square.

"Where's the old factory?" Amy asked.

"Finally demolished. Seems our towns have finally come together to support... this."

Amy chuckled. *Look at what teamwork can do. Honestly... this is the most gathered I've seen JD and Enfield... ever.*

They crossed underneath a giant, glowing red banner labeled *Callisto's Haven.* The inhabitants worked around the lot within this small, picturesque new town formed on the trail between Jadesfeld and New Enfield. Regular folk from Jadesfeld walked among the sea of cyan cloaks belonging to The Light. At the end of the lot was a magnificent stage, with an even more impressive cottage behind it, triple the size of the others.

Amy froze. Sidestepped with her eyes locked above. "Gma. Gargoyle." She released the croak in her throat.

Perched atop one of the quaint cottages crouched a gargoyle's statue, whose broad shoulders rivaled the thickness of its legs. The talons of its feet hung off the triangular edge of the cottage's roof. Its folded arms and expression, mixed with anger and pai,n bore down on passersby. The glorious wings on its back were drawn in, yet still towered over the rest of its body. The gargoyle's shadow loomed over Amy's entire body.

"It only confirms what we know." Rezna's eyes stayed on the statue until she crossed it. "The evil shall pass. Until then, make sure you stay out of its way."

They stopped midway to acknowledge the largest cottage of them all.

Silence followed them home and into the basement.

Rezna whipped around. "You were impressive today with how you handled that vengeful spirit. Launched the bloody pest right into the wall." She chuckled. "Caught me off guard. Well done." She made her way across from the room and hit her stretch routine.

"What are you talking about?" Amy asked.

"Oh, come off it! Humility will only get you so far. Now—" Rezna leapt from her frog stretch and regained her towering stature. "Are you ready for your next level of training?" Her arms conducted. "Back straight, arms out to your sides. Stretch, girl, stretch!"

Amy jumped from a frog stretch of her own, *bored as ever.* "Do we have to do this now? *Training?* I just had surgery."

"Today could be the end of your life. You would have wished you had trained. When I was your age, I'd chuck myself in the ocean and train underneath."

"Yes, I know. I almost drowned that one time we tried it."

"You wouldn't have drowned. Don't be dramatic."

"Brilliant, truly. We have more effective training methods in the modern era, Gma."

"Modernism." Rezna sighed, her head in her palm. "Did you even bother opening the book I gave you?"

"I scanned it."

"Excellent, this should be of no consequence to you. You'll have zero trouble mastering this new technique."

Despite the hunger in her belly at the idea of learning a new technique, *why bother? Why spend countless—*

"Cut the daydreaming," Rezna said. "Your head's always lounging in the clouds or smoking them up in my house."

"You sound like Demora."

"At least one of you is making common sense."

Chilly silence cut through the air at the slither of her last syllable

"New technique, you say." Amy offered a hand. "Let's have a go with it, then."

"Hm." Rezna paced, semi-circling back and forth with her arms behind her back. "You'll need all the tricks you can muster to make up for your loss of your aura. Today, you learn the first part of the Maaura style, the Shield Stance."

"A shield doesn't sound very technique-y."

A smirk from Rezna. "You'll have to dig deep within the depths of your soul to focus the energy needed for the shield. Only then can I teach you the next part of the Maaura style." Still pacing, she beckoned her granddaughter with a finger. "It's ready. Try to break my shield."

"You're just going to keep walking back and forth?"

"What if I told you I'm standing still?"

Amy questioned her visual perception as She followed her grandmother's movements. *What type of fuckery is this? I'll crack it.* She trekked forth. A few inches from Rezna, *passing by, passing by, passing by...* Lifted an arm. *Oh, I see.* Moved her left hand close—"Ah, fuck!" Reeled back, shaking out the static jolt.

"You still approach with imbalance," Rezna said. "Let me peel back some layers for you." She closed her eyes, still pacing.

A second Rezna faded into existence right in the middle of the *original's* path, their bodies unfazed by one another. The new Rezna, arms crossed in front of her like an addition symbol, leaned down and faced her palms toward Amy. "This is the base stance. It's your starting point. Launch any attack from here while keeping your defence secure. Your weakness lies behind you."

"What about the top and bottom?"

"That's one you'll have to figure out on your own. You only use the force with which you are given."

Amy shrugged, crouched, and mimicked the stance.

"Ta-ta. Dominant forearm on top for better leverage and effectiveness. Maaura Style-Major."

Amy rolled her eyes and put her right arm on top of her left.

"Forearms. Concentrate. Remember what brought you here." Rezna made her way over. She poked her fingers right into Amy's palms. "I'm still able to get through."

"I've noticed."

Rezna poked. Poked again. "Still able."

"Really? Would you like to try again?" Amy's constipated face looked past her relative.

Poke. Poke. Poke. "Still able to get through."

"This is bull—"

OOOOOOOooooooooOoooooooo

The walls rumbled with a summary of high notes trailing after one another.

Amy's head went on a swivel. "Wha— What the hell was that?"

"We have guests. Spectacular." Rezna strolled up the stairs.

Amy poked her head up behind her. "Is <u>that</u> our new doorbell?"

"It attracts the things that scare what we don't want to intrude."

When does she find the time?

At the kitchen table, the Devine women sat side by side.

Across from them, the woman who led it all, the leader of Callisto's Light: Madame Blé. Dressed in a red gothic-inspired dress with her cerulean cloak behind her, she smiled as her hands slid onto the table. "What a momentous occasion. So glad you both were home. Thank you for welcoming us in."

"Of course." Rezna gave a *polite* nod. "We're tight on time today, Ms. Blé. What's the meaning of this visit? Not to be rude."

"So don't! You won't! And please, it's Madame." Madame Blé's smile creased in. She placed a curious finger on her chin. "I was curious about your household's beliefs in Callisto's Doctrine." She held up a book of muddy red tones with silver embossments around its edges. "The Book of Callisto here guides me today onto your doorstep, The Light's first official visit in your community." She leaned forth, elbow sliding, her hand holding chin. "Including New Enfield."

"Yes," Rezna said. "You're welcomed."

"What is your faith denomination?" Blé eagerly awaited on an elbow.

"Our religious beliefs in this house cease to exist," Rezna said. "With all the respect in the World for what Callisto has done."

"I see." Madame Blé rubbed her candy apple-colored collar. "Do believe this is not the first time I have been in the home of <u>strange</u>. Of course, as in those championing a belief more suited to their lifestyle." She opened arms of embrace, leaning back in her chair. "It is all in Her Light. The Light welcomes all." Her giggle shrieked and filled the room for seconds before she cut it. "Though Callisto <u>literally</u> brought us into the light, Her Essence is still doubted to this day." The woman smiled as she reopened her hands. "We are not here to coax you into belief. Ms. Droûx and I came by to greet the exquisite woman who single-handedly held the towns of Jadesfeld and New Enfield together during the Saint Cloudy crisis."

Amy's eyes fell onto the table.

"It was a troubling time." Rezna poured herself a cup of tea and moved the pitcher towards Madame Blé. "Why is The Light making camp here?"

"We are here to inform you of The Initiative." From the corner came the cold, imposing voice of Ms. Droûx. She bore holes through the Devines somehow at the same time.

"Who's the initiator?" Amy asked.

"All in Callisto's Light," Madame Blé said. "We recognize your towns have dealt with a lack of resources for quite some time now."

"<u>Unimaginable</u> lack of resources," the statue-like figure of Ms. Droûx *chimed in*.

Rezna cut her an eye.

Snarky much?

"Our illustrious cult has created a refuge for your towns," Madame Blé said. "We have established a site that will stand forever, keeping a progressive eye on the people and casting away the offspring of Dalestone. We are hoping that you join our crusade in good faith to show everyone that Callisto will be there for us all when the time comes. A public vow to Her Light."

Rezna raised an eyebrow. "If this is about acting in your commercials, the answer is simply no. I will not be publicly or privately making a vow to anyone." She smiled. "With all due respect."

Madame Blé smiled. Fixed her bi-collar. "In the Haven, some watchful souls caught you inspecting around our camp. What say you, oh great Rezna Devine?"

"Your ambitions are... There's a word for it that died in me long ago."

"Charming," Amy said.

"Yes, that's the one." Rezna poured some more tea.

"We would love for <u>the</u> Rezna Devine, saviour of townsfolk, the Surgeon of Death herself, to officially join our ranks."

"I quite like that last bit, the Surgeon of Death. I didn't know you were capable of flattery, Madame."

"My capabilities will continue to surprise you, I'm sure. The title becomes yours once we make our agreement. You will receive every detail of our organization's mission. Cults of grand ambition are in decline, and it is a travesty. I can have you right at my side for cooperative, <u>genuine</u> changes in our community. Your reach would go wider than where you know."

"Your opposers—"

"Are irrelevant." Madame Blé's fingers drew circles in the air. "As you know, gossip spreads until it is no longer fashionable. The Light is here to continue proving those who doubt in Her power wrong by cleansing away the sin that is aching poor souls. We ask for a simple handshake and an offering." She reached out her open hand to Rezna.

"Offering?" Rezna sipped her tea. "Offering for what?"

"For Callisto, of course."

"What use would a dead woman have for an offering?"

Amy choked on her last sip of tea. Her eyes darted between all the women in the room.

"Maybe..." Ms. Droûx approached the table, one slow step

at a time. "There's a bigger cause here than your ego."

"Well…" Rezna finished her cup. "When you've solved your cause, you can come back to me and try to solve my ego."

"Awkward." Amy shut her bedroom door and hopped onto the bed.

Your request for news bulletins in Jadesfeld has an update. Would you like to hear it?

"Yeah, sure."

Another resident has been taken in by Callisto's Light for cursed symptoms this morning. The total number of confirmed cursed residents is currently seven.

"Ugh, no more news. Creaevix, play me the highlights from LCWF's press conference."

White ziccolights scattered along the wall opposite her and came together to craft a screen. A *buttercup-shaped* woman dressed in a bedazzled spiral of cloth racing around her curves stood tall into the camera.

Next to her, nearly offscreen in her wake, a shivering stick of butter, the reporter. He adjusted his tie and cleared his throat. **"Would you say it is your top priority, Ms. Glossum?"**

Glossum's Persian sand-colored skin flushed. **"I am my own orbit. My massive heart goes out to all those lives lost and affected down in my hometown of New Enfield."** The wrestler leaned *too close* to the camera and pointed her finger *straight into the soul.* **"With Callisto as my witness, I will shed a breath of light for your community. Remember who Her name is."**

1, 2, 3. 1, 2, 3. 1, 2, 3. Amy's curled fingers pressed into the meat of her palms in rhythm with her counts.

On-screen, the reporter's forced chuckle broke Glossum's catwalk strut away from the camera. "You heard her, remember who her name is. Though I'm not sure who's the 'Her' she's referring to in this instance."

The screen scrambled.

It was real? It got louder. The voices—

The voices in your head.

The voices in your head?

The voices, the voice, the voice, the voices in your head
ARE DRIVING YOU AROUND!

Amy spun to the screamer but faced the ziccolit screen and nothing else.

Just cool it, Devine. You're a loony bin, that's all it is.

On the screen, the scattered lights wiggled back together to form new images. A man with a gorgeous haircut pinned back in three buns on his head rose from a table full of media members. He adjusted his suit, popped his collar, and pointed a beefy arm toward a masked wrestler some seats away.

"You knew what was shaking, partner, moment you stepped in the spotlight and tangled with The Family." He pointed at the beautiful, golden LCWF Heavyweight Championship resting on a plaque in the middle of the table. **"Let me tell y'all in case yous forgot! The Marvellous Marone has been here, done that, and the only thing I haven't done is cement myself at the top. I brought The Family too far to go back to scraps now!"**

"This..." The masked wrestler opened his eyes. **"This is my lifeblood."**

The Marvellous Marone slammed onto the table. **"You haven't seen blood yet, pal."**

"This is ridiculous." Amy laughed.

"Axbakitii!" A reporter stood, waving, as his angel-winged mic flew up near the masked wrestler's face. **"You've never beaten Marone in developmental. What's your strategy this time on a grander stage?"**

"I have to win this. It's all or nothing, man. The past is the past, and I can only depend on the 8 Legs of Wisdom to guide me."

"Heh, yeah. Ey, we'll see about that," Marone held his arms up to the crowd. **"I say, the Double M is here to stay. Let's hear it, huh?!"**

"Barbaric." Amy shook her head. "Dedicated to an art that mangles you over time..." *I think I love it.*

Chitterchitterchitterchitt-irp   *Chitterchitterchitter-irp-chitterchitter-ch-irp*

Amy massaged her forehead. The book gifted by Rezna watched her from on top of her pillow. She released a deep sigh and picked it up. Flipped through it. Settled on a page. "'Using no way as way?' I can't do it." She covered her face with the book and sank into the bed. *I should retry the astral plane. Maybe my aura's just... hidden. My orange could still be inside. How did Gma create copies of herself and manage the Maaura Shield with invisiauraism?... That word's sticking. I think I'll keep it.* Amy jots it in her journal. *I wonder if I can manipulate the shadows I cast to guide me towards my light.* **Sigh.** *I gotta do some testing.* **Mmmm.** *A nap first... ....*

...   .

....

....

Save the children.
Save the children.
Save the children.
Save the children.

The broken melody rang through her mind.

Tao tried to teach us, but we wouldn't <u>listen</u>.

Accept it.

'It only confirms what we know. The evil shall pass. Until then, make sure you stay out of its way.'

Who are you?

<u>You.</u>

Amy's eyes shot open, and she dodged another ramming blow from above.

A pink snout huffed into her face.

Chapter Five: Maaura Shield

Chapter Six

Time! for change!

Archie the bat flew in front of her face and growled, then nipped her nose.

"Oh! Royal twit. Where've you been, anyway?" Amy rubbed her nose. With a mocking face, she asked, "How's the Animalia Kingdom? Wait. How—" Her hands touched the cold slab underneath her as she scurried to her feet. *Oh no.*

She scanned up and down the smoky Alleycat Ave., the toughest strip in her part of town. The long, winding alley was even more suspicious at night, with a few silent souls mucking about, rarely making eye contact with one another. *The real partygoers aren't out yet...* People in uninhibited rags of quality cotton, silk, and more scribbled on the walls.

A small child moved from one wall to another. *Based on the structure of his frame, his undeveloped stance, and the small cracks under his feet— obvious signs of strength instability—* Amy knew he could be no older than six. *Took me till seven to properly distribute my weight on each foot.*

She walked through the alley, rubbing her shoulders, searching the night air. *Save the children. Where'd that come from?*

Wasn't me... was it? Must be the schizophrenia. She stooped to the drawing child.

"You alright there, kid?" *Am I truly going mad?*

"Thrillaz!" The boy bounced to his feet. The gap from his missing front tooth was filled with sapphire. He gasped. "The moon's following! Do you have the time?"

"Moon's following? Time's a mystery to me lately." Amy turned to a checkered jacket fellow who leaned up against the wall, smoking a bong two sizes bigger than his head. "Excuse me, do you know the time?"

"Time! for **change!**" The bloke lifted a finger towards her and took a long drag from his spectacular bong. The smoke inside traveled up four pipes winding around one another before meeting at the top. "As of 5 p.m. today, we have won the **right!** to pick our name." He tipped the bong from its handle like a mug as smoke escaped into the sky from the corners of his mouth. "Now they send police forces to do 'checkups' on our facilities. Convenient."

"Pick a name? Who?" Amy asked.

"The nomads! The homeless, as _they_ call us!" The young boy said. "We deserve a name of pride!"

"Don't cha watch the news?" The man kicked the ground. "Now, if only we can come together on a name..."

"Why are you all drawing on the walls? What's that symbol?"

"It's for the homeless," the boy said. "Everyone deserves an icon."

The bong man gestured to the boy. "Sinclair here has come from Ducky's Way to help our sector with the protests. Marvelous idea to etch our symbol where they can't escape it."

More protests. "Super, I know a young lady who was initiated at Ducky, not long ago." *After Cloudy...*

"Our community's gotten a lot bigger," Sinclair said. "I

haven't been there since… Hm. I don't know. Wait, the time. Do you have it, Sir Jov?"

Sir Jov pulled aside his coat. His palm clutched an oversized GCID *from the 2050s.* "Forty-six past eleven."

"Eleven?!" Amy and Sinclair burst out.

"Do you have gum?" Sir Jov asked.

"Fresh out. ZenDrop?" Amy offered him one, but her eyes stayed on the moon. "Hey, Sinclair, what did you mean by the moon's following?"

"The moon follows us sometimes. Us kids, of course. It protects us. I gotta run, The Midnight Inferno's in town!" Sinclair said. "He's releasing a special track at midnight that's only available to Jadesfeld and NewEn! See ya!" He ran off into the darkness.

"Odd lad, sometimes," Sir Jov said, taking another tremendous puff from his pipe. "Idolizing some music artist. **Ppppbbbb.**"

Amy jerked away from the spittle his mouth made. "Well, he's been odd enough to help you."

"Do you have gum?"

"No."

The undead Amys followed her home.
'It only confirms what we know.'
You're gonna die out here.

Amy scribbled into her phoenix-scaled leather journal.

Nothing goes. I don't even feel like writing this crap.
Night confines me like a noose around my neck.
The odd ones stay out of favor.
When will it be time to tip over the plot?

She stopped. Scraped her pen back and forth across the page

as though covering up a horrendous mistake. She tossed the pen and sank into her seat, eyes penetrating the ceiling.

She waved her careless hands through the air. "Dead pen. Dead children. Dead everything."

Decades later, She laid on her back, legs up against the wall. Her face: a fresh canvas for emotion to be painted on. Her arms orchestrated through the air as each finger meticulously strummed as though playing on an invisible piano. She spoke with a hint of funk.

Black, shadowy letters materialized above her fingers and floated off.

Petrified.
It's the perfect term for what I'm feeling inside.
Petrified.
Couldn't save your life if you chose to die.

"Creaevix, time."

It's 2:27 a.m.

Amy ran her hands through her hair. "Alright, let's put the music away for now." Stared into space. "Ok, the astral plane provides conscious connection but not..." Her hands stroked the air again as She mumbled on.

Her ceiling: full of shadow letters.

I know I can crack— Closed her eyes.

"La Luz..."

Opened her veiny, reddened eyes.

"La Luz..."

"I think I've been kidnapped by extraterrestrials," blared from the source of light on Amy's face. The ceiling screen showed the claustrophobic set of *What's News In Jadesfeld?!* Their chief reporters, behind the desk.

"She found herself locked in a cellar of sorts and lost consciousness. Later, she discovered her dress and panties

had been ripped—"

"La Luuuz... Ella lo quiere..."

"Some citizens are voicing their concerns about the Gyaads—"

Amy rubbed her eyes. "Creaevix, time!"

7:17 a.m.

She unhooked the crooked latches around the board over her window.

Slid the board out of the slanted, homemade base.

Ripped the shades open.

Peered down at *her rival.*

"La Luz. Ella lo quiere… Ella quiere la luz y se alejó…" The man strummed his guitar as he strolled down the streets of Jadesfeld. "La Luz…"

"She remembered being operated on a warming table. Authorities say the woman was found in a barn—"

Amy replaced the board over her window. Held her forehead. "I need a smoothie."

Chitterchitterchitterchitt-irp

Amy gagged. *Never mind...*

You'll need more than that to survive.

She spun around the room. *I am going mad.*

"In other news, authorities have gained helpful information leading to the findings of an underground apartment, along with..."

"Found amidst the homeless raids, I'm sure." Amy sat on her bed, rubbing her temples.

"They believe the map and tools found belong to the serial rapist and murderer referred to as The Head Case."

Amy's half-opened eyes twitched and rolled. "Creaevix, what's on entertainment?"

Top stories this morning

Shadows flashed across her face as every wall in her room showed different images without sound. She pointed at a colorful media set on one screen where a young black artist she followed on WorldTome sat across the desk from *What's News In Jadesfeld?!*'s Lead Journalist, Pomwell Packlebee.

"He's here! And what an arrival!" Pomwell caressed the tips of his blue bowtie. **"The Midnight Inferno! Or the artist known as Jamari Wyst, who just dropped an already chart-climbing single, 'Wake The Light'"**

Black goo invaded her vision.

Deep breaths. Amy's eyes closed, her hands over her heart. A sunny day in the woods with Demora. *Not now.*

The goo slurped back up, out of sight.

Amy glanced at the interview at irregular intervals as she moved her hands across the air, more black letters being produced in greater numbers than before.

"Your controversial interview the day before set the Internet on fire! Now, let's get real, Jamari. Your path from age six to now. How have you sustained such a high work effort after so many years?"

"Doing the work. Keeping the checks. Paying it forward."

"But your lyrics aren't always shedding the best light, though, wouldn't you agree?"

"What are you asking, mate?"

"Exactly," Amy said, still focused on her task.

"Well, let's start there. Six years old, your first track, "Mummy's A Slut". You released that."

"Right, I did."

"Where you express your dissatisfaction with your mother's choices—"

"Right, she cheated on my pop, broke up my fam. I had to wait for four years to get any of the profits from that track because of the lawsuit she improperly imposed on me, which kept me in a box. Fourscore less seventy-four, a black boy's dreams, ignored. So I released it myself. I have every right to my music."

Amy walked out of her room with the screen of flashing

images following alongside her on the walls. Swatted away the pinging **!!!** notifications. "Creaevix, silence all WorldTome notes."

WorldTome silenced.

She raised an eyebrow at the knock behind her grandmother's closed bedroom door. Continued downstairs, not turning at the deep, throaty **hehehehehe** from behind the door.

On the wall screen, an LCWF advertisement featured stills of Axbakitii vs. The Marvellous Marone.

Amy tripped down the last step, her eyes glued to the promo.

"Will you turn down that racket?" Rezna called from the kitchen table.

Always gotta say something, can't watch nothing in this house—

The screen dimmed to the wall's natural white color as Amy approached the puzzling sight. "What's this?" She asked.

"Scrubbing." Rezna inspected a whirlpool of her vibrant verdigris green aura. "Scrub the aura on its photonic level and rip out the nasty bug that tried to invade. My shipment of the deceased's prep tools is late as well, and I have two freshly headless departed to look after."

"How should I do mine?" Amy asked. "Aura scrub."

"You're fine, love, don't worry."

"I was there too."

Rezna paused and shifted in her seat with low eyes. "The— Some curses are particular about who they..."

She never stutters. My aura's been shot to shit, huh?

Rezna continued. "...don't attract certain auras because..."

Not even a curse wants me.

And <u>now</u> she asks me how I feel.. "Normal." Amy took a seat beside her. "Shipments come late sometimes, no?"

"I'm usually given a heads-up when one is. Not sure what the bloody hold up is this time."

"Well, a bit is going on at the moment. This Head Case fucker is stirring the plot for our fun little town. Enfield isn't doing much with theirs, I reckon. Maybe you can contact their mortician for extra supplies."

"Language. I am the mortician for Enfield. Mrs. Beverly resigned last week. A killer in Jadesfeld or Enfield; doesn't matter, same difference." Rezna looks off. Shakes her head. "No killings for decades. Now, we've got multiple in the past two years. Surely not a random trend."

OOOOOOOooooooooooooooo

The doorbell **cried** its song.

"You have to change that."

"Guests." Rezna took a deep breath with closed eyes. She pushed her seat away from the table. "With word of my late deliveries. That's the wish."

Amy opened the front door and stood dumbfounded.

Genevieve Graves, the former headmistress of Highbridge Intermissionary School, sat at the kitchen table. She stirred her mug's steaming contents with her pinky.

"Not hot enough for you?" Rezna asked, fingers entwined across the table.

"More sugar?" Amy asked with a nervous smile at her Gma's side.

"Oh, it's scalding, thank you." Graves' gracious smile and frigid blue eyes ran over Amy. "As a former sleeper militant for the Jewish Proud, my skin's not the least bothered." She removed her finger and took a sip, her gaze returning to Rezna. "Your deliveries, I'm afraid, won't be coming. You've made an enemy of the cult by refusing their invitation."

"What's that baffling woman's circus show have to do with it?"

"She's motioned to instate a Chief Mortician of her choosing; one who will follow in Callisto's Light. Her words, not mine. Though I'm surprised you didn't mention to her— you're a former practitioner of spiritualism."

Rezna's eyes waged war with the woman's presence. "That's irrelevant to her and confidential to most. Here I was thinking you were just a schoolteacher."

"I can see the fire in your eyes. It's a shame the World hasn't had use for exorcisms."

"Well, the military's been out of demand since the end of the Twin Wars, hasn't it? Much longer."

Graves closed her half-opened mouth and looked off to the side. "Ah, she's back. Perhaps, Ms. Devine, we can continue this conversation in private." She turned to Amy. "She wanted to get something from the store before seeing you."

Amy looked between the two women—*Graves with charm, Rezna with destruction*— before *happily* removing herself from the table.

Demora stood in the middle of her plot's cemetery, kicking pebbles in her torn jeans and an emerald oversized puffer coat covering her furry white sweater. The sun's rays hit her hair in a manner that caused it to sparkle more golden than usual. She faced Amy. "Hey. You had a package out front. I didn't open it."

Amy takes the brown postage box and lifts its already ripped seal. "Yes, you did." Opens the top.

"New gloves?"

Amy holds up and assesses the brand-new black pair of gloves. "Please don't open my packages." She nods at the other orange paper bag in Demora's hand.

"Here, I got you these." Demora smiled and presented a ribbon-tied gift bag in her palm.

Amy scoffed, took the *gift*, and ripped it open. "Gee, ZenDrops, thanks. More of these should help with the fact that I got smashed by a truck. Intensive surgery. Your gesture of hard candy has been noted."

"Ames, c'mon. I know. I'm sorry—"

"Great! Now you can go fuck off living your life, and I can go fuck off and do the same." Amy turned on her heel.

Barely living.

"Ames, wait." Demora ran and stepped in front of her. "Let's catch up. It's been a murky scene around this place. I miss you."

"Demo, you don't get to pull up whenever you're not running off on your own adventures. I know you've been through hell, but I'm grieving too."

"I <u>murdered</u> someone, you don't—" Demora whispered with a lunge but pulled back. Nodded. "You get it. I recognize that now. Can't keep using that one." She looked into the sun. Exhaled. "I've been a bit selfish. In my own world. I should have been there for you, as you were for me. I won't be taking my eyes off of you again."

Amy crossed her arms and faced the same direction. "You could have called." Her chest swelled, but her expression softened. "Texted, at least."

"I know. I know." Demora looked at her feet. "Ever since that night, these images... I can't get out of my head. Voices. Whispering to me."

Amy got closer. "What type of voices?"

"Same garbage from that night. How worthless I am. How easy I was to manipulate." She raised an eyebrow. "What about you?"

Amy sniffled. Stared at the many gravestones on Rezna's plot.

The air out here will suffocate you.

'Until then, make sure you stay out of its way.'

"Just the usual. Everything in that crawl space. Fighting you."

Silence except for the passing wind.

"The book." Amy continued to rub her arms. "The feeling of my aura ripping from me is a pain I won't forget. Thanks to the technique <u>you</u> taught me." *I shouldn't have—*

"I never asked you to commit the Forbidden Act, you <u>had</u> to!

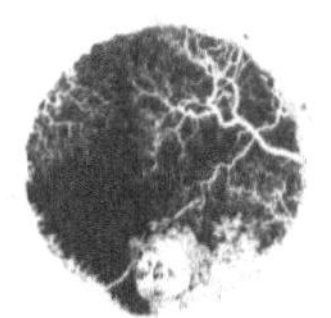

You knew the consequences as much as I did, but you <u>knew</u> it had to be done. I would have done the same thing!"

Amy inhaled before a gruff sigh that opened up another period of silence. "So. What have you been up to lately? How's the therapy? MHP treating you well?"

"Inconsequential. I zoned out during the third appointment and thereafter. Graves has been my refuge. She's teaching a traveling school. You should come to one of her classes, see if it's for you. I know it is."

"You? Schooling? What's Graves got on you?"

"Knowledge is growth. Growth fuels aura."

Aura. More of a curse word every day. Amy's immediate curiosity was extinguished by her missing sense of time and space. Committing herself to a routine, to studies and lectures and early mornings, once more? *Pass.*

"How's your aura healing?" Demora asked.

"It's not. It's still… colorless."

"I wouldn't worry about it. You'll find your way."

Thanks.

"Besides, you best not fall behind me in your training. Bet I could beat you pretty easily with your loss of aura."

"I'm not in the mood, Demora. If you came here to bully me into sparring, it won't work. Find some other way to get stronger."

"You have lost your fighting spirit, for sure. That Cloudy royally fixed your panties, huh?"

Amy tackled Demora to the ground. Sat on top of her with a fist hovering over her best friend's sneering face.

Demora's wild chuckle hit the air as she struggled against Amy's grip on her neck. "You <u>have</u> been training some! That's the Ames I know! The one who'll, no matter what, keep fighting and growing stronger. There she is."

"You're mad." Amy got off her and sat in the grass beside her.

Demora nodded with her hands behind her head, eyes in the sky. "Who isn't?"

Chapter Six: Time! for change!

Chapter Seven

The Rally

*S**he isn't you.*
Amy bolted upright, chest heaving in and out.

Chitterchitterchitterchitterchitterchitterchitterchitter chitterchitterchitter

Outside her open window, a Boeing 787-8 Dreamliner soared straight towards her.

Amy shielded her face right at the fiery impact.

The inferno engulfed everything in its path.

Her charring face shook violently as it burned away last.

"Creaevix, time!" Amy brought her hands down.

It's 9:27 a.m. You have sixteen messages from Demo.

A small smile crept from the corner of Amy's mouth. "Any relevant updates, Creaevix?"

Yes. You may...

"La Luz! Ella lo quiere..." The astounding vocals blended with the announcement of the Creaevix system.

"Are you fuck—? Creaevix, volume max, repeat please!"

You may find this headline interesting: Rezna Devine, Chief Mortician helming from Jadesfeld, revealed as a Spiritualist. The Sister Towns of Jadesfeld and New Enfield Plea For Her Intervention In Recent Crisis. Callisto's Light offers an invitation to today's rally.

"Oh."

Amy took soft steps into the cellar. Full stop upon laying eyes on her grandmother.

Rezna sat cross-legged on the floor, eyes closed, back straight, hands on her knees.

Amy opened her mouth.

"Before you ask," Rezna said, "I am fine. I am healing. And I'm praying for the strength not to kill my enemies."

"I figured. Who do you think was the anonymous source?"

Rezna's eye opened, stayed on Amy for an uncomfortable while, then closed again.

What was Graves thinking? "You're probably right. Will you attend the rally?" Amy asked. "You've been invited."

This time, both eyes fixed on Amy, *all too familiar for an explanation.*

"Right." Amy's eyes traveled the room. "What about people like your friend, Stella? News reports have more cases of demented folk with voices and visions by the day. Maybe you could—"

"Don't. You know why that's not possible."

"You can have an extra private practice. The symptoms. Seeing things others can't. Little odd, no? Same as Stella. Sounds right up our alley."

"I thought you were done saving people? Weren't you just telling me you 'just had surgery?'"

"It's not about me. If you can do something—"

"Haven't I done enough for this town?" Rezna stretched her arms, bent her back, cracked her neck, and got to her feet. "And the next one over? The young hero here feels another pulse in her heart to risk it all for the masses, again?"

Amy hugged herself. "How come you never told me about this whole spiritualist thing? You've always told me you worked in secret."

"There are some things one must keep to herself."

"They're calling for exorcisms if this goes on. But if it's a vengeful spirit, it could rip a less equipped spiritualist apart. Those people could die. Call your green-haired friend if you don't care to involve yourself."

"She's busy." Rezna closed her eyes. "There's something called self-preservation. Try it." She stretched and stretched *and stretched and stretched...*

Amy glared at her grandmother. "You're the Chief Mortician. You have the chance to prevent death."

Silence.

Amy stormed for the stairs. "Guess it's bad for business."

"Before you play hero again, remember where your aura stands."

Amy paused halfway up. She tapped a foot.

Not today.

She made her way up.

Amy, dressed head to toe in a flowing black veiled cloak, pulled out a lace scarf and unfolded it as She opened the front door. She froze, hands midway through wrapping her scarf.

On the front lawn, dozens of townsfolk smiled as they shivered from the escalating, violent winds. They carried baskets of food, quilts, ornaments, and more.

"Knocking on your door... I pulled the trigger..." *Walrus moustache on point,* the guitarist beat those strings while his voice crooned on. "Never knew Her Light could touch me without her neareeer! But my soul caught a glimpse... My heart skips...

Callisto's child, Rezna's gonna touch my sistuuuuhhhh!"

The crowd turned to him in a sudden and unified manner.

"Wha—Oh! Oh no." The guitarist spun to face everyone he could. "My sister died in a tornado. I'm just trying to talk to her."

Amy rang the doorbell.

OOOOOOOoooooooo*ooooooo!* The symphony of crooning notes alerted the crowd, causing off-looks and hung jaws.

"Hey Gma! You have guests!" She smiled at the guests. "She loves guests." Pointed behind her. "That's our new doorbell."

ChatteringChatteringChatteringChatteringChatteringChatterin gChattering The teeth went on *and on and on...* Black goo dripped from every corner.

Enough./**Enough.**

The cottages of Callisto's Haven had been draped in ziccolit confetti strings, all with a deep blood red. Short lines of townsfolk waited for The Light members in front of every cottage door. Each member took the forearms of those in front, closed their eyes, bowed their heads, and whispered prayers to them.

ChatteringChatteringChatteri Chatt... Ch... Ch...

Face covered with her scarf *and the sounds of chattering teeth behind her, finally being killed by the crowd noise,* Amy blended into the sea of spectators.

The black goo parading her vision slurped up out of view.

Behind her, six chattering, undead Amys rose into the air and sang, "It only confirms what we know."

Amy turned to face them, but they were gone. Faced forward—

"Stay out of the way!" The undead Hers slid up from her vision in multiple directions, disappearing into thin air.

Good riddance.

Formations of red ziccolights flew and merged into screens, displaying various angles of the front stage. The screens floated around multiple sections of the village. Behind the stage, the

Haven's biggest cottage, loomed over it all.

"This isn't right?!"

The crowd dispersed at one end of the Haven. Six members of Callisto's Light followed two detectives who forcibly led a walking pile of rags—Kiaixai— away from the event.

Kiaixai struggled against their grip. "Kiaixai's protest shall not be wavered in any way! The Light must pay for their discrepancies! On one day, or another!"

"You can't snatch a hat off someone, Mr. Kia," one of the detectives said.

"Kiai-xai!" The man in rags **roared**, his fist into the heavens.

"Right," the other Det said. "This is your fourth disturbance. Fifth if you count the restroom incident, now come on!"

Amy watched them carry him off, then relocated to the middle right of the crowd. She grabbed a biscuit from a cult member's passing tray and bit into its softness, closing her eyes with a grin. She opened them and turned, bumping into another passing cult member.

This hooded woman looked down on Amy with magnificent yellow eyes. She readjusted her cerulean hood over her porcelain blue skin. The towering presence shifted her gaze and put an extra pep in her step as she moved toward the stage.

A Gyaad in The Light? Their reach is far.

"Can I have your undivided attention?" A familiar *robotic* voice droned across the sky. On the screens above, Ms. Droûx stood behind the podium on stage.

Is it possible for anyone to have such a straight spine?

Behind Ms. Droûx sat a cast of misfits, some familiar, some not.

Oh? Mayor clocked out from vacation for once. Wow—No, wait, no. That's his brother again.

Amy lifted her left wrist. *More cracks, ugh.* Her GCID lit up. She tapped it twice.

Orange lights floated before her, forming into letters in seconds: Demo: Sry, not gonna make the cult's love fest. Catch ya later, tho!

Amy groaned. Swiped the *orange* message away. *Need to change that color.*

" —struck by horrific incidents that have forever scarred the minds of those we hold dear. It is my honour, duty, privilege, and absolute mission to ensure Callisto's Light watches over all its children." Ms. Droûx's assassin-stare scanned the crowd. "We're here today to rejoice in the warmth of the All-Mother and to rectify the loss of your safety. Let me introduce you to a few of our esteemed members. First, we have from the Child-Only Independent Community, Ducky's Way— c.Sinclair." Ms. Droûx slid to the side like an automatic glass door, her arms and head bowed.

The boy I met in Alleycat Way.

With a hop, c.Sinclair took center stage, greeted by roaring applause. "Thank you all for granting my community a voice here today. Um, of all the COICs available today, I'm proud to be Ducky's way. It's close to where my parents perished two years ago. It feels like I'm making a difference they'd approve of. My community is lucky to have elders with specialized deterrence methods to fortify the strength of my COIC's protection and, um… My fellow children and I will offer private surveillance for the towns of Jadesfeld and New Enfield. This will ensure, most importantly, that your children are safe. Thank you."

He bowed to the applause, then dashed to his seat as Ms. Droûx reentered the frame.

"Courageous. I now would like to present your Mayor—oh, excuse me, your Mayor's brother, who has recently been initiated into Callisto's—"

Amy's eyebrow raised at a *peculiar* sight behind some cottages.

Four members of The Light carried a black box that was as tall as five coffins stacked high and as wide as four coffins placed side by side.

Amy slid outside the crowd and strolled toward the back lot, tracking their movements. She rested against the corner of a cottage, pulled out a joint, and glanced at the workers. Struck the joint against the cottage's handrail once, twice, thrice—nothing. She scrunched her face at the unlit joint. Tried some more times.

"What are you spying on?"

Amy spun, catching her slipping joint.. A *rather burly* Light member approached her rear. "I wasn't—"

"Can't a girl hit a joint?" Madame Blé intercepted the man's approach.

"Of course, my Madame." The Light member bowed out.

Madame Blé shook her head. "These volunteers." She nodded over at Amy's joint. "Bit old school." Put her palm out. "May I?"

Amy handed her the joint.

"It takes a special kind of fire to burn our lumber. Terrible for igniting without the right source." Madame Blé pulled out a lighter.

"Bit old school," Amy said.

Madame Blé nodded *"yeah, that's true"* and put the lit joint between her lips, pulled deep. Let a little smoke out. Puffed. Deep.

I should warn her.

Madame Blé exhaled smoke from all facial orifices, reminiscent of a bearded Viking. "Huh." She inspected the joint and passed it back. "If you ever need a stronger plant, I can help." She gestured behind Amy. "I see you are curious, and the heart of the lion runs through your bloodline. Come. Let me show you exactly what is in store." She made off without waiting for a follower.

Amy proceeded with careful strides behind the elderly woman, who made way quicker than her age would suggest, disappearing behind the cottage.

Madame Blé welcomed her as She entered the cottage's open back door where the workers were. The inside's reddish wood decor overwhelmed the spot, with little furniture in sight, yet plenty of boxes, trinkets, and stage production equipment. Members moved things around, including the box She saw them bring in.

"You can leave that one there," Madame Blé told the workers as she beckoned Amy.

Amy stepped towards her and the indiscriminate box.

Madame Blé nodded to two others, and they disassembled the box by its folds, stripping each one after the other. After a few folds were off, the rest fell like dominoes.

A red velvet sheet covered a circular object. The members pulled it off.

"Here it is."

"What is this?" Amy moved up to the glass globe. The interior had a black seat that extended to its bottom, connecting to the exterior base the globe sat in.

"Portable birthing chamber," Madame Blé said. "We have a special member of The Light travelling with us. You will see her soon. Let's talk about you." She walked over to a set of folding chairs, sat, and tapped the one beside her.

Amy took the seat, almost knee to knee with her in the suffocating space, but kept her torso's distance. She squirmed. *Why does she remind me of Gma?* "Why are you trying to force my grandmother out?"

"That was never my intention. I simply wanted us to work together to create a solution. I was and am still willing to set aside ego if she and I both get what we desire. It's all in Her Light."

"Sure, but can it be done without an offering?" Amy crossed her arms. "What does that mean, anyway?"

Madame Blé smiled. "The tumultuous road to reach the status we have today can only accept absolutions. I can trust those who fully commit to Callisto's Light. It is a simple matter of trust and security."

"I can understand that, but forcing people to join your cause doesn't seem to be within 'Her Light'. Sketchy. To be honest."

"Mm. Never force. Only encourage. Once you have made your decision, I set you free. However, we have communities divided between the practices of The Light and your grandmother's. People are losing all that they know, all that they believe in, Callisto's Light. All because they found out your grandmother is—"

"Was," Amy interrupted.

M.Ble smiled. "Was a spiritualist. Stalling the hard work we must do here." Her eyes drooped, but her smile found passing members. Her attention returned to her guest.

"I can assure you my grandmother wants nothing to do with her former marker. You and her have an alliance there."

"That is reassuring. How do we go from here?"

"Let me talk to her. Convince her to talk to you, and we can squash this. Create balance between differences."

"I commend your honour here today. If you ever wanted a tour of our purpose within Her Light, I'd be happy to personally guide you."

Never. "I'll remember that. I'm okay for now, though."

"Well, the offer stands. To solidify my devotion to our agreement to work together harmoniously despite our egos— A parting gift." Madame Blé held out her hands.

A cult member placed a small orb-shaped sack in them.

Madame Blé presented it to Amy.

Amy took it and sniffed the concealed gift. Her eyes went wide. "Thanks."

"I cannot wait to hear your thoughts on my flower recommendation."

PECULIAR CASES OF SOMETHING DEVINE:

GRAVITY OF DEVOTION

CHAPTER SEVEN: THE RALLY

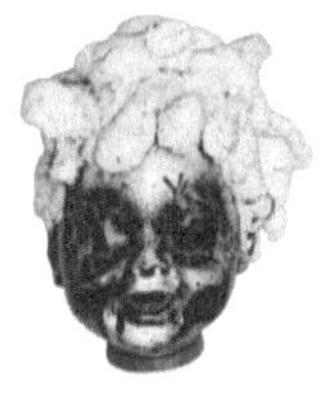

Chapter Eight

Where Are The Damned?

"That's a solid rec." Amy, with bloodshot eyes, reentered the dancing crowd. The blaring music waned in and out of amplification, moving through Amy, her hips swaying along. The hypnotic gospel track echoed through the sky.

On stage, in a white cloak that cascaded around his feet, the performer known as The Midnight Inferno moved his hips to the bend of the beat. An emerald T-shaped design was stitched from his pelvis to the top chest and across the length of each arm, shown in full whenever he expanded his arms.

... eyes...
I am Her hero
An angel in disguise
Floating on her eminence
to build a more beautiful World

Wake The Light

> **Crawling inside of me**
> **I won't care for the pain**
> **If it eliminates all my fear**

The tempo picked up.
Hands thrown to the sky, the crowd swayed with his words, many singing along.

> **Cast out doubt, bricking my resolve**
> **These chains recede humanity's evolve**
> **Don't run from the light,**
> **It belongs in your soul...**

> **Blaze your appetite and false perceptions**
> **It's time to renew; tonight's the lesson**
> **Paralyzed by the weight of others' obsessions**
> **This light will feed my expression**
> **Destroy any repression**

> **Wake The Light!**
> **Crawling inside of me**
> **I won't care for the pain**
> **If it eliminates all my fear**

> **Don't run**
> **Run**
> **Run**
> **Run—**

The stage exploded with fireworks.

> **I'll NEVER fall, cuz—**

The beat skipped a beat and fell into a disarraying looping track whose tempo outmatched the previous.

I'll be, mate, whoever you claim me to be!
And if I weren't, mate
Then why pretend just to agree?
All the media? They twist my story every chance they see!
Creaevix—fuck um! They won't touch my melody!
Cuz I am, mate, whatever you want to believe!
If I weren't, why bother with the fantasy?
Now they tryna break down who I choose to be
Bitch, PLEASE—I'mma "Stan" firm
There's NO rewriting me!

The Midnight Inferno raised the mic and a fist in the air. "Shout out to the Deity of Rap, R.I.P.!" He dropped the mic and waved to the crowd as he left the stage.

Rapturous applause punctuated Amy's eardrums.

"Ma-ri! Ma-ri! Ma-ri! Ma-ri! Ma-ri! Ma-ri!" A large section of devoted fans chanted above the rest.

Ms. Droûx slid center stage behind the returned podium. Scanned the crowd.

Almost silence fell to complete silence once her eyes landed on the cheering section.

"Wonderful. It is now my honour to bring forth the head of Callisto's Light and my sistermate, Madame Blé."

The most deafening applause of the afternoon.

Amy checked her ears for blood. Glazed eyes ran over the still-thundering crowd.

Madame Blé soaked it in at the podium. She raised her arms.

Silence fell.

"Undeniably <u>beautiful</u> expression." She touched her heart with both hands. "The lyrical prowess and angelic voice Mr. Inferno possesses stands with rocksidity amongst the test of time. As every rock on our planet knows itself to be most superior, Mr. Inferno is a force all of his own. And, oh! Such a young age. Oooh. The Youth! We must protect them."

"That's right!"

"Save us, Madame!"

"Luurng tirrrm curmmin!"

"It's impossible!"

"I'd die for you, my Madame!"

"Not our youth alone, but our civilization is in jeopardy. Before we dig further, allow me to welcome with gracious spirit our two special guests who have agreed to take a public vow of discovery through Callisto's Light. First, please join hands for Ms. Mali Cincius!"

Two seated guests helped a pregnant woman out of her seat. The preggo waved for the applause as she eased her way to Madame Blé's side. She curtseyed as best as she could.

"Ms. Cincius's story to reach our doorstep is harrowing, filled with the rare depravity of humanity's worst." Madame Blé held the preggo by the shoulders. "The path to restoration found its worth in Mali Cincius. For the soul of the universe guided remnants of Callisto's soul and harnessed it to life."

Applause.

Madame Blé squeezed her palms in prayer. "We carry life. Hope." Laid her wrinkled hands on and caressed the woman's womb slowly. "We carry the promise of a new tomorrow. If this is not Callisto's divinity at play... What is?" She took Mali's hands into her own. "Ms. Mali Cincius, will you join our ranks of glory?"

"Yes, my Madame." Mali bowed *with the voice of a boozed angel.* "I pledge my light to the Light of Callisto's and welcome the child she entrusted into my womb with her celestial energy."

Applause.

The hell does that mean? Amy bit into a fresh biscuit. Chugged water from a black canteen.

Madame Blé grabbed the podium. "Also here with us is the one who mothers all. The Mother of all mothers. The All-

Mother of all humankind. Carrying the burden of the World's children on her back. Revolutionizing what it means to see yourself in others. Give a superb welcome to Mother."

"Mother?""Mother! She's here!"

"I love Mother."

"Mother's real?"

That's what I'm saying.

Mother. Red veil, with pouchy cheeks hidden underneath, the middle-aged woman's grand cream and crimson dress wrapped around her in folds, widening as it neared the bottom of her feet. Her heavy eyes of sorrow fell over every inch of the crowd *as though examining each face individually. Knowing who they are.*

That was weird. What they say is true. Amy crossed her arms. *Feeling seen.* Smirked. *Kinda historical being here.*

Mother bowed to Madame Blé and then hugged Mali before taking the podium. "Thank you, my child. Thank you to all of my children here today. Witness this harmonious collection of souls who gather to make a change." She exhaled. Her chest pushed the podium.

Ms. Droûx caught and returned it sturdy.

"She's remarkable," a man next to Amy said. "Her bosom is immaculate."

"Truly," another agreed, placing a hand over heart. "As a prime mother would be."

Mother opened her hands to the crowd. "Know that these changes will prosper here and reach out to all of Earth's children. I am most grateful to be a part of this." She grabbed onto Mali's waist. She sucked in air through her nose, her eyes to the skies.

"Only a year ago, when Ms. Cincius's story found my being. The timing paralleled a momentous situation in my life. Our destinies—a point of unavoidable collision. I acknowledged that not all my children of Earth would be able to identify with one another in the same way as I, despite my intention to nurture all hearts and souls to be as one. The depression and self-ridicule ate into me. I lost hope."

Mali hugged her.

Mother kissed her forehead. "Then I heard Mali's story. Never sexed. Finding herself in the pains of death, only a mother knows, while walking the Fields of Correlation, stripped under this century's darkest red moon. In those fields, she woke up three months pregnant at 3:33 pm. The holy threes designating purity, adopting this beautiful woman as my own was only a divine translation."

Sobs? and applause.

Half a biscuit sat in Amy's open mouth. *No way she's claiming—*

"I, your Mother, pledge all my light and all of my heart to Callisto's Light."

Cheers joined the praise, followed by streams of ziccolights across the sky.

Scoff! A young man with a curved scar on his head ruffled his hair. His eyes darted everywhere, not settling on a particular spot. His torso shook out of sorts. "Bullshit." He pushed his way through the crowd.

"Bah. They'll say it's all scripted," an elderly gentleman in a wheelchair grunted, some feet away from Amy. "It's already starting with the younger generation. Someday, the people of tomorrow won't even believe Callisto existed. I was a boy when she passed. She paved the way for what we have today. We should cherish that."

"NO, THEY CAN'T FEAST ON ME!"

Cyan-cloaked members dragged the young man with the curved scar from the back of the crowd.

The disturbed man's head twisted from side to side. "NO! Why are they doing this?! I didn't fail you, Father! Why are you in me?!"

Cerulean cloaks directed them to a cottage's open door.

"What the fuck?" Amy hurried towards the back of the crowd. "What are they doing?! Hey! Stop! Stop—"

A Light member stepped in front of her. "It's alright, my child. That poor soul has been infected by something we will help him resolve. We're here to help The Damned."

Perplexed faces in the surrounding crowd watched Amy with everything but concern or understanding. *How am I the crazy one here?*

Light members rushed toward the cottage where the screaming man was taken. The one in front of Amy smiled and followed after them.

"Ugh, there's number five," a *cute* young woman with *orange* pigtails said. She moved closer to Amy. "Another year, another curse."

Tell me about it. They're all... used to this. While I locked myself away. Amy stopped herself from rolling her eyes at the "In Her Light" pin on the young woman's shirt. "You know what's up with the different colored cloaks?"

"Darker cloaks have higher rank." She beamed and twisted her pigtails. "I'm swearing myself into The Light first thing tomorrow morning. Gosh, I hope I become an understudy. Ready to make a difference!" She pointed to the stage. "M.Ble's back!"

Applause as Madame Blé hugged Mother and Mali. Then she took center stage, bringing with her a sudden silence.

"This..." She tapped her bony finger on the podium. "This is... We are... in a Callistonian state. Yet, there has been decay. As you see, the Damned are suffering. Every day. All things come from the power of Callisto. She granted us strength beyond the comprehension of our ancestors. She granted us wisdom far beyond our years. She granted us life beyond life."

Madame Blé stared over the crowd, then at Ms. Droûx, who nodded to her.

"Callisto's gifts include what lurks in the shadows. Now, I have watched—We have watched—as your police forces have failed you. They have failed to protect you from things they cannot even protect themselves from. No more. No... No, no, no, no. No more. The next time the forces of Dalestone try to invade the homes and heads of Callisto's children, we will eliminate the threat with such swift force that even your detectives shall resign, for they will have witnessed a <u>might</u> so strong that they know they can never again keep you safe. They will beg for our Light, as we are the warriors of Callisto. We, of course, will shelter them as well, for they will have finally realized the depths of their failure... and follow us into <u>The Light</u>."

Amy covered her ears as the crowd's approval proved too much. The relentless applause ate up the rest of the speech. *This exceeds the advertisements.*

"... Norma Jones!" Madame Blé left the stage, nodding at her replacement.

Been a while since I visited little Issa. I should... Amy smiled at her small friend's aunt, Ms. Jones, *looking healthier than ever.*

Norma Jones put up prayer hands for the applause she received as she stood behind the podium. "Sometimes you don't come back the same. It's in that decadent absurdism that we harbour in our routine personas. I'm no stranger to the bitter feelings that reality bestows upon us, but I have seen the light. In death... you're forced to recognise your morality."

Amy held her breath. *What are you doing, Norma? I mean, The Light are Deathwalker sympathizers, but— you can't—She wouldn't—they'll ostracize her—I've gotta—*

"I was nearly there." Norma nodded. "I saw enough of death to know I didn't want to cross over until I fulfilled my deeds for this Earth."

Sympathetic murmurs and applause filled the air.

"Such a brave woman."

"So close to death."

Amy exhaled her panic.

Behind Norma, ziccolights formed three white screens. A face appeared on each: Melanie Bates, her husband Codwell Bates, and *Norma's only child,* Jonathan Jones.

Amy stared at the boy's face on the last screen. *Jonathan. The way I last... how we last spoke... that damn curse ruined your face. Ruined you.*

Norma turned from the screens, steely eyes down on the podium. "My fam... my family was taken from me. The aftermath left more questions than answers. Hours of therapy for those poor children, including my niece. This year's death of that innocent boy is another test of our resolve. No child should take their own life. Trinks' legacy will go on."

"What's a bird without its voice?"

Amy half-smiled. She headed toward the back of the crowd with Norma's voice booming behind her. She picked up her pace after a slight crack in the woman's voice stabbed her heart. "As an ambassador for Jadesfeld and Founder of the Bates Foundation, my aim…"

Thoughts of death and all it brought stayed with Amy on her trek. *What am I even thinking? I should leave the detective work to <u>actual</u> detectives. But something's off with this cult, I can feel it. What are they doing to those victims? I can't find a single update on any of them after The Light took them in.* She shook her head and moved faster past her *mocking deathmates,* who floated above her. *As much as I want to ignore this… I can't.* Two of her doppelgangers walked alongside her.

She passed odd stares in the JPD without a stir. *Imagine if they saw my marching band.*

All of her doppelgangers snickered. Vanished.

She approached a steel round table in the cafeteria with two *out-of-place* detectives. *These American blokes dress funny.*

"Fabricated!" one of them shouted in a hushed manner *with a bowtie too tight and a mustache too long.*

"Expect us to rub two cents to get five," his partner responded, and he punctuated the point by pumping his thumb into the tongue of his red and white high-top sneakers. *Quite like those, actually.* The *foreign* detectives complained to one another as they sipped coffee.

Amy pointed down at the Det's high-tops. "Those them pump-like-a-sponge-to-cushion joints, yeah?"

The meek detective rose from his finger-pumping sneaker action and nodded.

"They're quite sick, good pick. You boys ain't from around

here." Amy sat at their table. "Maybe I could be of some help to you fellows."

"Aren't you some other Det's student? No thanks."

"Listen, miss, we're not interested in babysitting a—"

"—Non-existent."

"—junior Det, capiche?"

Amy checked her fingernails. "I'm just saying maybe I can get into places your warrants can't. Or places you're not trusted to be."

"Are you—breaking-and-entering—have you—"

"Lemme handle this, Rob. Whatchu talkin' about? You tryna get arrested?"

Amy leaned back in her chair and raised an eyebrow. "Look, fellas. Your American cowboyism hasn't won any hearts around this precinct, much less the community. You've been sent to help with this <u>awfully</u> dreadful Head Case. Now people with voices in their heads are popping up all over." She leaned in between them. "The cult's got your balls in a vice, and you boys need a waiver. Let me be the green thumb that sends you on your way. Catch me?"

The men gaped at her.

Amy walked out the sideswiping automatic glass doors of the Jadesfeld Police Department. She paused near a sunlit portion of the *more glorious than usual* front lot. She smirked at the silver Junior Detective badge gleaming in her right palm.

"I'm back."

CHAPTER EIGHT: WHERE ARE THE DAMNED?

Chapter Nine

Alleycat Blues: Torment Of The Dead

Another failure, Devine. Out for prayer. Amy grumbled under her breath. *Well, shit, where the hell does The Light pray that isn't the church?* She paused, hands on hips, staring back at the quiet of Callisto's Haven, *everyone seemingly on vacation elsewhere.* Continued her retreat from the middle of the small community. *If my investigation goes any colder, those out-of-town boys could turn me in to the precinct. Get me barred if I don't deliver. Oof!*

"Fuck." Amy held her head as she buckled under an invisible weight so strong it snapped back some fingers on her right hand. "What the—" She removed the glove on her right hand and stared at her middle finger, which was bent and stuck at an angle somewhere between the range of normal hyperextension and painful. She carefully peeled her finger forward to its normal position. Shook out and flexed her fingers. Cringed at the searing pain awakening within her deep scar. Looked up and studied the ground ahead of her. She walked towards *it.*

I feel something.

Her foot **crunched** on a darkened patch of dirt. "The hell?" She used the tip of her sneakers to kick some of the dirt up. *This weird patch shouldn't be here. Wait, that's a bit of deditrite soil.* Amy dug into the *fresh* earth, creating a small crater in seconds. A piece of ribbon caught around her finger. She pulled more of it out of the ground and then threw it aside, going back to digging.

Her hand uncovered a glass object peeking from beneath the dirt.

"What do we have here?" Amy doggily spread the earth aside, more of the object freed in the process: it sat on an old ball, another marble-like object coming into—

A finger, then the whole hand, punched out of the crater's center and grabbed her wrist.

"Motherfu—" Amy tugged her hand away and out of the foreign hand's grip.

The two marbles rose— dirt exploding up, revealing the head of a badly beaten woman, her jaw gnawing its way out of the ground.

"Oh, my—" Amy quickly assisted with uncovering the rest of the buried woman. She got half the woman's torso uncovered before Amy reeled back, eyes widened on the partially unburied figure.

Only the woman's jaw moved, gnawing at the air. Her upper body was thinner than it should be, while her lower body was *plumper than expected for her kind. Swollen, maybe.* The woman's veins were showing all over her body. Her head, not bruised, but merely decayed. *An undead. Ok, breathe, Devine, fuck. Fuck, it's one of them. I can't—*

The woman's face was stuck to one side, but her eyes were on Amy. A tear left one, then both her eyes. A haggard breath escaped her. "Please. Help."

Amy watched the woman, frozen, as the undead woman's cries strained in the windy air.

"Please."

"Please. Help. Can't... move."

"Please. Don't—don't leave... me."

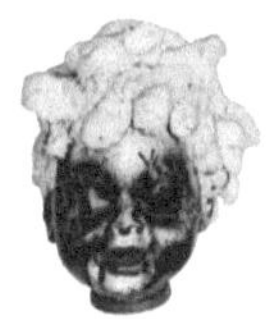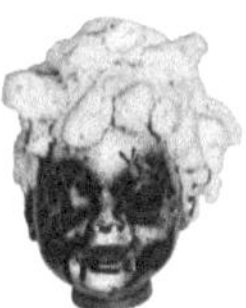

A familiar blue light blinded Amy's face as she forced her eyes to bore into the steel table before her instead.

A blue-colored hologram of the area inside Callisto's Haven where Amy undug the undead was spun around by a hand.

Its owner took off his crimson CrownEagle glasses and wiped them with a cloth. "You take trips to the Haven often, digging around in their dirt, Ms. Devine?"

"I was gonna inquire about joining The Light's understudy program." *Blech.* "No one was home and as I said—"

"Yes. You're quite familiar with deditrite thanks to your grandmother's profession." The detective sighed and sat across from her. He watched the hologram on the table slow from its spin. "I'm not accusing you of anything. Just making sure nothing's missed. It's my last chance."

"Come again?"

"I'm being reassigned across the country tomorrow morning. And we have these bodies turning up." He tossed his glasses on the table, rubbed his eyes, then wiped his white locs back as he exhaled.

"Where's your partner?"

"Playing darts at the pool hall, the bastard. Excuse my French. Only as comfortable because you're a det in training, I understand."

Amy nodded, warm from the acknowledgement. "Lemme guess. He's not thrilled about solving a crime targeting the undead."

"You didn't hear it from me. Not all of us hate the Angels."

"No. What's your name again, detective?"

"Detective Ryaant."

"Don't leave town. In case we have any more questions."

—Amy digs dirt, freeing more of the undead woman out of her early grave— the woman cries— Amy cries, a slight bit hysterical, as more of the woman is freed— the woman's face mushes into her cheek, both their tears mixing—

— "I'm sorry," Amy whispers—

— "It's okay," the undead woman replies—

"We'll be in touch, Ms. Devinve. The remaining JPD, of course."

Amy marched towards the precinct's exit, avoiding the stares.

"Hey-a!" Praisure popped over to her. "Jimmy's friend, right?"

Amy barely nodded, uncomfortable with stopping in her tracks.

"That was some nice detective work there, knowing where the victim was buried.""Yeah, it's no sweat. Learned about various soil types from my grandmother. Have a good one." Amy hauled ass towards the exit once more.

"Yeah," Praisure's voice called from behind. **"You too."**

In the background, bits and pieces of some voices of detectives she passed caught her ear.

"Yeah, she's the granddaughter of the mortician."

"Word, now? Rezna Devine's kin, huh? Last year with the uh—"

"Yup, that's her, alright."

"Saving the dead. Shudda left that rotter buried. What kind of human is she?"

Amy stopped at the exit door.

Not a breath behind her.

She exited the station.

You have to let go.

Why can I see you?

I don't know. Part of me remains... tied to you. Will you help them?

I'll help. Jonathan, wait!

'What's a bird without its voice?'

"Have you ever had your throat ripped out by a stripping crane? I wouldn't put it in the top five moments of my life..."

"Ah haha hahaha ha, quite... that's—"

"What I saw was worse. That girl's body was in shambles. She never should've been left out there alone. When have you last heard of an Enfield teen getting left behind during a school trip? Especially with headcounts every hour from start and finish? School outings throughout several neighbouring regions have a 100% successful return rate. What happened?"

"What is it you believe, Ms. Yamibel?"

"Hm."

"Do you need some water?"

"Yes, please."

"Here you go."

Gulp-ik. Gulp-ik. Gulpgulgul.

"Rotting throat ain't what it used to be. What I believe is irrelevant. It's the facts that are frightening. 'Eyes grey like the dead's.' Can you believe that's a hiss now? The living have always been society's tormentors. The dead simply watch."

"What are the facts, Ms Yamibel?"

"The facts are that the girl's mother lives three doors down from me in Euyrkm, and I've watched that sweet baby visit her mother for the past three years as if nothing's changed. Only one of my living children remains in contact with me. People have difficulty understanding what's outside their reality until they're confronted with unfamiliar challenges. Thrown into the unknown."

A crow sped past Amy's snoring noggin.

"And what do you see on the other side?"

"I see the depths of what fear can be. That girl never hid the _fact_ that she still loved her mother. Society hid how inappropriate they felt her decision was. 'One can't mingle with the dead and expect not to rot along with them.' That's what my ex-husband told me two days after my death, before I divorced him. The simple fact is, they left that girl behind that night, knowing for weeks we've had a starving, perverted murderer stalking for another helping of meat. This is another blatant attempt to harm my community."

"Is there—has there been any progress? Something the detectives haven't—"

"Oh, they'll progress when it's convenient." Gulp-ik. Gulp-ik. Gulpgulgul.

A murder of crows flew by Amy's still, unnerved slumber. Sorrowful wench of a girl...

"What do you want people to hear tonight?"

"Regrettably, there's nothing that'll resonate with broken ears. You choose to believe in what you know as gospel until the day comes when life shows you something... else."

I kicked and kicked and kicked her Devine ass—

"I'm an Angel. I have passed, but I walk this Earth in another form. The sooner humanity can accept my kind, the quicker we can create solutions. Sometimes those come by force."

Amy stirred awake. She shook the woman's greenish face from yesterday's news segment from her mind. Cradled her ambitious migraine with half-open eyes.

Gulp-ik. Gulp-ik. Gulpgulgul.

Astral Amy's hands and nose faded away.

Amy sat upright in the puffy, bright green lounge chaise.

Below her, a bustling section of Alleycat Ave.

Third time this week, we end up out here. What are we doing, Devine? Amy shivered. Stared at the bright Moon. Her heart thumped out of her chest. *You're alright. You are all right.*

Her eyes closed. *Deep breaths.*

"Creaevix, time."

It's 3:27 a.m.

"Interesting." Amy sat up, this time on her bed in her room. Splitting headache aside, she stretched with a little smile on her face. *More rested than I can remember.*

Amy pulled the globe-shaped sack—*courtesy of M.Blé*—out of her nightstand.

Unwrapped it.

Looked over the contents—a glass orb with moon symbols decorating it. Inside, filled to the brim with marijuana nuggets.

Amy's smile widened.

Dropped her twelve-inch caterpillar bong on the table.

Glass grinder hit down beside it, its cover popping off to reveal an oscillating rainbow light going around the razor-sharp blades.

Five minutes later, her reddened eyeballs followed the smoky trails circling her. "The old cat knows what she's talking about." She snatched her journal off the table's edge and slammed it open on her lap.

The moonlit sky peeked through the shades.

Amy shielded her face from it. Cleared the bong and waved the smoky air away. Stared back at the window, then down at the broken wooden boards that once adorned it.

Skirrrcht!

Amy grilled her closed bedroom door. "Unslept, annoying tokens." She picked up her pen, already in place at her last writing spot.

Swapch!

Took to the pages with vigor *but less anger than She's used to.*

Shut up! She clawed the sides of her head. *Thought I'd be cured by now.*

Amy jabbed the pen back to the page.

Perçeverance.

At what coçt?

What's the point of perçeverance if you're going to watch people die?

Swapch!

"The bloody hell!" Amy barked at her door. "Go away, or I'll show you real danger!" *These fucking tokens need to go. I should wake Gma, let her deal with her mess.*

Swapch! Swapch! Swapch! The thumps came from downstairs, left, right, all over the house.

Amy's head spun around her room and stopped at her window.

What the fuck?!

"What the fuck?" *Who—*

An ever-blinking set of eyeballs peered at her from outside her window.

The blinking stopped. The golden-streaked set of peepers dipped out of view.

Chapter Nine: Alleycat Blues: Torment Of The Dead

126

Chapter Ten

Haven Church

"Has she lost her fucking bloody Castillonian mind?!" Rezna's bloodshot eyeballs *bore holes in anything that moved* as she paced.

"So you did catch the cult's festival of love?" Amy said.

They stood in the basement in front of the ziccolit body of Norma Jones.

"I know," Zicco-Norma said. "The tone in the room when I told her I didn't think these 'night checks' were the greatest idea. I declined joining The Light, and her henchwoman looked ready to devour my soul. Unfortunately, it's all authorized under the Mayor. The nightly security checks were to be publicly announced three days before commencement." Shook her head. "Who follows regulation anymore?"

"I want her entire coven of disillusioned cretins and preggo bimbos out of my town."

"I'm afraid the Mayor's already granted them residency as well. 'Till the good work is done.'"

"Of course he has. Good work, what work does he know? Can't be here for more than a day or two, yet he makes all our decisions."

"Election's next year if you'd like to take a stab at it. I can't imagine you not winning against him."

"Do I give the impression of a politician?"

"Why don't you run, Norma?" Amy asked. "Gma could be your liaison of sorts. Help both our worlds."

Rezna and Norma stared at her, caught each other's eye, then stared into space.

"The undead Mayor." Zicco-Norma chuckled. "Wouldn't that be something..."

"I know your currency buys you privacy, Norma, but I'd still be careful on these lines. Anyhow, it's evident this woman's targeting us. I will not be harassed."

"My legal defences will make sure that if you or your 'tokens' have to intervene, you'll be taken care of. For now, let this one pass, and let's work on the long game, Rezna. This new initiative Blé introduced has some particularly awful annoyances still on the way." Zicco-Norma shuffled through some papers at her location. "The night checks are necessary, apparently, each night, every three hours, to make sure residents sleep with peace and aren't being possessed or harmed in any manner by unwanted supernatural forces. They're also opting for death portraits to be taken for grievance and new spiritual rituals, affixed—"

"Fuck off, for what?" Amy said.

"Tone," Rezna *warned*. She faced Zicco-Norma. "What the absolute hell is that about?"

"Oh. Something Victorian, remember you must die, etc, etc..."

"Latin originally. The Mayor approved?" Amy asked. "Does she remember we are living? Unlike her Callisto..."

"There are some contracts, monthly festivals, morning musical accompaniments, establishment of an in-house infirmary, rituals for protection and growth... uhh, what else? They're anal on curfews. Want people inside by 9 P.M. sharp so they can do their cleansing ritual throughout the towns."

Thoughts hit Amy fast, and her bowels begged for escape. All the nights, She would pass out at indiscriminate locations. How She made her way home with zero recollections…

Rezna stopped pacing. "I want to reinstall the bullet train."

"Well, that runs under their lot," Zicco-Norma said.

"I want to reinstall the bullet train to grant I, the Chief Mortician, more efficient travel to all communities I've worked with over the years. We'll need it in this new climate of terror. I'm sure the Mayor would agree, especially around election time. This would allow quick access to help throughout each of the nine vicinities that make up Camden Lot."

"But that's under their lot." Zicco-Norma grabbed her forehead.

"Chance can be a cruel operator."

"My bones can't take this anymore."

"Stick with me, honey, and you'll find I can be quite an ally." Rezna *smiled*. "Creaevix, time."

It's 4:39 a.m.

"I'll have the plans drawn up by this afternoon, and I'll stop by your office."

Sigh. "I'll see you then. Good day, ladies." Zicco-Norma blinked out of sight.

"Are you sure about this?" Amy asked.

"Sure does not certify comfort."

"Can we talk about the increasing amount of tokens in this house since last year?"

"What about them?"

"Are you— Are you preparing for something like Cloudy—" The heat rose in Amy's chest. "Something like Cloudy to happen again?" She gave a nervous corner smile. "The air is getting hot and phlemmy in here, no?" she added as She shrank away from her relative.

Rezna's *intrigued* eye *studied me*. "Its name still bores dread in you?"

Amy leaned into the wall and bowed her head away from

her grandmother's.

Rezna nodded. "The tokens are just a precaution. Some souls who pass can't let go. So they inhabit objects, usually something that they feel represents them well. A token. The ones in our home have agreed to keep an eye out for us while we shelter them." She moved up the stairs, but paused. Turned back. I don't know what The Light is here to accomplish in our town, but I do not trust it'll be in our best interests."

"Again, my apologies for that awful disturbance outside your window. That was an ill and rare miscommunication between myself and my staff. You see, we have some volunteers bestowed upon Callisto's Light by your Mayor. These... volunteers thought I said to start security checks outside homes at 4 a.m. My direction is and was to terminate the checks at that time, wrapping up on Wunmos Court. That individual that was outside your window is no longer under my employ. Not in my Light."

"All good." Amy kept her eyes on her.

Dull daylight around them, Amy walked alongside Madame Blé in Callisto's Haven.

The 4 p.m. tour was best. The hell if I was gonna wake up at 5 a.m. Light members populated the space in greater numbers *than I expected. I'm in the thick of it. Not a normal resident in sight, but me.*

Several Light members supported a kneeling, hysterically crying woman.

"Is she alright?" Amy asked.

"Oh." Madame Blé watched the scene unfold. "I will have to check in on that. Poor Lucia. Terribly nice girl."

They stopped in front of the largest cottage in Callisto's Haven.

"Welcome to Haven Church," Madame Blé said with an open arm towards the now-opening front doors. Two of her Light members smiled as they held the doors open for them with a friendly nod and a hand waving them inside the *massive church!*

"Thank you, dear angels. Do you know what is going on with our sweet Lucia?"

"No, Madame."

"No, my Madame."

"Alright then. Lovely day; have one, girls."

The church's interior seemed three times the size of its exterior, with the congregation area having enough seating for about ten kabaddi teams, while the sanctuary had twice that amount. The rest was your typical building of worship; stained glass depicted multiple images of the same woman with blue and grey hair doing different things: reading, conversing with others in lab coats, and feeding animals. Some members sat in the congregation, reading or praying.

As they reached the end of the nave, a member, hair colored and styled like a cherry, *skin smooth and flawless as chocolate milk,* moved from behind the altar and bent over to them with a bundle in her hands. Madame Blé took it and led them to the right, where a glass door awaited them.

"Celestia, is Lucia alright? She is out there balling her pure heart out?"

The cherry-haired girl behind Amy chuckled. "Oh, yeah. She failed another exam. That exam. Mrs. Mothershead got into her." Celestia cocked her head on Amy. "Yey."

Amy smiled back. "Hey."

"Celestia, do me a favour and run to Mrs. Mothershead's office and tell her I would like a meeting in two hours."

"You've got it, M.Blé." Lucia winked at Amy. "Seeya sometime."

"Later." Amy lost control of her smile as she and Madame Blé approached the door.

"Before we cross this threshold, I must inform you that no one is to pass any further without wearing the robes of Her honour." Madame Blé held the bundle out to Amy. "Then we may enter The Pits."

Madame Blé led the way down a bright staircase made of

dirt. "Normally, you would walk these stairs and the following path called Bridle Lane, before reaching a room where you are given your sacred cloak. Since this is only a tour, such a formal process is unnecessary."

Amy, donning one of the cyan cloaks of Callisto's Light, trailed cautiously behind her. She did a double-take at the steps, less dirt and more of a blue surface taking over the further down they went. "Is this blue limestone?"

M.Blé smiled. "We are fortunate enough to have this rare stone in abundance thanks to Her grand contributions. Callisto studied the loss of naturally occurring blue limestone for years, stockpiling samples to test her theory that it may be responsible for the biological advancement of 95% of all living beings."

"95? School taught us that only around 70% of life evolved."

They reached the lower level, The Pits, the floor completely covered in blue limestone.

"It is forbidden for today's schooling system to include the numbers within the Angels community in what they teach. Since no one can explain the complex existence of the undead, the education leaders of our World feel it unwise to mention. Not to mention the other forms of life unaccounted for."

As they moved down the hall of reflective walls, Amy peeked into the window of a room they passed by. Inside, several Light members in cyan cloaks like hers watched a presentation on the ziccolit wall screen. An instructor stood at the front of the room, lecturing as the video played. Swaying her hips.

Amy studied the woman's lips. "Schooling?"

Madame Blé waited for her some feet ahead. "That is one of our understudy classes."

"Understudy?"

"Those who decide to learn within the Church Haven's walls will eventually have earned their place within our ranks. Do you see there? Each understudy is marked with a star on their hood."

Amy peeped a yellow star on one of the hoods inside the classroom. "I see." She moved ahead. *Big fault? What big fault was that teacher talking about?*

Madame Blé's arms and face regarded the walls as old friends. "Each morning at 6 a.m., I walk every single hall of this church. Top to bottom."

Amy stared at the framed, harsh drawings along the wall. "These are all Lutheran Basquiats. That stamp. Are they— I was told these don't exist."

"They do. The great-great relative of one of the World's most formidable artists created his own series of thirty-three paintings to showcase some of the greatest achievements in the history of Callisto's Light. These are the only paintings ever done by the artist. He's one of our firmest believers."

Amy's eye stayed with one of the art pieces. A black figure stood under a purple sky in the middle of a raging fire. A shadow stood tall in the background.

Crick-ka.

What was that? Amy paused, staring at the wall beside her, in between contrasting paintings of a gloomy purple sky with black clouds. She turned her head, pretending to watch another class in session, and listened for the *faint grinding...* she heard a moment ago. *Floor plan rotation tech. Why would a church need shifting rooms?*

"My office is not much further," Madame Blé called from ahead.

She led them into a modest office that stood out for its red decor. "Please. Have a seat." Madame Blé sat behind her desk.

Amy sat across from her in one of two guest seats, eyes glued to a golden-framed letter signed by none other than *the Kay Reeves Estate, the Jackson Estate, and the Carey family— three of the most influential families in our society! 'In honour of the immense work Callisto's Light has done to pave a future of advancement for all.' Had no clue how far The Light's reach extends.*

"It is a bit much, I suppose, to frame it in such a way." M.Blé pointed to it. It is my reminder to keep going. Once upon a time, the Reeves family wanted nothing to do with us."

"What changed?"

"We saved their youngest daughter from a terrible fate." M.Blé took something out of her desk and held it towards Amy.

Amy took the red orb, twisted and popped it open. She pulled a golden chain with a glimmering blue key from inside it.

"That key belonged to Callisto. It is passed down and worn by every leader of The Light. It was the key to her home back in The States. I am not yet worthy of its splendour, which is why I have not yet worn it. Because of that man."

Amy took a look at the portrait hanging over the door that the cult leader pointed at. "Who is he?"

"The former leader of Callisto's Light. My former senior. See through my eyes how I only see through my cult."

.

.

.

FADE IN:

INT. CALLISTO CHURCH OF SUSSEX – DAY

A man in cerulean robes, draped around his feet and a crown with a red moon on his head, marches down the vast halls made up entirely of blue limestone. He claps his hands over passing candles, taking away their flames. Darkness left behind him.

> MADAME BLÉ (V.O.)
> This World, some ancient time ago, classified a cult as sinister. A label that stuck around for the adolescent years of Callisto's Light. Arch Priest Dictor was always ambitious, and on that day, I learned how much.

PRIEST DICTOR snuffs out the last candle and turns a corner.

INT. CALLISTO CHURCH OF SUSSEX - CRYPT - DAY

He shuffles through the dimly lit space between headstones. Stops at a statue of a warrior.

Lifts it from the bottom of one end.

Drags and pushes it feet away.

Looks down at the hidden door previously concealed.

INT. SECRET CHAMBER

Priest Dictor removes a padlock from a steel door. Opens it.

SECRET ROOM

FIVE PRISONERS, tied from head to toe like a mummy with only their eyes, nose, and mouth uncovered (but with a muzzle over each), shake in terror as the priest approaches them.

> MADAME BLÉ (V.O., CONT'D)
> He was the best of us. And the worst of us. Anyone who disagreed with The Light's progression would disappear without a trace. I had suspicions, but they earned me a lengthy suspension and much more trouble than I bargained for.

Priest Dictor prays over them as the room's lighting darkens.

The prisoners' **screams** fill the air...

> MADAME BLÉ (V.O., CONT'D)

It took weeks after my return,
but my research and persistence
during my "vacation" led me right
to the cellar where he held the
latest bunch.

EXT. COURTHOUSE - NIGHT

Priest Dictor, wearing a white jumpsuit,
is led down the steps by a detective,
rows of more dets behind them.

> MADAME BLÉ (V.O., CONT'D)
> It was one of the fastest trials
> of our time. The World Committee
> wanted to make an example of him,
> showing others that wicked ways
> would not be tolerated in our
> World. Though he never gave up
> the burial place of the bodies
> of the lives he took.

EXT. CALLISTO CHURCH OF SUSSEX - DAY

A decades-younger Madame Blé stands
behind a podium. A priest behind her
lowers a gold necklace with seven circles
over her head and around her neck.

> MADAME BLÉ (V.O., CONT'D)
> The day after his arrest, I was
> voted in as the new Arch of
> Callisto's Light. My first motion
> was to dismantle the mandatory
> use of the Arch title in favour
> of a leader's name of their
> choosing. Madame was my pick.

Young Madame Blé raises a hand, then
raises her other to cup it.

The crowd, a sea of blue cloaks, goes

wild for her.

>   MADAME BLÉ (V.O., CONT'D)
>   I will not pretend I did not want
>   the position. I just did not want
>   it that soon. It was unexpected,
>   as I was sure another was up next.

Young Madame Blé shares a glance with a
DISGRUNTLED OLDER LIGHT MEMBER also on
stage with her, several feet away. She
turns away from his glare and faces the
crowd with a smile.

**INT. CALLISTO CHURCH OF SUSSEX - ARCH OFFICE -
DAY**

An Older But Still Young Madame Blé sits
behind her grand desk, shuffling through
paperwork.

Two men lead the Disgruntled Older Light
Member into her office. He waves and points
an aggressive finger at M.Blé as she
calmly continues looking through her
paperwork.

>   MADAME BLÉ (V.O., CONT'D)
>   I fought for years, full of
>   betrayals, bigotry, and near
>   suspensions, to keep my rank. It
>   all paid out in the end, as the
>   truth shall prevail. Sometimes
>   with vigour.

She says something, eyes still on her
work.

The Disgruntled Older Light Member
explodes in a fit, nearly launching over
the desk.

The others restrain him. Drag him out of
the room.

FADE OUT.

.

.

.

Back in her current office: Priest Dictor's portrait.

"This is a reminder to me. Unholy cretins such as him exist out there. I'm only one force. I'm not strong enough to find them all. But in Her Light, I will die trying."

Madame Blé and Amy walked into a circular room. Along the walls, a painting full of harsh strokes spread from one end of the ceiling to another. The human figures in it danced around several fires in a sea of milky white.

Amy gasped. "Is that…"

"Luthern Basquiat's finest work: Callisto's return."

The room's walls rolled up, light shining in from underneath.

M.Blé reached the room's center and held her arms to the ceiling. "Here we have our immersive theatre. What I am about to show you is only supposed to be seen by our understudy group. I take it you will appreciate its glory."

"It's impressive, for sure. Lots of wealth to go around."

"Don't do that."

Amy faced a stoic M.Blé. "What?"

"You can fake as a charmer, but you do better as a revolutionary."

"Revo—" Amy pointed at herself. "Yeah, no."

"Don't sell yourself short, now." Madame Blé got closer to her than Amy expected, but she did not back away from the woman, despite wanting to. "The moment my organization arrived in town, you showed me your strength through eyes of inferno. You burned into me with your passion."

"Thanks for noticing. Newcomers in our town don't usually get the charm. Some lash out. I was curious which you are."

"The Light is a friend to all." Madame Blé's face grew somber. "Last year. You were one of the many unfortunate children affected by that curse, yes?"

Amy's body tightened. "I was."

"You are here for a reason. Do not ever let anyone tell you otherwise. Look."

Credits rolled on the screen, followed by a barren landscape filled with cornstalks surrounded by a river.

.

.

.

FADE IN:

EXT. VILLAGE - DAY

Hellish rainstorm. Families huddle under tents as others rush to gain cover elsewhere, some opting for the tallest cornstalks.

The limbs of all are skeletal.

                MADAME BLÉ (V.O.)
Humanity has not always been as fortunate as we are. We live in a golden area full of technological, medical, and financial advancements that our ancestors dared not even dream. What you see here… This is Hell.

A couple leaves behind their two kids, calling for someone.

EXT. VILLAGE RIVERSIDE - LATER

The storm has passed. The couple brush past large stalks and reaches a small clearing.

The father bursts into tears and falls to his knees. His spouse looks down, visibly shaken. Heads forward.

The feet of a small child stick out from under the river, the rest of the body submerged.

> MADAME BLÉ (V.O., CONT'D)
> A wise lawyer once said, 'Poverty is the worst form of violence.'

EXT. GUIZHOU - DAY

Dramatic cliffs and plunging river valleys twist throughout. Moss-dripped forests cover most areas. The rugged terrain hides villages of wooden stilt houses that hang on slopes with weathered, tilted charcoal roofs. Bamboo groves rustle in the wind.

BUSTLING MARKET TOWN

Dense fog owns the area. Still, inhabitants push through unfazed, making their marks. Women in Miao or Dong ethnic dresses sell dyed textiles, silver jewelry, and smoked meats to passersby.

On one side of the mountainous region, Barracks of rusted metal are bunched on top of one another in the populated urban area.

> MADAME BLÉ (V.O., CONT'D)
> Despite   their   situation,   I

witnessed some of the most courageous hearts dress like royalty while taking life one day at a time.

Youthful Madame Blé accepts a plate from one of the women selling.

> MADAME BLÉ (V.O., CONT'D)
> Every new place I went, I logged what I felt would most help the people and bring their civilization out of the growing decay. Not all communities were replenished after the Second War On Peculiars. After countries had laid massacres within themselves and with one another, humanity's most forgotten paid the heaviest prices.

EXT. MALAWI - DAY

An atmosphere cradled by a rugged necklace of mountains and rolling plateaus. Lake Malawi's vast blue shimmers as fishermen paddle canoes and cast nets.

VILLAGE

Villagers move past clusters of sunbaked, thatch-roofed huts with hand-formed mud bricks. Barefoot children play in dusty courtyards as chickens and goats run about on their own missions.

Two children draw water from a pipe into a bucket twice the size of their heads combined. Nearby, a child pushes another child into the stream, but an adult quickly scolds the child.

Youthful Madame Blé walks through the village handing out baskets with two cyan-cloaked Light members behind her. The receiving villagers open their baskets to find vegetables and fresh water jugs inside.

Youthful Madame Blé sees something in the distance.

INT. HUT - CONT

An emaciated woman sits in a straw chair with her head hanging off to the side and her hands dangling over the edges. A stream of water is carefully poured into her open mouth.

A young girl pours the water from a broken bowl she steadies in her small hands.

Youthful Madame Blé walks in. She rushes forth and turns to grab supplies from her members. Gasps. Eyes frozen on—

A man, thin to the point of bones peeking through skin, sits up in a dark corner of the room, only the whites of his eyes visible on his face.

A light member checks his pulse. Turns to M.Blé shaking his head.

> MADAME BLÉ (V.O., CONT'D)
> The entire family died that night. There just was not enough to go around to sustain life back then.

> MALI (V.O.)
> My Madame?

.

.

.

An inebriated-sounding voice echoed behind Madame Blé and Amy. One of the newest members of The Light, the pregnant Mali Cincius, stepped into the theater with nervous delight, giving Amy a small wave before focusing on M.Blé.

"Sorry for the interruption, but could we talk, Madame?" Her eyes sparkled once she noticed Amy, seemingly for the first time. "Ooooh, hi, new girl! I'm Mali."

"Hi Mali. I'm Amy."

"Oooh," Mali exclaimed again, but knelt over in pain this time. "Madame, it's quite urgent. I need you."

"Mali—" A tall, cyan-cloaked man dashed through the doorway. "Madame Blé."

"Ooaugh." Mali bent over again, clutching her stomach for dear life. "It's been nastily awful today, Madame."

"Oh, yes, yes. A bit of discomfort is necessary. You've got a fighter. Due to pop anyway now." M.Blé's girlish laugh slapped the air and infected Mali. Even caught an awkward chuckle from *Mali's guard.*

Amy gave a quick smile, taking a teeny step away from the *merry bunch. Something's off here. Bet she'll pop on Callisto Day. Ehk. The propaganda.*

"Excuse the interruption, M.Blé." The tall guard moved forward. The room's lighting illuminated the hints of blue within the eyes on his chiseled face. "It's my fault. I lost track of Mali. She's rather slippery."

M.Blé placed a gentle hand on his arm. "There, there, my boy. I pay you to keep her safe, which she is within these walls." She patted his face like a loving mother. "And you do it marvelously. Hunting her location is an endeavour of your design. We'll be at the pool. Come, Mali."

"The Infirmary is—"

"I'm aware," Madame Blé cut him short. "Will you do me a favour and run our security check from my office?"

"You've got it." The young man gave Amy a quizzical look before his departure.

Madame Blé locked arms with Mali and followed after, but doubled back to Amy. "Make yourself at home. Feel free to tour as long as you'd like, and I recommend sitting in on one of our classes. Till later, Amy." Placed her hand on Amy's arm. "Thanks for hearing me out, dearie."

Some two hours later, Amy exhausted her self-guided tour of almost every room she could find and also exhausted her patience in locating *wherever the hell Blé is now. Her meeting's surely up. Let's do one more check here.* Amy entered the office of Blé for the third time today, expecting it to be empty *again,* but stood stiff as the person behind the desk looked up at her with impatience.

"What are you doing in here?" The young man with blue pupils in his black irises shut the grey rectangular device he was *typing into?* a moment ago, and closed the drawer behind the desk. He stared back at her, his statuesque jaw hinging for an answer. "Access to this office is a limited privilege."

"You're right, I should have knocked." Amy took the seat in front of him. "Didn't do much the first time, and the door was cracked the same way I last saw it, so I wasn't confident Blé was in." Amy leaned forward, peeking at the grey block on the desk that he covered with his arms. "Is that a PC?"

"What do you know about PCs?" He opened another drawer and slid the *PC* inside. "And it's Madame Blé; show some respect."

"Sorry. I wasn't confident Madame Blé was in. What's your name?"

"Security."

"Oh. Well, nice to meet you, Mr. Security. My name is Amy."

"I've heard."

Amy half raised an eyebrow, *curious what he heard,* but her body eased. "I wanted to say goodbye to M.Blé before I left and thank her for the visit. Can you point me in the direction of the pool? I couldn't find it."

"No pool at 6 or 6. Daily maintenance, so no access."

"The Infirmary is—"

"I'm aware."

"...establishment of an in-house infirmary..."

"What about the Infirmary? I'd like to visit."

"Are you on the list? Friends and family only."

"Now, how do you know I'm not here to see someone?"

"Name?"

Amy leaned back, defeated, keeping her smile. "What were you doing in here?"

He remained stoic. "Security." Rose to his feet. "Now, if you'll excuse me, I have further work to get done." His arm gestured *politely* towards the exit. "I'll let Madame Blé know you were grateful for her hospitality."

"Sure." Amy got up. "Right, thanks." Started to walk away, but faced him with an inquiring finger. "One more thing. I was on this passage that led me to a sunken hall with some sparkling blue and white lights across the ceiling. Do you know what that is or where it leads?"

He shrugged. "Probably one of our many prayer halls. I'm not trying to be unhelpful. I'm no regular here, so still learning the layout myself."

"Lemme ask you one more question. I overheard some members chatting about a big fault of Callisto's. A teacher in one of your understudy classes was quizzing the students on the same thing. What is it? Callisto's One Big Fault?"

He shrugged. "May be a member exclusive."

"Oh. So you're not a member."

He gave her a *noble* bow. "Please, come back to visit one when you have a chance. The Madame will set you up personally, I'm told."

He doesn't wanna chat about it, either, huh? Amy held the door, half inside, half out, as she nodded. "Does she normally give out free testers inside the church?"

"Yes."

"Even down here? In The Pits?"

A small vein popped in the side of his head. "I'm just here as someone physically capable, in case things go awry."

Solid muscle. I'm shit for reading energy anymore, but something tells me he's no ordinary guard. In her quest for changing the World, what the hell is Blé hiding down here in The Pits? "Good day then—oh!"

Cherry-haired Celestia bumps into her as they stand inches from one another in the doorway. "My bad. Cute locs, by the way." She faced the lad behind the desk. "Hey! I need to run an errand. Can you let M.Blé know I'll need to push my a-cert meeting with her an hour later than planned?"

He nodded and retook the chair. "Done. Anything else I can do for you?"

"Oh, I see. Someone's got the big chair. Is Madame off-site?"

"Not as far as I know, but I'm in charge right now."

"Say less, fam." Celestia grabbed Amy's arm. "Can you help me?"

"Sure," Amy said, being pulled out the door. Gave Mr. Security a final nod before the door shut behind her.

Some time later, a stall door SLAMMED open. Amy and Celestia piled out, lips locked, their bodies a single noodle. They pulled apart, laughing, Amy fixing her hair; Celestia now fixing it for her.

"Thanks for your help," Celestia said.

"Likewise." Amy snorted. "Wow. So you didn't need to run any errands?"   "I certainly do. How could I pass up this detour?" She pulled Amy by the hips, their noses touching again.

The bathroom door took its turn slamming next, a red-faced Lucia storming in and past the two young women as she made her way to the sink. She dumped her handbag into it, some things falling out, and aggressively washed her face.

Celestia went to her. "Luce. Come now, what's the matter? Surely the old hog's words must've worn dry by now."

"I hate her!" Luce suddenly took a large amount of air through her nostrils, the sucking force immaculate. She reopened her eyes and stared at the other two in the mirror. "She's barking mad, that one! The devil in her bathes in Callisto's limelight."

"You should know better than to fail the big one."

"I didn't fail! I misspoke."

"What's the big one?"

Lucia looked at Amy as though seeing her for the first time. "Who are you?" She gathered her things and exited the lavatory.

Amy nodded. "Nice girl."

"She's had it rough today. Don't mind her."

"Can I ask you? What's Callisto's One Big Fault?"

For the first time today, Celestia wore no smile. Her expression, frozen as death itself, with eyes fixed on Amy. "What do you know about that?"

Amy didn't budge, not wanting to trigger any defensive movements in this *suddenly quiet environment, where I'm alone with a Light member, even as one I got friendly with.* "I. um—" Celestia burst into laughter. "I'm jerking you, beautiful."

"Oh, wow." Amy allowed herself to laugh, but still hadn't fully shaken off the strange curve in the convo.

"How was that, though? I've got a lead role in drama club coming up. Not feeling quite ready yet."

"I think you've got it."

"Please. About Callisto's One Big Fault? Hate to say, love, but it's a members' only kinda jazz. No offense. The Madame herself would untether and maim me if I blurted a clubhouse innie."

"Wait. Would she strike you?"

"Oh. **Psht**. Blé? No. But you know the older they get, you never know." Celestia took her by the back of her neck and leaned close, faces inches away. "You won't see me again. I'm too much of a muck-up for your grace."

"We'll see."

Celestia kissed her passionately, and Amy returned it.

They broke apart.

Amy watched every second of her leaving.

Hm. Maybe life isn't so shit after all.

Chapter Ten: Haven Church

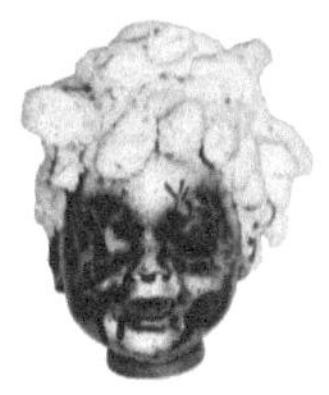

Chapter Eleven

The Singer

*I**must find out if The Light has ill intentions.* Amy slipped her bed off its frame. *For Gma's sake. And my own.* She stared down at *it.*

An orange and purple box *waited for her return to foolery, but passion.* Box in lap, Amy sat cross-legged on her unmattressed bed. *Blé. A creeper, sending eyes to peek at me after midnight? Humanitarian of the World? What aren't you saying, Blé? A night ago, it was easy just saying she's going down. But what the hell am I on about? Gma and her duke it out, and worse happens, is what? Well, I guess her influence could out Gma as Chief Mortician. Still. She's no demon, Devine. She's just a woman.*

Amy raised an eyebrow. *No matter how petty.*

"La Luz!..."

Amy pressed her eyelids together, hands squeezing the box. "8 A.M. Brilliant."

"Ella lo quiere..."

Amy took the lid off the box. Stared at its contents.

"La Luz! Ella lo quiere... Ella quiere la luz y se alejó..."

She pulled out a polished white mask, its face blank with slight blemishes and cracks all over.

"Knocking on your door, I pulled the trigger..."

What, they teaming up now? Amy laid the mask on a thigh and pulled a little silver instrument from her pocket. Squeezed it as its curved tip lit up white. She cleared her throat. "La la la la laaaaaa."

You're not good enough.

She poked the instrument into the open back of the mask, right into a black box where the chin sits. A stream of white aura connected between the instrument and the box base.

Amy forced out a sigh. "Me me me me meeee." Her eyes never left the connection, moving closer while turning the instrument with care clockwise or counter. "Creaevix, replay search on average voice modulator frequency."

Average frequencies can range between 3000 and 11000 ziccolights.

"Mamamamamamamamamamamamamamama... ow." She massaged her throat. Checked a red alert on her GCID: 70% "Dear, gotta get that voice right, but no louder than 65%." *Will this even gonna work?*

No. Throats get strangled out there.

She ignored *the voice from nowhere* and glanced at the two map drawings on either page of her open journal. *They've got twice-a-week meets at these four locations, but Blé and Droûx never attend. Blé spends her days blessing new supporters of The Light, never on any schedule, so it's difficult to isolate her. Droûx is never seen without Blé. Where does she go when Blé is alone? The singers have a backstage pass to spots A, B, and C, and this other location I haven't cracked yet. They go to this one daily. And nightly. Why at night?*

Amy groaned. "This setting is so hard to fucking get right. Come on, I can do it. Just feel for it. Creaevix, does swellboo density affect ziccolight range and power?"

By Nigerian director Gygi Adedeji, the movie "Brigade of the Bamboo Loyalists" was released on October 14, 213—

"Creaevix, stop!" *Movie was alright.* Amy rubbed the bridge of her nose. "Does swell-boo den-si-tee affect ziccolight range and power?"

No. However, higher power sources may cause swellboo to bend and disrupt nearby external sources.

"So I'll crank this up a bit... Zzzzzzzzzzzzzzzz zzzzzzzzzzz zzzzzzzzzz..." She tinkered away with her instrument until thought, emotion, and reality all meshed into one unbothered stream of flow.

Some twists and turns later, her eyes landed on her journal pages. *I'll take this trail from Jadesfeld straight through Enfield. I'll circle the West Markets twice, then double back to Enfield Square Central around 3:15, no later than 3:20. Most will be clocked out for the day, and those obsessive cult-yodeling hopefuls will clog the spot. Bleeding fucking eardrums everywhere. Hope that Shelly girl isn't there. Sorry, but if you're not gonna take your singing voice seriously, hun, you might as well pack it up.*

"Creaevix, time."

It's 12:18 p.m.

"Fuck." Amy inspected the front and rear of the mask as She swallowed the last of her plain, toasted, buttered bagel. *Had to eat. Feeling better. I'll leave on time.*

You've gotta go outside. Been doing that a lot lately. Increasing your chances of dying.

This schizo's getting out of hand. Been over two weeks. She ignored the laughter in her head and pulled an alabaster bundle from the box on her bed. "This is it." Her arms dropped. "This is a bad idea." *Who says they'd pick me, anyway?*

She got into the pants; four final hefty tugs to settle in.

Zipped up the all-white bodysuit, raising her chin.

Threw the black cloak over her shoulders.

Clasped the single platinum button on her chest, securing the cloak.

Caught her reflection in the mirror. Rolled one of her dreadlocks between her index and thumb. Touched the puff of her afro. *Grown a ton over the past year...*

With more of her hair hanging down in twisted locs, Amy grabbed the remaining afro portion and tied it back with a white band into a ponytail.

She put on The Mask. Strands of puffy black snow-like swellboo material slithered from the edges of The Mask and connected around the back of her head.

Oof, that's tight. But it works for now. Must find an easier way to wear this without cutting my hair. That's simply out of the question. "Creaevix, mirror, please."

The adjacent wall glowed white, its surface now reflective.

She stared at *the stranger and long-time secret friend*: The Singer. Opened her cloak, revealing the slick alabaster bodysuit. She inspected every inch. Nodded. "I can do this. Even if I have to "try out" for a month. There. A month's commitment. We can do it!" Cleared her throat.

Outside... Death awaits...

Amy unmasked, took sheets of paper out of the box, and rambled over the notes before tossing them to the floor. "I'll just make something up. Refuse to say her name." *Callisto this, Callisto that...* She scratched her throat. Cleared it. Itched again.

Needs to be convincing.

Save the childre—

No. It has to be about Callisto.

Bitch.

Amy sat at her desk. Scribbled in her journal with her right hand while her left pinched her clearing throat. "Creaevix, time."

It's 12:36 p.m.

"Fuck." She scribbled away. Scratched out. Scribbled. "Can't beat 'um... flatter them." *Let's knock it out. Be done.*

Bitch.

Amy searched her room for the intruder.

As always, alone.

Scribbled in her journal. Chomped on an Urhzunian donut. Took another bite.

Bolted to her feet. "Eh-eh-em." *Am I choking?* "Creaevix, what do you do when you're alone and choking?" She listened to the fuzzy instructions entering her head. Paced. Made a fist with her left hand and put the thumb side between her belly button and rib cage. Placed her right hand on top of that. Pushed in and up.

Moved behind her chair and aimed her belly over its backrest. *More force. Is that true?* Fingers plucked at the sides of her throat.

"Eeh-heh! Eh-eh-eh-eh-emheh" She downed an *eight-ounce* glass of water—*should've been more. Would I be choking if I could breathe?*

She asked Creaevix.

If you're able to breathe, speak or cough, then it's possible you might clear your own throat.

Not helpful. Eyes wide. *Wait.* "Creaevix, is it alright to drink..."

No, as this won't dislodge the blockage and may worsen the situation by causing a further blockage.

She shook her head. Scratched her neck. *So no fluids unless I want to compound the issue.* Amy forced a cough, trying to clear the burning sensation in her esophagus. Forced air from the back of her throat in a hawking manner.

Scratched it. Cleared it. Forced the air out.

Scratched it. Cleared it. Forced the air.

Scratched it. Cleared it. **Wheezed.**

Amy fell to a knee. Grabbed her throat. *No.* Her eyes dripped her anxiety as she feverishly wiped her face, scattered breaths growing raspier. Panting now. "Hi—I call..." Fell face forward, forehead first. Turned her head, which was damp from the pooling tears. "Now— ok." Her vision blurred. Within seconds, all She saw were black shapes pooling her eyesight as the ringing in her ears amplified.

She *"choked"* for hours.

The *inspiring* melody of Thelonious Monk's "'Round Midnight" filled the room.

Her wall's soft *orange* glow on her face, Amy lay sprawled on her bed, one arm draped over her chest, the other dangling off the bed. Opened her eyes. *Alright, we've got this.* She sat up. "This should work." Grabbed her GCID off the table. Stared at the time.

7:36 p.m.

She sighed. Peeped her shadow cast against the wall. Moved her arm around, playing with the shadow's direction.

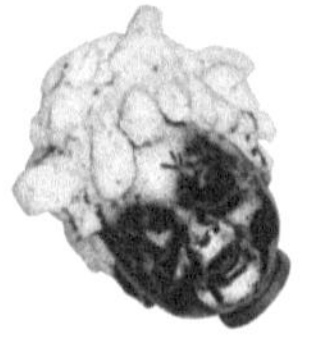
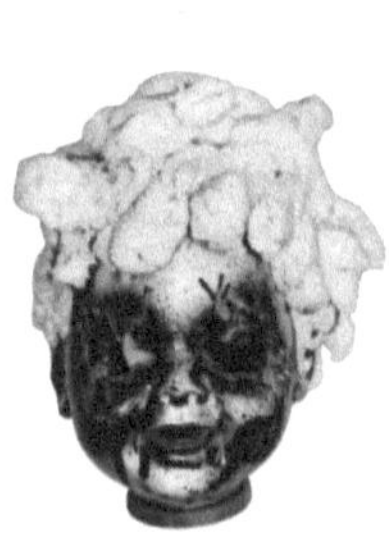
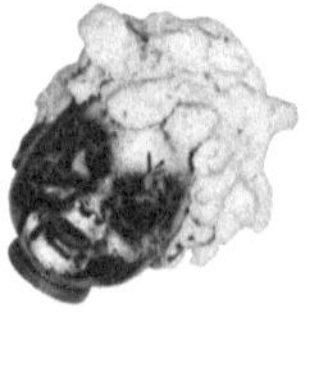

Put her GCID back down. "Tomorrow's a new day." Laid out. "Creaevix, lights out."

The *delicate piano* of "Summertime / Sometimes I Feel Like a Motherless Child" began.

Darkness *ate me.*

The chorus swelled.

"Breaking news!"

"What?" Amy's eyes fluttered open. "Creaevix, time."

10:01 a.m.

"How'd I miss the alarm?" Amy sat up in her bed. Scratched her bedhead with groggy eyes on the blurry images on her wall. "Can you pump the volume, Creaevix?"

"... and sources here at What's News In Jadesfeld?! have confirmed she is being

Couldn't sleep. Realized I need to recalibrate my mask to account for how much energy I'll be around when I'm traveling through the towns. The mask is like a black hole for electricity, including ziccolights. Don't want it to absorb too much.

'However, higher power sources may cause swellboo to bend and disrupt nearby external sources.'

Only my hands can show my light. I know the rest of it is there. My body is just so disconnected from it. Cooked myself for hours in the sun, trying to wake it up. It's no use.

Three days ago, I made a small breakthrough.

I call it the Palm Share. It creates a reflection of my

light onto another source and allows a tiny bit of my
energy to be temporarily absorbed by the source's
aura. First few times I tried it, I was fast asleep in
minutes because I had given away too much.

Maybe I'll try with another human someday.

I used up the last of my savings on some D-grade
glass, the weakest there is.

Used my Palm Share technique. My plan was to use
my shadows to draw out more of the light within me.

Only thing I ended up doing was blinding myself for
like thirty minutes. Wasn't my best idea. The energy
from the glass proved stronger than I thought. I
had to double-check it was actually D-grade. It was.

into the water filled sink. "There's the vision. Fuck. Huh? — watches her shadow in the water—

That gave me a new idea.

—Amy, wearing sunglasses, stands outside in the cemetery surrounding her home. She watches the deep purple skies, finding the moon—

The Moon lights us just as well as the Sun. At least for auraists.

—Amy's chest sunk in as her nostrils sucked in the rosemary air.

Its warmth, I'd argue, feels a bit stronger, too.

—A man smoking outside a bar in the UnderCity points Amy to an alley behind the bar—Amy makes her way down the dark alley—at the end of it, a large package awaits her—

Had to wait for a night when Gma was on a warehouse call bringing in new coffins.

—Amy stands inside another glass box—

Trick is, because the Moon gives off reflected sunlight, I could draw more power from the Sun indirectly. More than I could during the day or I'd risk boiling myself to a crisp.

—Amy, on her knees, covering her eyes—glass shattered all over her room floor again—

It didn't end up working, and I blinded myself for another 45 minutes. Only one eye this time.

But something else occurred to me.

—Amy walks into her room, wiping her face with a towel before tossing it in a corner—Remembers:

—The glass box absorbs her aura—spreads—blinding white light

Dark photons. The shadow of light. What if I can... but that's impossible? Dark photons have been proven, but we remain unable to interact with them. But under the Moon's light...

The Sun's light isn't as strong when reflected. But the energy is still there for the taking.

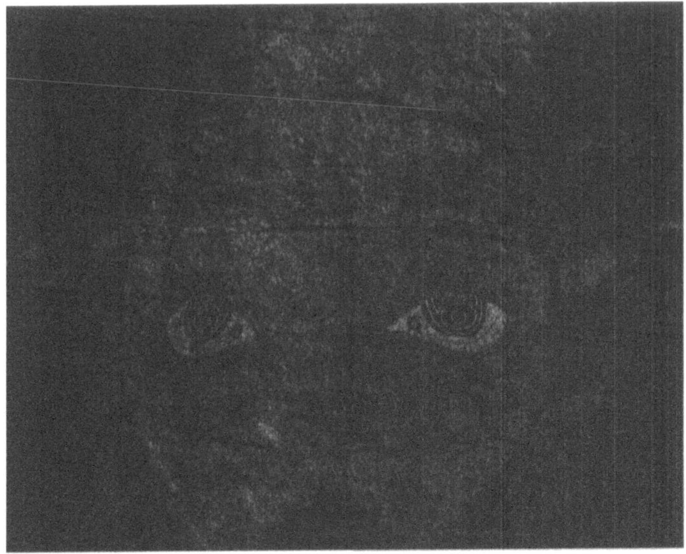

transported to a mental health institution."

"Wait, Creaevix, can I get a replay of this news story? Break it down in highlights for me."

Four videos appeared on the wall: top left, no sound, a woman with strange *makeup or mask?* fell to her knees, holding her head. She screamed into the sky, pulling at her brown dreadlocks.

"Sources say the young woman suffered some sort of mental breakdown stemming from an incident years prior. She dyed her hair to match that of her late mother, who we've learned perished in an accidental fire started by the girl..."

Top right, no sound, Enfield detectives guarded a barricaded crime scene. Their captain answered reporter questions.

"We can confirm she was found around 0400 hours in a state of shock after discovering a naked, drained corpse behind some fields. We're unable to say at this

time the cause of death. The young woman has been taken to a facility for further evaluation."

Bottom left, Jadesfeld reporter Debra Jackson.

Bottom right, Enfield reporter, Prince Thrillhawk.

Debra J: **I suppose you'll want to blame this one on the caring community of Jadesfeld, too.**

Prince T.: **All I'm saying is that if it weren't for the murder of the Bates last year <u>in Jadesfeld</u>, there would be no outbreak of bad luck with these curses now!**

Debra J: **"Bad luck? Really? Bad luck is what you're saying this is. The facts are clear. The Cloudy Curse was an anomaly no one could've predicted."**

Prince T.: **"Facts. Facts are irrelevant with the unprecedented puncture of murder! When will your town take responsibility?! She claimed her head was on fire!"**

Debra J: **"Are we forgetting that she's an Enfield resident?"**

Prince T.: **"Yet another victim of a psychotic episode, and she just happens to find a bloody corpse drained of its very life in some bushes! Convenient."**

Debra J: **"No human could have caused that type of damage, Prince, and you damn well know it! And she didn't dye her hair as your unreliable sources have it reported. We have it on record <u>from her</u> that the curse made her do it."**

Prince T.: **"You believe her?! She's a murderer!"**

"Jackson and Prince, at it again." Amy stared at the screaming woman in the top left video. "I've seen her before."

—cute, orange pigtails— "Another year, another curse." — "I'm swearing myself into The Light first thing tomorrow morning. Ready to make a difference!" —

Can't be a coincidence... Like me, she's lost her orange. Amy stood up. "Time to see what goes on in The Light." Her face winced. *But first—*

She used the loo five times within the hour. Showered once—

—Hairy insect legs peek out of the drain—

*—Amy **shrieks**— "FUCK!" Stumbles out of the tub, grabbing her towel off the rail as She falls to the bathroom floor—*

— and a half.

Chitterchitterchitterchitterchitterchitter

—Amy stares at the water going down the drain, nothing critters in sight—

Losing my fucking mind.

In her room, her breakfast plate grew cold under her stare. Her finger pushed the top half of her toasted bagel oozing with butter, revealing the chicken bits within.

Eyed the untouched smoothie.

Half the bagel lifted— a dozen hairy legs crawled out— more legs between her blueberries.

"FUCK!" She jumped out of her chair and pushed her plate away, knocking the smoothie off the desk.

Watched the liquid mess *she made* spread across the floor and under the bed.

Eyes on her plate: *free of critters.* "I'll fridge it for later." Rubbed her throat. Asked for time.

10:59 a.m.

She cracked her neck. *Bathroom break.*

11:33 a.m.

Still at her desk, She stretched while gazing at the board back over her window. *Bathroom break.*

12:16 p.m.

Sigh *Late again. Bathroom break.*

1:31 p.m.

She dressed in *her favorite mask,* relishing the disguise in the mirror again. The Singer. *We can do it. You're _fine_, Devine.*

So fucking late. Deep breath. "Dun-de-deh, Dun-de-deh, Dun-de-deh. Dun-de-deh, Dun-de-deh, Dun-de-deh. Dun-de-deh, Dun-de-deh."

Dun-de-deh, Dun-de-deh, Dun-de-deh.

Dun-de-deh, Dun-de-deh, Dun-de-deh.

Dun-de-deh, Dun-de-deh.

The replayed vocals echoed from The Mask and across the sky.

The Singer bounced with every step of the way, snapping her fingers as she vocalized. *1, 2, 3, 4*— "Doo-beh, doo-beh, doo-beh, doo-beh."

Doo-beh, doo-beh

doo-beh, doo-beh.

And 1, 2, 3— "La di da di da di daaa-di-da, la di da di da di daaa-di-da. La di da di da di da di la daaaaa..."

La di da di da di daaa-di-da

la di da di da di daaa-di-da.

La di da di da di da di la daaaaa...

Curious onlookers of Jadesfeld watched her, some stopping to listen.

The Singer kept her head forward. *Keep your nerve. I'm the only one in the World right now. Just me and the music.*

The Singer swallowed a chunk of air. Released. "I want to follow in your light—"

Dun-de-deh, Dun-de-deh, Dun-de-deh.

Dun-de-deh, Dun-de-deh, Dun-de-deh.

Dun-de-deh, Dun-de-deh.

The mask continued to play her recorded vocals. Each part rang in at a specific time along the melody.

"Said I want to follow in your light.

Doo-beh, doo-beh

doo-beh, doo-beh.

And I want to follow in your precious light..."

La di da di da di daaa-di-da

la di da di da di daaa-di-da.

La di da di da di da di la daaaaa...

Layers added to the melody *at the perfect spot.*

"I want to follow in your light.

Said I want to follow in your light.

And I want to follow in your precious light!"

The start of her melody echoed as each additional layer added a new dynamic to the tune.

The Singer moved towards the edge of the town.

The sharp air of New Enfield *slashed* her throat.

Cold as Dalestone. She cleared her throat. "I want to follow in your light." *Why do I feel nude? Oh, that's a nice scarmoricloak, lady. The wealth of the pot's hidden in Enfield! We should move here. Currency surely overstaying its welcome. Dread. Am I sounding like Gma? I'll ask Demora.* "And I want to follow in your precious light!"

"Here you go, love." A kind bowler hat tapped her wrist to The Singer's wrist.

"Thank you so much!" *Did I just get a tip?*

Cha-ching! One of her *favourite* sounds echoed inside The Mask. "Creaevix, turn on air mode." Her GCID's white light illuminated under the cloth of her left wrist. *Let's see if more generous folk are around.* "Let's go again." Cleared her throat. *1, 2, 3—* "I want to—" *Yeah, we should move out here. Now. Next question: how do I gain the Cult's favour? What if they're not accepting any more talent? I should have thought about that. Shit. What am I doing out here? I should probably—*

"Lovely tune!"

Cha-ching!

I'm amazing! Simply incredible, this lot. Way warmer than the Jadesfeld Jokers.

Cha-ching!

Why, thank you, darling! And a curtsy to you too! Oop—there's the fountain. Square should be...

Fuck. Packed as a mother— Ugh. Square's occupied, no! Lemme move up.

"Excuse me, citizen." A policebot roved her way. "You will need to clear this space as The Square has reached full capacity."

"Oh, ok. What? This way? Ok, but—"

"You are not able to stand here either, citizen. The Square has reached full capacity."

"Got it. This way? I just need to get—"

"Please, exit—"

Bloody bot. Language. Sorry.

Not sorry.

I <u>am</u> sorry. Shook her head. *Nevermind. I need to enter that square. Tapped her left wrist. What! 3:27?! Left too late. Fuck! Just had to get the bubble guts, Devine, didn't ya? Impossible.*

"Hey, it's cool. They can come with me."

Wha— Jamari Wyst, in the flesh. Eminence has its marvels. His skin is flawless. "Oh, thanks. I'm—thanks. You're Jamari Wyst."

"I see you're familiar with my work." His *starlit* smile grew under his *obnoxious, movie-star blockbuster* shades.

"Yeah, for sure."

"Let's see how you do in front of a sellout crowd." Jamari waved his hands apart. The crowd parted for him.

Ten hopeful performers climbed out of the sunken Enfield Square, *their instruments ignorant of anyone's personal space.*

Nice tune. The Singer gave a pound to *Mr. Jazz Didgeridoo.* Ducked *Mr. Pikasso Guitar's* large stringed instrument. She moved down each of the three square levels, Jamari in tow.

She reached the empty center of the bottom square level. Stared at the dozens upon dozens of faces elevated over her from every inch, every corner.

Jamari stood in front crowd, his arms folded and a smile worn as he tapped his foot.

He's trying to embarrass me. Cocky shit. She squeezed her fists.

Jamari's right eyebrow twitched. His mouth opened a pinch.

I'll show him.

Three blocks from home, mask off, Amy skipped a step, her black cloak wrapped around her. *Fucking sick! What a rush! Jamari's stupid face. HA.* She pumped her fist. Quickly re-concealed The Singer's fit with the cloak.

Hmph. *The Singer. Feels better when I'm Her.*

Her eyes narrowed on the backs of two people.

Demora and Graves exchanged words. Moved away from her block.

What the hell are they doing here? Where the hell are they going now?

She followed them at a *careful* distance, losing them thrice, *and that was before they reached the woods.* As she followed them deeper into the thick bushes, the last light of the day was swallowed by the towering trees.

This is a long way in the woods, Demo. Oh yeah. Her mom's birthday is coming up. Is it weird if I drop her parents a gift basket? They did babysit me once. Hm. If only they weren't so strict with their house rules and 'no visitors in their polished home'. What's this? Yuck. Can't come out this far in the woods without snailgators. Lemme watch out. Not tryna lose a foot like that one fellow. Ugh, moss. Wait, this is seamoss. *Ah, fuck!* "Shit!" She whispered with some stomps. "No, fuck, shit!"

"Surround her."

Seven silhouettes approached her faster than She could spin around.

PECULIAR CASES OF SOMETHING DEVINE:

GRAVITY OF DEVOTION

172

Chapter Twelve

The Students Of Graves

"First off, we weren't sneaking around. We came to pick <u>you</u> up, so where were you?" Demora said. "We were coming to ask you to attend tonight's class."

"Nearly got strangled by seamoss." Amy shook free of a few more strands. She analyzed the seven youthful souls *who jumped* her. Seven total, eight with Demora. Two double-takes— *Kassandra? That tall lad from The Light! JAMARI WYST?* Amy straightened her back, waiting for the explanation to come. *What are they up to, hidden in the forest late at night?* Her eyes found the moon. *Quite deep in the woods. Darker out here.*

The others watched her.

Amy stiffened her stance. "Is this the classroom's idea of some sort of gang initiation?" Folded her spaghetti arms. "Or weren't those outlawed?"

"Funny, coming from an outsider." A young woman with trapezoid braided buns behind falling braids stood taller than Jamari. She leaned over his shoulder, her eyes *scrutinizing* every aspect of Amy.

Love her jacket, though.

"Keep chill, Lil Sis," Jamari said. Nodded at Amy *as though old friends.* "Glad another soul-bearer can join us."

A wha— Cut your babyface charm. "What's Jamari Wyst doing here?" Amy dug the last piece of seamoss from her ear. "Is this some bit for your show?"

He flashed his trademark smile. "Callisto's blessings to you. I'm enchanted. I see you're familiar with my work."

"Here he goes…" several voices groaned in unison.

"What?! Anyhow—" Jamari went on, *uninterrupted by the gallery who wished his voice would cease its existence,* "I'm here for the same reason you are, New Girl."

"These," Graves said, cutting in the middle of all, "are the rest of the students. Students, let's show our newcomer what we're all about." She winked at *the newcomer.*

"Who is she?" An Asian boy with thick-rimmed decagon glasses leaned against a cherry tree with his hands behind his back. "I don't remember her credentials being validated."

Who's this mad scientist-looking—

"She's a far better spirit-wielder than any of you wish to be," Demora said.

Amy's horrified eyes dug into her. "What the fuck?"

"What?! Did I tell a lie?" "I don't know what you're talking about." Amy stepped close to her best friend, fists clenched. *How could she?*

Demo shrugged. "Your acting sus gives it away. We're all aura-wielders, it's chill."

"Ugggh." Jamari shivered. "That weird term again."

Are you fuckin— "What? Chill? For who? I got—" Amy, hand to forehead, turned from her so-called friend.

"Best spirit-wielder?" *Lil Sis scoffed.* "We'll have to see about that."

"Chill out, children." Kassandra sat on a stone perch sticking out of a tree's hole, checking under her fingernails.

"Well, class?" Graves smiled at them all. "Go on. Share yourselves."

Demora smirked. "As if you don't know." Raised her hand. Her fuchsia-pink aura flushed around it.

Furthest to the left, a familiar, tall and slender but chiseled young man raised his hand. Blue light particles converged, creating a *lapis lazuli* blue aura around his raised arm.

It is him. The one I saw in The Pits with the preggo, Mali. Mr. Stoicism himself. He's a student of Graves?

The slightly shorter Asian boy raised his fist. A *viridian* green aura with *malachite flickers* enclosed it.

One by one, the other students followed suit, their auras shining to life: a *milk chocolate* brown, *carnelian* red, yellow *Egyptian sand, rich* lilac *with bright shimmers.* The colors created a wonderful rainbow against the eerie backdrop of their surroundings.

Kassandra's right arm was free of any color or distortion. Two thin beads of sweat passed her eyes and now her mouth.

She's the perfect study! The concentration to maintain such a form... I have to journal this. She was the first instance of invisiauraism I witnessed. The genuine test of will. Maybe she can help me understand...

They're gonna kill you.

Nonsense. "What?" Amy searched the faces for the last question.

"She's a bit unstable, no?" *Mr. SmartyPants,* with the green aura, said. "What's on that brain of yours, Newcomer?"

"If you squeal—" Jamari cut his red-auraed hand across his neck.

"Careful." Demora's glare fixed on the group. She stepped ahead of her best friend.

"Who is this New Girl to you, Pink?!" Jamari spat at her. "What makes her belong—"

"Maybe cuz she's The One who contained Cloudy," Eyes shut, *Demo!* crossed her arms.

Most of the group's auras dropped from sight. Silence cut the cold, dry air.

All eyes on Amy.

Amy scratched at the heat rising in her chest. *I can't— She—* The instantaneous murmurs of the crowd grew.

What do I do? What are they gonna do? Her eyes searched for the nearest escape. *Nothing but dense woods. If I don't put out... Demo's got my back.*

The volumes of the students' voices rose, one chaotic symphony that She needed *to either run from or—*

Take out the trash.

Kill them all.

No—what? Who—

"That's ABsolutely ABsurd!" Jamari's chest puffed out.

"Doesn't equate," Mr. Smartypants said. "The raw energy it takes to contain... a spirit..." his words trailed off into a whisper as he stared into the distance.

"If true, it's an astounding feat." A young Asian woman approached Amy with a ball of lilac-purplish aura in her palm. She aimed it at Amy and peered through it like a telescope. She pulled a pin out from her exquisite hairstyle of five jelly-roll-shaped bundles. *Ms. JellyRoll* placed the pin inside her aura ball. The levitated pin spun. The sharp side pointed at Amy. "She has exponential spirit cycles."

I... do? I... I can't...

"That's—not real..." Lil Sis' voice went weak. "You can't... contain a spirit..." Her milk chocolate aura dimmed until nothing.

"I knew it!" A young woman with rambunctious curly hair and rosy caramel cheeks jumped forward. She punched her sand-colored fists of aura together with a *bubbly* lean and smile.

"Who are you?" Amy checked her over from her sandals to her head. *What the hell does she know?*

"She's not sharing," the brick-faced *Mr. Stoicism* said with an unimpressed glare. His blue eyes pierced through Amy, *but not as strongly as they pierced Demora's heart. She's so into him.*

The single bead of sweat that fell from her best friend's golden French blonde locks betrayed her in a way that Amy relished.

If she weren't soon to be deceased by my hands, I'd tease her for it.

Gossiping, little—

"Shan hiska," *Ms. Bubbly* said. "Let's let the newcomer take a second." She offered a welcoming hand. "Hi. My name's—"

"No names, please," Graves said, stepping between the students.

"Oh right, sorry." Ms. Bubbly curtsied. "I'm still in training."

"What is this, Professor?" Amy asked.

Those stone-blue eyes fell on her. "This is a safe space. It's your first class, so I understand if you need some time." Graves' smile flickered before dissolving. "We show our auras to identify and respect one another. The choice belongs to you."

Awkward silence.

"My... my aura's weak," Amy let out. *Loud and proud. More like weak and useless.* Her aura's fiery pit burned within her gut, wanting to breach the outside world. *But that's not me anymore.* "I'd like to save my strength if that's alright."

Graves smiled. "Wise choice."

Other voices sparked their opinion.

Amy took a deep breath. *Look at them. Hungry.* Fixed her grilling mug.

"That's enough, she has spoken." The professor paced around the group. "We all understood the position she was in before our small circle gained trust. Our World forces the best of us to hide in plain sight." She nodded over to the tallest section of bladed grass.

After a moment, a bright *saffron*-yellow aura beamed up taller than the blades.

"She acknowledges you," Graves said.

The space between the blades went dark.

"Here we go." Jamari chucked both shoulders forward, dusting one off. "It's rude to stay silent when spoken to." He threw a nasty look over at the blades.

The blades parted. Yellow eyes stared from deep within.

A 6'7 Gyaad stepped out with her veil-like substance— *the sheilv, they call it*— coiled around her from bottom to mid-neck. *Against the moonlight, she gleams brighter than her species does during the day. Another case for the Moon's usefulness...*

I've seen her before.

The Gyaad locked eyes with Amy. Bowed.

Oh, okay? Amy returned the gesture with an awkward version.

Graves patted Jamari's shoulder. "Our peer has always responded, Mr. Eminence." She moved away from the chuckle of students. Laid a soft hand on the Gyaad. "At birth, Gyaad voices are the softest. It takes time for them to control the power of their voice waves. Your lot won't be able to hear her without proper sound training. Well, almost all of you." She gave Demora a tight nod.

What the hell else is she getting up to? Amy's eyes bore between Demora and Graves. *How could she not tell <u>me</u> about <u>any</u> of this?*

"I feel a lot better now, to be honest," Jamari said. "Mutes scare me."

"Your ignorance scares me," Demora replied.

"Ditto," Mr. Stoicism agreed. "Wyst, you ever stop to measure the size of your head?"

"No time. I'm too busy moving, baby."

"Moving slow. Thinking slow..."

"Faster than you. England's most valuable Luxballer. My arse!" Jamari laughed.

"Damn straight! Twelve in the league!" Mr. Stoicism clenched his fists. "Try me. Any day, Wyst. Any. Day."

"Suure. Perhaps we give up your name, Mr.—"

"Please." Graves sighed. "No names."

"I don't get the point of this no-name game," Mr. Smartypants said.

"Maybe you'll have the chance to earn each other's names soon. Who's up for a challenge?"

"Bout time." Kassandra jumped down from her perch.

Graves turned to Amy. "For our newcomer, how much of the spirit world's origins do you know?"

Sweat trailed down Amy's back. Her breaths grew shorter with each passing second. *How do I answer that? They're all so open with it. I can't possibly... Gma would kill me. I'd kill me before that would happen.*

She blinked.

"What?" Amy took the hands of two blurry faces as they helped her off the ground.

"Are you alright?" Demora held Amy's face in her hand. "You were out for like a minute."

"Yeah." Amy held her *fuzzy* head, her vision off-center.

Graves came face-to-face, peering into her eyes. Stepped back. "Perhaps we should give our new friend some time—"

"No, go on," Amy said. "I want to know what all of this is about." "Very well." Graves' eyes stood on Amy. "Energy is inevitable. Living organisms have energy; the sun has energy. Magnetism between the forces causes the core of the spirit itself. Over generations, the core has become stronger until finally, and recently, the inevitable finally occurred: Our world witnessed the natural birth of a spirit that escaped into the external." She picked up her handbag and dug inside. "You will each be receiving one of these talismans." She handed something to Demora first and continued around to the others until she stopped in front of Amy. "This is your first choice, dear. You can walk away now, no hard feelings."

Amy grabbed the onyx-colored circular talisman out of the professor's hand. *Fucking Demo. Look at her. Unbothered. Wait till we get out of here.*

"Back to my earlier point..." Graves got down on hands and knees and brushed aside the earth. The tips of her fingers illuminated, white-hot as she dipped them deep in the soil. "We are relative to the core energy in the Earth, and it is always connected to us. It takes..."

What do I do? Go back to an empty existence full of insomniac episodes? Forget about the other auraists I'd just discovered after being told for so long that it would be decades, maybe, till I'd find another auraist out in the world. Gma's been giving me the same lecture since my toddler years: 'Keep it hidden until the world can be better.'

Now I'm exposed. Betrayed.

Graves' eyes grew a bright *coquelicot* red as her aura grew around her body.

Incredible shade. It's so... inviting. Like home. Amy wiped the sweat from her face. *She's melting me. Her aura. Its energy—*

"—with your knees. You must have at least a 57.65% synchronization with your aura to evenly distribute the weight."

57.65%! That's a tight calculation. Wait, what were the instructions?

The talismans in each student's hand levitated into the air, surfing the waves of Graves' red-orange aura.

"Brace yourselves." Graves flicked her wrist.

The talismans thrashed above their heads. Dropped into the hands of Amy, Demora, and the rest.

Amy's hand crashed into the ground, followed swiftly by her elbows, knees, and almost her face.

"Ho-shit!" Jamari caught his balance before toppling forward.

"What a task. How heavy are these things?" Mr. Smartypants wiped dirt off his free hand, then held himself up on his shaky knee.

The others fared a lot better, still on shaky legs, *although none too cool as Demora.*

Demora stared down at Amy, her mouth ajar. "Are you alright?!"

Wish she hadn't. "I'm fine." Amy got up and dusted off, leaving the talisman somewhere below— *shit-test-cant-tell-fuck-about-me—*

"I've seen all that needs to be seen," Graves said. She picked up Amy's talisman with ease. "It was a misstep. Don't worry." She handed it over and smiled. "Happens to the best of us."

Just kill me now.

"Alright, put them away." The professor waited till the final grunt and groan completed the task. "Who here thinks they are 57.65% in sync with their aura?"

Demora, Jamari, Mr. Stoicism, and Lil Sis raised their

hands.

Maybe there's hope for the rest of us poor souls with a sync less than 57.65.

"You'd all be wrong," Graves revealed. "Close, some of you. Close. However, not in sync."

Demora cast Graves a look before returning Amy's stare.

Graves clapped. "You're a phenomenal group. Something amazing awaits you at our next meeting. Your talismans will glow when it's time."

Couldn't get out of there faster... "Thanks for the heads up." Amy marched the streets and thrust her impatient hand back at the outpaced Demora, who tried to catch up.

"Listen, they had to know who they were dealing with! You're not just some newcomer. You're a master auraist—"

"Enough." *The sight of her— Grr!* "Doesn't matter anyway, my aura's to-shit."

You know it.

"Shut it!" Amy peeped Demo's shock. "Not you. It's the fucking schizo."

"Still dealing with that?"

Yes, Demo, we're not all self-appointed deities—

"You need some training." *OK, Gma.* Demora gave *her prideful nod.* "I'm sure we'll learn a lot from the professor."

"Your trust that easy to bargain?"

"Hey, wait up!" Jamari ran up behind them, wearing his hefty smile. "You guys see your number?"

Lil Sis strolled behind him. "You're breathing way too hard again, brother."

"Yeah, yeah. Look, check your talismans." Jamari flipped his palm around. His talisman wore an illuminated white number seven that danced in its center. "C'mon then. Let's see what you ladies are worth."

"Second?" Demora stared at her talisman.

Amy pulled her talisman out. Her jaw dropped.

A number one shimmered to life.

She inspected it against the sky. *Far out. This gleam is otherworldly.* "Where do you think she got these from? I've never seen this material before…"

"How'd you land first place?" Jamari asked. "You dropped yours instantly!"

"She got points for heart," Lil Sis *mocked.*

"Lay off." Demora's eyes *warned* the girl.

"Remarkable." Jamari took off his bomber jacket. "So, are you really the one who brought Cloudy to cower? What's possession like? Did you throw up? Did you kill anyone? Wait, you were possessed, right?"

"Read the room." Amy sized him up. *All these questions. Cloudy this, Cloudy that. Fuck Cloudy! He's not a fucking celebrity.*

HE'S ALWAYS WITH YOU.

Buzz off! Amy slapped her forehead. *Language.* Turned to the siblings. "How do your lot know Graves, anyway?"

"Long enough," Lil Sis replied.

"That's not an answer." Amy shook her head. *Deep breaths, Devine.*

"We met her in Cape Town on holiday," Jamari said. Nudged his sister with an elbow. "Gotta give a little to get a little, sis. It's all in Her Light. Anyway, Graves said she was organizing a traveling school where our talents can be amplified."

"Traveling school, huh? When did she find time for that?"

"After Cloudy, I imagine," Demora said.

Amy's eyes shot daggers into her.

"What?!"

"Watch how much you give, brother. She's still holding back." Lil Sis's audacious stare never left Amy, even from behind.

"I already told you, my aura's weak. And Demora, you're irresponsible and impossible. Thank you so much."

"You're so touchy!" Demora waved a hand. "It was a proud moment in your life. You contained a spirit, a <u>curse</u>! How many people can say that, truly?"   "Drop it."

"Welp, we're gonna head off," Jamari said, guiding his sister's shoulders. "Productive chat! See you two lovely ladies at the next meet."

"How long has this been going on?" Amy said once the siblings trailed away enough.

"Only about four months." Demora closed her eyes, *braced for it.*

Four fucking months.

"I'm sorry I haven't been so vocal, Ames."

"You've been plenty vocal tonight."

"Graves said she could help me learn to master my aura. It took some time for me to believe and even more time to say yes. I'm still uncertain."

"How did she know about your aura?"

"She can sense it, Ames. Truly sense it. A real, natural-born auraist. We didn't think we would find anyone like this... ever. What do you think?"

"I don't know. I merely signed on to save you from yourself."

"Oh, don't give me that roachweed. You're just as curious."

"Appetite's full for one night."

"I did find <u>something</u>, though. Look." Demora gave Amy a small piece of ancient-looking parchment paper.

"What's TSGL?" Amy flipped the parchment over twice. The letters were in bold and cursive, rich purple ink.

"We're gonna find out."

"No, <u>we're</u> not Demora." Amy shook her head. *Fuck Blé. Fuck TSGL, whatever the hell that is.* "I'm not Scooby Doo-ing this or any more shit for the rest of my life." *Gonna go watch some LCWF for the remainder of my existence. Watch others put their bodies on the line instead.*

Demora's deranged face got in hers. She threw her arms out at Amy, who trailed away ahead of her. "First off, Scooby-Doo is a superb detective and a stellar..."

Chapter Thirteen

It's Worse Than I Thought

Do you trust Graves? The words from the previous night lingered in Amy's pounding skull. She stared at an unopened package on her desk next to her cracked GCID, its screen with several fractures. She recoiled in her chair and sighed into the ceiling. *Too early. I barely slept.* She ripped the green packaging to shreds. *There it is.*

GCID Model X.

She pulled the new, sleeker GCID from its branded box. "Creaevix, sync new device."

GCID Model X found. Syncing information for Amy Devine.

...

Sync incomplete.

"What?" Amy looked at the back of the GCID's screen. "Oh, fuck me."

Her finger teased a large protruding needle on the back of

the device.

Looked at her wrist. A small hole in her skin pushed outside of her body.

Every upgrade's more of a nuisance than the last. She aimed the GCID's needle over the hole in her wrist. *Yup, too big. At least this model's not as bulky. Bullocks.* An eyebrow raised. *What if?* Amy stared outside her open window.

You're going to die out there.

"People die every day." Amy closed her eyes, feeling the breeze from outside. "Any time, anywhere."

You're going to die the worst.

¿Qué alimenta tu deseo?

"Hey Creaevix, ask Demora if we can meet thirty minutes later. I'll be a few. Say 3:15 to be safe."

Message sent.

She wasn't sure why her bowels betrayed her with absolute dominance. Her stomach ached in incrementing volumes with each layer of clothing She threw on.

Three bathroom trips later, She got her sneakers on.

Took them off. Ran for a last shot *on the throne.*

Chitterchitterchitterchitter-chit-irp-chit-irp

Checked under her toilet seat eight times in three minutes.

Cleaned herself.

Ran downstairs. Put her sneakers on again.

Where can I find the right dealer this early in the day? Chilly down this way. Thirty minutes from home, Amy trucked through the UnderCity, *searching, searching,* hugging herself, *searching.*

La La La La LA La La La Laaaaaa

She hugged tighter, eyes closed, and shook her head.

La La La La **LA** *La La La Laaaaaa*

She groaned.

La La La La **LA** *La La La Laaaaaa*

"Alright, enough!" She rounded on her undead chorus of doppelgangers.

Hehehe They slinkered away. Vanished into the shadows of nearby alleys.

Amy hung her head and quickened her pace through the shady gawkers around her. *Ever since last year's murders, there's been an uptick in 'spirit' business. People buying up illegal jars to stuff the souls of their deceased relatives in. Drugs inducing unconscious lucidity, enabling folks to know what death feels like. The Crevents are running free, selling all they can at the highest price. They're stuffed into every corner but no Dets on their case? Rubbish. Least I won't get mugged cuz they think I'm loony. Let's turn here—oh!*

Big Man, *literally on his name tag,* grunted as his belly bounced her back. "You've been truckin' round here for some time, li' lady. What I do for you?" He cracked his massive, *bruised* knuckles and thumped his fists together.

Close call. He seems cool. Who pissed him off? Amy boxed her knuckles together and bowed. "Respect to you, brother. Health and blessings. My GCID needs a reconfig. I've got an external unit, and the specs I want worked out are a little dicey. I would love to chat up an engineer in your camp."

He put up a finger. "One sec, please." Stunner shades looked off to his side. "Ya, Boss? Uh-huh. Hurd ya." Head back on Amy, "You can leave it 'ere and pickup in two 'ours. Whatcha need dun?"

"Oh, spectacular." Her eyes darted beyond him. "Your engineer near, or... Some technical spots are... I want some configs off the books. Hoping with some—"

"'Old on." Shades off to the side. "What's that? Oookay. Ok. Hurd ya." The man nodded to Amy, broad shoulders reassuring, "Pick up in two hours, 'round six. Boss Man says he's got you, no worries. Leave a list of wants."

"Who's your boss? Did you say six?" Amy clocked the glowing digits of the GCID on the man's wrist: 4:09 pm.

Fuck. Her eyes lit up. "You've got an external GCID? Wow, that's—"

Big Man lowered his shades. "You want it fixed or no?"

"Sorry. It's just— I've never seen anyone but me with an external one."

He continued to watch her.

"Right, yes. I want it fixed, go ahead. What's next?"

He cocked his head to the side. "Yeah, Boss. Oh, okay. Oh, 'old on." Looked at her. "Boss got a message. Ay, Creaevix, show the ting." Triangular lights burst to life over his GCID and danced over his forearm. The lights caved in all at once into a perfect sphere.

Amy moved around the spectacle with widened eyes. *What the absolute hell?* The cloudiness—*ugh*—within it dispersed in the middle. *Black lights inside, create seem to be spawning the shadowy grey effect forming the clouds. Such abnormal tech. This is not textbook Creaevix source code.*

Streams of blue lights danced out from underneath the clouds. They sped forth and shaped into a human figure.

The little man made of blue lights waved. "Afternoon, Miss. I understand you had some concerns about your device. I'd be happy to assist you." He lifted a hand, letting go of some lights that formed three hollow symbols to the left of him. "Here, you'll find my credentials."

A grotesque totem of lights hung in the air, made from three figures. A closer inspection helped make out each, from top to bottom: an octopus, a gargoyle, and a Phoenix.

Amy held her GCID up towards the glimmering man and his box of code.

Chime!

Amy reeled her arm back. A tidal wave of white lights blinked to life from her GCID's screen. They formed a white screen two times the size of her head.

On the screen, a web page with review after review, *mostly five stars,* and a certificate right in the middle.

Certified Light Engineer, The Engineer.

"You can provide Big Man here with all your wants for the device. Any questions, Miss?" The Engineer asked, with an infectious smile on the little blue human.

Yeah, what's your <u>name</u>? 4:14, fuck. "Last name, Devine." Amy swatted her lightscreen away and offered her GCID arm to Big Man.

She didn't answer. Fuck, she must be livid. Amy crept through the hills at the edge of the Jadesfeld Woods. *What is happening?*

Dozens of JPD detectives sprawled across the vast greenery. Some trees were uprooted, and bushes were torn to shreds around the spot.

Wait, I don't have to hide anymore. Fuck it. Amy made her way into the nearest clearing.

Investigative scientists worked behind strips of yellow and white lights that spiraled together like DNA strands. CRIME SCENE – DO NOT PASS in black light flashed across the strands.

Amy pulled her JPD Junior Det badge out of her jeans pocket. Flashed it as she passed by the curious Dets. Sighed and frowned at the word TEMP in the middle of the badge before pocketing it.

Several clearings over, one figure towered over the others: General Aba. The seven-foot gorilla led a team of detectives around *some octillerian* device. Its bagpipe-shaped body wore a badge with the symbol of an octopus on it. The device stood on four wickedly crooked flat bottom legs. Four more mechanical arms shot up into the air, prompting the detectives to jump back.

"Excuse me, Detective Sellers?" Amy approached the back of a white-haired Det, conferring with some peers. "What's going on?"

"Hey, that's Jimmy's pet project," a rough detective's voice carried across from the field.

Several chuckles followed.

I should ignore— Amy rounded on him. "Last I checked, Jimmy's on holiday after his stellar case work. When was your last case closed, Peters? Or you, O'Donnell? Hm."

Oooooos! across the field.

"Not helping your case," Det. Sellers said. "Listen, kid." He waved her over in private. "I know you and Jim had an arrangement, but that's where it ends. The precinct's got no time to be training a non-certified Junior right now, ya know?"

Amy pulled away from his hand on her shoulder. "No, I don't. All I know is your pissing buddies have been selling me and Jimmy short, and I'm sick of it. I thought you were one of the few with some sense left."

"Look." He leaned in. "There's been a hammering on the numbers last quarter. The entire department doesn't have the man hours to take on anything less than a detecti—"

"Are you joking? What about Detective Lonsmith? And those U.S. blokes? And that other new kid?"

"Lonsmith, she's moving downstream next week. I didn't make the call to the States. And the kid, it's uh..."

"Ey-yo! I'm ready!" A fresh face *looking like he flew out of the womb two seconds ago* ran over to the group behind them, flashing his shiny new Junior Detective badge. *Non-temp, I bet.*

"Hey! That's my boy! Get in here. Let's work him! Keep him feeding us coffee."

Barks of laughter.

Amy stared into Det. Seller's face.

"I got no say in any of it." He shrugged.

"We got actual detective work we're doing here, sweetheart!" *Another smirking, usually more grumpy detective yelled with a rancid breath that could level Great London.* "So, can you let us get it done? I'm in no need for a pet of my own and I already got scrappy kids at home."

Amy pointed a threatening finger at him. Opened her

mouth.

"My daughter will whoop your daughter's ass, Haglee," a one-eyed detective called out.

"She see better than you?" Another voice answered, followed by more chuckles from the entire lot.

"Devine." The unmistakable callous voice of General Aba came over Amy's shoulder. Gorilla years did well on him, but his scowls showed the age of his hatred for humankind. He faced the grumpy detective before turning to the rest of the *smart-asses*. "If you think that casually using the word <u>pet</u> is humorous, let me remind you of the years you kept my kind enslaved as <u>your</u> <u>pets</u>. Factually, with some still kept in captivity today."

The wind cracked the silence as the field of detectives shifted to their work.

"Ho! Hey-ho!" Praisure, the cowboy detective, *lumberjack of a man,* rolled up and lined himself between Aba and the JPD Squads. "Easy fellas. How's it do, lil lady?" He tipped his classic black Stetson. "Aba, my main G, how's it going, cowboy? What's that sweet lil device you got over there?"

Aba grunted. "I suspected some ill energies in this kidnapping. My device will confirm my suspicions." Aba refocused on Amy. "You. Aren't you the missing's companion? When's the last time you've seen—"

"Kidnapping? Who? <u>Demora?</u>" Amy laughed.

Several detectives slunked further away from them.

Amy's smile diminished. "Demora?"

"Careful with those deets, Aba," Praisure said. "We don't know nothing for nothing. No use getting the folks riled."

"You sympathize so deeply." Aba's breath let out a **huff**.

I'm plenty riled, bloody bastard. Amy grilled Aba. *If he did anything to her—*

"We must gain knowledge of <u>her</u>—" Aba gave an exclusive nod to Amy, "whereabouts at the time of the struggle."

"There was a <u>struggle?</u>" Amy's body rocked on her wobbly knees.

—<u>Amy, a mannequin, scrapes her hollow eyes—her face cracks—</u>

<u>*pieces fall—*</u>

She held the knot in her stomach forcing her spine to bow. Her breaths shortened.

"Might be that tortured, twisted son of a bitch," a detective strolling by said, his head deep in the hovering lightscreen in front of him. "Going around fucking the skulls of the dead."

Praisure smacked his bulky thigh. "Dag nabbit, Jannison! Now, why you goin' round spillin' all that conjecture?"

"Didn't your wife leave you, Jannison?" another detective yelled. "Go handle that!"

"They say..." Detective Jannison peeked out from behind his lightscreen, "He's trying to resurrect the souls through himself. Kinda like that other twisted fucker them years back." He moved past them. "What was his name?" he whispered.

"If he's only fucking corpses, why are we chasing after him?" A bushy-eyed detective hollered.

"Because some of those corpses are still living, Charly."

"They may breathe, but they ain't living!"

"Just do the job!"

"Maybe we should start releasing the names of the victims. Maybe it helps."

"Samsone!" Det. Jannison recalled some feet away. "No, his name was Candemseve... right? Hm... No..."

"GIT outta here!" Praisure brushed off the detectives and turned to Amy. "Easy wit me now, it'll be alright. Them fucknuts got the wrong shoe worn to a cookout. Lay of the land shows other than they think. That's why the bounty hunter is here." He pressed a hand on his chest. "When you last got a-knockin' from her, Ms. Devine, was it?"

Amy's blank stare surveyed the destroyed landscape. *Looks like a struggle to me.* "Huh?"

"When's the last you spoke to her?"

"She was waiting for me..." Amy's fingers dug into the earth. She sank her butt onto the ground. *There they go again, talking like she's actually been kidnapped! What a bloody tale! It's such a rare occurrence and Demora of all?! Taking the piss to a new level.*

"She was accosted about an hour and a half ago," Aba said. "I don't have time for this. Can you forward me the details, Praisure? I came to aid the human authorities in their investigation, not to fobolize with miscreants." He marched off.

She can't be... "Kidnapped?..." Amy's voice flew away with the wind.

"Squad B, we gotta roll out," a detective called from somewhere. "They found another dead one!"

Amy's heart sank.

"Man in his eighties! Let's roll!"

Amy closed her eyes with a sigh. Took a deep breath and held it. Let it out. Repeated the process.

"Ah, the world's gone tits and I've got ass." Praisure exhaled, scratching his head. He nodded across different areas of the field. "See, them detectives got their methods. Aba's got his. I've got mine. They don't call me the Kidnapper Sheriff for nothing."

"Who calls you that?" Amy watched the grass blow in the wind.

"You're right. That sounds horrible. I reckon—doesn't matter. We're gonna find your friend." *The suddenly gleeful man* pulled out a circular device with a thin-necked tube that **coughed**. "You got any DNA from her?"

Kidnapped. "Maybe. I think." *Her old hair brush. Wait, no, chucked it—burned it, fuck! I was mad then. All else is insignificant now. Demo... Kidnapped...*

This—

I have her old basketball shoes. Maybe...

—doesn't—

Stupid brain dipped into vats of vacancy, as usual...

—make—

Dare I think of anything more comprehensive than <u>maybe</u>.

—sense.

"I'll go home and raid my room. How does that thing work?" Amy pointed to the object in his hands.

Praisure massaged the back of his neck. "Reckon Jimmy trusts you. See, I don't give a damn a-detective nine-to-nine, tell ya. Jimmy, he's sorted, despite his department's stigma. And I respect loyalty to friends."

"What stigma?"

"Never heard such blasphemy. They've been hating on him for his handling of that Saint Cloudy case. Says he should've brought in the boys and not—" he pointed at her, "'some teenage girl.' Not my words." His hands went up in defense.

Cloudy, Cloudy, Cloudy. Even when she's missing, he's still fucking relevant— "Yeah. Well, they always want Jimmy to <u>do the thing</u>." Amy's face twitched. "Scratch his balls and share a pint while regurgitating their barbaric manners."

"Jim's an ace, no argument there."

"Fuck um. What's your plan?"

He leaned in closer with the device as it **coughed** away like a hushed child's whispering, looping cough. "I've been picking up some irregular energies already. My tracker here can tune into the lower frequencies of us Evos and fine-tune the output to attract higher ones. Reading's been off the charts on my tracker since I came into this town. I can never really pinpoint, but that's where my innate tracking ability comes in."

His device does what I used to do... The thought ate at her *like a malnourished cannibal.*

"I need lots of info." Praisure slapped the device off when a group of detectives passed by. "Time to go covert. Get me what you can by the end of the day, and I'll swing by to pick it up. Some of these jobs can take weeks with little to no info."

Weeks.

Weeks.

Weeks.

Weeks?

Chapter Thirteen: It's Worse Than I Thought

May as well send me off to Mickelspiff, Burt

Fobolize:- to create fictitious, misinspired, or absurdly insignificant conversation with another, who does not stand at the current communicationist level as the other party(ies)

Aba = jerk

Octillerian - relating to Octipi community, its people, or their language; having Octipi origins; objects have 8 orifices

<u>What the hell is General Aba doing working with the Octipi community? Why's he helping us humans anyway? Big Man's boss had a similar octopus symbol in his code. Are they connected?</u>

<u>Praisure's tracker has to work. 'My tracker here can tune into the lower frequencies of us Evos and fine-tune the output to attract higher ones. Reading's been off the charts on my tracker since I came into this town. I can never really pinpoint, but that's where my innate tracking ability comes in.'</u>

<u>Maybe I can...</u>

<u>—Amy closes her eyes—takes deep breaths—Come on, focus, Devine. Focus on her. Feel her aura—</u>

<u>—-seconds pass—</u>

<u>—minutes pass—</u>

<u>—Amy opens her eyes—"Bullocks"—</u>

                    AMY (V.O.)
          I remember the first time we
          ventured out here. We had just
          knocked some pastries from
          Baker Greggi's shop. It was a
          hard year for Gma's business
          and Demora's parents used to
          have her on a strict 1500
          calorie diet. Wanted her to go
          into ballet. They said she had
          to be light on her feet.

FADE IN:

EXT. ENFIELD FOREST - NIGHT

Bulbs of light illuminate over the heads
of several members of a large SEARCH
PARTY spread out end to end.

Slowly, WE MOVE IN on a small section
where Amy sits on a log, someone at her
side.

                    AMY
          We were just hungry. Ran all
          the way out here. After we lost
          him, we spent hours in this
          spot, talking. Enjoying our
          stolen goods. She… I was always
          the one that needed protecting.
          How could this happen?

NEARING HER: Ambient light flushes the
face of Amy and the woman standing next
to her— MADAME BLÉ. A NERDY LIGHT MEMBER
approaches them.

                    NERDY LIGHT MEMBER
          Madame, our third and final
          support team has returned from
          Enfield Depths.

He creates a circle of light in the air
with his finger. Inside of it, a dozen
dots of light in arrow formation move
towards the edge and outside of the
circle.

                    NERDY LIGHT MEMBER (CONT'D)
          We've covered everything up to
          what's forbidden with Animalia
          Act II. A local residing within
          the Depths allowed us to
          inspect a bit past that point
          and they've also confirmed no
          humans have been past that
          point in months. I, uh… I'm not
          sure what more we can get done
          tonight. Morning should provide
          a different perspective.

                    MADAME BLÉ
               (Nods)
          Well done. Tell everyone that I
          want Support Team A to set up
          camp in this area for tonight.

                    AMY
          I don't want anyone else
          disappearing on account of your
          generosity.

                    MADAME BLÉ
          Let me assure you, The Light
          has devotees skilled in all
          walks of life. We can handle
          ourselves. This isn't our first
          search party, dearie.

   (To Nerdy Light Member)
I will have Team B switch
places with them in the
morning.

    NERDY LIGHT MEMBER
Yes, my Madame.

He leaves them alone again.

    VOICE (O.S.)
I'll take tonight's shift.

MR. STOICISM walks up to them with
reddened eyes.

    MR. STOICISM
I couldn't— I didn't find her.
I'm sorry.

Amy gives him a small smile and nod.

He returns it and walks off, disappearing
into the dark night.

Amy stares into the vast night.

    MADAME BLÉ
We will find her. We will find
them.

    AMY
Them?

    MADAME BLÉ
One of our members has gone
missing as well. You're
familiar with her— Celestia. We
only found her cloak among some
bushes in the Haven.

                    AMY
          Fuck. Who would… I'll stay,
          too. Used to camp out in that
          big tree over there.

Madame Blé places a hand on Amy's
shoulder.

                    MADAME BLÉ
          I will find her. You've been
          awake for twenty-six hours.

               (Leans down)
          Trust me when I say, when we
          find the bastard who did this,
          we will rain all of Her might
          down on their pitiful soul.

Amy looks up at her.

                    MADAME BLÉ
          We are warriors. Go home. Get
          proper rest in a proper bed.
          For when we find the culprit,
          you will need your strength to
          support your friend's return.

Madame Blé squeezes her shoulder.

Amy's left hand rests on top of hers.

                    AMY
          Thank you, Madame Blé.

FADE OUT.

                    AMY (V.O.)
          I meant to ask you, Madame.

```
What is Callisto's One Big
Fault?



          MADAME BLÉ (V.O.)
Ah, yes. It is just a fairytale
that some of our members
believe in. There is no answer.
It is only a hypothetical
exploration. I allow this
timeless debate to be discussed
within the safety of the Haven
because I believe you must
always question what you
believe in.
```

Chapter Thirteen: It's Worse Than I Thought

Chapter Fourteen

A Blink Changes Everything

"**L**a luz..."
Hell never existed.
"**La luz...**"
Now it does.
"**La luz...**"
I gave him everything.
"**Ella lo quiere...**"
Shoes. Joint tips we shared. I picked every strand of Demo's blonde hair for hours off of shirts. Scarfs. Her jorts and bras. All gathered from the years of her presence. Beautiful years.
"**Ella quiere la luz y se alejóoooo...**"
'I'll go to infinity to fulfill my duty,' he told me.
I don't have infinity. The nightmare loops with each passing day. Waking up deep into this fabricated timeline. This couldn't happen in my world. Must be a nightmare.
'**What's a bird without its voice?**'
Seventy-two hours. *Nothing else matters.* It only took *22.5*

hours for Praisure to disbar her from being his aide. *Less than a full day, and I cause a wreck.* The last *49.5* hours spent in her room weren't enough to remove her from the *deafening* critics in her head—*external and internal, imaginary. So loud.* Louder than the sounds of happiness outside her home. *It's nice to hear children playing in town again.* The weight in her chest sunk deeper than She anticipated.

The first week went by.

I've traced every inch of this stupid town. Nothing changes...

"Knocking on your door... I crushed the mirror... That captivated my interest in your heart's consi-duhhhh..."

I've paraded up and down and through Enfield's city of currency cunts. The Singer failed. I failed. Prostituting my voice for claps and awe. NO information. No one knows a THING!

Amy SMASHED her left forearm on the desk.

Opened her eyes. Stared down at the square blue chip on the inside of her left wrist.

GCID xTIer lit up on its smooth screen.

Shook her wrist.

Shards of the GCID screen fell onto the table.

There goes my custom. Funds down the drain. She removed the GCID from her wrist.

Picked up one of the tiny shards.

Teased its sharpness over her right wrist.

Plucked a little at the vein.

Spotted the edges of her scarred backhand. *Rubbish!* "Fuck!" She tossed the shard— and GCID— across the room.

Amy trucked through Jadesfeld's freezing winds in a hurry—

—through the UnderCity—

She stood in front of Big Man.

"Again?" He asked.

"How much for rush service?"

Amy, in her room, behind her desk. "Creaevix, any messages from Praisure?"

No new messages.

"Can you call him?"

Calling Praisure...

She cleared her hoarse throat.

No response. Leave a voicemail?

"Ok, let's leave it."

Bing!

"Hey P! Ames again, so sorry again about the other day—"
Amy marches through the halls of the Jadesfeld Police Department, screaming, hands pinned to her sides—tosses papers off desks—sits alone in a holding cell—

"I was off my rocker, that's for sure. Just wanted to say, waiting patiently for updates. Totally cool. But I do—I would like it if you called me at my house. Please, okay. Thanks, bruv. End message."

Groans from the underbelly lead to an exhaled puff of air.

"Shit. Creaevix, can we go straight to vmail, Praisure."

Voice Mailing Praisure

Bing!

"Hey love, me again. Sorry, I just quickly wanted to say my GCID may be out of commission. It is—"
Amy screams into the glass outside Jadesfeld PD—smashes her hands into a panel of the building—it falls—SHATTERS—

"—So please dial me when you hear something. Anything at all. Thank you so much. End message." *I should write.*

She understood the last straw *why* he did it. *Kinda.* Offering herself as bait to lure Demora's captor in. Maybe it was the way

She *demanded*. A trade for trade bounty was a gruesome deal, yet it seemed fair. Perhaps She'd die sacrificing herself for Demora. Her body cringed at the desperation in her voice.

Ready to die.

That's my worth.   *That's my worth?*

She scanned her room for the voice *in my head.* Shook it off.

The second week went by.

"She teeeeeells meeeeeee. She tells me where to goOoooooo…"

She grilled the ***NOISE*** coming from the streets outside.

"She tells me not to wane… She tells me, not in vain…"

ANOTHER voice adds:

"She fills me up. She holds me down. When I'm fantasizing, She's always around."

Three voices intertwine, almost sounding like one:

"Ny-uh-uh-A! Nyuh-uh uh!

Uh-ny-uh-uh, ny-uhuh uh-uh nyuh-uuuh uh!

Ny-uh-uh, ny-uh-uh uh!"

—Amy's HANDS SWIPE THE SHADES SHUT—

Minutes, hours, I don't know— later, She sat beside her reboarded-up window. "Creaevix, what does Shan Hiska mean?"

Shan Hiska means to 'drink the wind' or 'get some air' usually meant to collect oneself after a disturbance

Hm. Fine, I'll write that down. I don't know what else to write, anyway. This used to feel easy. Why can't I write? Words make little sense, and nothing means <u>anything</u> to me anymore.

Brain's porridge.

If I'm so useless, why do I care so much?

If she dies...

It's your fault. You are <u>not</u> strong enough. Always late...

Everyone <u>seemingly</u> looking for her... they don't love her. Only one person who cares.

Truly.

I need to find her. She'd do the same.

Amy placed a foot inside her pant leg.

Blinked.

Amy sat on the floor, head spinning all around her room. Got up.

Jeans on, shirt—

Blinked.

Eyes transfixed. Sat on the bed's edge. *What is happening?* She lifted herself.

Blinked.

Parts skipping... what...

Blinked.

Don't have time for this nonsen—

Blinked.

On her ass on the floor. Rolled onto her stomach, face eating the floor. *I'm useless.*

SLAMMED her fist into the floor, denting it. "Fuck!"

Maybe we tell the old lady.

Oh, she doesn't care. Amy sighed. *May as well talk to the voices in my head.* "She'll just tell me to train it off or some nobdickish procedure. I'll punch my way through this like she expects me to." Her weak punch hit the air.

Crashed face-first into her bed. Thrashed her hands into it.

Stared at the ceiling. Asked for the time. *How did two hours pass?*

Her head deep in a book— *surrounded by a pile of clothing that needed washing.* The book's title on the cover: *If You Have A Soul, You May Experience This.* She kicked some overturned books concealed in between the bundles of clothes. *Can't even give me as many options as letters in the title.* She tossed the book on top of more piled under her desk. "I can't find anything on this fucking condition."

She blinked.

Found herself standing, face inches from the wall.

She **groaned** at the ceiling. *If it's aura related— which I'm 100% sure it is— I'm dipped in shit.*

Blinked.

On the toilet. She fidgeted with her fingers. "Had to use it. Had to."

No identity.

"Shut the— who the fu—" Her eyes flared around the room's soft bluish-white tones—sighed into her palm.

She.

Who is She?

Chitterchitter-chit-irp-chit-irp

Amy squealed as her body trembled and swatted invisible intruders off her arms. "I'm gonna be late. Library closes soon." Cleaned herself. Flushed the toilet.

I can't figure it out.

She can't figure it out.

Barnabas? Is that you—

Come home!

"Barnabas?" Amy asked. She swatted her hand away. "Get the fuck— who the fu—"

*I'm rolling in the **NOooOoooooooooooooooooooooooooo***

Ooooooooooooooooooooooooooooooo

Oooooooooooooooooooooooo

ooooooow—

Stop.

"Creaevix, any messages from Praisure yet?"

Chitterchitterchitterchitter

No new messages.

"Right, but any from Praisure?"
Chitterchitterchitterchitter

No new messages.

"Bloody hell."
Chitterchitterchitterchitter
She flicked her tongue in anguish. *I could swear these fucking hairy baby creatures clutched the tip of her tongue. The babies were the worst. The adult raccooroaches are more efficient in their goal.* She shivered. "Come on, Praisure. Please. Find <u>something</u>."
He doesn't wanna call you. Get it through your—
Chitterchitterchitterchitter
Get it through your—
Chitterchitterchitterchitter
—through your—
Always eyes on me...
Chitterchitterchitterchitter
Get it—
Chitterchitterchitterchitter
Staring through my window at night.
—through your—
Chitterchitterchitterchitter
—your—
<u>*—The green-haired spiritualist peers—*</u>
—your—
There are gaping corpses staring at your soul.
Get it through your thick skull!
She kneeled in front of her bedroom wall. Tapped her forehead on it in beats. "Rambling again." Palmed the *gaping hole*

of her ears until the ***chitterchitter*** sound ceased.

She turned. Her eyes locked with her own.

Her reflection on the wall smiled back.

"I can do this. Gotta get out, I can—"

"Devine." A ziccolit Rezna appeared behind her.

"Gma, I—"

"Interesting call I got. You broke your house arrest. Again."

—Amy, in front of Big Man— 'It's not ready yet' he says —
"What's the point of rush service if—" —

Amy raised a finger.

"You've broken your house arrest fifteen times in two weeks!"

Amy nodded and opened her mouth.

"No need to lie," Zicco-Rezna said. "Luckily for you, once again, your cowboy connections have spared your demise. Praisure kept you from further punishment. I was ripe for either decision since you can't seem to keep yourself out of trouble."

"I-broke-my-GCID! I just wanted to get an update—"

"Thankfully, the Chief has respect for me and sympathy for the children affected by Cloudy—"

"Can you not bring that name up right now? I just—"

"He's willing to shave your multiple house-breaking offences if I promised to talk to you—"

"No-one's-done-a <u>thing</u> yet! Nothing found!"

"—and made you promise not to cause any more trouble—"

"At least The Light has started some kind of campaign—"

"Enough."

"Demora's out there!" Amy massaged the burn in her throat.

Zicco-Rezna stared hard into her eyes. Her eyes softened. She sighed. "I'll let you know if I hear anything about Demora. With Norma's help wrangling the detectives, we <u>will</u> <u>find</u> <u>her</u>. You have my absolute promise."

Amy's shoulders fell. She collapsed on her bed, facing the boarded window.

"For both our sakes. Please. Can you promise not to give Madame Blé and her circus more fuel? Stay put."

"Fine." Amy sat up. Turned to face—

Gma was gone.

Amy turned to her wall mirror. "I'm forever doused in the dread of Dalestone." With an eyebrow raised, "I should write that down."

She blinked.

Dodged the hand clawing out from her mirror image.

The reflection—normal again.

I thought I'd be better by now. "Maybe it's something else... I can't leave, but I can't stay here tripping bollocks either." *I can't help Demora in this state.* "Creaevix, can you get out a message to Archie— *the white bat flew madly around Amy's head as she scribbled away at her desk*— by connecting through the Animalia Kingdom—somehow? Is there a hotline?"

Out of my capability, I'm afraid.

"Marvelous. It can do a zillion things but can't— never mind. Focus."

Focus.

She punched the air in front of her in calculated increments, one fist after the other.

Focus.

Her right fist smashed into the wall. Pulled back.

Shook her head at the small crater that now existed. *Gma's gonna kill me.*

Ran down the hall into the lavatory.

I'll wake up. She stared at the ice cube-like tiles under her feet. *I'll just wake up.* Shifted her butt on the toilet. *I'll wake up.* Feet rocked to and fro. *That's it. Wake up.*

.

.

.

.

.

"WAKE UP!" She coughed blood.

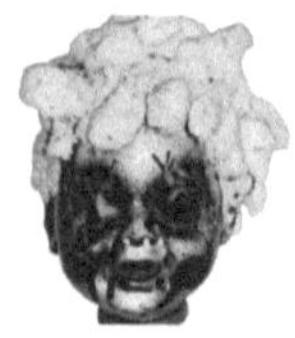   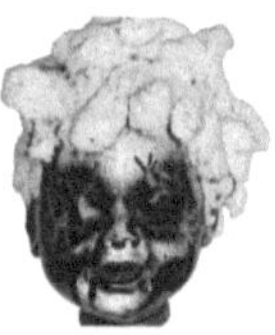

The third week came in.

Amy climbed down the last step into the basement and gawked at its cleanliness. *How many more times will I check down here? All these storage craters of only Rezna knows what.* She slipped past extra metallic slabs for the dead and rows of filing cabinets from a century unlived by Amy.

Amy opened each file cabinet. Rolled her eyes at the medical documents inside. *Files upon files upon files of the deceased.* She shivered.

You'll be one soon.

She faced the door that She dreaded more than most.

The morgue's prep room.

She opened into the surgical tidiness of the silver room. *Walking in a warm dream,* She squirmed *in the mere existence of a room made for butchering the dead.*

In the back corner, *missing the red mark,* the door frame leading to the secret room. *Found a capture box for Cloud—IT last year. Could use another assist.* She felt around the edges of where the door used to lie. *Besides the frame, it's a solid wall now. Keep dreaming an opening will appear. I could punch through this easy. Probably. I can't feel any warmth inside. It's always been warmest right here. It's just—gone.* She turned away. *If there was anything in here that could help find Demora, Gma would have used it already.*

PING!

"Creaevix, play message!"

Playing new message from Madame Blé.

"Good day, dear. I was unable to reach your GCID, so I hope you receive this in a timely fashion. The Mayor has agreed to fund an exhaustive search party for all those still missing. I have secured an additional budget for a rally that I did not need, and it will be used for your friend and our missing member. We hope to broaden our search outside of the sister towns. You are welcome to our Haven whenever you would like. Our prayers are with you. Stay strong."

Amy sulked towards the exit.

She sat on her room floor, head between her legs. *Why Demo? She was doing more with her life than me. Exploring her aura. Learning more about herself and our World. Why is she the one taken by some mad fucker? Who decides THAT, <u>Callisto</u>? Worshipping some dead woman. Absurd.* Amy pulled at her locs. *My best friend's gone and I can't do a damn thing!*

A single tear fell on the side of her socks. She watched it soak in. "I'm useless."

Behind Amy, white streams of white light rose and peeled off her body—HER AURA. It hovered behind her, shaping itself.

Took human shape. The shape: AURA AMY.

She isn't you.

"I could be out there right now, ripping some asshole's throat apart." Amy picked at her toes. "Jim wouldn't approve." A soft chuckle escaped her. *Jimmy. I wish you were here, mate.* "What would he tell me?"

Can you even hear me anymore?

"Oh yeah, forever doused in the dread of dalestone." She snatched her journal off the table and picked a *marvelous* purple pen from in between some of her untwisted braids. Picked at them. "I need to get something done with this hair, too. Another problem to add…" Stabbed her pen into blank pages.

Her aura worked behind her. Aura Amy's fingers strung left and right, sewing her light meticulously inch by inch. Roots of luminous streams expelled from her fingertips and branched to several parts of the ceiling. Her eyeballs ran up in her sockets, replaced by bulging bulbs of chaotic electricity. Her mouth let out a croak. It spat out strings of white light.

The aura strings zipped across the room and stuck to the walls and ceiling.

Meanwhile, Amy, unbeknownst to the magic behind and around her, stopped her obsessive *puncture* of the page She wrote on and bit the pen's tip.

White aura strands swiftly removed the latches and wooden board over her beaten down, cracked wooden shutters covering the window.

She put her pen tip onto the page.

Blinked.

Her sentence was already written.

"How—" She put pen to paper.

Blinked.

More words on the page.

"What. Is happening?" Amy stared at the words that *betrayed* her. Her head slowly rolled up. Eyes widened, jaw dropped, staring at the complexity of the white aura webbing surrounding her. *Behind me, I can feel—*

Aura Amy smiled and waved.

"What. Is. Happening?" Amy looked down. "I've gone completely mad."

Aura Amy's head cocked to the side. *"You're losing the plot."*

"I'm losing something, all right. I need to make sure you're here <u>actually</u> before I commit myself."

"Since you were too distracted to take further action, I sent out a signal for us."

"Act on what? Signal?"

"Seeing a doc, love."

"You, what?"

"I sent out a signal."

"I'm talking to myself."

"You always do."

Amy rose on shaky feet. She ran to her window and stuck her head out. "No."

White lines of her aura coursed up the side of her house and shot into the sky like upside-down lightning bolts.

"Please tell me you can take it down."

"How? What does it matter unless you get better and we find Demora? I had to step in."

"You can't—There are rules, and I would appreciate it personally if you didn't hijack my—"

"Our life as I am you as much as you are me. For I am your shadow, and I am here to stay. Despite your every plea."

Amy just stared at *her. Me? Wha*— "Right, well, you're more of a manifestation of my innate ability..." Her eyes narrowed. "One I need to get under control."

"That's arrogant." Aura Amy nodded. *"It's the SUTBAA."*

"How'd you know I was worried about SUT—"

"I'm you."

"Please. Says the fractures of light masquerading my essence. Sending out <u>death</u> signals for the entire World to come on in and axe us."

"Don't be such a theatre show. They'll just assume your Creaevix is zonked. Ooo, Archie should be here soon."

"How'd you—"

Something **banged** into the door, capturing both Amys' attention. **Bang. Bang. Bang.**

Aura Amy waved her arm to the side, and the door opened with her movement.

Archie the bat zoomed inside, almost tackling Amy, instead crashed into the pile of books under her desk.

Amy smiled as the bat gathered himself and flew up to her face. "Good to see you again, my love."

Archie hugged her face, *his wings now big enough to wrap around my head!*

Human news doesn't travel fast.

Did he— Amy stepped back as the bat let go. "Yeah, my head's in a spin."

Archie flapped around with anxious vigor.

Amy nuzzled her face against his. Stared into those big eyes. "You can't smell her out, can you?"

Archie's ears went down. Shook his head.

Such a good boy, no matter! Aura Amy put her hands on her hips and stepped between the two. *"Where could she be that Archie can't smell her? What's the game plan?"*

Amy bit her lip. "I don't know if I should go through with this. Maybe Gma's right."

"You're looosing THEeee pa-LO-tah."

"This is happening so fast." Amy punched her palm a few times and her eye landed on the book Gma gave her to study. "It's like what that Sifu philosopher says. Something something about opportunities."

"I like it!" Aura Amy punched the air.

Amy nodded at her aura version. Then to Archie. "How would you like to invite your friends over for a party?"

"I am thrilled when we're slow. It scares me that UnderCity medical assistance is becoming the trend. Folks losing their minds. The absent Mayor— scared to let the public know what's really going on. Grave times we're in. What was it like when you gained consciousness, Ms. Devine?"

Amy shrugged. "It's been a bitch. Like I had an out-of-body experience, you could say. I completed the action, but I wasn't there for the event. You get me?"

The six walls around her were adorned with medical certifications from several vicinities throughout London and beyond.

She treats in Amsterdam? Paris, Jamaica, Beijing...

"If it's Class 3 drugs, it wouldn't be the first." Dr. Qindox's stubby finger clicked the button on her headband. A string of blue light cast onto Amy's face.

"I get a slight headache. More like a migraine right before it starts."

"The images you see, what would you call them? Nightmare scenarios?" Her surgical gloved hands pressed pressure points in different sections, then opened each of Amy's eyes. "Hallucinations with an exceeding sense of self-worthlessness?"

Amy gave a slight nod. "Could it be... that curse going around?"

"Oh, curse. Pshh. Rubbish, love." Dr. Qindox checked each of her nostrils. "No people are suffering from the shit that's hit this town since last year. Murder opened up a can of worms. Besides, you don't seem tormented like those poor souls, love." She smiled. Dipped her nose, her eyes peeking from the top of her lenses. "Any strange vaginal discharges? Moles formed? Mouth foaming? Taking illegal pharmaceuticals?"

"No, none of that. Could—" Amy gulped. "Could SUTBAA—"

"Oh, no. But It'd watch for that too. Uncommon and a bitch to get rid of once diagnosed."

Amy raised an eyebrow. "Marijuana, wouldn't...?"

"That's harmless. Are you sure you aren't taking <u>anything</u> extra? No potions you got on the OffNet? Any forbidden species you're harbouring in your home?"

Define forbidden. "None of the above. Feels like I'm on *Questions For Miles.*"

"You're in the underground, love. Don't get offended. Our most frequent patients are only ailed by their self-manifested dread."

"I'll take my offences as they come. Something to keep me alive."

Dr. Qindox laughed. "Very good. Dr. Vinity told me you had a lovely charm."

"Thanks for allowing the short notice, doc. Any idea what's going on with me?"

The doctor kicked her closet door open. An old-school twenty-five-inch monitor with chrome wings flew next to her.

Its screen cut on. Showed a picture of Amy's brain.

"Remarkable. You have a split stem, midbrain, one side larger than the other. See here?" She pointed it out. "It's quite difficult to determine exactly. Your symptoms present as a composite of anterograde and retrograde amnesia types known as global amnesia."

"My memory's fine. I just... miss steps."

"Sort of like Retroactive Amnesia."

"Come again? That makes little sense."

"I've seen it once, in another case. Your stress levels are clearly part of the blame. It's a matter of narrowing down what else."

"Retroactive Amnesia. So if I'm doing things I <u>wanted</u> to do... It's like... intuition? But I don't control it?"

"That's a cute way to look at it. Who says you're in control? Not quite. Whatever stresses your mind is under renders you incapable of focusing on multiple primaries. Have you eaten today?"

"No."

"Have you had a glass of water?"

"No."

"Have you at least showered before coming to see me?"

"Of course!"

"Hmm." The doctor analyzed every inch of the diagrams on her monitor.

Amy beat on her knees as She waited.

The light dimmed in the room. Returned solid after some seconds.

"What sort of meds can you recommend me, doc?"

"Nothing for this. I'm not even sure what <u>this</u> is." The doctor's eyes finally sat on her. "I'd like you to return for special testing to see if we can narrow this down. Something's disrupting your system."

Amy released a breath of air. "There's got to be some remedy in the meantime. Please. Whatever it takes. <u>Today</u>."

Dr. Qindox sighed. "Well. There is one thing you can try to cope with and maybe prevent an episode."

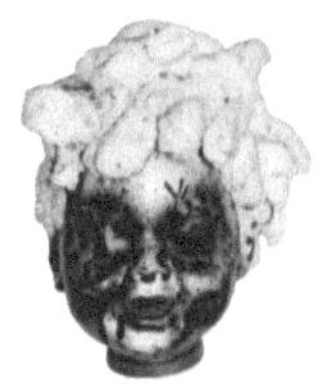

Chapter Fifteen

Public Combat

Amy strolled under the moonlit sky, a joint kissed between her lips. *Doc's orders.* She stared ahead at the dusty granite streets infused with marble gems that twinkled around the midnight hour. Glanced up at a shadowed figure nested high within the greenery of an oak tree.

"Damn gargoyles. I guess it's comforting. Kill whatever's eating the lot."

White aura rose from her back, twisted, and formed into the top half-torso of Aura Amy.

Oh, the lovely, wonderful soul of this sad, sad young adult woman traveled hopelessly within her imperfect shell, knowing her host was destined to see them both to doom.

"The poet returns," Amy said. "You should get a gig, bring in some UDs for us."

Oh, I wouldn't want to spoil your wretched plans to off-yourself. Why ruin the fun in that? It's not like it affects us both. Oh, wait, it does. The spirit rolled her eyes and crossed her arms. *"Nice to be out for once under the moonlight. While conscious."*

Amy's eyes trembled on the moon. Her eyes narrowed on it. Looked off into distant space.

Aura Amy stepped in front of her. *"Are you kidding me?"*

"What?"

"We share a brain. You're hoping to get kidnapped!"

Amy turned away from her.

"So you can find Demo."

"It was just a silly thought."

"Right..." The spirit's eyes lingered on her host. She leaned in near her ear. *"Why haven't we gone out much anyway? A girl needs to spread her wings."*

"Because death is out here."

"Death exists everywhere."

"I'd rather die in solitude than..."

"You'd rather we die intentionally."

Amy bit the air. Let it out. "I can't take this anymore."

Tough shit.

Amy wheeled around to face solitude. "I must be cursed." Moved forward. "Maybe Stella's infected me with hers. Curse, are you latching on to me?"

You wish! That would give you some reason to take action.

"You're right. I was hoping for the curse." *What a day. Wonder if Jimmy's having a much better day than I am. Bet he is.*

He's not you.

Who are you talking about now?

Jimmy. You were thinking about him again.

Stay out of my head.

Quite hard to do. Aura Amy reappeared behind Amy. She burned out alongside her host, though attached at their soles. *"How am I supposed to do that?"*

"Are you mad?! You need to get <u>back</u> inside!"

"You need to gather yourself for both our sakes." The aura flipped her hair back and twirled the ends of it. *"Besides,*

no one's out. There's been murder."

Amy stopped. Stared ahead. Lips quivered. "Mother of Rupert's Pit... It's gotten worse."

"I remember that case." Aura Amy tapped her chin. *"Such a traumatising—oh."*

Blocks away, Amy's Jadesfeld home stood out, illuminated bright white against the dark skies. *To make matters worse,* a solid beam of light shot out from the house's roof, high into the clouds.

"Is it too late to believe in Callisto?" Amy asked. She turned to her aura self. "You've ruined us."

"You've ruined us."

"That's not fair." Amy groaned and stomped her feet, body shaking from head to toe *in her tantrum.*

"Did that help?"

Amy pushed forward as her aura form slithered back into her body.

I'm sorry, alright! I didn't know it would—I just wanted to send a signal out. I thought the roof was best because I figured Archie could spot us from his bat cave. I was right! But that is not the point. I thought maybe through the—

"You thought. Remarkable. Did you think about shutting off the Unidentified Alien signal once he arrived? Town already thinks we've got aliens running around snatching people up."

That's right! We could blame it on aliens!

Amy shook her head *in disgust.*

Hey!

Walked onto her block, head hung.

I didn't know it would do that to the entire house! I... ugh!

Stopped to assess the field of spectators.

A crowd shouted across the street from her home, some in their pajamas.

Kiaixai, draped in layered cloaks madder than before, rode atop a floating stage right in front of the crowd.

"This majestic disturbance showcases the truth we run from. This beam from the heavens, this white light, topples the blue overcast of Callisto's mad—bark off mad women!"

Several members of Callisto's light tugged at several strands of Kiaixai's cloth. He wrestled them off before pushing the final man's face away. Cleared his throat.

An arm yanked him straight onto the ground.

The rest of the members cleared the way for the one who stood over him.

Ms. Droûx, arms stiff at her sides, peered down. "What's the problem now?"

"Kiaixai had a right to his civil protest. Yet your governmental ways acted as a blockade for his efforts. What's left is the fight for freedom!"

Ms. Droûx sighed.

Kiaixai puffed out his chest and pointed a finger straight at her. "A challenge for the heart of the people! And to drop Kiaixai's fines!"

Ms. Droûx cracked her neck and nodded. "You want a challenge, Mr. Kiaixai? Let us commence!" Her echoed voice boomed over the crowd and beyond as her eyes scanned the lot. "Any objectors?!"

The crowd's sweat answered her.

"Kiaixai accepted! Enraged, he jumped to his feet! He pointed with the ambitious heart of an orphaned, food-deprived son. Kiaixai accepted the madwoman's duel!" He bent over into a pose resembling a bent-neck eagle with its wings spread.

I've seen that stance in one of Gma's ancient books. Are they about to throw down? Here, in Jadesfeld? I've gotta get closer. "Sir, excuse me." *Watch it, woman. Yeah, yeah, it's me, the daughter of disaster. Granddaughter of the spiritualist, spawn of hell, whatever.* Amy slipped to the front row of the crowd. *Organised combat in Jadesfeld. Ha! Demo will...* She rubbed her arm, picking at nothing.

"It's her!"

"She's the girl of the Woman."

"The Mortician?"

"Is the house possessed?"

"Callisto's upset with us!"

"What's the story?"

"I wanna see the fight right now."

Kiaixai pointed back at Amy's blinding house. "Let this symbol of great hope serve as evidence of our true ally. Cast out Callisto's Light!"

I think I quite like Kiaixai.

Ms. Droûx stalked towards him, holding up her dress to move quicker.

Kiaixai lunged with a hammer throw, followed by his palm aimed at Ms Droûx's gut.

Ms. Droûx lazily dodged his efforts quicker than he could block her palm strike to his face. "1." She froze over him with hungry eyes and one hand on the other in front of her.

Kiaixai rose on shallow legs and threw a weak punch.

Caught by Droûx.

His arm bent upwards, out of shape. His body lifted off the ground— thrown spine first in a seamless sweeping motion.

"2." Ms. Droûx yawned in a faux manner.

Kiaixai peeled his upper torso off the ground and hopped on an arm. Sent flying grasshopper kicks towards her dodging midsection.

Ms. Droûx punted his latest kick away and grabbed his other leg. Lifted him off the ground—windmilled him—smashed his body into the unforgiving granite.

"Arrrrrh!" The shaking man pulled a bloody piece of marble from above his eye socket.

"3." Ms. Droûx gripped down onto his shoulders.

"Ahhh, wha—" He cried out as her fingers dug into him.

"Up you go, then." Ms. Droûx brought him to his feet, still holding him with a tight grip. "Turn around now." She flipped him around to face her and slapped his face once. Twice.

Slap. Slap. Slap. Slap. Slap. Slap. Slap. Slap.

"That's for the number of petitions I've had to deal with

because of you." Her knee found his gut, which bent him over.

"This is for prayers towards you reaching a new light," the woman said, staring off into the clouds. "Callisto's Light." Ms. Droûx flipped him, opposite of facing her, and held his face to the sky. She tossed his body down onto his floating stage, sending the splintered bits and pieces flying, hitting members of the crowd.

"Finally." Ms. Droûx stepped over his body and craned her neck *so deep I thought she'd break it.* "For equivalent pain and suffering." Squatted over him and punched him in the face.

His tooth flew across the street. He smiled. "Her big fault. **Twaa!** I know all about Her! I know all about the big fault she is!"

Callisto's One Big Fault? Amy moved closer.

Ms. Droûx smashed her fist down again. Again. Each fist took turns finding his face, shoulder, arm, chest, everywhere— *with intelligent fists and accuracy*— never taking her attention off the task.

Bloody madwoman. Is she—

More teeth flew around his head.

"That's enough." Amy grabbed Ms. Droûx's arm and pulled it. *Fuck? She's strong as shit.*

Ms. Droûx yanked away and spat at Amy's feet. "You dare touch me? His concession hasn't ended the duel yet, child. This lost soul asked for a spar, after all."

"K...Kiaixai..." He attempted to turn over. Gave up halfway. His hands reached toward Amy's house. "There's no room... to surrender... in decadence. K-Kiaixai came to see the spiritualist."

"He's done." Amy stepped closer to Ms. Droûx.

The woman stooped to her, nose to nose. "You reek of ambition clouded by low morals."

HOWLING WIND blew Amy's hair past her flushed cheeks.

Can't keep it, sissy—

Kiaixai shuddered on the ground with violent, jolting force.

His head trembled. The back of it hit the ground every other second. His body jerked up and followed suit.

Amy stooped over him. "Should I—" Her arms hung *uselessly* over him, unsure what to do. "Help him!" She barked at the *nonchalant Droûx.*

"Seems like a simple seizure." The woman shrugged. She peered into Amy's eyes. "You care to spar?"

"Enough!" Rezna marched over from the cemetery and got in between Amy and Ms. Droûx. "If you want to lay a hand on my granddaughter, I'm afraid you'll have to inspire me first."

Ms. Droûx brought her hands together, mid-air at her waist. "If that's what it takes."

"Some religion!" Rezna spat. She pointed out several members of the nosy crowd, then down at Kiaixai. "Don't stand around like fossils of an inert species! Get this man medical attention!" She twirled off with Amy in tow.

The GCID-powered lightscreens of several townspeople blinked to life as they called emergency services. Others scratched their heads or wandered off.

"NOOOOO!" Kiaixai choked himself with one hand while the other punched small craters into the ground. **"GET OUT OF ME!"** His voice had multiple pitches.

Amy and Rezna turned back to the man's body.

He jerked up— **"NO!"** — paused midair— **"She would never say that!"** —then smacked down. Again. Again. Again.

"Kiaixai loathed the day his wife took her life, for he could have done better to save her!"

"He loathed!"

"He loathed!"

"HE LOATHED!"

Amy shielded her eyes from the blinding white light illuminating every wall as She followed her grandmother into their home. She closed the front door.

Rezna, now wearing her black designer shades, pushed past the staircase. Spun to face Amy.

"That was crazy," Amy said. "Can you believe that? A spar in Jadesfeld."

"Cut the noise!" Rezna barked. "I come home to my entire house lit up bright as a Christmas ornament. You know I despise that wretched holiday! To make matters worse, my home was <u>filled</u> to the brim with drunken <u>bats</u>?!"

Amy scoped the damage of Archie's party, *the kitchen, telling the worst of it.* "Oh yeah, bad swarm. I don't know what happened. I went out to search for Archie. Thought he could sort 'um out. Don't know how—"

"Cut. The noise." Rezna slashed her throat. Gestured to the walls, tapped her ears—*no one's listening to us, paranoid woman—* then to the basement door.

Amy rolled her eyes as She trailed down the last step, thankful for the darkness of the cellar.

Rezna paced. Ripped her shades off. "Down here is the only place I can cut off access to that fucking system." She bent towards Amy. "You're lying defeats you, yet you still do it! Where were you?"

Amy sighed. "I had to go see a doctor."

"Why?"

"I've been having these memory lapses… *Yawn, yawn, yawn. When it started? Why's it matter, Gma? This back-and-forth is what I <u>tried</u> to avoid. Always on my case. Can't breathe for a second without tarnishing the pedestal of the great Rezna Devine.* …could have first happened that day at Stella's, but I'm not sure."

Rezna resigned onto her throne with a sigh. Rubbed her temples. She got on the floor and crossed both legs. Her eyes found Amy again, *and they felt… sympathetic.*

"The doctor said it's like some kind of retroactive amnesia of sorts? It's confusing, but yeah. Answers elude me."

"You trusted a stranger over your own blood."

"I— I was nervous that I was losing it. And she <u>is</u> a doctor."

"And you spark up a light show. Was that a brilliant plan?"

Amy dug her hands into her pockets. "I didn't exactly do it on purpose. I think."

"Unbelievable. Who do you think is best equipped to guide you through these situations, Amy? A common doctor or someone like you with aura?"

Oof, first name call out, huh? She's furious. "I had to get better now so I could find Demora. Couldn't wait for you. I couldn't wait for Praisure. I should be out there looking for her every second!"

"You tried that and got yourself behind bars!"

"I can't be locked up here either while she's somewhere out there!"

"You—" Rezna stroked her forehead. "We've discussed this to exhaustion. I am working with Norma to make the damn authorities to do their bloody job! Demora is a fighter! She will not be fell by some pervert! We have to play this one smart. That cult has excommunicated more souls than the number of its members. If they were even to catch a whiff of our aura… being labeled Peculiars would only be the start of our troubles."

"Is there ever a moment to rise?"

"When you are ready."

"You only ever care about your self-preservation. I can handle myself."

"How did that go for you last year?" Rezna closed her eyes and brought her hands together in a triangle pose. **Scoffed**. "Handle yourself," she muttered under her breath.

Amy stared down at her. *SO high and mighty. Un-fucking—* "Cloudy was a little shit who needed to be locked away! No one else was listening!" *I can't deal with her shit anymore. That's it.* "I did what I had to!"

"My self-preservation, by the way, is what has kept us safe—"

"It didn't keep her safe!"

Rezna's eyes bore into her. "It has kept everything that we believe in and are building safe. You can choose to listen, or you can choose to get yourself killed. Or <u>worse</u>. The path is yours, girl. Be careful which you choose and where you walk."

Brrrrrrriiiiiiiiiiing!

Both women jumped in anger.

"WHAT <u>now</u>?" Rezna *demanded from the walls.*

Message from Praisure. 'I found Demora.'

Amy stood beside Praisure. They faced a glass window leading into one of the interrogation rooms of Jadesfeld PD.

Only half of Demora's silhouette was visible in the dark room. Facing the wall.

"She's been right in that corner ever since," Praisure said. "She shut the light off as soon as she came in. Hasn't said a word. Hasn't moved. Hell, I ain't even seen her blink." His eyes floated on top of the dark boats of his sunken skin; the bags almost met his cheeks. The overgrown beard, other facial hair, wrinkled clothes and missing lens on his tear-drop aviator sunglasses weren't a match for the distant look in his eyes.

Amy followed his unshaken stare from the interrogation room where Demora was. *It's the kind of look one gets when they've realized something terrible and hauntingly life-changing about something or one close to them.* "Are you alright?"

Sigh. "Just growing tired of all the senseless violence goin' round. But today, we got a win against evil intentions." He gave Amy a weak smile. "Good luck, lil lady. You got this."

"Thank you for finding her."

Amy entered the dark room. Shut the door, sealing away the *much-needed* light from the hall. She trailed along the wall, inching closer to her best friend's back. "Demo?"

Demora's head turned a hair, her peripheral on Amy. "Never again."

"How are you feeling?" Amy leaned down behind her.

"I'm tired of being second. Last fiddle. All the time. A puppet."

Amy opened her mouth *but found no words. I've been running around trying to save you, but I can't. Even though you're right here... I'm still useless. What do you say to someone at the edge of a cliff?*

Demora's fist smashed into the metallic flooring, leaving a dent behind. "I have been made a victim twice! Twice! That's enough. Never again. NEVER again! NEVER!"

Amy reached toward her, hands lingering over her best friend's shoulder.

Demora's body heaved out of breath without turning.

Amy placed her arms around her.

Demo's body shifted closer into the embrace.

"Who did this?" Amy whispered. "I'll kill them. Who took you?"

Demora's body fell, relaxed into the sea of Amy's love. No tears streamed, though she tried to form some sort of response through the chokes of her sore throat. "I don't know."

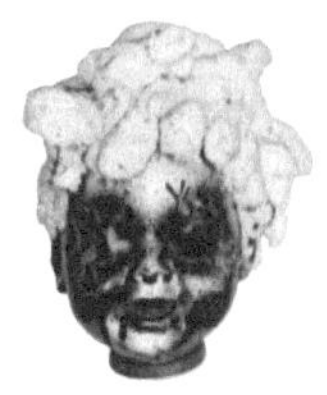

Chapter Sixteen

Dreams Are Made Of This

A flurry of chaotic shadows rushed across the arena. Matter of pumice origin hung from the ceiling, with tips that dripped black gooeyness. In the middle of it all lay a field of squares, and inside each were letters marked A through Z.

Two female figures stood together, their faces obscured in darkness.

Kassandra?

"They're already on their last leg." Kassandra's faceless body turned to her partner. The grooves in her smooth face flesh wiggled as she spoke. "Keep feeding sacrifices to my ally's ability, and I'll protect our clear path to victory."

Her partner nodded, squirming under the flesh of her faceless skin. "We're floating on the stars and beyond!" the distorted, scratchy voice echoed.

"Great." Kassandra pointed across the field at Amy. "I sacrifice my— deeeeeee— and my partner's ally to bring out the level four— Disrupter!"

The shadows rose above Amy as she turned to her side. *Where's my partner?*

"If any of my opponents have two allies on the field, my ally can move and attack twice."

"What?!" A voice called from the emptiness beside Amy.

"Noooo!" Amy fell back as clouds of grey trailed around her. *Why'd I do that?*

"Activate my facedown card!"

Red eyes, inside an overcast cloud of shadow, pounced.

Amy ducked as the shadows closed over her. *Should've activated my facedown card...*

"Next turn, this match is over. You failed." A hole spread in the middle of Kassandra's facial skin. A laugh came out of it.

Amy fell into a pit of darkness. *It's over... I should have waited to use my...*

Tormented by the scum of the past.

I stayed up every night for some multitude of hours, bloodshot eyes on my window with every passing light or sound from the outside. Planes of the World's past crash into my space, crash into my mess. I've been discovering myself in the darkness, trying to find comfort here because it's restless elsewhere. Might as well develop it where I can and stash myself into a bubble of solace.

Thing is... I don't want to fit into a bubble.

.

.

"We can't attack her monsters anymore." Amy grabbed the edges of a podium. "We can find a way to win without hurting her."

"She made the play," said a distorted voice from the empty slot beside her. "It was her choice."

.

.

Heart palpitations are growing more frequent by the day. What's outside my window?

Who?

I wrote a new song today. It's shit, but I'm trying, so... What day is it?

Blind to my own needs with a migraine for a pincer squeezing my knowledge. I can't escape.

Left kick, right kick, spin. Jab right, left cross. C'mon, gather your stance together, Devine.

My fucking head. I still need to do crunches. Here we go.

Connect this strand to that. Fuck. How the hell did she do it? If my aura's smarter than me, what use am I?

The work needs doing. Gonna start daily with the squats and crunches, then go straight into journaling. I should aura train... I'm too weak.

...three brief meals evened throughout the day to keep the fuel going...

... one long shower. One brief shower. Three...

This is all rubbish.

You're gonna die for your efforts.

.

.

"Return! Your Mother's Dread!" Faceless Kassandra stood on a single leg— her right one missing. The left arm was also missing, but the right clenched its fist.

She's not gonna make it. We have to stop this now. If I attack her, she's done for. But I have to win. How do I earn both results? "No! My ally...." *This isn't good...*

A Knight, clad in shadows, fell to its knees, green sparks flying from between the clouds of its sizzling body.

"And the fun doesn't stop there!" Kassandra's Faceless Partner said.

That voice. I know her. From where?

"Let's take out her Princess. Go! Destroy it!"

A faceless damsel in shrouds dropped her swordisc with a **clang**. She screamed. Tiny holes of light burned throughout her body.

The empty podium beside Amy vibrated. "This sucks for us both. I know I said we've got this. But I'm out of options."

Amy turned to her Invisible Partner. "Hey, you did your best."

"You're going to give up so easily?" Kassandra pushed her Faceless Partner.

Here they go again...

"Shut UP!" The jitters behind Kass' Faceless Partner's flesh overtook her entire body. "You got us stuck in this cuz you're too stubb—"

That's it! They don't understand each other! The smile crept in on Amy's face. She removed it.

Dangle Dolly... Echoed throughout the dark arena.

Not this song again. Amy searched for the source.

Whiiiiiiirrrrrrrrrr A machine clad in clouds floated beside her.

Amy closed her eyes. Deep breath in... out. In... out. Her breaths synced to perfection with the rhythm of the machine.

Her eyes opened. *This is it. I'm not losing to you again.* "Your turn ends now!" Amy raised her hand to the heavens. "I play—Show Your Grace! Ends your turn immediately. Since you forced my partner's ally to attack me!" *That's not all.* "My survival—Shadows of Oracle! Take her Your Mother's Dread!" *And now the grand setup.* She smirked. "Grand Wisdom!" *It's over.* "I end my turn by discarding Your Mother's Dread, since I can't use it." *This has to be it. My partner...*

The space beside her grew thick purple shadows.

Never did I think <u>you</u> were what I needed all along... And <u>you</u>, of all the people...

"No. This can't be it!" Kassandra's Faceless Partner dipped out of frame.

"This is NOT over!" Faceless Kassandra charged over to her Faceless Partner. "You must have something of use there. This is NO time for weakness!"

They're scrambling. Is this how victory feels? Ended her turn. This is it. All because she ignored the most basic rule. Not even a rule. The essence of what the game is. She broke the one measurable aspect this game is designed for.

"Activate Your Mother's Dread!" the space beside Amy echoed.

There you go, partner. We're close to the finish line...

"Twice The Fun! Now I can play two allies!"

An overcast of shadows loomed over Amy and her invisible mate.

"Allegory Of Saints! Bring back her Ruins Of Vengeance!"

That's right. End this cruel game, partner.

The overcast of three prominent figures loomed over the faceless pairing of Kassandra and her partner.

"I can also bring back..."

This is too easy.

"You remember how this felt, don't you? Take her—"

Kassandra pounded her arms down with a world-shaking **CLONG**. Her face flesh opened. LAUGHED.

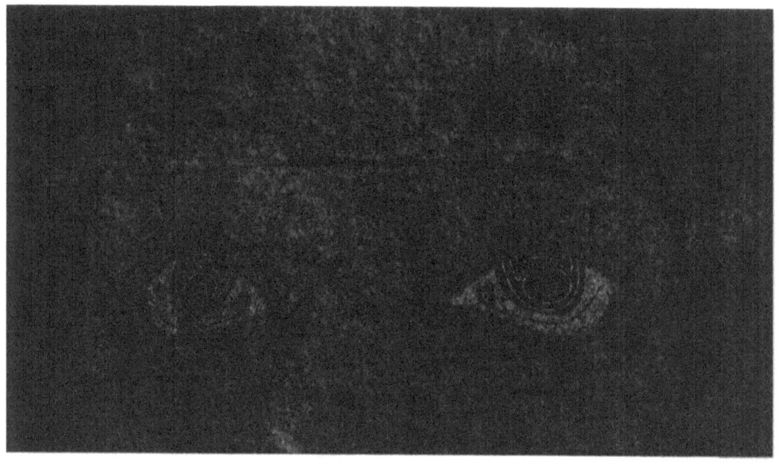

Days flipped through like a captivating novel, whose contents I'd rather undigest on one end of things. On the other, I felt a strange growth inside. Pain lingered on the faces and routines of the three women now living together in this household. Seeing Demo's face regularly made the days easier. The nights, less scary. Fewer nightmares. But when the nightmares came...

Even though the cacophony of freelance vocalists no longer disturbed my sleep as much, I still wake each morning as though late for life's purpose.

Demora stared out the window on some of those mornings, wondering the same after our dread-filled convos. 4 a.m. starts to 2 a.m. ends. Her sleep returned to a normal five-hour timeframe over the past few days. Couldn't blame her, not with my abusive nocturnal patterns. By the second week, she already got herself out the door. How'd she do it? Took me months to step outside after Cloudy.

I get a kick outta the kick that others get from their kicks. Good times.

—The Singer holds her fists to her chest as she sings— What went right that day?

—Humans and hybrids alike made space as some Gyaads graced their way near the front of the audience—The blue faces of the Gyaads stood out above the crowd; the shortest of them, seven feet tall—

They are quite the marvel... —The Singer swallows her bold stare and grasps the butterflies in her gut— Focus on the task.

—One of the Gyaads in the front row laughs— The harmony slaps my heart.

—"She's so lovely," the Gyaad says as she whips around, twirling her veil-like exterior. "Isn't she?"

"A voice that could rival our Great Sister's summer quartet."

"Don't let our sister hear you say that."

The Gyaad beauties share trebling laughter— Not of this World, and it reels the spirit from derangement's depths.

I'd die and be happy right now.

Bad times.

—The blackened energy creeps its way to her middle fingertip—Amy's entire body convulses. Eyes roll back—

—'Amy... reconsider your decision. Bond with me'—

—Amy curls her right hand into a fist—Smoke rises from her blackened right hand—A deep burn sizzles into the skin of her backhand—runs up her middle finger—

—Her orange aura ball swirls around the Book of Clouds— the book's black and white aura circles inside of it— My lost aura.

Maybe I shouldn't have trapped Cloudy's spirit. Amy watched her reflection in the mirror tremble as She stared at her scarred right hand. *But what would have happened if I didn't?*

Good. Bad. Useless terms, anyway.

—The smiling face of Jonathan Jones— decays until the flesh melts— Good ends up bad if you live long enough. Any good I've done will be outweighed by the evil to come. And the evil that has already happened. It's all pointless to play this good and bad game. It's a child's fairytale. A Santa Claus or a Tooth Fairy. Rubbish once you're old enough to know better.

Amy sat across from Aura Amy on the bed. *My spirit grows wiser every day. As I die daily, she rises. I have to learn to live with her, outgrowing me. I may disappoint her in the end, never finding myself, or not being strong enough to go on, and she'll wander off in the wind.* "You were trying to help. I appreciate you."

"I'm terribly sorry." Aura Amy bowed her head. *"I'm understanding more about your human world. There are rules to your World. Things to consider before action."* She raised an eyebrow. *"Though too much contemplation can be cancerous to growth."*

"Let's agree on trust." Amy smiled at the bright spirit before her. "Can you trust me to get us through our next nineteen years?"

"I'll try." She smiled back. *"Joking. We'll do it together."*

Alone, Amy jots in her journal.

My aura's a mess. So am I. Dr. Qindox's latest round of tests has confirmed I show signs of one thing. Statistically Unlikely To Be Agreeable Ailment. Yeah, it could be the SUTBAA. Disillusioning my brain. Causing me to question things without deeper context. Without proof. And, of course, nothing else is known about this rare ailment. Could be what's causing the amnesia. Retroactive or otherwise.

Amy and Demora sat across from each other on

Amy's bed.

"I'm sure their trip to Antarctica is going lovely." Demora rolled her eyes.

"Can't believe how ghost they've been. As soon as they're back, I'm going over there with you to remind them of a thing or two."

"My knight in dazzling armour." Her friend grinned. "They've been talking about shipping me to some boarding school."

Amy chuckled. "Good luck to them with your track record."

"Bug off!" Demora shoved Amy.

"Language." "Yeah, yeah."

Knock. Knock.

"Yeah?" In unison.

Rezna smiled in the open doorway. Seeing you two together again fills me with gratitude. Truly. Demora, please stay with us as long as you'd like. I've informed your parents, and I take it they'll be heading back soon after the wisdom I gifted them."

I love her.

"I've been asked by the city council to attend a conference in New Enfield. This cursed spirit going around is shaking their core. Time to get this railway started. You girls can stay out of trouble while I'm gone?"

"Of course. Do they have any leads yet?" Amy asked.

"None. I'll keep you informed as I receive info. And please. Stay within the city limits for the time being. There'll be extra protection around the house."

"More tokens?" Demora rubbed one hand on top of the other.

"Perhaps we can lessen the tokens?" Amy's eyes zoomed between Rezna and Demora.

"Rezna nodded her understanding. "I'll let them know to stay out of the common areas and your room, girls. Keep your wit, and don't anger them. Especially the one in the basement. She's particularly nasty."

"She???" Amy and Demo said.

Rezna's head tilted on a book lodged into the wall. "No tassels in the house, please, ladies. My salary isn't exorbitant enough to cover idle behaviour." The door closed behind her with a gentle click.

After the aged woman's steps retreated down the stairs, Demo said, "She's a mad one." Her eyebrow raised with a smirk. She dug in her pocket. "Speaking of idle behaviour—" She pulled out her glowing talisman.

"Is Graves insane?" Amy snatched the talisman from her and tossed it on the bed. "You just got back! You can't go to that meeting tonight."

"<u>We</u> can go. And we will. We should. We owe it to ourselves, don't we?"

"I don't think you're in any—"

"Besides, with everything going on, we need to get stronger. This is training times ten, working with Graves. You've seen what she can do!"

Amy rolled her eyes. "Graves has all the answers, huh?"

"I don't know. It's better than sitting here reminiscing."

"You were gone for weeks, Demora! Weeks!"

"And my aura still burns!" The blond firecracker jumped up from the bed. She grabbed her chest and tried to gather her raspy breath. "For three fucking weeks, I suffered pain unlike—" Her fists clenched. "Then they tossed me to the side. Like I was nothing."

"What do you mean? They <u>let</u> you go?"

"Lunch, girls!" Rezna's voice came from down under.

"If you want to stay in this room rotting away for the rest of your life, then have at it. I'll be at that meeting. Make up your mind. By 10 p.m. tonight. That's the time the students meet." Demora stormed out and slammed the door shut behind her.

They let her go? Why would they let her go?

Cancerous.

Amy shook her head. She reclined against her headboard.

The **moaning** hands of her undead doppelgangers stretched across Amy's body. They cradled her.

"Sorry, sis, nothing personal, but you have to go down."

Amy's mouth frowned. "Are you the most wanted?"

"If I were, you'd already be in your cell."

Amy wiped her swollen, bloody lip and spat a wad. She faced a coliseum made for ancient games. Shielded her eyes against the blinding light flickering above the spectator stands.

The Judges, hidden in the shadows within the stands, gazed down on her.

One of their vicious fangs moved forward. "Something... odd... that one."

Amy grilled them.

WHAM! The wind punched her throat.

Amy fell to her knees. Bled from her eyes.

She respawned.

Punched in the throat again.

And again.

And again.

And again.

"This is one game you'll never win." Demora stalked towards her with narrowed eyes and a crooked smile growing by the second. "Dangle Dolly, can you feel me?"

"Demo, cut it out." Amy backed away from her. Caught herself off balance on the edge of a platform.

Peered down into the bottomless pit.

"Dangle Dolly, won't you trust me?" Demora

GRABBED her face. "WAKE UP."

"I can't move." Amy struggled against her best friend's grip. *I can't move.* Held her throat. *I can't speak!* Her mouth flesh stitched itself together, leaving a crawling sensation under her skin. Each eyelid followed suit. She mimed herself away from the pit. *Stop, Demo, please! STOP!*

The sounds of her thumping heart quieted. Chilling silence enveloped her mind. The sound of unrecognizable laughter echoed inside Amy's trembling body.

I own you.

Amy linked arms with another girl.

The girl's sporty yellow jacket arm squeezed the hold. Diamond-shaped buns nodded to Amy. "Now or never!"

Amy nodded back. "Let's do it."

"GO! Don't let them pass!"

Try to stop me.

Amy and her shadow-covered teammate sped right through a pair of linked arms.

"They're coming! Get ready!"

A hand grabbed Amy's arm.

Amy stared at it, frozen in time. She grasshopper-kicked its missing owner—the grasp relinquished with a squeal.

Amy smiled.

Sporty yellow jacket girl hugged her. "We did it!" She pulled away. Blinked out of sight.

Amy gasped. Plump veins swelled even bigger in her face, turning grey, and pulsed with an urge to bust. "I can't... I ca—" She grabbed her throat and stepped back as her eyes bulged out of her sockets. Her fingers curled into her palms as her mouth dripped with excess saliva. Each part of the skin peeled in sections. Her eyes grew red streaks, bombarding her irises.

Amy's shriveling carcass rasped for air. **SCREAMED**.

Amy jumped up, sweat dripping from every pore. Touched her heart. Slowed her breaths. Peered over at Demora, who slept unbothered beside her.

Checked her newly fixed blinking GCID xTier.

Orange lights illuminate her face.

Read the message from *Madame Blé.*

Amy sat in silence for a while. Took another look over at the Demora. Then back at her GCID. She rubbed its screen in a circular motion.

Sorry. I just got my best friend back. I'd like to spend as much time with her as possible.

Amy nodded to herself, satisfied with the message she sent. Went to place her GCID on the desk— its screen lit up again. She checked it.

Madame Blé: I understand. Take your time. You are both welcome at the Haven anytime. You're in my thoughts and prayers. Take care.

She's up late as hell. Amy thought about it for a moment, staring at the wall.

Swiped the orange letters away.

Placed her GCID back on her desk. Cuddled up behind Demora.

"This vocal instrument inside your throat..." The back of Dr. Qindox dug through a set of conjoined desks angled along three of the four suffocating walls. She wheeled to different sections of the desk. "Who's the installing surgeon?"

"No clue," Amy said. She leaned against the window, dangling her feet off the smaller-than-twin-sized hospital bed. Surveyed this much smaller office space around her. "Someone at Dagenham General."

"Let's start keeping track of these names, huh?"

"Aye-aye." Amy saluted.

"Meantime, I'll call over and match charts. Now." Dr. Qindox spun towards her and put her glasses over her hazel and green irises. "Let's hook you in."

That's quite the shiner. Amy's eyes fell from the doctor's face. "Never got to try V4."

"Well, you're in for a treat, dear. Please shut off your..." Dr. Qindox frowned. "Where's your GCID? Thought you had an outie?"

Amy squirmed at the word *outie.* "Left it home today." *No need to be tracked like a criminal.*

"Okay." Dr. Qindox shrugged and moved forward with her contraption. She rested the long-legged spherical device next to her patient.

Amy apologized for her foot's slight tap on one of the device's legs and followed the directions to shift left, then right, then a little more left until the doctor gave her the okay. She nuzzled into the headpiece. The nine nodes stemming down from the oscillating crown blinked white and blue one by one around her head.

"Legally required to say this next part." The doc cleared her throat. "Thank you for trusting in my medically cleared and capable hands. You have been prescribed a twenty-minute dose of existographic therapy. You will now enter the environment simulated by the accredited XipiOsun V5."

"Ooh. V5."

The machine whirred on, and a chromatic voice let out, ***"Open your eyes. Revitalize."***

"Open your eyes. Revitalize." Dr. Qindox repeated. "Enjoy your trip."

.

.

.

.

.

.

Round 5

.

.

DING!

"Come on!" A shadowed figure bobbed and weaved forward.

His speed is ridiculous. I'll have to catch him off guard.

"You gonna stand there and model? Or you came to fight?" The handsome boxer floated around, his footwork a blur.

Amy growled as she got to her feet.

"Come on! Get them dukes up!" His feet danced towards her.

They clashed in the middle of a faded yellow world. They were the only two blips in the ongoing space of nothingness.

His lightning-fast jab tested her block. Tested again. One more.

Amy ATE a hook that knocked her several feet back.

Still on her, his precise fists tapped her noggin. He jumped back to dodge, but danced forward in a mad dash, delivering hook-jab combos.

Amy fought out and away from him, but *the yellow sandbox* they were in seemed to close in around her as his fists forced her into an invisible corner. She slid left— threw punches— **BAM—BA-BAM BAM!**

"Oooh, you've got the moves, kid! Just do something else with that anger."

The phenomenal Atzra[2] Rutt[1] is coaching me on temper. What a time. Oh shi—

"Made you look! Watch out now!" He burst through her guard and delivered an uppercut to her bone-jarred chin. Kept launching—His fists of glee blurred at all angles around her— crosses, hooks, and uppercuts rained—

That gleam in his eye. Full belief in every blow. I need that.

Amy shifted out of his barrage and tapped his chin twice.

He came back—**WheeeEP—BAM BAM BAM— THUP—TAP— THUP—TA— BOOM— THUT THUT THUT THUT— SWIISH-SAP—DUN DUN—THWAP— BOOM—THWAP— BOOM!**

Amy staggered back on wobbly legs, arms windmilling to gain balance. She caught herself on straighter legs. PUNCHED her gloves together and charged forth with a smile.

.

.

.

.

.

.

"That was... refreshing." As the headpiece lifted off her head, a sigh followed, and Amy's gaze wandered around the room.

Dr. Qindox gave a knowing smile. "The new update rewards the player the more they're into the game. Breaking down your opponent's moves, dodging, landing successful blows, and even shit-talk, the game rewards your neurotransmitters for everything you do that your spirit favours. It accounts for your mishaps, too. Rounds you out a bit for us. I'll have your full report sent by morning."

Amy stared at her shaky, clenched fists, biting her lip. "I feel like I can take on anything."

"Be careful. That wears off unexpectedly. It's a strict therapeutic massage of your response nerves." Dr. Qindox gave her an orange lollipop.

Amy shook out her shoulders with rapid blinks. *Game surely woke me up.*

"You're rewarded for pushing yourself to beat the game, even if you end up losing." Dr. Qindox shrugged. "Statistics say most do, by the way. Never seen a victor myself." Winked her black eye.

"Quite the shiner there, doc." Amy nodded to the bruise. "And why the downgrade?" She gestured to the clutter-heavy medical office they stood in. "No offence."

"I thought you'd never ask!" the doctor laughed as she steadied her patient's trembling stance away from the XipiOsun V5. "I don't know, dear. A few years earlier, and I could've taken out all twelve of them." Her acoustic laugh dwindled to a snicker, then a throat-clearing frown. "Just some hooligans stealing my office supplies, probably for illegal pharmaceuticals. Had to switch to a more discreet location."

"Are you okay?" Amy scrunched her face. *Is it the same group that took Demo?*

"You be careful out there," Dr. Qindox said, yanking her gloves off. "Some are here to witness humanity's downfall."

Chapter Seventeen

The Prison Games

"If you didn't have to have another smoothie, we'd be there already."

"Relax, it's fine." *It's a safer breakfast. No one's ever choked on a smoothie.* Amy picked at her throat. *I think...* "You've been through a lot. No one's clocking you."

"Don't even mention that. Can't stand pity parties." Demora navigated through the tall, deep brown and blackish green stalks as the pair traveled deeper into the woods. "Watch for—"

"Yeah, snailgators. Turns out, they've migrated from our part of town. Conservationists have tracked their movements west, which I find odd. Snailgators are territorial, so the likelihood of them just up and leaving is—"

Demora put a hand up to Amy. "Promise me you'll get outside more."

Amy grabbed her friend's hand, halting her movement into the shorter blades of the pasture ahead. "Before we entertain an audience, are you sure you're ready for this?"

With a sigh, her green eyes rolled, and her hands tossed in the wind. "Yes, I am fine, Ames. Quite pumped, if I'm honest. So you can dismantle your suspicions."

"Are you gonna tell me why they let you go?"

"I exhibited great behaviour."

"Demo, this is serious. I know this is tough for you to relive, but we could learn from your experience and help save others."

"Would you stop trying to— experimentize with me? Hark, Amy, you're a nagging vulture. But even those mangy birds are more pleasant to talk to."

"They didn't... hurt-hurt you, did they? Like— rape?"

"Oh—you're for the love of dread!" Demo said in an urgent, hushed whisper. "Maybe they're not into blonds, and I helped them figure it out!" She shook Amy's shoulder with her free hand. "For the last time, I don't know!"

"You can tell me before we meet the swarm." Amy grabbed her shoulder in return. "Have you told your MHP about—"

"Drop it!" Demora pulled from her grasp. "Knew I shouldn't have told you anything..." She pushed through, stomping into a clearing, the blades closing behind her.

Following, Amy threw her hands up in frustration. "No one's on time for squat these days!" She stretched into the open circular field. Froze.

Through the silver birches, a pair of bright yellow eyes peered at her.

Amy cleared her throat and looked away.

"Hi, call me On Time." Lil Sis, arms crossed, stood to the side, her eyes shifting between the two latest arrivals.

Graves sat in a circle on the ground with Ms. Bubbly, Mr. Stoicism, and Mr. SmartyPants. Behind them, Jamari and Ms. JellyRoll paused their conversation to observe the newcomers.

"Bout time," Jamari said. "It's ten past 10." He checked an *exuberant* old-school Rolex on his wrist. "Make that eleven past 10. You know we're supposed to be here no later than seven minutes past the hour, Pink."

Oddly specific number.

"Buzz off," Mr. Stoicism said, rising on his feet. "You're insufferable, Mr. Rap Star."

"That massively undercuts my talents."

Mr. Stocism walked over to Demora. "Are you alright? You didn't need to be here."

"Off." Demora smacked his hands away. "I've got a hand on my schedule."

"Just saying…" He sulked away.

"May I have a word?" Graves beckoned to Demora.

"Let the pity party begin," Demora *threw* in Amy's face.

Amy winked and patted her back as she set off.

"You and your friend." Ms. Bubbly appeared beside Amy, *a little closer than we're acquainted…* "Your ordeal. I didn't think I'd see either of you again. How is she doing? And you?"

"Oh." *Guess I'll smile and pretend I've been through something.* "I'm glad she's home." Offered her a handshake. "I'm A—"

"Oop—no names." Giggling, Ms. Bubbly took her hand.

The vibrations from the giggles shot warm tickles up Amy's arm that soon flushed across her entire body. She shook it off and broke the handshake. "What's with this no-name business?"

"Fraid the Professor won't say. I think we're gonna play some type of game." She leaned into Amy's ear, a curl of her hair grazing her lobe. "I'm Vedessia," she whispered. Winked. "And I know your name. Now we are even." She hopped off and jumped right into a chat with Ms. JellyRoll.

"How?" *Now we're even? First the other night, now this? What the hell __does__ she know? Stupid, cute dimples…* A berry hit her forehead from above. "Ow."

"Your funeral home don't get news or Internet?" Kassandra stretched out, perched between two thick branches in a tree overhead. She hopped down in front of Amy.

Amy picked up the *bullet* that *attacked* her. "Smartiberiies grow out here?"

"Ya." Kassandra's teeth chomped one *with ease?* "You're the only other soul your friend hangs with, and her name's plastered in every report. You do math?" She nodded towards Vedessia— *why is she cheering?*—in conversation with Mr. Stoicism. "Her head's always in the clouds. We're not here to play games. Graves will push our spirits to the limit." Her head cocked towards Amy.

"Are you ready?"

"Surprised you're here. You didn't want to hear me talk about aura last year." "That's cuz your irrelevance precedes you." Kassandra shrugged, chomped *another?!* berry and walked off.

Her teeth must be made of steel.

"Alright, gather around students." Graves moved to the middle of the patch. "Thank you all for clearing your schedules this week. Tonight, you begin to test the depth of your training. With time, the hope is for you to cultivate complete mastery of your spirit. A recognition of your efforts awaits at the end of your trials, courtesy of The Society of Great London."

"The what?" "Who?" Multiple voices spoke their minds.

The professor's arms simmered them down. "All over the world, secret societies exist practicing methods of honing the spirit. There are forms, abilities, and levels you all have yet to uncover."

"Peculiar levels, it seems," Mr. SmartyPants said.

"We don't use that term around here, love," Lil Sis said with a side-eye.

"If you're referring to my use of the word with its given definition, which is to be strange or unusual, I can't imagine why you'd waste your breath clocking me."

"She can waste her breath as she sees fit, Mr. Knockoff Brix Shades." Jamari chewed a twig and spat.

"Thanks?" Lil Sis said.

"A fraction of the statement you prescribed may be true," Mr. SmartyPants replied, "But I'll have you know these glasses were crafted by the personal optician to the Emperor."

"Who's Emperor?" Jamari asked.

Mr. Smartypants sighed. "How could I expect someone like you to understand royalty?" He ran his fingers along his shiny glass frames.

Graves put her hands up. "At ease, boys. You'll have plenty of chances for healthy competition inside the structure."

"Structure?" Amy asked.

"I'll explain in a moment. Right now, I'd like everyone to present their talismans."

The murmurs died out. Graves waited as each student held out their talismans in front of them. Demora nodded to Amy.

Amy copied the others, flipping her talisman's bright white number one— *same color as my aura*— to face the other talismans in the circle. Each of the students' talismans had numbers lit in their respective aura colors as well.

Brilliant scarlet circles of aura formed around each talisman. The ring-enclosed talismans rose out of the students' hands and suspended above their heads.

"Concentrate your spirits," Graves said. "You're going to create a solid barrier around yourselves that can't be penetrated."

Demora's sparkling fuchsia-pink aura burst around her. The flames of pink ceased into a solid outline around her entire body as she folded her arms.

Ms. Bubbly/Vedessia's sand-colored aura spiraled around her like sand in an hourglass. It highlighted her cheekbones *and graced her hips.*

Mr. Stoicism's lapis lazuli blue outline rose from his feet to his head in seconds.

The viridian green aura jolted around Mr. Smartypants. He smirked at the others.

Jamari flared his nose. He stomped his foot, and his carnelian aura flashed around him.

His sister took a deep breath with her eyes closed and mouthed something. Her milk chocolate aura twinkled to life and formed a box around her. The aura box shrank until only an outline against her form.

Ms. JellyRoll's lilac aura danced off her in lightning-strike waves before fitting her outline.

Kassandra's hair stood on end as a gust of wind circled her.

The blades behind them shifted to the side. The Gyaad's incredible stature stood out above them all. With closed eyes, a rainbow of light rose from beneath her feet. The lights swirled around her until they reached the top of her head. It shimmered over her, raining down a sunny saffron shade of brilliance.

The others gawked at the sight.

"Well done, everyone." Graves turned to Amy. "It's alright if you decline. I won't ask you to do anything you're not comfortable with. This showing of your aura, however, is a requirement to move forward, as it's an act of trust amongst the group. It's your call."

On the spot... What am I even doing here? They're all here to figure out the depths of their soul. I already know mine. "It was so nice to meet you all. I wish you the best." Amy backed up and, with averted eyes, made her way out of the circle.

"Wait!" Demora glared at her. "I wasn't... I wasn't sure if I'd see you again after... it happened. I only came back for two reasons. To prove myself to be more than what I felt in that moment. And because of you." Wetness betrayed the corners of her eyes. Her eyes fell to her feet. "Each passing day I was gone, I ran out of reasons to live. Everything we've been through... none of it would have mattered if you weren't there." Her swift hand wiped the corner of her eye. "You were the constant reason I should go on. I needed to come back to show you the best of me." Demo clenched her fist in front of her. "I will not stand for you walking away now!" She shot a small stone in Amy's direction. "Not now, not ever!"

Amy's frozen soul gazed at *the unusual display of emotion from her best mate.*

"You belong here!" Demora pointed her indexes to the ground.

I don't know if— Amy stared at the palms of her hands.

"You can do it," Demora said. "You belong here."

Thanks for the confidence boost, Demo. I don't know what I'd do without you. Amy realigned with the others, her eyes never leaving Demora's. *Can I still— Shut up. Let's do this.* Her back straightened. Fists clenched at her sides. Deep breaths. *Concentrate. Concentrate. Aura, if you can hear me, now's the time to trust me.* She closed her eyes.

Deep breaths. Deep breaths. Find the source. Her eyes opened. *I am the source.*

Her palms EXPLODED in her WHITE AURA. *Ok, basic step done. C'mon Devine.* Closed her eyes again. *Aura is always with you. Otherwise, you'd be dead. Aura is always with you.*

Eternities for her, but seconds for the rest, a whirlpool of tiny white lights surrounded her, trapping her in its core. The rotation sped up. The white lights fired at her body, bit by bit, sticking to every curve.

Amy opened her eyes. Her exterior wore a solid outline of her blanket-like white aura.

Graves had her head down, eyes closed. *Smiling.*

"Seashell white," Mr. SmartyPants said. "Very vogue hue in the 2090s, perhaps."

"Quite the observation. Very well then." Graves moved from student to student, inspecting their aura outlines. "While keeping your auras in this state, you'll kneel into a comfortable deep squat, keeping your back as parallel to the ground as allowed. Have at it."

Demora stooped first, her balance unwavering. The others followed suit, Amy being last.

What's next, a Do-si-do?

"I warn you to steady yourselves, as this next part will prove challenging. Keep steady as your talismans lower on the middle of your backs."

The hovering talismans above each classmate made their way toward their owners' backs.

Amy's eyes followed the talismans' graceful fall. *How did Graves become such a young master? Who trained her? Gma always says I'll be well into my forties before—*

—Rezna's lips part— **'truly capturing aura's raw essence'**

A raindrop fell on Amy's nose.

Her eyes went wide as the token's weight hit her palm.

She blinked.

"Ugh." Amy wiped her chin free of dirt. "You've got to be fucking kidding me." She transferred the wet mud from her hands to her denim jeans. Got to her knees. A body or two collided somewhere around her, but the sting of the moment kept her focus on recovery. She dusted her *thankfully* dark pant legs off.

Demora, Vedessia, Kassandra, Mr. Stoicism, and Ms. JellyRoll remained squatted, with the latter two buckling worse than the others.

Kassandra's face remained as unbothered as ever, yet somehow almost snarling at the same time.

The rain stormed down.

Is Graves responsible for the downpour, too? No... Maybe?

Graves sat on a stump, fanning herself with a Druich leaf. The *super* meaty veins of the slouching, grey leaf exhaled small pockets of mist into her face.

Is she enjoying this?

"Oof!" Graves dropped the leaf, dug a small notepad out of her pocket, and jotted. "Leaf miners... Quite an idea..." she mumbled to herself.

Mr. Stoicism went down. "Dammit!" He clenched his muddy fist.

Ms. JellyRoll fell to her knees. "Must train harder..." She let out between breaths.

Kassandra *met her match.* Eyes like blades, on her knees and she pounded her fists into the slush.

Demora's eyes locked with Amy's, then went back to Vedessia's.

Vedessia smiled in return.

Appetite in her eye. There's something more to that girl.

Demora's eyes jerked off center but refocused.

"All right, I've seen enough," Graves said. "Otherwise, we'll be here all night with these two."

Demora and Vedessia dropped their auras. Their heavy breaths created mists in the rainfall. Demo's eyes moved on and stayed with Graves.

"Congratulations," the professor said. "You're quite the group."

Amy stared at the bright number 10 on her talisman. *Most of us.*

"You are all about to witness the power of the Prison Games."

Everyone stared at Professor Graves.

A weak sound escaped Mr. Stoicism as he gawked at her from his bent-over position. "Professor, did you say—"

"Did she say we're going to prison?" Jamari exclaimed.

"Not literally, I hope," Lil Sis said.

Graves stepped ahead of them. "Stand back a little. This will take some doing." She outstretched her arms, fingertips pointed to the ground.

A slight rumble came from under the earth.

Specks of red light shone out from several spots on the ground.

Worms of Graves' red aura wiggled out of the ground, prompting the students to jump away to avoid rising clusters of dirt.

Amy stepped back as a shadow cast up her midsection.

"This is mad," Jamari said.

Mr. Stoicism's jaw dropped. "Fucking hell…"

"What is this?" Ms. JellyRoll's stare fixed on the monument rising before her.

They all gazed at the shadow towering over them.

Graves relaxed her arms. "If you have a mind, you can create a prison."

Red aura vines whipped around a block of dirt as it rumbled its way further out of the ground. Dirt fell from the roof of the monstrous structure as it *finished its birth*. Its roots dressed the structure's rounded angles.

At the front, a single pitch-black entrance awaited them.

Feels… feels like something's calling from the inside.

"Is this thing stable?" Lil Sis asked. "We're not going in there. Are we?"

Ms. JellyRoll scoped the structure with an eye through her lilac aura ball. Her hairpin within the ball bounced around. "This reading is off the charts."

Graves nodded. "I suspect your lot shouldn't take more than a week to complete this game."

"A week?!"

"This is what I told my agent I'd be away for a week? Prison?"

"Weeeek? I've got a package coming tomorrow."

"Really."

"How—what?"

"You can't be serious."

"Dreadful."

Graves's silent smile brought silence. "You'll have many opportunities to leave whenever you like."

"That would be pointless." Mr. Smartypants's eyes analzyed the structure from top to bottom, then turned to the others. "We'd forfeit whatever we intend to gain from the Prison Games, no?"

"That's correct. Anyone wishing to bow out now, please step aside, and we'll discuss in a moment. For the rest of you willing to go on, please step inside."

"Bottoms up." Jamari strode forth, flipping his talisman high and catching it. He repeated the process on his way to the dark opening.

"Your brother's thick head is rather ballsy." Mr. Stoicism shook his head.

"Runs in the fam." Lil Sis followed her brother into the structure's infinite darkness.

"Perfect." Demora went for it next.

Amy took a step but paused to gape at the mouth of the mound. *Can I defend myself? If things go...*

"Shan hiska." Vedessia smiled at her and then floated ahead.

Amy's eyes narrowed on her back. *What's she playing at?* "I'm drinking the wind, alright." She went into her pocket and discreetly checked her GCID screen from within it. *Out of sight, out of mind. Plus, wearing this thing only adds another glaring difference between me and all of them. I don't think they've noticed.* She ran ahead to catch up to Demora.

Kassandra stepped inside the *prison's* hole last. As she crossed, a dirt wall rumbled down, taking time to fill the gap between the students and the outside world.

Graves bowed to them from what felt like *a mile away.* "Good luck, everyone! I'll see you shortly."

Last call, Devine. You can still get out of this.

"Last call for cowards." Jamari's snicker raised the hairs on Amy's arms.

"Away from your eminent privilege, the coward will be you, Wyst," Mr. Stoicism said.

"Don't use my name, fleabait. Respect the rules."

"Coming from you? That's funny."

"Is this staycation of ours going to be a bag of yammering testicles?" Mr. SmartyPants' voice came from somewhere behind. "I prefer stimulation of a greater source, gentlemen."

"Pause," Jamari said.

"We'll have food, right?" Vedessia's soft voice quivered. "I'm already starving."

Darkness ate them all.

*—A man, made of whirlpooling shadows in a — Dashing— suit made of twitching clouds, **SCREAMS** in Amy's ear—his fists plummet her into the dirt ground— his arms and legs contort around her limbs, locking her in place—*

*—the heads of children with glassy blue eyes **LAUGH** as they twirl around Amy's head— a giant baby head **CRIES**—grows larger as it spirals towards her—the mouth opens at the last spiral and swallows Amy whole—*

—Amy, on her knees inside a glass box, yells without sound at the ceiling of her captivity—

—Amy wrestles Demora inside a prison cell made of crumbling dirt walls—Amy shoves Demora into an endless black hole—

—Amy sits at her desk in her room, writing in her journal—

I wasn't sure what I was thinking.

Why would she help me?

But I had to try.

—Amy slows her run, catches her breath as she approaches—

—CELL 4—

— "Hey, can I—" stares inside the cell—

—the earth walls were as black as scorched meat—

—Kassandra lounges on her throne of vines—E'oné sits on the bed—

—Amy nods to her. Turned to Kassandra. "Can I talk to you?" —

— "No." Kass turns away—

— "Please. Just two minutes. I'm begging you for just two."

—Kass rolls her eyes. Nods to E'oné—

—E'oné gets up, half-smiles at Amy, and leaves the two alone in the cell—

—*Amy staggers forward and holds the bed's railing to steady herself. "You have no reason to help me. I'm sorry I've been a nuisance. But please, remember what we went through last year. With Cloudy." —*

—*Kass shifts in her seat. Crosses her arms. "What is it?" —*

— *"You owe me no favors, but I'm asking you for one now. This is life or death." —*

—*Amy walks up to her. Raises her hand. Her white aura bursts to life over it—*

—*Kass frowns at the gesture. Uncrosses her arms. Her hand creeps up. Takes Amy's in it—*

—*Amy's eyes lock with her. Callisto's Light are Demora's kidnappers—*

—*Kassanda's eyes widen—*

— *"I don't believe he played a part in it. But I need to find out before he's hurt. Or worse. By Demora. Please, don't let her get anywhere near Jamari—*

AFTER

Chapter Eighteen

Smile of Blé

On the third and final night of the Prison Games, Amy walked home alone, after avoiding the buddy system suggestion by those left standing. She equally ignored the incessant ringing inside her head, drowning out her thoughts of what to do in the wake of her betrayal. Every step required patience. For herself. *"Eres sólo ficción para tu alma. Alma es tu Prime. Es Overbeing. Debes escucharlo. Listen."* Each time her foot hit the ground, the statement screamed out of her ears, tired of *my cabeza's cage. Estupido. Muy estupido.* "I just got her back…" Her eyes found the dirt road she traveled. "And I've already lost Demo again."

She got home right around midnight, but didn't go inside. Instead, despite the nerves pinching her spine, she sat on her front porch and stared up at the Moon. Counted the stars. Or the bats. Her phantom feet carried her inside the house and up to her room, only to return to her seat on the front porch, her cracked GCID in hand. *I've gotta breaking this thing in angry fits.* She rubbed the screen clockwise, and it glowed in response. "Call Demo."

Call has been forwarded to voicemail. Would you like to leave a message?

Amy rubbed the screen again. "Give me a second."

Waiting...

She shut her eyes, letting the GCID's warmth soak her face with its light. "Ok, ready."

Please leave your message after the tone

Ving!

"I..." Amy tapped the GCID screen against her forehead. Stopped and stared straight. "I can't hide it anymore, Demo. I can't pretend I don't know that look in your eye because every time I do, I see murder. And another part of me dies." Amy chuckled. "We're just kids. Fucking bloody kids who had no business seeing what we've seen." Her face fell into a distant gaze that looked far away at nothing. "I hear Cloudy's voice every day. I heard it every waking minute, the first six months after the capture. That first week after Cloudy, I <u>listened</u> to it <u>every second</u>. I was so sure I would die before that week was out, if not by my own hand, then by the massive ache in my chest. No. I wanted to die. In those moments, I learned I was weaker than I hoped for. Being in the outside World had a different meaning for me. It meant survival. Yes, I was hurting inside, but being out here..." Amy's scarred right hand traced the wind blowing by. "Living through one day was my gold medal. So, of course, being in my own home gave me the best odds of survival. Gma's here. Her tokens are here. Where would I need to go?"

Amy stood up and paced from one end of her house to the next. "You've always been able to just pick up and go, no matter the weather. I fear for you. After you were taken, I actually prayed. I prayed to Callisto that you'd come home safe. I ran out of options because I was too weak to do anything for you myself." Amy leaned against her porch bannister, her eyes getting lost in the landscape again. "I'm sorry. For everything. I just want you to let me in. Whatever you're planning, please, before you do anything... can I be by your side? No tricks. No more murder. This can't lead to more murder. I can't."

She crushed her GCID in her scarred right hand. Looked down at some broken pieces raining down from her palm.

Her chin rose, her distant stare returning.

She wore the same face the next morning. "I lost someone last year. *Myself.* I try to recover, but I can't let go of the pain. It's almost like I need it, the pain, just to keep me sane. Keep me feeling alive in some way, but I also want it to go away. I don't know what to do anymore. I don't know what's right or what's not. All I know is I need a little faith." Tears welled up in the corner of her eye.

Madame Blé reached her hand out, almost touching Amy's head, but took it back and let it drop on her own knee. "Sorry, old habit. The result of too many times a godmother. You didn't do it."

"Do what?"

"Fake as a charmer."

"Feeling more revolutionary these days." Amy smiled back at <u>this bitch</u>— *but, look at her. How could that face be the cause of such evil?* "It's okay." *What if... what if Blé had nothing to do with Demora's kidnapping or with any of the others? If she isn't the one responsible, it must be...* "Can I ask, why do you employ Droûx? She's a bit cold and brutal, no?"

M.Blé's girlish chuckling squeal simmered more quickly than it normally does for Amy's likening. "Oh, <u>Ms.</u> Droûx is a butterfly stuck in its triply hardened cocoon. I have never met anyone else who has gone through the wringer more times than most and still gets up in the morning. This World has softened us humans. It is all too easy now. We carve messages in their air with our fancy devices. Service time at any restaurant never surpasses ten minutes. Poverty is all but extinct in over 95% of our World. Ms. Droûx, I am afraid, still lives in a world that predates our own, stuck somewhere after the climax of the Second War On Peculiars. Her family name once drew admiration across London, but has suffered losses and a tarnishment that cannot be undone. Her devotion to Callisto's vision of harmony and advancement for all is only rivaled by my own. She may be tough. She is also bound by her faith in the greater good."

They sat in the guest seats at M. Blé's desk, facing one another.

Madame Blé's face scrunched up. Her shoulders squeezed into her torso, as though cold, and her eyes looked along the floor, past Amy. "We still haven't found Celestia. I fear it's my doing. I've always sent her on errand after errand through each town or city we visit, and she never fails to deliver. Detectives found terribly covered tracks leading back to where she was **snatched**." M.Blé bites down on air; lips cursing an unseen presence. "She's the best spoken of us, and her leadership skills far exceed most. That girl has no family except for us. No friends outside the church. Wherever and whoever they are, those who took her must pray... "

M.Blé's mouth curled into a sharp smile, both warm *and disarming.* "I apologize for my blunt words, but I do not feel pity for those who prey on others. It tears me apart to see the young suffer. I can see the brightness in you. I am only sorry you will miss the next ceremony for our newest members. In time. I know you will rise in our ranks in under a year."

"In under a year." *The smile of Blé* haunted her for the following days, as Amy spent most of her hours in the lower level of Haven Church: The Pits. Listening. Taking notes. Oblivious to all but the instructor. *And the churning in the walls.* She gave polite smiles here and there when it was warranted. After every class or sermon, she donned her cyan cloak in silent solidarity with her new reality. *A member of The Light, through and through.*

On the fourth day, *with not one peep from Demora,* Amy decided—*it's time.*

She arrived early in the afternoon. Callisto's Haven bustled with the energy of mating rabbits, unlike anything Amy had seen before. The few citizens there and members of The Light drank bottles of *boozy mead—the smell of it— Light sure knows how to party—* and conversed in circles around performers. Ballet dancers, an assortment of instrumentalists, and fire starters worked their artistic charms over their groups. The chaotic mesh of sounds pounded the air with a broken melody *that, at the same time, sounds completely cohesive.*

The audience members tossed *play money* at the feet of the performers. *Yuck/Yech! Peasbeating in public should be a crime. Some respect for artists. Much of their audience isn't even watching the show. The performers are background noise to their intoxicated socializing. Huh?*

A firestarter Amy instantly recognized stood on top of a small stage. His mahogany skin peeled back in small folds. He bent down in his beige, high-waisted trousers, and his entire body quaked. Bright red streaks grew all over his naked torso, feet and arms. He growled into the skies, jets of thin blue flames pushing from every exposed pore. The flame strips doubled in size as the firestarter beat his chest and began performing a *ritualistic dance I've seen marked on the walls inside the church.*

The man's magma-colored eyes looked in her direction. His smile tore across his face.

Amy averted her gaze and kept rolling by, itching her elbow the deeper She got into the crowd.

A woman whose name she could never remember sat at a small wooden table in front of the Haven Church doors. Amy found her smile, slapped it on, and walked up the short steps. "Good afternoon, lovely to see you again. Killer skirt! Love the purple. What's this?" *Too much, Devine, stay cool.*

"Charmed to see you again, darling. We've had to update security with the unfortunate events, as of late. From now on, anyone coming in or out of the church is to be signed in or out here first." She let loose a childish giggle.

"Oh, makes sense."

"Are you risen and ready for another glorious day on your mission?"

"Risen and ready."

"Sorry!" A drunk man stumbled into the table, dropping the contents within his hand with a **clatter**. "Hi, miss. I'd—**gulp.** I'm ready for my last refill, please."

The *patient* front desk woman shook her head with a smile. "No worries, you'll just have to head over to cabin C right over there." She pointed. "Remember, Mr. Brooks? Cabin C. Over there." Her finger pointed towards the right cabin.

Amy's eyes stayed on the *ACTUAL COIN?* and *a REAL NOTE?* Until the drunk man snatched both up and hobbled away. "Was he holding <u>real</u>, hard currency? Where did he—"

"That is correct, sugar."

"Are they—" Amy's arm presented the crowd as though the front desk woman hadn't seen them before. "No offense, but they're peasbeating, right? They're not using <u>real</u> <u>hard</u> currency?"

"You got it again! No peasbeaters here! Believers 'round the World donate their hard-earned extra earnings towards Her Light. During the last seven days before the new year, they can come to any sanctioned site such as ours, and we provide them with physical assets equal to their UD donations. They spread their wealth as they see fit while here. Then they return their donations to us. Sort of like a closure between you and your donations."

"Those are two-pound coins and ten-pound notes! I've never even seen a twenty-pounder or a single coin 'cept online in my entire life!"

The plum cheeks of the front desk woman grew redder as she smiled. "<u>She</u> <u>does</u> work in mysterious ways, wontya say? Wouldn't you agree Her Light shines brighter than we'll ever truly know?"

"I'm learning. Thanks." *They're all fucking insane. And loaded.* Amy started to walk past her, but stepped back. "Hey, just curious. When can I take a cloak of Callisto's Light home?"

"It took me three years to earn a cloak in Her Light. Don't you worry. When your time comes, you'll already know it."

Amy said her goodbyes and headed through the doors of

Haven Church. *Three years??? I don't have that much time. Gotta get to that infirmary and talk to him today. If I'm caught or if I don't get the answers I need... Demo, where are you? Fuck! Just* <u>please</u> *don't do anything drastic. Shit. Perhaps I can somehow get my hands on a cloak. Last resort. And unless Jamari gets back to me, I don't know if The Singer's got a shot with the cult, either.*

After passing the nave and entering the door for The Pits on the right, she met another roadblock, no longer faced with a rack of available cloaks. A man half her size manned the entrance to a new room at the end of Bridle Lane.

"Name and affiliation," he asked, tapping his fingers along the doorframe of the freshly constructed cloakroom.

"Amy Devine. I'm an understudy."

The cloak attendant smacked his hands together, and when he pulled them apart, a white screen made of shimmering yellowish ziccolights expanded within his hands. "Search Amy Devine." His face, half-covered by the screen, his unconcealed eye bore a hole through Amy. **Zi-Pop!** The man's stare became the most adorable smile a second later. "You're all clear."

A minute later, he stepped out of the cloakroom and handed her a bundled cloak.

A wind of the cloak's freshness blew in Amy's face, and her body's frigidness softened. "Thank you. Is that a new update?" She pointed to the man's screen, still behind him.

"Oh, yeah. Don't get your hopes up. It's only been rolled out to a few organizations for beta testing. Bless-ed be The Light."

"Blessed." Amy pressed forward to the left and went down the winding dirt staircase that slowly turned blue. Checked her cracked GCID screen, with only some glass pieces left. The exposed metal underneath crackled with a warm yellow glow that snaked its way around the interior. *Gonna shock myself. This GCID is wrecked. My pockets need a blessing. Gave my last UDs up for a new strap. I hope The Engineer cooks something up soon.* She continued onto the lower level, already hearing the faint grinding mechanism within the reflective walls. *In good time. Let's get through the slog of it.*

That slug was pretty hefty today. After a thirty-minute class went thirty minutes longer than expected, Amy put the pep in her steps as she exited Classroom A and made her way through the sparkling blue limestone corridors. *Forget lunch. No sweat, I'll make it.* She checked her GCID as she kept a polite pace past Light members and hopefuls alike. *Tried* to smile and nod her way past an older Light member named Ms. Hacy, but the woman caught her hands in hers and waddled alongside Amy. It took a few minutes till Amy found her exit from the conversation, which was one of the last minutes she could spare. *I'd win the bet, knowing I may run into Storytime Hacy. Almost there.*

The archway leading to the sunken room before the pool door welcomed her with zero light. With *less than a minute left,* she rushed through the dark on soft hops. Waited in front of the iron door to the poolroom. Closed her eyes and took a deep but quiet breath.

"What are you doing here?"

Amy's head swiveled as the rest of her body froze, her outstretched hand not daring to reach any further for the door's handle. Heavy steps approached her right side. A shadow emerged from the dark.

278

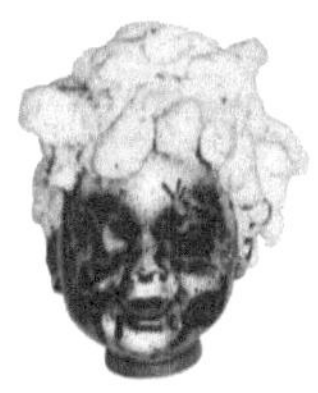

Chapter Nineteen

Infirmary

"They needed someone with a cool head to keep guard. These possessed folk. **Hark.** If you ask me, they should be in an institution. Anyway, the pool's closed." Mr. Stoicism kept his arms folded as he stopped only a few feet away from her.

"I know." Amy rummaged through her thoughts, careful with her next words. "I was hoping to get into the infirmary."

"The infirmary?" He smirked *in unbelievable*. "Right, a well-trained ear could hear past the soundproofing. <u>You</u> tracked it?"

"I've been following the pattern. Shifting wall tech only works universally, moving the rooms on this level every other hour. I tracked the movement of the gallery, and it's always the same: clockwise once, twice counterclockwise, and then shifts back to the outer track while two rooms, classroom four and the lounge, move to the inner track. Tracked the library, just to be sure."

"I'm impressed, but to no avail. During pool maintenance hours, the infirmary is moved here because it's closed to visitors.

Family or not. Only senior members are allowed in right now."

"You don't feel that's a bit odd, Pudersmitt?"

"Maintenance? No, I don't. What are you after, Devine?"

"I need to visit my friend; he's been here for some time now."

"Is he family? Why don't you just come during normal visiting hours?"

"He's not family. He's a— friend."

"You must work on your poker face because that wasn't the slightest bit convincing."

"Ok, thanks." Amy sighed. "You're right. He's an acquaintance. I'll try not to be too long. I just need to talk to him."

"Give the message to me. I'll run it by whoever it is."

"It needs to come from me. Please, I'm asking for a couple minutes, and then I'll be on my way."

"What's your <u>friend's</u> name?"

"His name is Kiaixai."

"Oh, no. Can't do, sorry."

"It's important."

"I'm sure it always is with you."

Amy stepped back to look him up and down. "What does that mean?"

Pudersmitt's jaw tightened on one side. He *chewed on the words his mouth was cooking next.* "Can we not pretend you have the cleanest record?"

"<u>Excuse</u> me?" Realization washed over her expression. "What—"

"Thousands in civil charges for various offences. You average five out of six civil strikes <u>annually</u>. Breaking into the underground trolley system. Defacing City Hall. <u>Scrubbing cams?</u>"

"How do you know all of this? My records are sealed, and last I checked, you're not a detective or higher. Did Ang—"

"Oh, leave Hideko out of it; he's too smart for you. He

bested you once. Get over it. His countrymen fall to him regularly. Consider yourself lucky. Anyway, why should I partake in your criminal behaviour?"

"Criminal? <u>Criminal</u>. Please. Spare me the dramatics. At least I did all my "crimes" for fun; no one was in the crosshairs. I wasn't the one scheming my way through the Prison Games with secret alliances. Or crawling on my knees, begging someone to be my partner."

"You—" He pointed an *indignant* finger at her. "There's nothing wrong with showing respect for a woman's choice. Bloody brilliant! You're an honest criminal, <u>at least</u>. It's no wonder you moped around alone most of your time in the Prison Games, stuck in your head puzzles. None of which helped, by the look of your rank at the end."

"Okay, Mr. 'This is unfair! Professor, that's not fair, nor that, or that. Everything's unfair!'" Amy's arms returned to her sides after waving in the air madly through her ranting mockery. "<u>At least</u> I can show respect without groveling. No, instead, I should learn from you, and watch my partner <u>steal</u> points from others, yet still work with him. Class act, you are."

"Don't ever question my class! You have some nerve. Only one of us has the stomach to toss their <u>best friend</u> into a black hole so casually."

Amy thought of a million ways Pudersmitt's head could leave his carcass. The fire inside of her simmered with the appearance of a strange reality. Her body eased from its puffed state. "You spoke to Demora?"

Pudersmitt was a brooding trunk. A slight satisfaction teased over his lips.

"You've been talking to her? Where is she? Is she alright?"

"That's the wrong order of questions. Have you stopped to think about how she's feeling?"

Amy scrunched her eyes in protest.

"Or are you too busy trying to do things your way?"

"Of course, I feel— you have no idea how I feel. All of this is because I love her. I don't want her to do something that she knows will tear her apart."

"Sounds controlling."

Scoff. "You've stepped into our life for two seconds and think you've got the whole story?" *Don't do this with him now, Ames. He can wait.* "Amy's nostrils forced air out. "Listen—"

"No, you listen." Pudersmitt leaned close to her, eyes traveling all around before settling on her. "You made me look like an imbecile before, but that was the last time. I'm not letting you through."

"I made you— Did I make you—"

They bickered over each other, their fists inching ahead of their bodies as they got closer. Their harsh whispers towards one another, cut short by the **WHOOSH** of air brought by the opening iron door behind them.

"I thought I heard voices out here." The head of the Cult's resident pregnant woman, Mali Cincius, poked out from behind the door. "Oh! Dekkie, I was hoping it was you. So glad you're here." She stepped out, letting the door **SLAM** behind her with echoing results.

Dekkie??

"Mali, this is not a great time." Pudersmitt shuttered as—

Mali placed an arm around his neck and smiled at Amy. "Hi, I'm Mali. Dekkie, is this the cute girl you keep running off to meet with?"

"Wha— absolutely not! I never said—"

Her eyes are glossy. Amy shook Mali's hand. "Nice to meet you, I'm Amy, an understudy here."

Pudersmitt got between them. "Yes, yes, we're all delighted to meet one another. Amy was just on her way."

"Dekkie." Mali shoved Pudersmitt aside and moved in the middle of them. "This is so unlike you; imposing yourself between women. Why are you so nervous? She is your girlfriend, isn't she?"

"She is NOT—"

Mali faced Amy completely. "I'm so sorry, he's not usually this wound up. In fact, he's always been the perfect gentleman. I don't know what he's thinking today." Her infectious, warm smile grew as she took Amy's hand. "I was just on my way out for a walk. Would you like to join me?"

"No, Mali, we've been through this." Pudersmitt took Mali's arms and guided her back towards the iron door. "It's best you stay inside until your meds wear off, okay? Come on."

"What kind of meds do they have a pregnant woman drugged up on?" Amy asked.

"Ah." Mali stood in front of the door's handle, gently pushing aside Pudersmitt's attempts at opening it. "The drugs help the little bugger's chittering go down." She tapped her belly lovingly.

"Mali, come on now." Pudersmitt turned the handle forty-five degrees and pulled it open by a hair.

Mali's butt pushed the door close again **SLAM**, her eyes still smiling at Amy.

"Mali…"

Amy gripped his shoulder tightly. "She says she wants to go for a walk. Is she not here of her own free will?"

He looked back at her with burning eyes while still trying to get the pregnant woman through the door.

Mali's bum kept shutting the door. "Why so weird today, Mr. Gloomersmiit?" Her finger tapped his nose.

"I'm just trying to visit a friend," Amy said.

"And I said no." Pudersmitt finally opened the door successfully and guided Mali past it.

"It's about who took her." *Can't say kidnapping. How about "vacation?" A little more subtle.* "On that vacation. We know who took Demo."

The buzzing silence answered her. She would have thought he didn't hear her if it weren't for the twitching of his spiked ear tips. Pudersmitt turned to her with quivering eyes. "What did you say?" He abandoned his efforts at containing Mali.

No turning back now. The longer this remains unresolved, the angrier Demora gets. Then there's no telling what she'll do. "In the prison she recognized Mr. Eminent's whistle. You know who he's with."

Pudersmitt's bottom lip curled. "Ja—"

Amy's eyes darted to Mali, then back onto Pudersmitt.

"Dekkie, <u>you've</u> been to the cooler? What on Earth for, smiling too hard?"

"Mal, would you give us a second?" Pudersmitt nodded away from the *distraught, but sheepishly waiting, pregnant woman.*

Amy trailed behind his beckoning arm, stubborn in her steps. Once they were a touch out of Mali's earshot, Amy relaxed her body and stared straight into Pudersmitt's piercing blue eyes. "How is Demo feeling?"

At that very moment, as though the past twelve months had never happened, a pulsing wave of heat came from Pudersmitt's body and flushed against Amy's skin. *Sure as night, I can feel his aura.*

"She's pissed, but she's sitting right. You know, she's..." He stood there *absent. In his thoughts. Maybe reliving moments with her. Moments he had with her. Alone. Moments I'm not a part of.*

The temperature dropped in the space between the two of them. *One, for sure, maybe both, lost in their helplessness.*

A *bouncing?* warmth drew close behind Amy's back.

"Don't be a bore, Dekkie." Mali placed a hand on his shoulder, *looking somewhere beyond his head.* "Let the girl see her friend. It's all we've got in this World." She teetered slightly away, playing with her fingers. "I had a friend once. Course, that was before she slept with my fiancé—ex-fiance— and gave him three kids. She's got cancer now."

"This is not a story I need to hear again, nor does she."

"Oh, but Dekkie, here's the part you didn't hear. It struck again. Our most intellectual deity, Karma. See, my ex-best friend got cancer. I was the first and only at her bedside. The others in her life disappeared. Her children joined the nearest COIC on an "unfit home" condition and had their full independence in under a month. My ex-best friend—let's call her, fuck it, Jarcy— was a sketch mother, I hear. Husband left her for a huntress, and now they're missioning all over the Sahara as we speak. She called me after realizing how gravely she messed up back in the day."

Mali gazes lovingly at the two of them from behind. "Oh,

how she broke my brother's heart as we were fresh in the working world, and gave my brother a quick case of AIDS. For two years, it ravaged him." Tears welled in her eyes. "He's got two fingers working on each hand. Almost all toes. I can't talk about the rest without the little one turning."

Mali held her belly. Her eyeballs looped around her sockets as she seesawed off her heels and the balls of her feet. "Jarcy mowed down a child with my auto in a drunken oopsie and got off because she was… intertwined with our home city's mayor. I got fined out of attending university. Still paying it back. But there I was. Sitting with my cancer-stricken ex-bestie, listening to her story for two hours. I almost went back. Then, I remembered when my mother died and Jarcy was too busy getting her back blown out to make the funeral. She showed up hours after the reception. Now there Jarcy lay; her skin shriveled ninety years her senior. Her family, friends and everything else—gone. And who does she call? Me. Should I give her the chance to hurry me again?"

"Mali, I'm sorry about your friend, but we really need to get a move on." *Pudersmitt swallowed the rest of his impatience for once.* Checked his watch. "Amy, how positive are you—how positive are either of you about this new development?"

"I'd never doubt Demora's judgement, much less her senses."

Pudersmitt watched her with a stiff, pointed eyebrow. Grunted.

"To live with cancer." Mali sighed *dreamily.* "Anywho, will you let sweet Amy see her friend, please?" The preggo touched Amy's cheek.

"Come on. We'll take this to our <u>Graves</u>." Amy gave a warm smile to Mali while removing the dazed woman's hand from her face. Locked eyes with *Pudersmitt.*

His mouth opened in response, but nothing came out. His eyes narrowed on her. His stoic stare widened into a broad, *hyena smile.* His eyes were fuller, and his ears stood on end. "A war is best served with precise speed." He led the way.

"Wow. That was such a lovely smile." Mali went after him. "Why do you seem so upset, Dekkie?"

Amy stood back for a bit, letting Pudersmitt open the door, and allowing him and Mali to go through first, leading into a sparkling, floral pink hallway. *This could be a trap. I'll have to trust Pudersmitt's love for Demo means it won't be. Unless he plans on trapping me in some wicked scheme to "help her."* She looked at her cracked GCID's small green light. *Still service here.* She took off her device and placed it in the darkest corner of the room before taking a stance back in the doorway. *Here goes.*

Chapter Nineteen: The Infirmary

INFIRMARY

CULT'S EYE RECORDS

By

CALLISTO'S LIGHT

Date: scrubbed

FADE IN:

INT. HAVEN CHURCH - INFIRMARY - DAY

PUDERSMITT's steps echo down the pink hall, ahead of AMY and MALI. Amy watches her reflection in the shine of the walls.

                    AMY
          Wasn't expecting this decor.

                    PUDERSMITT
          Madame Blé ensures the patients
          have a welcoming and peaceful
          atmosphere.

                    AMY
          Right.

                    (V.O.)
          He must not be convinced about
          the cult's hand in Demora's
          kidnapping.

                    MALI
          She's an honest saint. I'd still
          be selling bootleg coins up north
          if it wasn't for her.

                    PUDERSMITT
          You were a bootlegger?

                    MALI
          The best. I specialised in
          antiques. Most Creaevix systems
          that still accept coins aren't
          equipped to handle coins older
          than AC50. Had a comfy existence
          until Dets caught up with me.
          Before my trial, Madame Blé showed
          up and offered the Dets an
          alternative. Without Callisto,

> I would have never been found.
> Her essence sent the great Madame
> to me.

                    AMY
          Yes, I'm sure.

                    PUDERSMITT
               (an eye on Amy)
          Callisto is responsible for all
          our gifts. We must've forget that.

Mali rambles on about her bootlegger
deeds.

                    AMY (V.O.)
          *He's still deciding. I need to
          be ready in case he wagers against
          me. Do I have a chance against
          him?*

The faces of the STUDENTS OF GRAVES flash
in Amy's mind.

FLASH: LIL SIS aka E'ONÉ WYST raises an
eyebrow.

FLASH: A cocky smile on JAMARI WYST.

FLASH: Pudersmitt's stoic face complains.

FLASH: KASSANDRA's cutthroat grill.

FLASH: VEDESSIA aka MS. BUBBLY's
infectious smile.

FLASH: MS. LING aka MS. JELLYROLL's
inquiring stare, eyes lit with her lilac-
purple aura.

FLASH: HIDEKO ANG aka MR. SMARTYPANTS
snickers, his shade of green flickering in
his mad eyes.

FLASH: VYAILA aka THE GYAAD GIRL's yellow eyes penetrate.

FLASH: DEMORA smiles with confidence.

> AMY (V.O.)
> *Every one of them had an advantage over me in the Prison Games. I hate to admit it. They outclassed me in every single game. I barely hung on.*

> PUDERSMITT (O.S.)
> This way.

Amy wakes from the daydream and peers down the lit path he guides them towards. Opposite, a chain-link gate blocked access down another path shrouded in darkness.

> AMY
> What's down there?

> PUDERSMITT
> Some patients are too far gone.

He and Mali walk the other path, leaving Amy to linger by the gate.

Deep down the gated hall, eyes filled with golden veiny streaks stare straight back at her.

Amy turns away. Makes for the other path.

> GOLDEN PEEPERS (O.S.)
> (from behind)
> He smells something in you.

As Amy catches up, the trio reaches another hall end, this one with only one path to their right.

Midway down the new hall, a guard donned in a cyan coat stood in front of a wooden threshold protruding from the ground. Distant voices in the air behind him.

> GUARD
> What's the meaning of this, Pudersmitt? No visitors.
>
> (points to Mali)
> And get her to bed rest.

> MALI
> I'm quite awake, actually. Do you see these stars?

> PUDERSMITT
> I will, but I need you to let my friend here get in to see her friend.

> MALI
> Yes, let sweet Amy through, pretty please, Mr. Guardsman. Or the Huffy Man behind you will gobble you up.

They all turn to her. The guard checks his back.

> GUARD
> How much they got her on?

> PUDERSMITT
> Please. We'll just take a few minutes.

> GUARD
> And hear Droûx's mouth again? I think not. Out of question, out

of story. I told you. You gotsta stop stroking your soft spot for the ladies before you lose all your mojo around here. And before you try to—

The man stumbles back, a quarter of his former height. Pudersmitt looms over him.

PUDERSMITT
She needs to see her friend. You would deny a lady such a genuine and pure request? I've had just about enough of your lectures, Stuley, and I am not interested in your faux bravado. I'm sure your father wouldn't approve of your antics.

GUARD STULEY
Hey! There's no need to bring the old man into this! Now I'm sorry, but you can't keep asking me to hand out favours for every poor soul you come across!

PUDERSMITT
As I said, I'm sure your father wouldn't approve of your antics. Especially not with all the funding my family provides to The Light. I will bring as many visitors in here as I please, and you'll allow it in good faith.

GUARD STULEY
Hey now, who do you think—

Pudersmitt backs him into the NEAR-INVISIBLE soft netting over the threshold. His back inflates, almost blocking the guard entirely.

                    PUDERSMITT
          This is not a debate. One more
          visitor for the night. Unless
          you'd like to reacquaint yourself
          with the nomad lifestyle you so
          loathed back when the cult found
          you digging for straps in the
          caves. You're the only nomad I
          know who was one, not by choice,
          but by design. Your design.

The guard lowers his head, blocking most
of it in the shadows of the corner wall.

                    GUARD STULEY
          Who is it?

                    PUDERSMITT
          Kiaixai.

The guard groans.
                    GUARD STULEY
          Had to be that imbecile? Five
          minutes, kid, alright? I can give
          you five.

                    PUDERSMITT
          Ten.

                    GUARD STULEY
          Wha— ugh. Sure.

The side of Pudersmitt's face turns to

the others— *wearing that awful hyena grin.*

> AMY (V.O.)
> *What the hell?*

> PUDERSMITT
> Let's make it.

The guard waves his hand over the threshold. The fine strands of the netting glow white and retract down past the wooden threshold.

The voices of patients ahead amplify. The trio moves past the hunched guard and into—

INT. INFIRMARY BLOCK B - CONT

Moans in anguish *welcome* them.

Sparkling marble floors and walls greet them, too.

> AMY (V.O.)
> *The truth can be blinding.*

The trio hit the first set of patient rooms a few steps in. The doors of each room—a pink shade lighter than the walls, with knee-length windows. Glistens in the light. Inside the left room, a man smiles at them. Presses the wall. A green square lights up on it under his hand. He waves.

> POLITE PATIENT
> Good evening.

> AMY & MALI
> Evening.

In a room on the opposite side, two women

break from a kiss and continue their muffled conversation while they shave their armpit and leg, respectfully.

                    AMY
          At least they have sizable cells.

                    PUDERSMITT
          Their <u>rooms</u> are more than three
          times the size of your average
          human. They're allowed out in the
          fields behind the Haven for
          recreation three times a day.
          They are all willingly here; my
          family's legal team has gone over
          all of their medical contracts.
          They want to be cured.

                    AMY
          Okay.

                    (V.O.)
          Allowed. I doubt Kiaixai is here
          willingly.

                    MALI
          Madame Blé ensures every one of
          our patients has a five-star
          experience. Privacy tech—

                    (burps)
          'Cuse me. Privacy tech gives them
          the comfort they need. Amenities
          they've got up the wazoo as well
          as access—

A bifocaled man in the room they're approaching is on a call, a ziccolit woman across from him.

                    BIFOCALED PATIENT
          Yes, dear. They're feeding me five
          times a day! Don't you worry about
          me, okay? Doctor's results say that
          I…

                    PATIENT IN ADJACENT ROOM
Turn   your   Llisto-licking
transparency setting off, Mulvy!
We ain't all got to hear your
conjecture! Where's my cousin?
Stuzy!

          (To the passing group)
Evening, y'alls.

               MALI
They've got access to the outside
world all they'd like, though
most prefer the solitude they
find here.

               AMY
How long has this place been
operating?

               PUDERSMITT
Right after the rally, it became
fully operational. There were
plans drawn up for it before The
Light's arrival.

The grumblings from patients grow louder
as they pass each room, *as though a
symphony for our arrival.*

Amy freezes in front of one of the rooms.
Stoops to a knee in front of its window.

               AMY
Hey. Do you remember me? From
the rally?

Inside the darkened room, a young woman
with frazzled dreadlocks to match her
expression sits against the furthest
wall, hugging her knees.

               AMY

Hi. How are you, love?

Covered in shadow with only the eyeballs barely visible, the patient's vacant but hardened stare meets her.

> FRAZZLED LOC PATIENT
> I had orange pigtails, but I burned them out. I've been bad. Bad.

> AMY
> What do you mean? What happened?

The young woman glares back at Amy.

> AMY (CONT'T)
> Are they hurting you?

Amy swallows and shifts in her kneeled stance. Her eyes can't stay on the young woman's *face of malice.*

> FRAZZLED LOC PATIENT
> You're one of them. Why would I talk to you?

> AMY
> Huh? Who—

Amy looks down at her cyan cloak of Callisto's Light. Pinches the material. Strangles it in her fist.

> PUDERSMITT (O.S.)
> He's here.

Pudersmitt beckons from several rooms over.

> PUDERSMITT
> We're here, Stuley!

CUT TO:

KIAIXAI'S ROOM

Pudersmitt and Mali peer in from the outside. The polished door splits in the middle, each end zipping up and down out of sight.

> MALI
> This one's alive, right?

Amy jogs into view. Tosses aside the cult's cloak she no longer wore. Enters. Inspects the *cell*.

> AMY (V.O.)
> *Same bland pink as the rest.*
>
> (eyes widen)
> *Kiaixai, look at you. What did they—*

KIAIXAI, *free of his usual heavy coat,* knelt in the prayer position. The shadows in his cell give his body the outline of a stick figure. He looks right through Amy, who sits cross-legged in front of him.

> AMY
> Hey Kiaixai, it's good to see you.

He gave her a faint nod.

> AMY
> How are you feeling?

> KIAIXAI
> Better.

                    AMY
Do you remember me? The daughter
of the spiritualist.

                    KIAIXAI
Mm muh. Spiritualist.

                    AMY
I wanted to thank you for believing
in my grandmother. I'm not sure
what you had planned when you
arrived in town, but I think it
worked. I know it did.

                    KIAIXAI
Mm. Better.

                    PUDERSMITT (O.S.)
You're wasting your time.

Amy looks deep into Kiaixai's eyes.

                    AMY
Do you want to be here, Kiaixai?

Kiaixai's head nods off in one direction.

                    AMY (con't)
Are you sure?

Kiaixai swipes the floor in an arch. Taps
it.

                    KIAIXAI
Mm, hm. Better.

                    PUDERSMITT (O.S.)
Remember, we're on borrowed time
here, **Devine.**

His last word echoes down the halls.

Without turning to face him and with

clenched teeth—

                    AMY
          Yes. Got it.

She gets closer to Kiaixai. His eyes
bulge on the scar on the back of her
right hand.

                    KIAIXAI
          The unusual scar...

Amy checks what he's looking at. Her
tight face lightens with *understanding*.

                    AMY
          That's right.

                    KIAIXAI
          It seeks truth.

                    AMY
                (squints)
          What do you—

                    PUDERSMITT (O.S.)
          So do we, buddy.

Amy rolls her eyes. Looks deep into
Kiaixai.

                    AMY
          If anything changes about how
          you feel, let me know. Even after
          I leave here today, ask for Amy
          Devine. Okay?

Kiaixai barely nods back.

                    AMY (V.O.)
          I'm not even sure this is
          registering with him. I'll speak
          his language.

Kiaixai's still nodding.

> AMY
> (Lowers her voice)
> Amy recognized that Kiaixai was right. His protests tried to warn them. There's more to their message, and Kiaixai knew.

Kiaixai looks up at her.

> AMY
> Amy needed Kiaixai to tell her something else. She'll listen.

She leans towards him, inches from his prayer hands. Puts her hand out.

Kiaixai looks at her hand.

His hand **claps** into hers.

> KIAIXAI
> Mm. Kiaixai was grateful that she always tried to listen. He now wondered what it was she wanted to know.

Amy smiles.

> AMY
> What is Callisto's One Big Fault?

A moment of silence.

Kiaixai chuckles, still gazing at the floor. His fingers drag across it in an arch motion.

> KIAIXAI
> Better. It's all a jest.

Amy's body deflates.

> PUDERSMITT (O.S.)

> (SIGHS)
> What am I doing?

> MALI (O.S.)
> The best you can, love.

> PUDERSMITT (O.S.)
> He's got no fight left in him.

Amy perks up.

> AMY
> Kiaixai, what's the last thing you remember after your fight with Droûx?

Kiaixai flinches at the name. Pulls away from her and goes back to his prayer position.

> PUDERSMITT (O.S.)
> I say we call it a wrap. Clearly he's a lost cause.

Amy grills Pudersmitt.

> AMY
> With the amount of drugs your lot has got him on—

> (Waves off her rant)
> He's responding.

> PUDERSMITT
> "Your lot". Huh. For your information, the only word your "friend" or acquaintance or whatnot has ever uttered is "better". So I hate to say you're not making groundbreaking waves out here.

Pudersmitt steps into the room. Kiaixai shuffles back, still in prayer position, knees scraping the floor.

                    KIAIXAI
          No...

                    PUDERSMITT
          Ask him if he knows about Demora's
          disappearance.

                    MALI
          Disappearance?

                    KIAIXAI
          No?

                    (points at Pudersmitt)
          You copoodle with them.

Amy's face *considers*.

                    Pudersmitt
          What? I'd never hurt her.

                    MALI
          Hurt who?

                    AMY
          You're scaring him. Step. Out.

                    PUDERSMITT
          You're oversharing. Not getting
          to the point.

                    AMY
                    (finger waves up and down
                    Pudersmitt's body)
          And this helps?

Pudersmitt huffs. Steps back into the hall.

Amy faces Kiaixai but keeps some distance from the stuttering stick of a man.

                    AMY
              (Lowers voice)
         It's okay, it's just me here. I
         have a friend, dear to my heart.

              (Quieter)
         They took her. I want to make
         sure no one else gets taken.

Kiaixai's sad eyes look directly into hers. Tears form.

                    KIAIXAI
         More will be taken. It won't stop.

                    MALI
         Taken?

                    KIAIXAI
         It's too late.

The door to his room slams shut. Amy and Pudersmitt meet at it from opposite sides.

                    PUDERSMITT
         You locked her in there!

                    GUARD STULEY (O.S.)
         Oh shit!

Pudersmitt bangs against the door.

                    PUDERSMITT
         Today, STULEY! Right now!

                    GUARD STULEY (O.S.)
         I'm working on it! I couldn't
         see past your massive block! Once
         I do, you're all OUT! At once!

> KIAIXAI (O.S.)
> (breathless)
> Listen to me.

Amy flinches at the breath on the back of her neck. Turns—

Kiaixai's in her face.

> KIAIXAI
> Do not wager against them or they will cut out your tongue and make you her vessel their advantage is deep their numbers are large, modest here, but large elsewhere and they will make you her puppet.

Amy's lips try to find the words.

> AMY
> What are they planning?

Guard Stuley's **SCREEEEEAM** rips the air. Approaches—

RACES past them with a diaper-wearing patient straddled on his upper back— biting into his head. Stuley's eyes GLOW WHITE—

The door **whirs** open *slowly*.

Pudersmitt uses his body to shield Mali and beckons Amy forward.

Kiaixai sits cross-legged on the ground. Tears falling. Wearing a Cheshire smile. Rocks back and forth.

> KIAIXAI
> Maybe there's a chance after all.

Amy keeps her eyes on him as she backs into the hall. Pudersmitt tries to scoop her behind him, but she smacks his hand off. Her eyes widen.

On both sides of them, dozens of patients—THE DAMNED—are either exiting or have exited their rooms and wander looking clueless. Their EYES GLOW WHITE.

Pudersmitt's arms shield the two women behind him.

One of The Damned, red Einstein hair, points to Pudersmitt.

>   RED EINSTEIN-HAIRED PATIENT
>   Don't lay hands on the innocent!

The others follow his finger and trail towards the POI.

>   PUDERSMITT
>   Careful now. Steady.

His arms guide Amy and Mali as he leads them towards the exit. Another patient scratches her rump and stomps her feet behind them.

>   RUMP-SCRATCHING PATIENT
>   Don't you hurt the innocent one!

>   PATIENT 1
>   He is, isn't he?

>   PATIENT 2
>   What should we do?

>   PATIENT 3
>   It hurts. It hurts.

Amy watches their guard as Pudersmitt

leads Mali closer to the exit.

                    AMY
          Where'd the guard go? Is he
          alright?

                    PUDERSMITT
          He'll be fine, he's got a hard
          head.   Probably   went   for
          reinforcements.

                    AMY
          His eyes were glowing. White.

                    PUDERSMITT
          I know.

                    AMY
          Is he infected?

                    PUDERSMITT
          Probably. That patient must've
          infected him. We'll all be cursed
          soon if we don't get out of here.
          Don't touch a single one of them.

A PATIENT HAS A FINGER HOVERING INCHES
FROM PUDERSMITT'S FOREHEAD.

                    PUDERSMITT
          How—

                    MALI (O.S.)
               (breaking)
          Dekkie…

A **CACKLING** PATIENT wiggles their finger
over Mali's head. Adds another wiggling
finger near her pregnant belly.

                    CACKLING PATIENT
          Don't touch a single one! Don't
          you do it!

> (snarl grows, eyes quiver
> on them all, still
> **cackling** but *darker,
> throaty*)
> YOU WON'T HURT THE INNOCENT!

MONTAGE OF CHAOS ENSUES:

Patients cry out things:

> **"Don't you dare!"**
>
> **"The ripples are 'rupting"**
>
> **"Hands may not frolic!"**
>
> **"NIGGER?!"**

A constant moaning stutter wanes low to loud and back from groups of patients, different groups, at different times.)

Patients close in.

The trio squeezes together, back to back.

> PUDERSMITT
> MALI, CLOSE YOUR EYES!

She does.

> PUDERSMITT
> (To Amy)
> NO CAMS!

Amy's knowing glance catches his.

> PUDERSMITT (CONT'D)
> Don't let them touch you! Worse time to shake a curse.

> *AMY (V.O.)*
> *I'm already cursed.*

A faint white glow flickers in Amy's eye.

                    AMY
          They won't even remember this.

                    PUDERSMITT
          How do you know?

                    AMY
          Trust me. Someone's who's been
          cursed. We have to fight our way
          out.

Pudersmitt puts his head down. Looks at
the *swarm around them.*

                    PUDERSMITT
               Right.

THE DAMNED RUSH THEM FROM ALL ANGLES.

Her WHITE AURA illuminates like a
peaceful tide over her arms and legs.
Throws her arms back—body t-shaped—spins
her fist into nearest nose—back fist
BLASTING a chin. Her legs take turns
roundhouse kicking away oncoming waves of
saliva-dripping patients.

SAME TIME AS

Pudersmitt's aura EXPLODES—knocking the
Cackling Patient and other nearby
patients off their feet—before becoming a
thin blue outline around his body.
SMASHES a stiff elbow into the face of the
patient in front of him, turning them
around 180 degrees. Grabs them from
behind and uses their body as a shield
while using their arms as battering rams
to take down foes.

                    PUDERSMITT
          Just keep your eyes closed, Mail.

I swear it, no harm will come to
you.

> AMY (V.O.)
> *The hell? Something in his eye
> is different. Unhinged.*

The Cackling Patient SLAPS A HAND over
Amy's shoulder from behind.

> CACKLING PATIENT
> (through cackles)
> I got you-i got you-eh-AH-got
> you I got you I—

OVER AMY'S SHOULDER—

The cackler's hand only hovers inches
from it—a THIN LINE OF HER AURA in
between them.

> CACKLING PATIENT
> (through cackles)
> You gotdam nigg—

Amy kicks back, sending the cackler
flying into a group, downing them.

> AMY (V.O.)
> *Nigger? Really had to bring that
> old-fashioned back, huh?*

SNUFFS a patient about to claw into
Mali's face with both hands—

—at the same time, Pudersmitt's fist meets
that attacker's belly- the attacker flies
off ahead of them, crashing into the wall,
then the floor.

> PUDERSMITT
> Follow my warmth, Mali!

Eyes sealed, her hands feel out. She

nods.

Amy, Pudersmitt, take turns BOUNCING back opposition from both sides, crisscrossing each other, back and front—the light trail of their auras lingering for seconds after each blow, creating mini rainbows of white and blue light.

They mow down and protect Mali down the hall. The onslaught starts to overwhelm them as patients leap off the backs of others to reach them. Amy swings a broken patient room door off its hinge and into a leaper.

AMY (V.O.)
Batshit. Needed to happen.

Pudersmitt pounces over her—SLAPS a patient into a row of others—Pudersmitt's foot dents the wall as he bends on that knee, balanced parallel to the floor. The seconds go by as he remains suspended with a *teeny* pendulum movement.

Amy (V.O.)
(Eyes shaking at the
sight)
How—

Pudersmitt, eyes *hungry, tracking the next meal,* remains horizontally challenged as he knocks off a few persistent pats swarming Mali.

He rejoins them on the floor, with most of The Damned groggily recouping. His aura dims out; a second later, so does Amy's.

PUDERSMITT
Where the fuck is everyone?

He leads them three rooms away from the guard's post.

AWAAAAAAAAAAAAAAAAAAAAAAAAAAAA-NO-NO-NOOOOOOOAAAAAAAAAAA...!

A patient pushes, struggles within the grips of three Damned.

Two of The Damned rattle the almost-off door of another patient.

A pair of Damned fight over a squealing patient under them.

                    PUDERSMITT
          Dammit!

                    AMY
          They attacking the calm patients!

The source of the earlier **scream continues**— The Frazzled Loc Patient fights off two Damned—to be taken down by six others. They grab her by her locs and drag her further back into a pocket and behind and out of sight into the closing opening made where more of the Damned are on their feet. Shoulders hulking. Grins gnawing. Eyes flickering between a white glow and their natural color. Bodies leaning.

                    PUDERSMITT
          Shit.

                    MALI
          Can I open my eyes now?

She does.

                    MALI (CONT'D)
          Oh no.

She closes them again.

Pudersmitt bangs against the invisible wall over the wooden threshold. No one on the other side to answer him.

                    PUDERSMITT
          We need help! SOMEONE!

The Damned mob creeps towards them like broken-armed mummies—

Triple their speed—

Amy and Pudersmitt's respective auras burst bright once more, outlining their entire bodies as they step in front of Mali.

                    MALI (O.S.)
          Please…

The Damned smash into the weight of Amy and Pudersmitt, pushed back from touching Mali, but their grabby hands are too close for comfort.

The struggle brings Amy and Pudersmitt to their knees, Mali clamoring behind them in the corner.

                    MALI (CONT'D)
               (eyes still closed,
                praying)
          Callisto, please save us.

White light OVERTAKES Amy's eyes.

                    PUDERSMITT
               (shields Mali's eyes)
          Devine?

White aura WASHES the scene.

FADE OUT.

FADE IN:

INT. INFIRMARY BLOCK B - DAY

A high-pitched **wail** slices the air.

The Damned Patients have starving eyes ahead of them. They drool, some moan, all with jerky movements as they creep towards their target.

BIFOCALED PATIENT'S ROOM

A hidden compartment underneath a bed is accessed. Fingers punch in a code. One of the patient room doors snaps shut just as some Damned reach the front of it. Their dazed glowing gaze stares inside.

The Bifocaled Patient cowers back onto his bed.

BIFOCALED PATIENT
Creaevix, call wife.

Calling…

Outside his cell, Damned patients drag the screaming Frazzled Loc Patient by her long dreadlocks.

                    FRAZZLED LOC PATIENT
     NO! Please wait, STOP!

               (cries)
     No, this can't…

She's dragged out of sight, her pleas
drowned out by the moans and
indistinguishable words from the Damned
mob.

A growing darkness overtakes the light in
the hall.

                    BIFOCALED PATIENT
          What the hell?

BACK IN THE HALL

Kiaixai stands far behind the mob's
action. Eyes focused on something.

                    KIAIXAI
          It's in her light, after all.
          She will be in danger… if they
          find out.

The hall's darkness rises on and around
him.

Towards the other end closest to the
exit, the mouths of the Damned hang open
as a shadow looks over more of the crowd
with each passing second.

The Cackling Patient shuts up. Takes
hesitant steps back.

                    PUDERSMITT (V.O.)
          I'm not sure what I saw. It was
          living, breathing. The heat in
          there became almost unbearable.

Pudersmitt covers Mali's already closed eyes. She pulls herself into his arms, burying her face in his chest. Wraps her arms around him. He hugs her instinctively.

> MALI
> What's going on, Dekkie?

Pudersmitt just stares. They're covered in the still-growing shadow.

> PUDERSMITT
> It'll be alright. Maybe over soon.

> MALI
> Amy, are you okay? Is she okay?

> PUDERSMITT (V.O.)
> A nightmare on two feet. Best I can describe it.

The Frazzled Loc Patient's eyes quiver as The Damned, holding handfuls of her hair, shares her attention on whatever's coming.

HOOOOOOOOWHAAAAAAAAAAAAAAAM!

Like bowling pins, the Damned hair-pullers are sent flying away by a massive gust of wind. In its wake, black, pulsing electric sparks whip and dance around the Frazzled Loc Patient. She shields herself. Uncovers, in shock, but unharmed.

> PUDERSMITT (V.O.)
> Everything after happened so fast.

CUT TO:

```
Blurred vision. Two blotches above slowly
become clearer. Faces.

DEMORA and Pudersmitt.

                PUDERSMITT (V.O.)
       I brought you here right after.
```

FADE OUT.

Chapter Twenty

The Plan Before Euyrkm

A*ginormous* twinkling chandelier spins from the ceiling in the center of a lavish hotel suite. The walls were draped in holly vines. Artwork on the wall ascended in a stair-step pattern; watercolor and glass paintings, abstract images stretched in between connecting them, a small assortment of sculptures designed as though trying to claw out of the wall, and even a gold-plated miniature piano with the signature of its *most eminent owner and beloved musician. And the amount of furniture in here can fit a museum.*

Amy sat opposite Demora and Pudersmitt at a circular card table near one corner of the vast suite. Amy pulled a card from a deck of cards. "Did it have a face?" She asked, playing a card, then shuffling her hand.

"Face? No. Well, not that I could see." Pudersmitt met Demora's eye and shrugged. "We were only behind it."

"Did you see any other distinctions?"

"I don't remember any." Pudersmitt frowned. He pulled open one of the table's drawers and took out some plastic coins. Slid three over to Amy. "Run me. I do remember one thing. It looked like it wore a crown." "A crown?"

"I'd said so. What?" His last question to Demora was met with an even more annoyed glare from her than before.

Demora tossed some coins towards his side. "Run me. Has it been long enough? I don't see how this game calms you."

Pudersmitt and Amy share a stare. The cautious young man smiled and handed a card to Demora.

No need for him to suffer for me. Amy leaned forward, her hand out. "Demo, I—"

Demora moved further back, out of her reach. "I think we don't need to enable any more of her suicidal experiments."

"I didn't do it on purpose, Demo!"

"So tell me right now that you haven't been working on this deranged, demented, psychotic, cracked, loony—"   "I get it."

"Bonkers, nutty—"

"Alright, I get it."

"Do you?!" Demora's hand slammed the table at the end of her first word. "Have you? Tell me right now, you haven't been trying to do exactly what I asked you not to do and pursue this impossible task of burning out your aura?"

Amy stared at the spot where her hand landed. *Not a dent.* "It's not burning out my aura." She bobbed her head, trying to find the right words. "It's more like a cook."   "A cook?"

"You gather the right ingredients and then—"   "You gain a fever that knocks you straight on your ass, knocked, because one shouldn't be cooking their aura."

"Knocked, blinked, it's all the same. I always come-to."
"Except for when you won't."

"Course I will, Demo, will you stop—"

"Will you stop—" "How about we remember the genuine issue at hand?" Pudersmitt placed a card down to emphasize his point.

The card: Queen of Spades, with a stylistic portrait of Madame Blé.

Demora's unwavering glare stayed on it. "Why do monsters get printed in the paper? Madame Eminent on card decks." **Hark.**

"She won't for long," Pudersmitt assured her with his eyes more than his words. "Got a little backtrack with yesterday's events."

What happened to me? I need to know. Amy sipped her tea with care, swirling her mug with the eye of a well-learned wine taster. "Out for twelve hours, huh?"

Pudersmitt nodded. "We're glad you're here, though. We've been talking about bringing you in." *His usual choice of clothing defies him. Looks like he's been training today.* Dressed down in a pale blue tank top with grey sweats, his muscular physique was now quite apparent as his sweaty arms naturally flexed.

"Bringing me in on what?"

"The plan," he presented with pride, pushing his chest and arms out.

A spot of sweat landed on Amy's arm. Wiped it off. "You've clearly been training hard on it."

"Training? No. Haven't trained since yesterday, I think."

"You don't have to lie. I can see the sweat pouring off of you."

"Not everything is training, Amy." Demora ended flatly, *seeing where this is going, but what is she— Oh! Oh. Oh, ew, no, oh—*

"With me? Here?"

"Don't be weird, Amy. This is one room of many; you're fine."

Amy looked between the two of them. "I don't think I will be."

"Back to the plan," Pudersmitt interjected, coming back to the table with a towel in hand and wiping himself down.

Amy feigned vomiting. "Like seriously, how long ago before I woke up?"

"Anyway." Demora tossed a card at her. "We're going to burn down the Haven."

"You're wha—"

"Only the church." Pudersmitt cut in, keeping his eye on Demora *until she gave him a nod of confirmation.* "When no one's inside. The plan is to draw out Blé. Get her up in arms, and she'll throw a protest about it. She can't help solid publicity."

"Craves it," Demora added, glaring at the playing card with Blé's on it.   Amy watched her. "How do you know she'll do that? And someone's always at the church, remember?"

Pudersmitt nodded. "Well, with the infirmary shut down, the detectives are keeping a tighter leash."

"They shut down the infirmary?"

"And moved all the patients to Lakewood. Blé's addicted to the podium." Pudersmitt drew a box in mid-air and, seconds later, a yellowish-grey box popped into existence. He took the box and turned it to Amy, a webpage displayed on it. "She'll find any reason to grab the stage after an injustice to her cult. Did so here ten years back when someone flooded her prayer room in Brisbane. Or here in '66 when she got locked out of a town hall in the U.S. for visiting too much. She staged a four-day-long protest outside the gates." He pointed out more items on the screen. "Every time, she put on a parade."

"This new tech is killer." Amy flicked the box back towards him, and he caught it. But so what? So what, the old bat throws a parade? And, just gonna say it— don't either of you think that burning down a church is maybe a little drastic, or no? Not to mention collateral damage."

"No one will be inside," Demora answered, *annoyingly.*

"How are you ensuring that?"

"Bugs," Pudersmitt said *matter-of-factly*

as though I'm supposed to know what that means. "They're insects, don't be rude. What about them?"

Pudersmitt got out of his chair like it was Yuletide. "You gave me the brilliant idea. Turns out—wait." He sped over to a backpack on his couch, yanked something out, and then ran back over to them with it concealed within his jacked, chiselled hands. *How frequent does he train his hands? What does he do, hit jagged steel?*

Demora's face gave away a quick look of sympathy before making it stoic once more.

"What's this?" Amy's curiosity bent her forth, despite her uneasy eye on Demo's uncomfortable nature.

"This—" Pudersmitt revealed the object—a jar with two fuzzy slippers—*NO*—

Amy sprang out of her seat, launching her chair into the next wall. She stabbed a finger at the jar, then at Pudersmitt. "You— What the fuck are you doing with those fuckers? I mean, what the fuck?!"

"I know it's strange, but it's perfect." He tapped Demora for support. "Tell her."

Demora side-eyed him, then his jar, *now on the table—* "This is your part of the plan."

"Once you told us about them, I got curious. Father made me take up an insectology excursion for a year. I've gotten great at tracking down nests. Given the old marble landscape of your town, it's the perfect honeypot for these guys." Pudersmitt tapped the jar—

Inside, two baby raccooroaches scatter at his poke of the glass enclosing them, but their furry oval bodies were too bunched up together to move around much. The faint grey bands along their abdomens twitched—twitched faster, like TV static.

Amy's whole body shook away from the sight. Her body fell to the side, and her feet carried her into the suite's kitchen, opening the fridge. She picked out her half-finished glass of water, but it shook in her hand before reaching her mouth. Her lips quivered. She returned the cup to the fridge, slammed the door, and took deep breaths.

"They're gone," Demora's voice called out.

Amy faced the two and the now bare table. "What the fuck?" Made her way slowly from the kitchen back across the room. "Why?"

"Whoever exterminated these lads did a poor job," Pudersmitt said. "I found a small nest just outside town limits before hitting Enfield. Your raccooroaches—"

"They're not <u>mine</u>."

"They enjoy sitting in marble, cooling down from their aggressive feeding habits. Someone forgot to clear all cracks. In another six months, your lot could be seeing another infestation. They won't be here for long. I called a specialist. They'll be here on Tuesday."

"That's a little less than a week. And your plan?"

"It's happening in three days." Demora stood. "We need your answer. Noon, three days from now." "What?"

Demora approached her. "Amy, you've made it clear that you are going to do things your way, despite this being my battle. Now, I've taken the time. I've planned it out. Are you going to help me or not?"

That look in her eye. "Is that even enough time to fill me in? If I choose on the day?"

"It will be."

"Let's say your plan works. Plant the critters. Start the fire. A parade is thrown. Isn't that only helping Blé?"

"She won't be around for long," Demora's monotone voice answered.

Amy stepped closer to her. "Demo, you can't be thinking— we can't—"

"We're going to nab her," Pudersmitt *clarified.* "In one swift move, we snatch and contain her."

"So, kidnap the kidnapper. Sure, just karma. Then what?"

Pudersmitt's face *lost its mojo. It fell onto Demo—* He cleared his throat. Nodded over to Demora. "She won't tell me. But she's promised not to kill or mutilate her."

Demora nodded. "I do promise that. On my aura."

Amy gave a slow nod back. "That's comforting. What are you going to do to her? Or with her?"

Demora smiled. "You'll just have to trust me. Can you?"

She's already made her decision. This isn't happening in three days; it's happening sooner. If I had to take a guess... She's probably planning on doing this a day before the deadline. Sooner, if something else pisses her off. What the hell do you want with Blé, Demo? Amy sighed. "Of course I do."

"Yeah? On your aura?"

"On my aura. Can you make me a promise?"

Demora *wanted to groan. Look at her throat, swallowing it.*

"Depends. I will try my best."

"I need you to promise me not to go after Jamari. No harm or contact."

Demora's nose jerked, cheeks flushed, and her hair jumped on end in small spots only noticeable by her long-time best friend... *but her eyes never blinked.* She nodded. "You've got it, Ames."

She's telling the truth. Never mind how much it hurts her. "Thank you." Amy looked at Pudersmitt.

Demora also clocked him. Raised an eyebrow.

It took him some seconds, but his face gained recognition and he answered, "OH, yes. I will not touch Mr. Eminent. Scout's honour."

"Good." Amy shook her head and regained her seat. "I've still got to figure out what the hell Callisto's One Big Fault is."

"What did you say?" Demo knelt in front of her. "Where'd you hear that?" "It's been all over the cult. They worship over the secret like gold, so it must be important. I thought Kiaixai may have known, but I got nothing. What?"

Demora's eyes searched the floor. "Wherever they held me, damn cult members kept repeating that over and over. Callisto's One Big Fault. Before they let me go, they said it wasn't my fault. Told me it's all in Callisto's One Big Fault. It's one of the few things I can remember, and it's been eating at me."

"I'm gonna find out." Amy took Demo's hands in her own. "Come with me. We can figure it out together."

"I've got to maintain a few things for my plan." Demora pulled away and stood. "Three days, Amy. And if you choose to stay out of it, you won't interfere, right?"

Amy rose to meet her eyes. "I promise."

"Good. See you in three."

Amy stepped outside the closing glass doors of the foreboding *REGALURCHI* hotel and onto the busy Enfield streets north of Square Central. She closed up the white robe she borrowed from the front desk, tight around her, and moved through the crowd of thick coat-wearing citizens. *Season's starting to bite. Not even my aura's warmth is enough.* She fought to keep the long robe from dragging along the ground, to no avail. A **buzz** stopped her momentum, much to the other pedestrians' annoyance.

Amy pulled into the nearest alley and answered her GCID's random call. "Hello?"

"Amy Devine?"   "Yeah, you got her. You sound—"

"It's me. From the infirmary. And the rally. Can you meet me?"

"Orange pigtails?"

"Yes."

Amy checked her surroundings. "Sure. Where are you?"

"Euyrkm."

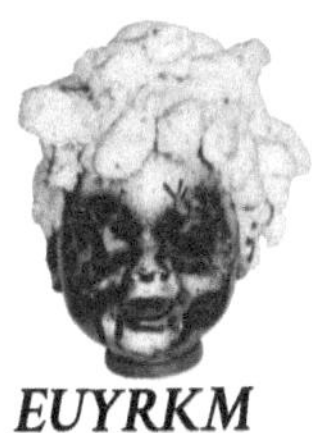

EUYRKM

FADE IN:

EXT. ABOVE EUYRKM - DAY

A dingy green marble wall spirals out of
the ground and around the small community
of low-rise huts. The space between huts
is a maze. Not much plant life inside the
walls, but an abundance outside of them.
Indistinguishable creatures lurk on the
perimeter.

EXT. EUYRKM BORDER - DAY

Someone stands at the point on the wall
that spirals into the ground, facing a
tunnel's path winding to the left.

> CURSE INSIDE MARMI (V.O.)
> **You'll get her killed. You
> selfish little bitch.**

The hoarse voice snickers.

Footsteps from the tunnel.

> CURSE INSIDE MARMI (V.O.)
> **It's not too late. There's still time. Or is this another situation like your mother, where you refuse to listen and she pays the price?**

The sweat on MARMI's face blinds her. She wipes her eyes. Opens them.

Raw, shiny flesh stretched over bone in unnatural folds as the corner of the mouth curled up its permanent heat-etched grimace. The twisted, melted jaw chews on the air. Some more of its teeth fall at Marmi's feet.

Marmi steps back and curls away—but the image is gone.

The footsteps reach their loudest. From the path, AMY emerges.

Marmi watches the smiling newcomer approach.

> MARMI (V.O.)
> I don't know what you did, but… you were standing there in the aftermath. All the crazy patients were down. You had this look in your eye. Peace. Then you passed out.

> AMY (V.O.)
> And you couldn't see much else? No details stood out?

> MARMI (V.O.)
> I wasn't close enough. There were black sparks around me

when you took out the other
patients.

EXT. EUYRKM - DAY

Everything is either bronze or bamboo.
Huts with bronze metal sheets for doors
neighbor each other by inches, all
closed. Down the block's road of pebbles
and dust, arms bend the *flexmetal* sheets
from roof to ground, closing off the last
few huts.

Marmi and Amy walk side by side along the
cement tiles of the road's path.

> MARMI
> Nobody listens to Kiaixai. You
> did.

> AMY
> When someone's screaming in a
> room, it's insane to ignore
> them.

> (off Marmi's look)
> It's a saying my Gma has.
> *Though not sure she believes in
> it anymore.*

> MARMI
> I suppose. They're not keeping
> anyone in the infirmary against
> their will. But I can't explain
> the feeling I always have. It's
> like I wanted to leave less and
> less every day.

GRAVITY OF DEVOTION

                    AMY
How'd you know I was talking to
Kiaixai? You were at least
eleven cells down that hall.
You could hear us?

                    MARMI
Almost everything.

                    (Smirks)
I can tell it's been nagging at
you. The way you look at me…

                    AMY
               (Averts eyes)
Have you told—

                    MARMI
I haven't told anyone about
your snatched friend. Read
about her kidnapping online.
Thought she looked familiar.

                    AMY
Familiar how?

                    MARMI
She's been down here in Euyrkm
once or twice.

                    AMY
Visiting someone?

Marmi huffs out an air of frustration.

                    MARMI
I don't know. I don't follow
her around.

                    AMY (V.O.)
The hell is Demo doing in
Euyrkm?

          (clocks Marmi's mild temper)
In the Infirmary, ever hear
anything noteworthy?

                    MARMI
No. Every second I spent in
that hell-for-a-clinic, I
listened to every word spoken.
Waiting for an opening.

                    AMY
Did you ever try to escape?

                    MARMI
I hate admitting it, but the
cult's treatments are actually
effective. Outside the infirmary,
I couldn't control the visions.
Even if I could, I knew I'd end
up dying of fright or going
insane.

                    AMY
How are the visions now?

                    MARMI (V.O.)
*She's unhinged. That power she
used to wipe out those psycho
patients in the infirmary.
Still, I wonder. Is her power
stronger than this curse inside
of me?*

Amy watches her, waiting for a reply.

                    MARMI
I haven't had one since last
week.

          CURSE INSIDE MARMI (V.O.)
Good. Girl.

MINUTES LATER

They stand feet away from one of the
closed-off huts.

>   MARMI
> You'll have to excuse them. The
> community is not fond of
> outsiders.

>   AMY
> I can't imagine why.

>   MARMI
> Wasn't always like this, I'm
> told. You change with the
> times.
>
>   (fully faces Amy)
> Are you ill? You're sweating,
> and you're getting pale.

>   AMY
> Oh, no, I'm not ill at all. I'm
> solid.

>   *CURSE INSIDE MARMI (V.O.)*
>   *(singsong voice)*
> **She's lyyyyyying.**

Marmi steps up to Amy's face. Her hands
grab over her shoulders without touching.

>   MARMI
> I need to know. Are—You— "ill"?

>   *CURSE INSIDE MARMI (V.O.)*
>   *(singsong voice)*

**Course she is, you dim cunt! Look at
her! That girl hasn't eaten anything solid
in 90 days!**

Amy backs away from her.

> AMY
> (V.O.)
> *She means cursed.*
>
> (shakes head)
>
> No, I'm not. Are you okay?
>
> CURSE INSIDE MARMI (V.O.)
> (singsong voice)
> **Listen to your mum. Skin her now, save her for later. You'd wear her flesh well, my love.**

Marmi got closer.

> MARMI
> I CANNOT risk bringing you into any of these huts if you're ill. These people have suffered enough and I'll be damned if one or more of them gets ill because of my carelessness in letting an outsider come here. Now, I'll ask you one more time: Are. You. Ill?

Amy relaxes her arms at her sides.

> AMY
> I understand your concern. I swear to you I am solid. Not ill at all. It's...

EXT. BLUEBAN'S HUT - SAME TIME

A finger bends the bottom of the bronze sheet door a few inches off the ground. A grey eye creeps from the pitch black within the hut.

                    AMY (O.S.)
          It's just that I've always been
          afraid of corpses.

The eye slips from view. The finger lets
the sheet fall close.

BACK OUTSIDE

                    AMY
          It's nothing to do with the
          concept of death. I've never
          been sure why I get so afraid.
          I see myself sometimes, dead.
          Not a flinch. Or a whisper
          outside of final bodily
          functions. At times, my corpses
          follow me around. Laughing.
          Taunting me with my worst
          fears. Now that I think about
          it, it's the fact that when I
          am really gone, there won't be
          any laughter or talking or
          moving. No more traveling
          around town, as I please. No
          more secrets. No more pain. No
          love. Not even death, well, at
          least a second time if I come
          back the first. It's all just
          gone. Everything about me,
          everything I knew. Speaking out
          loud about now shits my pants.
          I've never even talked this
          much about it, not even to my
          best friend.

                  (V.O. to herself)
          *There you go, Devine. Deep
          breath in.*

            (takes it, then through
            pursed lips)

Out.

> (releases)
> *You're alright, Devine. You're
> okay.*

Amy continues to steady her breathing—
Marmi, also the first to see me talk
myself through this exercise.

A silent Marmi watches until the ritual
is done. Eyes blinking *on a schedule.
Trying too hard to be normal.*

Marmi bows.

> MARMI
> Thank you for saving my friend.
> If anyone else had found her
> outside the Haven that day,
> odds are great I would have
> never seen her again.

> AMY
> It was the right thing to do.

> MARMI
> Where does your "right" thing
> draw the line?

Amy's right thumb and index finger rub
together in a circle.

> AMY
> I'd rather not find out.

Marmi turns her back, facing the hut.

> MARMI
> Come on. When we're inside, get
> right to the point.

She leads the way. Amy lingers before following.

INT. BLUEBAN'S HUT - DAY

The silhouettes of Marmi and Amy stand inside the dark hut, the blinding sun outside behind them.

                    CORP MOTHER (O.S.)
          Close the door.

Marmi pulls down the door, leaving them without light.

                    CORP MOTHER (O.S.)
          Any more sunlight and I could
          eat my flesh straight off the
          bone.

Snickers in the dark. The outline of the motherly, cautious voice appears on the right. A growing thin line of soft light grows all over the room, revealing the edges of a couch or two, some tables, a pet dish…

The outlines of the hut's inhabitants— *five, no six of them— come into view.* Their eyes are most visible; all of them shiny grey balls, peering at their *hopeful guest?*

A spotlight blasts over Marmi and Amy's heads.

Amy thrusts her hand forward.

                    AMY
          It's lovely to meet you. I'm

Amy.

The shape of a big, beautiful woman leans forward on the widest of the three couches. CORP MOTHER. Her face— what I can see— is painted like a star's. She snickers in delight.

> CORP MOTHER
> Lovely! Did she say lovely to meet? Lovely? Wow! You can call me Corp Mother! Well, I guess we're best friends then, after all, no? What say you, family?

~~Someone~~ (confirmed: SHELBY) on the far left points at Amy.

> SHELBY
> She's an outsider. She can't be trusted.

A swift arm knocks into him. The tall one **shrieks** in joy.

> TALL SHRIEKER
> You're a— (**shrieks**) riot! (**shrieks**) We will be her friend, won't we?

His shriek continues, and his devilish glance is shared with an even taller set of eyes across the room.

> TALLEST EYES
> I'll be her best friend.

A leather-skinned toddler crawls closest to Amy. *With every breath, his eyes rotate in their sockets…*

> LEATHERED-SKIN TODDLER
> Can we take her to the playpen?
> I will show you all of my toys.

The family laughs. *Longer than comfortable. Am I dead meat here?*

> AMY
> I understand one of your own might have some information I'm looking for. About Callisto's One Big Fault.

> LEATHERED-SKIN TODDLER
> So what if they did? What is it to you? Could I play with you then?

> TALL SHRIEKER
> Easy— (**shrieks**) there, chum. (**shrieks**) If we keep her here any longer, we might have to— (**shrieks**)

> TALLEST EYES
> I'm not impressed. Let's get started now.

LEATHERED-SKIN TODDLER	TALL SHRIEKER
Excellent. What a fine day is churning.	I second that. No need to waste any more fluid breath.

Corp Mother raised two fingers that clawed at the air.

> CORP MOTHER
> Enough!

The sharp bite of her tone echoes between them all.

                    CORP MOTHER (CON'T)
Amy, huh? What a common name.
The one I've given you isn't
mine. You're worth it outranked
here. Lucky you got this far.
You'll be luckier if we let you
leave. You can call me Corp
Mother because your fear of
corpses still keeps your bed
wet at night. Whether that's
piss or tears is your concern,
honey.

Snickers.

                    AMY (V.O.)
*So Marmi's not the only one who
heard me. They think they've
got an advantage over me
because of my fear. They're
only half right. I'll play into
it.*

Amy leans into them with a clenched fist.

                    AMY
               (clears throat)
I w-will not argue with you nor
cause you harm. I s-simply—

          LEATHERED-SKIN TODDLER & TALL
          SHRIEKER
W-w-w-w-wa-s-s-ssss!

               TALL SHRIEKER
             (**shrieks**)
She's a regular Aristotle!

Corp Mother raises a hand.

Silence.

                    CORP MOTHER
          What if we do know what
          Callisto's One Big Fault is and
          we don't tell you? Will you
          kill us then?

                    AMY
          No. Never.

                    CORP MOTHER
          Am I not worthy of your
          bloodshedding capabilities?

Amy froze, breath caught in her throat.

Corp Mother's faded grey mouth creeps
into the spotlight. Three-quarters of it
hangs down on one side, teeth always
showing. She chews. Smiles.

                    CORP MOTHER (CONT'D)
          You BEFS. I've seen the
          way your lot so easily
          slaughter my people. Tell
          me, child. Have you
          counted the seconds it
          takes for your blood to
          pool in your noggin? Here.
          Let me show you.

Something CLAMPS Amy's feet stiff. The
world spins around her— metal clinking—

Till she's upside down. So is Corp
Mother. The two of them surrounded by
darkness, with small hopes of light
peeking from holes above them. The smell
of rot invades the nostrils.

                    CORP MOTHER (CONT'D)
          Too much blood at the back of
          our heads— boom! Rupture. Takes

me three minutes before I have
to be rushed to our medical
practitioner to undo what
damage can be undone.

                AMY
Why are we—

                CORP MOTHER
Why's it so important to you?!

                AMY
What?

                CORP MOTHER
Callisto's One Big Fault?
What's your aim?

                AMY
I'm sorry, I can't say. It
could get the wrong people in
trouble. Some, very close to
me. But it's important that I
find out. Please. I must—

                CORP MOTHER
You must know nothing! You dare
ask us to betray a secret of
The Light?! Amongst you relics
of human life, Callisto's Light
are THE ONLY ones who see Her
vision for the future and show
us the respect we deserve. To
betray a secret of The Light is
a treacherous act! I hear you
have already stirred up trouble
in the Haven Church. You're
just another outsider looking
to rip the church open from
within—

                AMY
I'm an understudy! I've been

          learning—

                    CORP MOTHER
          QUIET!

                    MARMI (O.S.)
          She's telling the truth!

Corp Mother's eyes zip back and forth
across the floorboard above them. Smiles.

                    CORP MOTHER
          Ah! So she's a traitor in their
          ranks?

                    (Eyes return to Amy)
          How even more delicious—

                    STRONG, WEATHERED VOICE
          Enough of your Prey Pen! Let
          her up!

Corp Mother growls.

The world spins again—

Amy drops to her knees, back inside the
hut's front room. Eyes each of the undead
licking their teeth at her. Spots two new
faces exiting a door behind them.

The undead teenager, OCTOBER, leads with
a familiar bandaged and bruised face,
walking up beside her.

                    AMY
                    (Slowly rises)
          Stella.

STELLA's busted lips curl up into a
smile.

                    STELLA
          It's nice to see you again,

dear. I'm sorry for the harsh
nature of our hosts, but we
live in troubling times.

                    AMY
What happened to you?

                    STELLA
Ah.

Her feet labor themselves into
an open solo couch where she
plops down next to Corp Mother.

                    CORP MOTHER
That is none of your concern,
outsider.

                    STELLA
This outsider happens to be the
granddaughter of Rezna Devine.

GASPS and a **SHRIEK** from the gallery. All
the undead eyes in the room stare at Amy
without blinking. Except for Corp Mother.
She looks… disappointed?

                    CORP MOTHER
The question is… is she as
powerful?

                    OCTOBER
            (points at Amy with a grin)
She broke all the windows at the
Jadesfeld detective headquarters. With
her bare hands.

Corp Mother raises her half-torn eyebrow.

                    CORP MOTHER
I can break a window just fine.

                    AMY

I was… under duress.

                    OCTOBER
And the Angels speak of a girl
who wears her GCID on the
outside, who saved the children
from Cloudy last year.

                    AMY
I didn't—

Amy's eyes get lost in the *accusation*.

Corp Mother takes a long look at Stella.
Stella responds with a small nod.

                    CORP MOTHER
Still. No matter the past. Is
she strong enough for this?

                    AMY
Strong enough for what?

                    CORP MOTHER
The Pirate.

                    STELLA
I took on Milard three days
ago.

                    AMY
You found him?

                    STELLA
                    (nods)
He wasn't too keen on
remembering what he took from
me. But I gave him no choice.
If only I had a bit more
strength. I could've ended him.
That bottomless bastard.

                    AMY
Gma told me you were one of the
strongest fighters she knew.

                  STELLA
Oof. Past tense.

             (chuckles)
I've won a tournament or two.
Give me your hand.

Amy hesitates. Breaks the tiny distance
between them and lays her hand in
Stella's.

They watch each other. Amy starts to look
off, but her head snaps back onto the
chuckling old woman.

                    AMY
     That...

             (V.O.)
Her aura's incredible!
Forceful. Trembling up my hand
and coursing through my body.
I've never felt this sort of
power before. Not even from
Gma. Stella can't be stronger.
Can she?

             (shakes the sting off her
             hand)
It's very impressive.

                  STELLA
Oh, no need to sugarcoat. It's
nothing compared to the Devine
bloodline.

                    AMY
          But...

                    (V.O.)
          *She's joking, right? If I
          weren't so paranoid about
          flipping through the floorboards
          again, my legs would give way
          to the mini quakes her aura's
          shelling out. Hell, if she
          wanted to, she could flip me
          either way.*

                    STELLA
          When my kids were born, the
          only training I was interested
          in was learning how I can be a
          better mother. After they were
          gone, I gave up everything. I
          got hooked on trying to locate
          this predator. And I almost had
          him. By Callisto's grace, I
          almost had him.

Stella groans, face grimacing in pain.

                    STELLA (CONT'D)
          This pirate bastard is tough.
          He's not even an aura wielder,
          but his innate power is strong.
          Considerable enough to match
          Rezna, I suppose. Maybe. The
          years are unkind to us all.

                    CORP MOTHER
              (nods over to Amy)
          And she's the answer? BWA!

She laughs. Amy frowns. Fists tighten as
the sharp laughter continues to assault
the eardrums in the room.

                    AMY
What am I missing here? What do
you want me to do?

October steps out from the shadows with
prayer hands reaching out to Amy.

                  OCTOBER
Marmi said you can help us out.
Bring him down. For good.

Amy stares at her blankly for some
seconds before her face fights off a range
of emotions. Looks at Stella as though
punched in the stomach. Switches her
sight to Corp Mother.

                    AMY
You wouldn't even hear me out
before, and now… I should get
my hands dirty for you, that
it?

The matriarch of living corpses leans
back, lounges in her seat.

                CORP MOTHER
I can't help it since your
people never hear us. Deaf ears
are a kindness. Now, you've
been here long enough. You know
the price. Do what needs doing.
Doing otherwise could mean my
true extinction.

        THE OTHER CORPSES IN THE ROOM
Not the true extinction!

                  OCTOBER
Mum, she can do this. I believe
it!

                    AMY
          What are you expecting me to
          do?

Corp Mother's crooked smile drools.

                    CORP MOTHER
          Shelby! Where's Shelby?

                    TALL SHRIEKER
          He's here— oh.

                    TALLEST EYES
          Where'd Shelby go?

                    OCTOBER
          Shelby?

                    LEATHERED-SKIN TODDLER
          Think he went to the loo.

                    CORP MOTHER
          Shelby! Dammit I need my…

                    TALL SHRIEKER
          I could get it, Ma.

                    CORP MOTHER
          You know only Shelby holds it.
          One sec—

Corp Mother struggles to get out of her
seat. Her family tries to help, but she
smacks all of their help away and manages
to stand on her own. She rotates her
pelvis, holds her hips, and shuffles
towards a dresser on one side of the
room.

                    CORP MOTHER
          Damn hip's gone rot before the
          legs. If I have to grab it, the

journey'll kill me.

> LEATHERED-SKIN TODDLER
> Let us, Mum. We can—

> CORP MOTHER
> Never! Now shut—

She gives him the zip mouth motion.

Stella shakes her head.

> STELLA
> You should really train these children soon. It's getting too dangerous out here. Leaving it to you and Shelby alone... can't imagine if...

> CORP MOTHER
> Keep your cleanflesh ideas to your own, Stella. I know what's best for my children. They're still here, aren't they?

In a blink, Stella presses Corp Mother against the wall with one arm into her chest. The arm threatens in small quakes to shoot upwards.

> STELLA
> I may not have much left in me, but I've got more than enough, no less than a fourth of my strength... and it's all I need to wipe your head clean off right now.

> MARMI
> Hey, easy gyals...

Marmi's face *is shitting herself. By the*

look in Corp Mother's eyes— scared but defiant— this uneasy partnership may be reaching its boiling point.

                    AMY
          Stella, let's keep a cool head,
          yeah?

Stella releases her death grip.

                    STELLA
          Amy, do me a favour and check
          for her little brat outside.
          He's known to wander.

Amy makes her way.

                    AMY
          Right.

Marmi mouths, "Thanks", as Amy approaches.

Amy's eyebrows raise in acknowledgement.

She steps on a floorboard.

The world spins—

Metal clinks—

The smell of rot flushes her once again.

                    AURA AMY (V.O.)
               Host, watch out!

A warm blanket of white aura caresses the neck and back of Amy's head.

The darkness jumps at her from behind— angled teeth open—

SLICE!

Amy's neck yanks up— she turns— her fist

coming with her—

SMASHES a nose— something sprays all over her—

The world spins— metal clinking—

Amy drops onto her butt. Her eyes, nostrils, and mouth wide. Her entire upper body is covered in reddish-brown and grey liquids. She's frozen. Not breathing— *I wouldn't dare!*

LATER, SOMEWHERE OUTSIDE

Amy, fully clothed, stands under a shower, water wiping away her filth. Similar vacant expression on her face.

LATER, BACK INSIDE HUT

Amy stands in front of Corp Mother, her children, and Stella.

They stand in front of a tied-up Shelby sitting on the floor, grilling them all.

> CORP MOTHER
> It seems you've forgotten the true meaning of Euyrkm, my son. How long have you worked with the pirate?

Shelby spits at her feet. *Instinctively* flinches.

Corp Mother's sad face just watches him.

> CORP MOTHER
> I won't hit you. Son, if nothing else, please help me stop what he's doing to our people.

                    SHELBY
Our people are fools! Always
have been. Meaning of Euyrkm my
ass. We are Angels. We
outnumber the cleanflesh at this
point, no? We can have
everything! Take it from them.
Devour them and shove them into
boxes for later food for our
people. They've had the Earth
long enough and look what
they've done with it!

                    TALL EYES
You're disgusting.

                    SHELBY
At least the pirate's doing
something!

He cackles. Thrashes in his bondage so
hard his skin pushes and tears off from
the tightness against the rope.

                    SHELBY (CONT'D)
The piss-poor undead. That's
all we ever were to the rest of
the World. Stopping Milard
ruins our one chance to gain
strength over them.

He throws a head towards the *cleanflesh*
humans in the room. Locks eyes with Amy.

                    SHELBY (CONT'D)
I almost had your head. I don't
know how you dodged that. The
luck...

Amy holds the back of her neck.

BACK OF HER NECK: A long scratch goes end
to end.

Amy looks at the smear of blood on her finger. Locks eyes with Shelby.

                    CORP MOTHER
          Oh, Shelby…

She drops to her knees in front of him. Gazes into him with teary eyes.

                    CORP MOTHER (CONT'D)
          I've got Rachel.

Shelby's cackles get caught in his throat. He breathes harsh air every other second. His eyes travel the room, then back to his mother.

                    SHELBY
          What do you— She's dead. The
          true extinction got her.

Corp Mother shakes her head. Shelby's teary eyes stay with his mother.

                    SHELBY (CONT'D)
          I saw it.

                    CORP MOTHER
        She survived.

Corp Mother takes something out of her pocket and shows it to him.

Shelby goes wild.

                    SHELBY
          NO! NO—RACHEL! NOOOOO! You hear
          me, NO!

                    CORP MOTHER
          I know you switched it out with
          the real one some time ago. The
          lies end here, Shelby.

                    SHELBY
          FINE! Let me see her! Let me—

                    CORP MOTHER
          The pirate, Shelby. Where's the
          pirate?

Shelby searches the floor for answers.

                    CORP MOTHER (CONT'D)
          Or, I rip Rachel apart.

                    SHELBY
          NO! Wait! Wait wait wait— I
          don't know where the pirate is,
          he never tells me. We meet in
          the forest most the time, but I
          know he'll be at another
          initiation ceremony in a few
          nights. That's all I know,
          please, mother! Where is she?!

Corp Mother stands.

                    CORP MOTHER
          You'll never know.

She turns and walks away from him. She
nods for the others to exit.

                    SHELBY
          Oh, whatever the pirate does
          doesn't stop in your shit town
          or the next over. It will never
          end. It's worldwide. I've seen
          how they protect Milard. You
          can't touch him! Once he's done
          here, it's on to the next area.
          Not like you can stop him. Look
          what he did to her.

                    (Nods to Stella. Locks
                    eyes with Amy.)

And you're less experienced. Smaller. Naive. You think everything's going to be alright. You haven't grown enough or lived enough life to know better. I sympathize for you. Me eating your head wasn't personal, lovely. It was a kindness. Just look at you. Battered internally.

(Sniffs)
There are just some things we can sniff out that the highly regarded cleanflesh can't comprehend. You're wasting your time with this pursuit of the cult. They're probably covering up for the bloke. Power is everything. My people may banish me from Euyrkm, but I will be accepted into another community of Angels. After all, there's no prison to lock me up.

Amy's chest puffs up, and she stalks towards him with clenched fists.

SHELBY (CONT'D)
Once the Angels are strong enough, we'll rip everything from you. Then we'll rip you, children and all.

(Snickers)
I once watched Milard crush an 8-year-old witness'—

Corp Mother TWISTS and RIPS Shelby's head

off. Tosses it at her feet. STOMPS on it.

> TALL SHRIEKER
> Euyrkm, Ma! We don't kill our
> own!

Corp Mother gives him a lazy eye.

> CORP MOTHER
> We also don't rape and murder
> the innocent. Especially not
> children. Clean this up.

She moves right up to a still-huffing Amy.

> CORP MOTHER
> Now I've lost a child because
> of you. Here.

She rushes something into Amy's hand.
Squeezes it in her hand.

> CORP MOTHER (CONT'D)
> That's enough trust for
> decades. From Euyrkm!
>
> (points behind her, at
> October)
> You may have saved my daughter,
> but I do not trust you,
> cleanflesh.

Amy unclenches the softness in her hand.

> AMY
> (*SEES IT*, Drops it)
> Fuck!

Corp Mother catches it before it hits the
floor.

> CORP MOTHER
> Don't you dare drop it! It's
> sacred.

                    STELLA
          Well if you give someone a
          rotting member unexpectedly,
          you can expect them to drop it.

Corp Mother stuffs it in Amy's hand again.

Amy takes it. Pockets it without looking
at it.

                    AMY
          Is that…

                    CORP MOTHER
          Rachel's dried big toe. It'll
          get you passage back here at
          the gate.

                    AMY
          I didn't see any gate coming
          in.

                    CORP MOTHER
          That's because you had help.

Marmi shrinks against the wall.

                    AMY
          How will any of your people get
          back inside without this?

                    CORP MOTHER
          Why would we leave to go out
          there with your kind?

Amy looks off. *Right*.

                    CORP MOTHER (CONT'D)
          You want your precious
          information? Bring us the
          pirate's head on a platter. And
          the clock's ticking! Our flesh

decays daily. If it weren't for
our spirit, we'd rot quicker
than the hate we get.

EXT. EUYRKM - DAY

Undead neighbors leave their huts and
look down the road.

In the distance, Amy, Stella, and Marmi
make their way towards the outskirts of
the community.

INT. BLUEBAN'S HUT - SAME

Corp Mother and October gaze out their
door.

Behind them, the undead children mop,
sweep, and reorganize the room.

> CORP MOTHER
> You can find out what the big
> secret is for the girl? Tell me
> you can.

> OCTOBER
> I can find out.

> CORP MOTHER
> You better. Or else she'll come
> back expecting. Doubt she'll
> try to be our friend then.

> MARMI (O.S.)
> Why do we need her?

MARMI appears from behind them.

> MARMI
> I'm controlling the curse's
> power better everyday.

Corp Mother points outside the door to where the Other Marmi, Amy and Stella disappear around a corner.

                    CORP MOTHER
          Your illusion is clever. We sit
          tight. Let the girl risk
          herself and if she can't get it
          done, then we will.

                    OCTOBER
          She will.

                    CORP MOTHER
               (Looks at her)
          You're full of belief, child.
          Keep that.

FADE OUT.

After Euyrkm

*T*hree days. Demo gave me three days.

A day before, Amy and Stella stood outside the gates of Euyrkm, unknowingly constructing what would be their last conversation for a very long time, but it was also one of their most important ones...

"You best keep your grandmother out of this."

"Stella, what were they referring to? What is true extinction?"

"The true extinction is what they believe happens from a void, where the soul is put out for good."

"That's impossible. Aura doesn't... disappear. It becomes part of chairs and trees, and mostly just wanders after you're gone."

"That is fact. I've even heard of a special place in the States where souls congregate. Still, the Angels believe it can be extinguished as well. The meaning of Euyrkm, I take it, you're unfamiliar"

"I researched. Euyrkm means life beyond life."

"It has a few other meanings. The one Corp Mother meant is "never eat man". You must never repeat that. With the perceived weakness that meaning exhibits, the outside world would eat them alive. Fear is the only thing that keeps the Angels safe. It's a bit superstitious to me, but I empathise. Who am I to devalue the beliefs of another? I wish we could all recognise each other's breaths and that we are all still living so long as we feel. I can trust you to keep Euyrkm's

secrets quiet?"

"Of course."

"I knew so. You are the spawn of Rezna Devine. She's worried for you. Told me you and Ms. Demora disappeared for a few days."

Sigh. "I needed to get away for a bit. Demo too. Gma hasn't been home since I've gotten back. Has she said anything else about my delinquency?"

"No, and no worries, I'm not here to report for side A or B. After the year you've had, not sure I'd leave my residence either."

"..."

"Amy, when will you start to realise what you've done is your strength?"

"What do you mean?"

"Well, for context, I've chased the pirate down so hard for my children. And to stop him from causing further damage to innocence. He's raped and pillaged his way to a position of power. He victimises the Angels and calls it a service to Callisto. Uses their unique qualities to expand his empire. Somehow, he's drawing from their strengths to increase his own. Draining their bodies. Mangled Angel corpses, turning up in the open. No shame, no remorse from that bastard. Truth is, I know your grandmother could take him out. However, she is getting older, and the battle may just kill her. She is trying to avoid getting involved, at least physically. I have tried to help by giving fragments of information to the detectives anonymously. But they don't care about the undead. To outright name the pirate is suicide. Learning how deeply connected he is— **scoff** —and knowing he's a part of Callisto's light... He'd be gone before they could find him."

"And how exactly do the Angels expect me to capture him?"

"Trust me when I say I was against sending you on this mission, but they outnumbered me. But a deal with an Angel is a deal set in stone. What I suggest? Avoid physical confrontation. Trap him. When he's caught, you call me. I'll do the rest."

"How am I supposed to trap him?"

"You've done it before."

"Clou— That was different. And I can't split my aura again."

"Oh no, there's no need for that at all. After Cloudy, your

Grandmother told me your innate abilities have yet to reach their limit."

— In a bubble of flustering thoughts, Amy stops walking. Her gaze bores into the older woman's broad back, the muscles showing through creases in the swamp grey fabric. —

"She said that?"

"Milard, the pirate's beliefs run so deep within him that they've convinced him he is some sort of deity. Now his actions contradict his vision. Don't make his mistake. See your vision."

"I... I don't have a vision."

DAY 2

Amy's gaze staggered off center as she remembered some of Stella's last words from the previous day.

"Learn from your enemy. What cuts you most inside? What vile thought makes you turn and scratch at your skull, wanting to solve but can't find the way? Think about the things that possess you deeper than some sick, vengeful spirit ever could."

A list formed in her head as Amy winced at her building tears that nearly won their exit.

"Are you listening to me?" The sharp stare of her grandmother closed in on her, the heat from Rezna's mouth a minty fluster up Amy's nose.

Their hour-long argument this evening had lost most of its robust punches and digs at one another for who should feel this way or that way, or what could have been done— all the usual arguments came to the table. However, one new piece of information gave Rezna the most scorching rise. Amy realized she had hurt her grandmother, tugging at an immeasurable scar buried inside.

Rezna's voice cracked out, "How dare you?"

DAY 1

Twenty-seven hours before this *delightful* conversation, Amy woke up impressed with the nine hours of sleep she got. The evening, quiet, with a household still free of Rezna Devine, didn't feel as empty as Amy imagined it would. *It usually feels so empty when Gma's not home. Maybe I've gotten over that. Just feels so full right now. Clustered.*

Her GCID buzzed on her bedroom desk *again*. *Fuck.* She grabbed it, waved her hand on top, and a ziccolit screen expanded in front of her. Incoming messages rolled in:

```
Jamari: Ay, I let everyone know to be there
              on time.

 Your boy's got an early morning gig.

 My sis'll send me the deets in a few.

        Hope to see you there!
```

Amy threw her GCID across the desk. Flinched in annoyance as it slid off and landed with a **clang** on the floor. *Jamari keeps pushing for info on my background, but still no meeting with Blé. Perhaps he doesn't trust me enough yet. Not even sure I can face that woman right now. Certainly no time to hang out with the old prison gang. Besides, Demo won't be there. Too busy planning her church fire. Fuck that's bleak. When did we start burning churches? I'm still not convinced she'll go through with it.*

Her GCID buzzed.

How could I face them, anyway? Every student of Graves outclasses me in one or more ways. I was a joke for the entire Prison Games. Lost so much, some to better players—

Hideko Ang's sneering face occupied her mind.

—some convincing players. Little bitch ass Ang. She caught a glimpse of the *Hallow's Journey* book lying on her bed and returned her eye to it. *Not a total loss. It's an entertaining read, at least.* She buried her face into her arms atop her desk. *I've slept so long, yet I'm still so tired. Finding Milard. How? Let's say I catch him. Great job, Ames. Now call up Stella and she'll do the rest. In her condition, what if she's unable? Autofalls onto me.*

"Bring us the pirate's head on a platter."

Amy paces in her room, the resulting rumination lasting

for about three hours before she *came to my senses. I've got to act. Bring the Angels the pirate, and they'll let me in on Callisto's One Big Fault. It's got to be the key. Why so hush-hush about it? It's the best chance I've got at stopping the cult before Demora arsons them out.*

Amy turned in her chair to face the webpage on her ziccolit wall. She asked Creaevix to scroll the current page and "initiate hand gestures, please." *The cult has a history of using code names for coordinates.*

She opened the drawer under her desk and pulled her journal from it. Jotted. *Mapping out the coordinates for Callisto's One Big Fault leads me to a location on a whole other continent. That's malark— nonsense. Currently, three missing cases in Jadesfeld. Where would the cult keep them? If not, the now-closed infirmary. All patients moved to local hospitals. At least something good came from that venture. Can the same be said for my shadow form? What does it look like?*

—Marmi's hard stare—
Black sparks.
—Deklance's worrisome face—
Crown.
—E'oné's quivering eyes—
A face. Mean.
Black sparks.
Crown.
A face. Mean.
Take down Milard. Within their ranks.
Impossible.
Simply won't happen.
I could go back to the Haven. See the aftermath of the Infirmary incident.
Don't go back.
No go.
I may run into Milard. If he's even there. Never saw him once.
Fool's game.
Or maybe I did and was too stupid to realize. Amy clamped the

side of her head with her scarred right hand. A tear **bubbled** on the hammock of her bottom eyelid. *I should have died the day I met Cloudy.*

{—In the middle of an open field of greenery, Amy stood with her eyes closed against the bustling winds around her—}

I should have just died.

{—The blunt winds ripped flowers and grass all around her—}

And let him use me as a vessel for his rage.

{—Gathering winds ball up and shoot straight into Amy's open mouth—}

Amy stared at her scar. "Why won't you go away?" She sighed. "Doesn't matter." *I chose my path.*

Truth is, ever since the Prison Games, my blinking spells have gotten even more erratic and random. They happen so fast once I recover. It's like nothing happened. I noticed those tiny pockets of missing time, regardless. Did my interaction with other aura users worsen my condition?

Amy tore the page out that she had just written on. Crumpled it in her hand. *No.* Uncrumpled the page and flattened it out on the desk. Placed it back where it came and closed the journal, leaving the edges of the ripped page sticking out. *Leave it as a reminder to myself.*

"Amy, when will you start to realise what you've done is your strength?"

Amy removed her comfy T-shirt and sweats and got dressed in knee-cut black denims and her fuckery shirt. *I don't know if that's true. I've got to be ready. This is where I'm at. No matter how I got here. I'll bring Milard down.* "Talk a big game, but you're stuck behind her front door, Devine. Creaevix, track all physical activity and provide me with a report by the numbers exactly one day from now. Track the usuals."

Understood. Tracking your activity now.

She spent the next two hours practicing the same side kick and cross punch, alternating sides. Sat in the middle of her bedroom floor after reading the book gifted by Rezna. "No limitation as limitation." She scoured the Internet for more books by the Sifu philosopher and studied digital texts. Highlighted the most potent points to her while ordering and then eating a burrito bowl from her favorite Mexican restaurant in Endfield—*they have all the best spots. I'd be a pinched-penny away from poverty if I lived any closer.* With a full belly, she managed to get onto and laid out atop her home's roof, breathing deep as an audiobook delving into the history of Callisto's Light played from a ten-year-old ZiccoCube travel-sized device that rested beside her head. She drew and took notes in her journal under the ghostly moon glow.

(things learned about the cult

- Function as a traveling church, and there are laws protecting and governing them

- Blé has a World Committee block of the highest level, keeping her history before the age of 18 confidential

- Droûx has been known to act as head of security without an official title

- Settled disputes with public spars, challenges ,games

- Third wealthiest organization in the World)

More research *and distractions* on the little-known/barely documented fighting style of the Frightciety of scared-to-fight fighters, Asian royal titles, apparition sightings, hummutt psychology, luggerauto advancements in the past five years, rare swellboo weaponry, *zilch on the fabled Soul Game we played in the Prison Games,* Animalia Gems scores across the league, the lambyolks' connection to evohumans, latest Mickelspiff incarcerations...

Morning arrived with thirty new pages filled with her musings.

Scattered throughout her day, She went through a plethora of motions:

At different times, performed sets of bicep curls, lunges, Romanian deadlifts, leg raises, and rounds of squats.

Ignored Creaevix's warnings about physical overload.

Opened up Rezna's chest of games and played chess first, then Go with Creaevix as her opponent, with levels maximized to mimic professional-level players across the World.

—Gyaads sway and cheer as The Singer performs in Enfield Square—

Used the basement's messy layout of storage obstacles and artifacts as a mini track she ran for short sessions at a time.

—A man with a mangled face laughs, only one side of his mouth able to move—

Hit some bodyweight exercises here and there.

—Rezna's body disappears behind black clouds—

Ate when She got starving.

*—**Squelch!** Pristine plops on her bloody head—*

Swallowed nineteen fluid ounces of water every 3 hours.

—Cheneley the Undead juggles his severed head—

Your physical activity report is ready.

By the mark of twenty-four hours later, Creaevix read out her stats in the kitchen:

300 pushups

500 situps

600 crunches.

314,914 steps...

The front door opened.

Amy looked back from the kitchen table.

Rezna Devine emerged from the shadows of the hall.

DAY 2

Rezna knew. And despite Amy's insistence that She was doing it to keep track of the cult's activities and the fact that—

"They took Demora. They're the ones!"

"I heard you the first time." Rezna's voice echoed throughout the basement. She took a seat in her favorite chair and massaged her forehead.

Amy moved towards her with intensity in every step. "Then why am I always screaming on the inside when we talk?"

"You don't get it. You do not get it. You never do." Rezna's eyes regarded *the stranger* in front of her. "This isn't a one-way deal. You gave her access. She's learned as much about you as you have about her, I'm sure of it."

"You can't know that!"

"I've made a life of needing to know how my enemy thinks. You've given away our leverage."

"But the pirate who hurt Stella's kids also hides within their ranks."

"And he must remain there, for if all you're telling me is true, this battle goes deeper than we've anticipated or are equipped for. If they find out what we really are…"

"They won't. Not if we move with caution. I…" For the third time tonight, Amy almost spilt the tea. She wrestled with whether to tell her grandmother about the plan to capture Milard. *She'll try to lock me in this house somehow. Not tryna repeat my fifteenth birthday. How can I make her understand? Nothing's more important right now than stopping The Light.* "I know why you're so angry with me about Cloudy."

Rezna groaned. "Ugh, again with the doll. We've been through this. The longer you give that doll residence in your mind, the tighter the bond between you and it. You need to focus on building your strength. Forget what you can't control."

"Enough with the self-preservation monologues! I can't— I'm not you, Gma. I can't just stand around and watch innocent people getting hurt and claim I'm doing it for the greater good of my Peculiar World. I know you must care somewhere inside."

"You shouldn't place bets on broken horses."

"What broke you so bad that you have to ignore—"

"I'm referring to you."

Amy froze in her spot, arms inches away from Rezna, but they fell flatly at her side.

"Your spirit's taken the worst of all hits. Splitting itself to house a curse that's now floating in some offshore prison. Your confidence is shot. You only began leaving the house some weeks ago after nearly a year of isolation. Even as you speak to me, it's as though something else is speaking for you. Your fear or your nerves, I can't figure which or if it's any of the two." Rezna leaned forward with her hands clasped and pointed at Amy. "How can you put yourself on the front lines for others when you barely have any fight left for you?"

She wouldn't know why until a short time after tonight, but Amy felt rage. For the first time in a while, pure rage filled her heart. Her lips quivered before her response. "In a world that ignores the small voices, what do you expect? If I hadn't stopped Cloudy last year, all of those children would end up dead! Maybe not then, or by now, or even within ten years, but eventually the hate inside that cursed doll's spirit would have rotted them whole. Why can't you see that? I do everything you ask. Everything. I read the books you gave me, spent the entire day training, kept my head down, and all for what? So that when it matters, I can hide while others are suffering?" Amy kneeled before her, her hands *begging*. "I understand you're scared."

Rezna raised an eye.

"Last year, Cloudy caught you. If you can get caught, then what does it say about my chances of survival? But fear isn't... it can't be our downfall. We have to—"

Rezna stood fast. "How dare you?"

"How dare I what? How dare I place myself in the company of devils to find out how they operate? It's more than the detectives or anyone else is doing."

"You're impossible! Fuck! You're just like your mother!"

"Let me guess; that's why she died? For giving a damn?"

"She died a victim—"

"Because YOU were too scared to act! Too scared to fight at her and my father's side!"

"The Class Ones cursed them! By that time, I was no longer a fighter."

"You've never stopped being a fighter, and you placed the burden on me."

"Fine! A burden they would have wanted you to carry.

Fight, Amy, fight! But do so—"

"In fear? Your excuses for not fighting add up to the same thing. You should have either died alongside them or they could have had a chance to still be here with you. And me."

"That's naive thinking. My job was and is to preserve our culture, the ways of auraists, and nothing more."

"I can't live by that code." Amy walked away from her and started up the stairs.

"Then you'll die by theirs."

Amy PUNCHED a hole through the wall.

Rezna's flinch left her with a hand holding her up against her chair.

Amy turned to her without meeting her eye. "Maybe I should die. That's it, isn't it? I wasn't meant to make it this far. I cheated death. Now it torments me. I was supposed to die with them."

"No." Rezna regained her height. "That was never your future."

"I wish it had been." Amy went up the stairs.

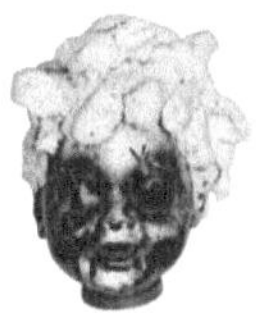

She wanted nothing more than to sleep forever. Amy laid down on her bed and tucked herself under her covers. Tossed and turned as her GCID buzzed several times on her desk. She smacked her lips. Snatched it up.

A ziccolit screen popped up.

Unknown: Your new device is ready for pickup.

"Great." She swiped away, and the next message flew onto

the screen.

Jamari: There's an initiation ceremony tonight. Sorry for the last-minute notice, I just found out.

There'll be performances and special guests and all.

Perfect night for a debut. If you're down and willing.

You could come chill as well and just spectate.

Your call. Let me know.

"Milard likes to grab the corpses when they're fresh."

With Stella's words ringing in her head, Amy got out of bed.

Chapter X

(DIRECTOR'S CUT)

                MADAME BLÉ (V.O.)
        I see all
        through the eyes of my members.

FADE IN:

INT. C.L. QUARTERS - HEAD OFFICE - DAY

DIRECTOR swallows the final piece of his
Urhzunian donut. Wipes his hand full of
crumbs on his shirt and raises the other
towards ENGINEER, who operates the URx
camera next to him.

~~The~~ MADAME BLÉ~~, fewer wrinkles on her
face,~~ sits behind her grand desk and
smiles at the camera. Three perfectly
aligned glass towers stand behind her.

                MADAME BLÉ

We are here on this miraculous
year of AC81—

                DIRECTOR
Wait—cut! Let's run that back.
Play it again, Bian.

                ENGINEER
Yup.

                DIRECTOR
Hey, doing great, M.Blé. We're
just gonna run that back again.
Swing it around, you know? Get
a different angle.

                MADAME BLÉ
Of course. Say, Mr. Riverman,
that Alaskan documentary last
season— Did you write that on
the way to MeccaCast?

                DIRECTOR
Oh yeah, yeah. Seen a little of
that, huh?

                MADAME BLÉ
The piece on the Camp Phoenix
Rupture quite took me. Tell me.
Are you a follower of The
Light?

                DIRECTOR
Oh yeah! Huge devotee! Ever
since I was a little kid, you
know. I owe my success to my
rocks! Tekwun and Tektu—

Director points to two men in purple
dashiki robes. TEKTU waves, his long,
twisted ponytail of dreadlocks whipping

around. TEKWUN appears behind him, avoids
the whipping ponytail, drops a box,
winks, and waves. He scratches his curly
mohawk.

> TEKWUN
> Hey Mel, I found a bunch of re-
> rolls in the back.

> DIRECTOR
> SICK! Oh—let's get rolling.

Director moves up close to ENGINEER.

> DIRECTOR
> How we looking, Bian? Also,
> what's uh—
>
> (whispers)
> AC81? Do we need it?

> ENGINEER
> It's 2170. Ninety-one years
> since her death. Callisto's.

> DIRECTOR
> Ah, copy, copy. Okay, let's get
> set. Madame, you ready?

Madame Blé nods.

> DIRECTOR
> All right! 3, 2, 1, action!

> MADAME BLÉ
> Here we are, miraculously in
> the year AC81, 42nd day, where
> we will witness a delinquency
> of Dalestone's might.
> Sanctioned on this day, an
> exorcism for one.

Madame Blé gestures towards one of three female members of the cult lined up against the wall.

> MADAME BLÉ (CONT'D)
> May we have the subject?

SISTER C, middle of the group, opens the door and stands in the doorway. She nods outside.

Madame Blé smiles as her arms welcome someone in front of her.

HOST, 20s, ~~beautiful, gorgeous, STUNNING, sexy, cute, attractive~~ (idiot director, simplify) gives a short bow in her orange ruffled knee-length tunic.

> HOST
> Life's blessings to you,
> Madame.

She takes the seat in front of the desk. Her fingers massage one another, left hand over right, right hand over left, back and forth, back and forth with the rubbing.

> MADAME BLÉ
> Unnerve yourself, dear. We are
> having a conversation, that is
> all. First, some prerequisites.
> Can you please confirm your
> identity?

> HOST
> Metzka Rui.

> MADAME BLÉ
> Age?

Host swallows hard. Her lips smack
together.

> HOST
> Ss— sah— Sorry. I get confused.

> MADAME BLÉ
> Take your time, dear.

> HOST
> Twenty-nine.

> MADAME BLÉ
> Why are you here today?

Host massages her belly; her mouth hung
open over it.

> HOST
> There's something inside of me.
> It teases me.

> MADAME BLÉ
> Would you want this demon, this
> parasite, expelled?

> HOST
> It's no demon. Demons don't
> exist.

> MADAME BLÉ
> I know, dear. Colorful language
> to explain the intricacies of
> human degradation.

> HOST
> It's not human.

SCRAAAAAK!

Vicious claws cut their way through the
host's green pumps.

Madame Blé—poker face.

                    MADAME BLÉ
          Restraints.

Black bands spit out from the arms, legs,
and back of Host's chair. Wrap tight
around her limbs—Four bands on each.

Madame Blé smiles.

                    MADAME BLÉ (CONT'D)
          To move further, we will need
          your consent, dear. Do you wish
          to vanquish this soul from your
          vessel?

Host's clawed nails scrape into the
wooden floor.

She sways to and fro, staring into her
lap.

                    HOST
          Take my body.

                    MADAME BLÉ
          Miss Rui, you must look me in
          the eye and give me your honest
          consent.

Host's head creeps up. Bumps have taken
over her face. They rise as long and thin
as porcupine quills. Her stammering,
teary, sniffling face lines up to Madame
Blé's.

                    HOST
          I consent. Please help me.
          Please, please get rid of it.

Madame Blé raises her palms to the skies.
A low hum reverberates from her pursed

lips. She lowers her arms.

>   MADAME BLÉ
>   Callisto, I take your hand—

She raises a hand as though expecting
someone to help her up.

>   MADAME BLÉ (CONT'D)
>   —enclose in my other—

Blé's free palm raises to cup the other.

>   MADAME BLÉ (CONT'D)
>   —fueling my soul with your
>   essence.

Sisters A, C, and E drop to their knees
alongside the wall. They mimic her
motions, heads bowed.

>   MADAME BLÉ (CONT'D)
>   Guide us in restoring this
>   vessel to its purity, bestowed
>   upon birth.

>   SISTERS
>   Bestowed upon birth.

>   MADAME BLÉ
>   Risen in light.

>   SISTERS
>   Risen in light.

>   MADAME BLÉ
>   Cast through the fire of life.

>   SISTERS
>   Cast through the fire of life.

MADAME BLÉ
Now lost in trenches.

SISTERS
Now lost in trenches.

MADAME BLÉ
Help us burn away her sins.

SISTERS
Help us burn away her sins.

MADAME BLÉ
The continuous fire, blossoming
through the night.

SISTERS
The continuous fire, blossoming
through the night.

Host cranes her neck to one side,
gargling. Her neck contorts until her
chin points to the ceiling. Her mouth
releases a longwinded **croak.**

HOST
Save me, Sister.

Her head spins back the opposite way—her
body follows, flipping her over and out of
view.

All lights **fiiiff** out. Pitch black.

DIRECTOR
Hey, what happened? Bian, you
got that on tape? Bian? Bi?

TEKTU
What's going on? Tekwun?
Brother, where are you?

Red FLASHED in front of Madame Blé's face in the dark.

                    MADAME BLÉ
          She's circling us.

Something scrapes across a surface. One long continuous **scraaaaaaaaaaaaaaaaaaaaaaaaaaaaaaaaaaaaaaaaaaape**!

                    DIRECTOR
          What's that noise?

                    TEKTU
          It's coming from everywhere.

                    MADAME BLÉ
          It is time, Ms. Droûx.

Cool, almost bluish white light illuminates the glass honeycomb towers behind Madame Blé. Blood red ~~light~~ spirit flushes into each like smoke.

A **hum** spreads across the entire room.

                    DIRECTOR
                 (wipes sweat)
          Oh shit!

In the top corner of the room, nearest the door—a weathered, dripping cocoon nestles in a web of wet beige matter. Host's head sits on top of the cocoon, her face contorted into three parts, each with one big yellow eye in the middle. Her deformed mouth hangs open as it discharges amber fluids. Teeth sharpened and crooked. Her split open chest cavity reveals Host's bare arms covered by strips of her torn sleeves. Underneath her exterior, her bare legs hang ~~uselessly~~ like a trampled tail.

Behind its cocoon, two prickly crustacean spider legs extend. Each one dangles the naked, stiff bodies of Tekwun and Engineer upside down from their penises. Webbing is over each of their eyes and open mouths.

The creature snarls at Madame Blé.

Madame Blé stands up and opens her arms to the creature.

> MADAME BLÉ
> You are not authorized to dwell in this sacred flesh nor cross the barrier. By the light of Callisto.

The creature lunges forward.

It smashes into an invisible barrier that reveals itself in patches: a wall of blood-red ~~light~~ spirit.

Madame Blé claps her hands together. Inhales deep. Opens her arms. Exhales.

The spirit wall obeys her movement, spreading to open a hole in the middle.

> MADAME BLÉ
> Come into the light, child.

The creature drops its victims. Six spider legs shoot out its abdomen.

The creature scurries towards the opening of the spirit wall.

Madame Blé waits as though awaiting a hug from a loved one. Clenches her fists.

The three eyes of the creature stop short of the tip of Madame Blé's nose. It spits and snarls in her face as its jaw chomps at her.

The opening has shrunk TIGHT around the creature's neck.

MADAME BLÉ
And now we cast you out.

MS. DROÛX appears on the other side of the spirit barrier and aligns herself with the creature and Madame Blé.

She holds up a spherical device—the Vyktrex Core—to the opening of the spirit wall. The device's core sparkles with harsh white vibrance.

The creature whips its body towards Ms. Droûx.

Its head passes the opening in the spirit wall.

Ms. Droûx underhands her Vyktrex Core at the creature.

It hits the top of the creature's head. Levitates above it.

RESHAPES—diamond-shaped. Four other diamond-shaped edges slice their way out from its core. Their edges sparkle white.

The blood-smoke red spirit escapes from the tops of each glass tower behind Blé and trails towards the creature.

The spirit wall SNAPS in a ball around the creature's entire body, except for its bubbling head. Steam squeezes out of its pores. The screaming creature drops to the floor.

Flailing in the spirit-net, the creature's body shrinks to human size, except the head.

On her knees, still screaming within the net, her head grows back to normal. The Host. Engorged veins pump in and out on her bruised face. She quivers. Coughs up blood.

The blood streaks stiffen in the air, suspended.

They pull back inside Host's mouth, holding it open.

Her neck cranks back to gaze at the Vyktrex Core over her head. Her body struggles against every movement she makes. A bulge grows in her throat. Her neck enlarges like a toad's vocal sac, blood shooting out.

A cream-colored ~~light~~ spirit forces itself out of her mouth.

The core of the Vyktrex whirs, its small mechanical parts twisting and turning.

The spirit net enclosing Host peels up off her body.

Combines with the blood-smoke spirit and wraps around—entraps the cream.

The combined spirits SUCK into the Vyktrex Core with a **SWOOP**—Captured.

The room's natural light returns.

The Vyktrex Core spins in mid-air. Stops. Mechanically twists and transforms back into a sphere. Overhands itself back to Ms. Droûx.

She catches it in a palm and sticks it onto one of her belt's metallic squares. Her hand reaches forward—

INT. CENTRAL COTTAGE - MAIN OFFICE - DAY (PRESENT)

Ms. Droûx turns a small knob on an old-school box monitor taking away the screen's video.

> MS. DROÛX
> Cannot believe your town still has these… boxes.

She walks past—

REZNA DEVINE, who watches her every move. She sits across from—

Madame Blé, at her desk. Smiles. She takes in the view outside her window: Her members working on various tasks.

Ms. Droûx, hand over hand in front of her, stands beside M.Ble.

> MADAME BLÉ
> A spurt possessed her. Unfortunately, this spurt descended from arachnids, which, as you are aware, makes for a horrible concoction. It's mannequin form is nearly untraceable!

                    (shakes head)
          Poor girl. Just strolling past
          a department store when a
          mannequin jumped through the
          window and latched onto her.
          Unluckily for it, she was the
          daughter of a town Noble. Her
          father deduced something was
          amiss with his beloved daughter
          in short order.

Rezna's hand smoothes over the desk.

Ms. Droûx's nose upturns at the gesture.

                    MADAME BLÉ (CONT'D)
          They expelled the spurt from
          her body, killing it in the
          process. However, its spirit
          found her again some hours
          later, and when it took her
          over this time…

                    (squeezes fist)
          Its power owned her. Her
          father's currency could not buy
          that solution.

Rezna strokes the desk. Nods.

Ms. Droûx peers into her.

                    MADAME BLÉ (CONT'D)
          Until he believed in The Light.
          Though he found us, we believe
          we found him. As you saw, we
          are well-equipped to perform a
          level-three exorcism. That
          young woman is now married with
          her second child on the way.
          So, if your concerns involve
          potential possessions in town,
          we— Ms. Droûx and I— are here.

                    MS. DROÛX
          Do you have a problem with our
          furniture?

Rezna doesn't even look up.

                    REZNA
          Wondering how long you've had
          this desk. Remarkable texture.
          Your little capture device orbs
          are— fun.

                    (looks up)
          Now, Ms. Blé—

                    MADAME BLÉ
          Madame.

                    REZNA
                    (looks off, then returns)
          M.Blé is proper form as well,
          yes?

Madame Blé nods. Gestures to carry on.

                    REZNA (CONT'D)
          Take a look at these
          communities. They forgot what
          murder was, and it shook their
          foundation. Time flies. A year
          in, and we're back to murder.
          And while I respect your
          ambition, the last I checked,
          neither you nor your colleague—

She flicks a finger at Ms. Droûx without a
look.

                    REZNA (CONT'D)
          —are certified to practice
          exorcisms. Spiritualists, like
          myself, I'll add—

She winks at Ms. Droûx.

                    REZNA (CONT'D)
          —remain the only certified
          exorcists in this World. Even
          if your cult's influences have
          garnered you unauthorized
          privileges before, as far as
          this vicinity goes, I am the
          only Spiritualist. Regarding
          matters of possession, I
          outrank you technically and
          legally. I am obligated to
          investigate any potential
          possession in the vicinity of
          my station.

Madame Blé's straight smile crinkles at a
corner.

                    MADAME BLÉ
          Come now, Rezna. It is obvious
          you d-d-don't—

~~She clears her throat.~~

~~Ms. Droûx's eyebrows jump, watches her
leader quake from her childhood stutter.~~

                    MADAME BLÉ (CONT'D)
          —even want the job. You are
          tired. Let us help you. We can
          foster a smooth partnership
          where you are The Face, and we
          do the dirty work.

Madame Blé pours herself some tea. Offers
Rezna a cup.

Rezna puts up a gentle hand and shakes
her head.

                    MADAME BLÉ
     I mean, Spiritualist, **auhshh**!

          (giggles)
     Charming, but such ritualistic
     methods. Some old footage we
     have of Spiritualists—

                    MS DROÛX
     Barbaric.

Rezna **sighs** in her seat.

                    REZNA
     This World's always been stuck
     between the past and the
     future, hasn't it?

                    MS DROÛX
     No. Only you.

                    REZNA
     Does your constipated imp come
     with an off-button?

Ms. Droûx steps closer to Rezna.

Who's unmoved.

Ms. Droûx leans to her face.

                    MS. DROÛX
     The Devine family sure loves to
     salt their wounds. The
     uninhibited nature stirs me.
     Perhaps Ms. Devine…

                    MADAME BLÉ
     Now Ms. Droüx.

          (giggles)
     We do not muscle the help.

Jadesfeld and New Enfield's extraordinary cooperation is a genuine source of liberating spirit.

Rezna rises, her eyes never leaving Ms. Droûx's.

                    REZNA
Check your Overbeing.

          (Turns to Blé)
I hope that on your next day of birth, you gain further wisdom.

Rezna pops open her graphite-colored tote. Pulls out and drops a box of Urhzunian donuts on the desk.

                 REZNA (CONT'D)
Consider it a peace offering. You're right. Cooperation is key. It's vital in this jungle of a World we inhabit. You'll hear about an exciting expansion being revitalized soon.

          (Smiles)
Looking forward to our partnership.

Rezna turns on her heel. Makes for the door.

                 MADAME BLÉ
It will be as fruitful as the one I am building with Amy.

Rezna pauses.

                 MADAME BLÉ (CONT'D)

                    Oh. She did not tell you she
                    was one of my understudies?

The side of Rezna's face glared back.

                    REZNA
               Stay away from my
               granddaughter.

She strides out of the office.

Ms. Droûx slams the door behind her.

Madame Blé opens the box of Urhzunian
donuts and sniffs. Her nose scrunches up
as she peers down upon the red, squiggly
jelly lines with green pusberries oozing
on top.

                    MADAME BLÉ
               Scrumptious.

She pushes the box away.

Ms. Droûx stares darts into the door.

                    MS. DROÛX
               Rezna. Devine.
               What are we doing about her?

                    MADAME BLÉ
               Miserable old fart. What is she
               talking about?

Ms. Droûx stares into space. Scans the
air around her head.

                    MS. DROÛX
               Oh dear.

                    MADAME BLÉ
               What is it?

                    MS. DROÛX

She's attempting to expand her reach through a long-defunct transportation project. A bullet train extension that will create a line between the closest cities and transfer points to some locations beyond her scope.

                MADAME BLÉ
Extension? What does <u>she</u> need <u>reach</u> for?

                MS. DROÛX
If we don't get hold of this, we'll be removed from our plot, disrupting our operations.

                MADAME BLÉ
What is your read on her? We get a read, we can send The Vengeance on her.

Ms. Droûx scans her airspace.

                MS. DROÛX
She is just a miserable old woman.

                MADAME BLÉ
Hmph! I'll say. Any recoveries from the Infirmary?

                MS. DROÛX
I've run through the nurses, guards, and etceteras, and all say the system malfunctioned, locking them out from the Infirmary Block B. They say Deklance got Mali to safety, but some of the patients, although high as blubbering robins, mention a third person.

                    MADAME BLÉ
               (leans in, fingers
               entwined)
Who?

                    MS. DROÛX
No one knows or can give a
comprehensible description.
Even Stuley's off his rocker.
Supposed to be guarding the
door, but his mind is lost at
the moment. The meds aren't
working for him either.

                    MADAME BLÉ
               (sighs)
We should throw a rally. But no
time. We are so close. Have you
spoken to V about the
procedure?

                    MS. DROÛX
I ran it by her. She's taking
some time but seeing the better
light. She'll come to terms
shortly. I know it.

                    MADAME BLÉ
We should prep The Source. How
far apart are the contractions?

                    MS. DROÛX
About twenty to thirty seconds
apart.

                    MADAME BLÉ
Bring it down to ten seconds.
We are almost there. I know.

                    MS. DROÛX
We should wait.

                    MADAME BLÉ
          No. We cannot—

The door bursts open. Sister A, greying
hair, hustles in.

                    SISTER A
          Sisters, sorry to interrupt. We
          have Creaevix producers on the
          line for you. Young Jamari has
          done a follow-up to his rally
          performance the other day.

Madame Blé throws her hands up.

                    MADAME BLÉ
          Well, what do they want me to
          do, muzzle the boy?

               (sighs)
          I will deal with it. Ms. Droux,
          please find the boy and see if
          his friend is available.

                    MS. DROÛX
          Hmph.

                    MADAME BLÉ
          Is this next test going to
          work?

                    MS. DROÛX
          We shall see. It's a match, but
          the output… may not be high
          enough.

FADE OUT.

Chapter Twenty-Two

Meeting Of The Cult

*I*diotic *directions and frivolous...* Walking through the echoes of a time she had never known, Amy's eyes got lost in the architecture and the simplicity of this detailed old-school entertainment lounge. Every smell filled her nostrils with hope and wonder. Fond memories of her childhood adventures flooded her mind. Every surface she grazed her hands over warmed her fingertips, even the cool touch of the ice machine. She walked, pausing in spots to gaze at the lights and sounds from the chief attraction: the bowling lanes.

Right across from the nine lanes were alleys of parlor games, board games, foosball and other tabletop activities — the assortments of leisure too broad for Amy's brain to manage all at once.

Her body struggled to pull away from the smells of toasted pineapple and glazed chicken dipped in honey, escaping the food stand she passed by. Her battle paid off when The Man Behind the Stand handed her a carton full to the brim of buttered popcorn *for free? And a glass of iced tea to top it off??*

"It's complimentary with every visit," the man said.

Amy's mouth went ajar. *Heaven is here.*

She munched while passing each of the immaculate oiled lanes, watching the few patrons make their moves.

She moved towards the last lane at the end of the spot.

A dreadlocked young man scribbled away in his notebook. Big Man stood guard at his side.

Amy nodded to Big Man.

The young man sprang his legs off the ball return and faced Big Man. "Aay, give me a minute alone here, big bro."

"Copy, big boss." Big Man smashed his fist into his palm. Nodded to Amy as he passed her. "Ay!" He pointed towards a group of kids and ran after them. "Ay! No running on that, lil twerp!"

Amy raised a brow as she approached the *Big Boss*. "So you're the Boss Man giving complex instructions to get here?"

"Aaay." He shrugged with ease. His arm waved her into his row. "Please, have a seat."

"I'm kinda in a hurry."

"Yeah, on the run." He nodded. "I get that." He placed his notebook underneath his foot. "I sent you through my special entrance cuz I figured you'd appreciate lowkey. Seems your style."

Oh, did you? Is it? "Well, thank you for noticing," Amy said sarcastically. She pointed around the spot. "Is this the front for your <u>other</u> operations?"

"Crackdowns are always crackdowns. My special brand of chronic hits a little harder than people are used to. It's harmless. Yet, when the order of rulers is upturned, foot always gotta be on the neck."

Amy pointed at his notebook. "Scared I'll steal your ideas, but trust me with your special entrance?"

"We've had some vengeful drafts here recently. I like to keep my foot on top of things, too."

"Why the invite? You trust me? Or trying to control me?"

"Never said that. I wanted to meet my top customer. Find out why she's been unconscious all over town, reeking of my product. Bad for business."

Amy's expression melted. She stiffened her stance, locking eyes with him. "So, threats?"

"Never. Understanding. My cousin visited Enfield last year to see a friend of his. His friend's little boy, my cuz fostered in a sports program." He stared down at his feet, his smile gone. "The kid's never been the same since. Lost his entire family to that Cloudy curse."

Amy's face winced.

His eyes traveled over Amy until meeting her eyes. "Kid told my cousin a girl saved them. A girl who wore her GCID outside of her skin. Definitely an anomaly."

Amy looked off towards the pins down the alley. Her hands drummed against her sides.

"Don't worry. You won't find any policing authorities in here. And the kids that could remember are few, and their loyalty knows the risk you took for them."

She sat in the opposite row of the lane. *Another one in the mix.* "Never knew a place like this existed underground."

"I wanted to create a spot where people could come and be themselves. No expectations."

"A hideout? For you, too?"

He smirked. "I like to keep my peace. There are always changes needed in the established order. I'd rather move through the shadows with knowledge. 'Rip the pages out of the script so they who rule can't continue reading.' Help the people help themselves. Privately."

A smirk escaped the corner of Amy's mouth. "Authphrix Fortheen Kay, *World Down Under.* Read that book a few times."

"Well, I appreciate the reads."

"Wait, you're—"

"Now you know a secret about me."

Amy chuckled. "Bravo, chap. It's one of my favorite reads, by the way."

His palm thumped over his heart thrice.

Amy frowned. *Gma does that.*

He handed her a black velvet pouch. "For your bat. Noticed he might have a bit of a muscle fracture. This should help. It's safe for bats. Infused with some of my product made especially for his kind." He chuckled. "Little guy loves it."

"Thanks?" Amy stared at the bag. "How'd you know—"

"Listen. It's not my business what you do in your spare time. But when you pass out right before a Detective raid, and your bat has to help navigate Big Man carrying you to your home, Big Man's not at his post. Detectives would've caught you out there with an unlicensed strain. Bad for you and me both."

"A—I—" Amy's head cocked to the side. *Who ARE you?*

"No worries. Your bat looked after you the whole time. I think he even threatened to claw out Big Man's eyes." His laughter captivated the air around them.

"Thank you again, I suppose. And my GCID upgrade?"

He pulled a teeny triangular black onyx glass out of his pocket. Four teenier hooks shot out from the edges of it.

"This will hook underneath your top three layers of skin. Won't be moving anywhere. Need to sync it closer to your head for a few weeks, so I'm thinking upper chest. Takes an extremely steady hand to get the perfect link location cuz the tech's a bit more complex with this one. May I?"

Amy nodded at his open hand. Got up and sat beside him. Leaned her chest towards him.

With his eyes laser-focused on a spot between her collarbones, he beckoned her to raise her chin. His steady hands aimed the GCID over the spot on her chest he focused on.

Amy looked him over. "What's your name?"

"Hold still for me a little longer, please." He stilled himself.

She became a mannequin.

He stuck the new hardware to her chest in one swift motion. Backed away, studying it.

CHIRP! The GCID screen lit up with white light.

Oscillating lights illuminated his face. "Wait for it." His eyes followed the sequence, the lights still on his smile. "There! Full power." He checked her eyes. "Now, look me in the eye."

Amy raised her brows as she maintained eye contact.

"How do you feel?" he asked.

"Fine."

"Solid."

At eye level to her left, groups of various white characters floated out in front of her.

Z.
x0??????
??????
??????

What kind of tech...? The random strings unravel one character after the other, one line after another. He's no normal engineer.

"That second line shows how to contact me," he said. "Just enter the code. There's a plethora of features I'm sure you'll find uses for in no time. It'll be hard pressed for this thing to break or even scratch, so go crazy. Whatever you do."

"Z?" Amy's smile met the changing characters before her. She waved them away with her hand. "Z, The Engineer. Well, Mr. Z, or Kay, from America, I presume? Can you make it untraceable?"

He grinned and nodded. "Already built-in. Had to find out who you were before I gave this to you."

Amy scoffed, half-smiling *at his nature.* "Who am I?"

He took out a miniature square device.

What is that? It looks like Jimmy's cellular from who knows what year. This guy's got his own network, too?

His fingers traced across the screen of his device. After a few strokes, he looked back up and nodded at her expression. "It's called a smartphone. Old school tech."

Letters and numbers made of black light materialized on Amy's right. She frowned at them. "I don't get it."

"If we meet again, I'll elaborate cuz I'll have the answers by then." He got to his feet and stretched.

"Yeah?" Amy rose. Folded her arms. "What if the authorities shut you down before then?"

"Authorities couldn't shut me down if they wanted to. I got a modest operation, and they believe various sources are at the head. Those sources don't even know who I am. JD Chief himself gets my product delivered to him. Dets puff their chests for show, never knowing who's who. Besides, I'm always in the wind."

"And you trust me?"

"Never said that." He shrugged. "Maybe us outcasts gotta stick together, same way you stuck up for them kids. Just the right thing to do."

"A great cult is worth its message." Jamari sipped his IcyJel! branded smoothie. "Mmm. The greatest. Cookies Strawbaganza…"

Amy leaned over her smoothie bowl. Her finger drew a smiling face in it.

"Anyway," Jamari continued, "Industry tries to make a muppet out of you when they can. You ready for the lights?"

"How'd you figure out who I was?"

"It's like I told you before, your voice. Studious vocalist like myself can ride the waves between your vocal patterns. That corny layering effect couldn't fool me."

"Corn your ass!" Amy laughed.

"You seriously got a heck of a tuner on you, something I think the cult sees some value in. I'm always down to sponsor another talented artist. Maybe get you a feature?"

"I don't know about all that…"

"It's simple, mate. The more exposure you have, the more they'll listen."

"You mean—like the singers outside my window every morning?"

"Told you, we're not here for muppetry. I'm talking about The Light's club within the club. Who, yours truly, runs with. Giving them special recs for new members and whatnot. Stick with me."

"You mean I could become a mem—"

"Oooh, you want to become a full-fledged member!"

Absolutely not. "I would love to!"

"Sick! This would give me major bonus points with Madam Blé. Been on the naughty list lately."

"Everything all right?"

"Nothing the Midnight Inferno can't take care of."

Amy smiled and leaned back in her seat, his words reverberating through her head.

Across the spacious restaurant, a little girl laughed with her burger in hand as she ate with her family. She turned around. "Mother—"

Amy's head whipped back to meet Jamari's. Threw her thumb back. "You sure no one can see us?"

"It's all in Her Light. Relax. I got a guy in bubbleoptics."

Amy's finger poked to the side. She yanked her finger back from the bouncy bubble that regained its transparency. "Like Mr. SmartyPants?"

"Better. No bugs required."

"You know that's an offensive term now. Animalia'll crawl up your ass if you're not careful, Mari.

"I'm working on it. One character defect at a time."

"Right. Well, then." Amy cleared her throat. She put a hand over her heart. Chin tucked up. "What shall I have to do in Her light?"

"That's not funny."

"What, no humor in The Light?"

"Not me. Madame Blé wouldn't like it."

"Ah. I won't embarrass you, but I must remain disguised for personal reasons."

"Yeah, that's fine, love, just don't make a muck of me out there. Be on time, too! We'll be meeting at our secret spot later on tonight. You come by in your mask and cape, or whatever, and hang out of sight for a minute. I'll give you the special shock entrance treatment, Midnight Inferno Style." He pounded the table and sat back with every tooth on display. "Can't wait till you see the performance I cooked up. It's gonna be like a movie, mate. Going to do your *Follow In Your Light* number again?"

"I can cook up some fresh."

"There's The Artist. Love the new look, by the way." He pointed out her GCID hooked on her chest and then up to her hairstyle— dreadlocks mixed with afro parts, all waving to one side or another, some with red bands around them. "Mind if I offer some suggestions?"

Amy scratched the back of her head. "About the look or the music?"

"For you, my prison sister—" Jamari's shades lowered. "I got time. I can dabble in both."

Last place I expected to be. Entire hair twisted in dreadlocks, Amy ran her fingers between the strands. *This ends tonight. Then one more day of training and I'll be ready for Milard.* "Mary J. Waana, call Demo."

The GCID on her chest lit up.

Calling Demo

"C'mon..."

Call not connected.

"Any messages at all?"

That's a negative.

Amy, neck to toe in her outfit as The Singer, rolled her eyes at her GCID's reply. *Demo, where the fuck are you? Fingers crossed that she's training herself to death and not planning anyone's. This will be over once we have evidence. Playing Jamari like this feels cheap,* but if he's in on it... If not, I hope he'll understand what I'm gonna do. If a bit of deceit means stopping The Light, then so be it.

Mind your Overbeing.

I am over being done with this cult. We rid Jadesfeld of them once and for all.

We just spent near three days in prison. What about Gma?

Hell with her and her lavish conferences. A train won't stop a group of kidnappers. I'm doing something besides training. Nothing to tell, anyway. Demora's on a warpath. <u>We</u> saw it in her eyes. She's gonna rip that cult apart if it's the last thing she does. We have to beat her to it and do it the right way.

Ooooooh, the right way, who knows the right way? Lemme guess—Us?

The right way is not letting my best friend place more blood on her hands or get herself killed when there's an easier method.

Nooooow, She's a fighter. Look at us.

Amy stopped. Took a breath. Kept moving. "If she would just answer me... Maybe it is best she's not here. I can only control her so much."

Control is crazy. We should have stayed at their little clubhouse in the Haven.

There was nothing incriminating there. And no one home to question.

Could've torched it, maybe. What do you expect to find out here? Why perform in their marching band?

Cuz their marching band gets us access to whatever's out here. Maybe where they kept Demora. Need a name for you. It feels weird calling you Amy or my aura.

But I am both.

Ace. How's Ace?

I don't hate it. Why not let Demo skin the bastards?

"Are you sure you're my aura?" Amy searched the surrounding wilderness. "I sound crazy."

Sometimes, you could use a little more of her or even Rezna, but I digress. She isn't you. Why not give this to

Praisure?

Praisure's gotta be clean. Can't afford anyone getting unnecessarily tangled or hurt.

Aura Amy/*Ace* siphoned from her host and peered over her shoulder. *"Except us?"*

"We're just getting in, doing a brief show. *I don't know about pledging our soul to The Light. But if we can find that chamber they kept Demora in, we can blow up their entire operation. Pics, vids, whatever we can get in. Tonight is about getting in favor."*

"Hmph." Ace tapped Amy's forehead. *And what if they don't like your little performance?*

Well, that's mean.

What if we—

Will you stop?! They took Demora. Pried on my privacy—

"So, this is about your pride?"

—gave Gma hell and "tried to run her out of town."

You're not listening...

8 AM wake-ups! They took Demora. That pompous Blé smiled in my face over and over, knowing what she'd done. Her and her imp. She took Demora! Could've loaded my weed with poison!

Why do you always have to justify your anger? Just be. *"And if you're upset that Demora surpassed you in the prison, you can say it."*

Amy twirled onto her. "What? I'm not I'm not upset about that."

You're hungry now to prove yourself because you've been in the desert too long. Ace raised a brow. I can hear it inside you.

Are we ever on the same page? Can you do me a favor? Follow MY lead.

You mind your appetite, don't overfill on the hunger. Ace slinked back into her host. *"Or you'll get us both killed..."* she whispered before becoming one with Amy.

I've come a long way since Cloudy. Amy dipped behind some bushes, eyes peering ahead. *Look at their little fan club.*

EXT. LOT - NIGHT

Cloaked members of The Light move about a rectangular lot full of shrubbery all around it. Several dozen hooded members loiter in the space, their whispers breaking the silence.

On one end of the lot, MADAME BLÉ stands with JAMARI. Glass towers illuminate either side of a path with red light behind them.

                    MADAME BLÉ
          You won't let us down, isn't
          that right, Mr. Wyst?

                    JAMARI
          I got you, M.Blé. Relax, she'll
          be here.

                    MADAME BLÉ
          She?

                    JAMARI
          See? Partial surprise now since
          I've already spoiled.

                    MADAME BLÉ
          She, he, qui— it does not
          matter. We want to ensure that
          we do not let our members down.

                    JAMARI
          I've got a spiffy performance,
          just in case.

Madame Blé eyes him.

Ms. Droûx's scarlet-gloved hand comes down on her shoulder.

An ear-to-ear smile creases on Madame Blé's mouth.

> MADAME BLÉ
> Come, Jamari, let's get
> settled.

The lenses of Jamari's blockbuster shades brighten. Ziccolights form a keyboard in front of him.

BEHIND THE BUSHES

AMY covers her glowing GCID.

> AMY
> Mary J. Waana, ghost mode.
> Bring up messages.

Black letters on top of white light BLINK TO LIFE in front of her. She snatches the paragraph and moves it behind the bushes.

Hang back. When I start my set, there will be four beats. You come in on the third one.

> AMY
> (whispers)
> Let's respond—Copy that. You
> were right, J. It's a fucking
> party out here.

Facts. More than I've ever seen.

IN THE LOT

The deep cerulean cloaks of the hooded

bodies gather around the center.

Ms. Droûx claps twice.

The members break their huddles and hurry towards the outskirts. All align on the outline of the lot.

Ms. Droûx moves into the center and claps twice.

Silence falls.

Ms. Droûx scans the members.

> MS. DROÛX
> Thank you, members of The Light, for being here on this special occasion. Tonight is about the restoration of humanity's faith. On this night, we fulfill our promise. But first, initiation.

A dozen bodies or so made their way to the center and formed a circle around her, heads bowed.

> MS. DROÛX
> We stand before Callisto, sharing in Her light.

The members pull off their cloaks, revealing their full nudity to the World.

Jamari, under his hood, takes a step back. Stares at the other hooded members on his sides.

> JAMARI
> Ight, not my cup of tea. But good for them?

Ms. Droûx's eyes each nude member around
her.

                    MS. DROÛX
          In unity, we stand.

The hooded members around the lot raise
their hands to the sky.

Ms. Droûx walks up to each of the nude
invitees in the circle. She stops at one
of them.

                    MS. DROÛX
          Do you give your all to Her
          Light?

                    NUDE INVITEE 1
          I do, I swear it.

Ms. Droûx moves to the next member.

                    MS. DROÛX
          Do you give your all to Her
          Light?

                    NUDE INVITEE 2
          I do, I swear it.

Ms. Droûx slides in front of the next
nude body.

                    MS. DROÛX
          Do you give your all to Her
          Light?

                    NUDE INVITEE 3
          I do, I swear it.

Ms. Droûx moves down the line of nudity.

One after the other, they swear it.

Ms. Droûx took the last swear. She moved

back to the center of the naked group.

> MS. DROÛX
> All those before us shed
> enlightenment that we will use
> to prosper. Heed caution, for
> what you consume becomes you.
> For the World is our church,
> and we shall obey it.

Ms. Droûx's fingernail teases her wrist.
Then, DIGS INTO it. Slits her left arm
from wrist to elbow.

The nude invitees open their mouths.

Ms. Droûx hovers her dripping arm over
the first of the waiting mouths.

> MS. DROÛX
> As Callisto is in me, I now let
> her into you.

Drops of blood leak into the first mouth,
some slipping onto the lips.

Ms. Droûx moves to the next open mouth.

Blood drips in.

> MS. DROÛX
> As Callisto is in me, I now let
> her into you.

She continues down the line…

> MS. DROÛX
> As Callisto is in me, I now let
> her into you.

> MS. DROÛX
> As Callisto is in me, I now let
> her into you.

Ms. Droûx, back at the center, hands behind her. Her eyes scan each of them. She nods.

GULPS hit the air as the invitees swallow their human wine. One finishes his swallow, wipes his white, bloody beard, and searches the night sky.

> NUDE INVITEE ?
> Mother, cleanse my soul, for I have sinned before you.

He bows into the dirt.

BEHIND THE BUSHES

Amy's dropped jaw.

> AMY
> That's the Mayor's brother…

BACK AT THE LOT

One by one, one after the other, the bloody-mouthed newbies follow the example of the first.

> NUDE INVITEE ?
> Mother, cleanse my soul, for I have sinned before you.

> NUDE INVITEE ?
> Mother, cleanse—

> NUDE INVITEE ?
> …my soul—

> NUDE INVITEE ?
> …for I have—

> NUDE INVITEE ?
> …have sinned before you.

                    NUDE INVITEE ?
          ...before you.

                    NUDE INVITEE ?
          ...you.

Ms. Droûx closes her eyes.

                    MS. DROÛX
          Are you proud of your sins?

                    NUDE INVITEE ?
          No.

                    NUDE INVITEE ?
          No.

                    NUDE INVITEE ?
          No.

                    NUDE INVITEE ?
          No.

Ms. Droûx opens her eyes.

                    MS. DROÛX
          Will you do better in Her
          light?

                    NUDE INVITEE ?
          I swear it.

                    NUDE INVITEE ?
          I swear it.

                    NUDE INVITEE ?
          I swear it.

                    MS. DROÛX
          Penance awaits.

The invitees pull blades from their cloak
bundles.

They SLIT the meat of one of their index fingers and paint the coming blood into one of their palms. They SPIT in their palms to seal the deal. Their fingers swirl the concoction in their hands.

All raise their cupped palms to the sky, one hand supporting the back of the other. They turn their hands to drip their fluid mixture in front of them.

Ms. Droûx cups her hands in front of her.

> MS. DROÛX
> Absolution awaits. You were left, now, right. You've paid penance. That's all She asks. As for you all? Forgiven and written back into glory.

Applause from the entire lot.

The nude newbies raise their hands in celebration. Some shout their freedom to the skies.

Members congratulate and cheer them on.

> MS. DROÛX
> Yes. Now.

All members line up along the lot's outskirts, the naked invitees throwing back on their cloaks.

> MS. DROÛX
> You've all been gracious in Her message. Courageous for your sacrifices. The time has almost come.

A dozen hooded members sprint forth. Create a circle around Ms. Droûx.

                    MS. DROÛX
          I give you, Madame Blé, Master
          of Ceremony.

Thunderous applause.

Madame Blé rises from her chair and
stretches. She takes long strides as she
waves to her devotees.

A Queen to the blind. Stupid cunting bit—

She stands alongside Ms. Droûx.

                    MADAME BLÉ
          Welcome, all children of
          Callisto.

                    Member ?
          Welcome, your grace!

                    Member ?
          We are in the light!

                    Member ?
          Give us salvation!

                    MADAME BLÉ
          Your votes have brought
          salvation once again! We have
          found many suitable for the
          task and will reveal the
          nominees later. But right now—

She motions behind her.

                    MADAME BLÉ (CONT'D)
          I give you our Carrier!

A hooded member guides the arm of the
preggo, MALI CINCIUS, who flows into the
lot in an elegant white dress.

Mali cushions into Madame Blé's embrace.

> MALI CINCIUS

Ahhwk!

She steps back and grabs her swelling belly.

> MALI CINCIUS
> It hurts so bad.

> MADAME BLÉ
> Bad and good do not exist, my
> dearest. Only necessity. Are
> you ready to fulfill Her Light?

Mali surveys the surrounding members, Ms. Droûx's *ever-bothered face,* and returns to Madame Blé's loving smile.

> MALI CINCIUS
> I'm ready, my Madame.

> MADAME BLÉ
> Lie down on Her Earth.

Ms. Droûx ~~and her grimace~~ help Mali into a sitting position on the ground.

Mali settles back on her elbows. Eyes roll up to Madame Blé. They share a nod.

> MADAME BLÉ
> Let the birthing commence.

Ms. Droûx stares into Madame Blé's eyes.

Madame Blé nods to her.

Ms. Droûx gazes at the night sky.

> MS. DROÛX
> Bring Her Light.

Her droning voice echoes through the night.

> MS. DROÛX (CONT'D)
> Bring Her Light.

Mali's body flinches with a lasting **groan**. Holds her chest. Pushes her hand downwards, on top of her belly.

> MS. DROÛX (CONT'D)
> Bring Her Light. Bring Her Light. Bring Her Light. Bring Her Light. Bring Her Light.

Mali **screams** a cat's trampled tail of horror.

> MS. DROÛX (CONT'D)
> Bring Her Light. Bring Her Light. Bring Her Light. Bring Her Light.

> CROWD 1 (O.S.)
> Bring Her Light.

A part of the crowd recites a beat behind her words.

Ms. Droûx bends to Mali's ear.

> MS. DROÛX
> Breathe, girl. Open yourself.
>
> (stands up straight)
> Bring Her Light.

She stands back up straight.

> MS. DROÛX (CONT'D)
> Bring Her Light.

                    CROWD 1
          Bring Her Light.

                    CROWD 2 (O.S.)
          Bring Her Light.

More join in another beat after their
leaders.

Mali's tears stream down her face.

                    CROWD 3 (O.S.)
          Bring Her Light.

The missing part of the crowd chimes in a
beat after the last group.

Mali's eyes go wide. BLOOD TEARS fall
from them. Her cries fill the air. Her
pupils whiten, and veins push out of her
face and neck.

          MS. DROÛX & CROWDS 1, 2, & 3
          Bring Bring Bring Bring

            Her   Her   Her   Her

              Light. Light. Light. Light.

SQUELCH! Mali groans in passion,
desperation, and anguish.

          MS. DROÛX & CROWDS 1, 2, & 3
          (CONT'D)
          Bring Bring Bring Bring

            Her   Her   Her   Her

              Light. Light. Light. Light.

Madame Blé bends between Mali's open
legs. Her hands await the pitch.

MADAME BLÉ
Bring. Her. Light.

MS. DROÛX & CROWDS 1, 2, & 3
Bring Bring Bring Bring

Her   Her   Her   Her

Light. Light. Light. Light.

MADAME BLÉ
Bring. Her. Light.

SQUELCH! Kaw-kee-oock-keeeeeee!

MADAME BLÉ
Bring. Her. Light.

MS. DROÛX & CROWDS 1, 2, & 3
Bring Bring Bring Bring

Her   Her   Her   Her

Light. Light. Light. Light.

MADAME BLÉ
Bring. Her. Light. Light.

SQUELCH-aaaaaaack!

A string of blood squirts into Madame Blé's face, followed by a healthy spray that lasts for seconds. Remnants drip from her mouth. She flashes a toothy smile.

MADAME BLÉ
Bring. Her. Light.

                MS. DROÛX & CROWDS 1, 2, & 3
          Bring   Bring   Bring   Bring

            Her   Her   Her   Her

            Light. Light. Light. Light.
                      MADAME BLÉ
          Bring. Her. Light. Light.

Mali's eyes roll back. Shrieks
inconceivable pain—

Squaaaaalp!

Mali **BAWLS, SHRIEKS** between catching
breaths. Grabs over her heart—**RIPS** the
cloth of her dress, exposing her breast.

She drops. Passes out.

Madame Blé peers into something in her
arms.

                      MALI
               (weak, eyes a pinch open)
          It's all… in Her light. Right,
          Madame?

Madame Blé nods.

                      MADAME BLÉ
          Get her to rest.

Two hooded members grab Mali by her head
and legs. They carry her away.

~~Madame Blé's eyes remain fixed on whatever
the hell she's cradling in her hands with
the utmost tenderness~~.

Madame Blé straightens her blood-soaked
chest and raises her hands to the crowd,

showing off the birthed.

In her hands, an infant spurt uncoils its vine-like limbs from its human-like body. A molasses-like substance drips.

The spurt's belly spreads open. A shiny object within it.

A tear falls from Madame Blé's eye.

                    MADAME BLÉ
          It is here. The Source.

In the spurt's hands—A crescent-shaped object. Its smooth, ghost-white surface sparkles in the moon's brilliance.

                    MADAME BLÉ (CONT'D)
          The Source of her glorious
          return.

She takes the object from the spurt's belly. Cradles the gleaming object to her face.

The infant spurt drops from her arms. **Squalls** up at M.Ble.

Madame Blé raises The Source to the heavens.

Ms. Droûx picks up the foot-stomping infant spurt and takes center field in front of a waltzing Madame Blé.

                    MS. DROÛX
          There are cults that exist off
          the idea of breaking one to the
          point of death to understand
          what comes after. What I offer—
          what we offer—is the promise of
          faith. Faith delivering

absolution in the acceptance
that we are all transcended...

FADE OUT.

Chapter ?

HIStory

You can call him less than that if you'd like. His humanity was stolen by his vision. Removed from most of his desires, he wasn't half as bad as many expected of him. But mind my bias towards my sibling…

Afforded a handsome life from our father's acquisition efforts, we had more than necessary by World Committee standards. This meant ample free time for the family to indulge in reckless behavior.

My brother and I never really saw eye to eye. I was dedicated to my studies, somewhat of an obsessive. Daily, I found new topics to explore as I searched for answers to the mysteries of the spirit. Humanity has come a long way, yet still, there are missing pieces to understand. Evolution was kind to us. Not everyone understood what that meant. I was one of the chosen few who did.

My fifth birthday was the first nightmare. I totaled my nanny's auto by accident, as a child does when they can't control their strength. By age eighteen, things got out of control. My brother? There for many occasions. All the destroyed rooms. Fights and other rambunctious activities. He'd cover for me. Helped me repair any damages. Attractive monetary gifts to keep the right ones quiet.

My brother respected my gift and said he'd always keep me safe. Regardless of the obstacles, he had a knack for thriving in every situation. Running became his sanctuary, a means to distance himself from the weight of his shame. Always seeking external adventure fit for an appetite as extraneous as his. One day, he found an adventure too overwhelming for his conscience to endure...

BROTHER VENGEANCE (V.O.)
I miss murder. It was simple.
Miscreants could be gone at the
speed of light.

Sure, I was no better than them. Popped into 'CLUB WONDER' daily. Pops owned half. Fucked my days away, my choice on the piece of ass. The men were <u>always</u> BETTER. They gave it like the needy scoundrels they are, but couldn't take it HARDER than they could <u>give</u>. Pussys. Speaking of which, the pouches were <u>DE</u>licious. Feeding my oral fixation on their succulent nectar. Tits, ass, pouch; fuck um all which ways you wanted—they LOVED it. Asked Daddy to give um more, so I gave. Fucking spirits in that pool of the richest and filthiest. They were all the same, but how could I judge um? My ancestral cesspool kept its tombs like the Pharaohs in Africa.

So, I started from what I know.

Use the wealth to get the power I need.

Unleash the power on the Undeserving.

It was easy getting to the initial 45%. They lived unapologetically. History taught um nothing.

Meanwhile, I trained.

I wasn't ready. Even after training. After all, who in their right mind would commit honest murder? How could I ever be ready?

Till that day.

Knightship rolled-in a-storm. There I was, getting my usual fix of head and illegal drugs before I knew what happened. I never got the sound of the eKton out of my head. **POP!** Murder. Murder. Right in front of me. I'd never seen anything like it before. It's not like the cinema. There's a lingering smell about it, even to this day, it violates my nostrils. His head, split in three. His brains were scattered across my lap like missing pieces of ancient jigsaws. *'We found Herrix! He swung first—we all saw it. Knight Donally's swordrifle misfired! Accidental discharge,'* they said on the record. It's easy enough to scrub a cam; who's gonna challenge them? Typically, Knightship are standup gents, but this call was personal. Knight lost a sister last year to a 'Peculiar attack.' Herrix had nothing to do with that...

I thought the worst was over till they marched every soul in the spot into the showroom. Club Wonder's finest! All lined up for the pickings. Customers, you stand by, too! In case you're harbouring Peculiar interests. All the <u>Knights</u> cared about was who their Peculiar target was.

Then they stood back... and in rolled the Americans. CIA. Collaborative Intelligence Agency, making friendly rounds in Wales in a spot where they got '<u>intelligence</u>' about some Most Wanteds in town. No mercy. No way out. Unforgiven for imaginary transgressions. They scanned us all. I had never been scanned before; I was too rich for that experience. Currency protected me my whole life, but at that moment, it didn't matter.

They found their next mark. **POP!** More murder. Poor Yudith. To my surprise, I was witness to two more murders that day. Stepping over poor Yudith, next target up—they looked <u>her</u> in the eye. No, not her, I thought a thousand times over, praying in my head. I'd never prayed before. What need does the wealthy have to pray? Kaily from the glorious metropolis of Miami. Six years ago, we met. Now her head eating his fucking eKton —*in London? Is that legal?* — My younger mind wondered…

I tried to bargain. *"Hey, leave her be! She's innocent!"*

'Innocent?' Mr. CIA said. *'Who gave her the right to run from the mess she mixed in back home?'*

"She says it was an accident," I tried to tell him.

'Take him.'

An eKton in my fucking face —*its scythe for a handle cutting into my cheek*— Never been this close to one before —*I wait for its scythe to extend and slice off my neck. Made only in America, the fucking bloodthirsty scoundrels*— My haunted eyes on the grim reaper before me.

Is this it? Am I next?

Course not. I'm rich.

'He's Droûx's boy!' a shining Knight let out! *'Droûx blood has eminence here.'*

'No problem, Knight. We're just going to teach him some manners. A visual lesson… to remember who the enemy is.'

I staggered as they dragged me front row to see her face. One last time. Another **POP!** —*brains splatter from the electrical charge onto my lips, eyes, neck*— and she was gone. Murder. I was over. Who I thought I was… over. No, it wasn't love for Kaily, not the romantic kind, anyway. She was the second-best head I ever received in my life. Our conversations hours past dusk reminded me why humanity mattered despite the free World of chains we live in. She exhibited the brilliance of gentle expression, and every step she took brightened the darkest path. She reminded me of the beauty… in everything.

Except them.

Our World is beautiful, but there are parasites that need expunging. I learned some years later that murder never truly left our World. It was only diminished into obscurity by wealth, and its power rested with those at the top of society's hierarchy. Including my dear family. Generations of slaughter. Not by hand, but through drugs, drink, and depression; the unholy

Deities of existence.

From the moment I got home and sat on my couch painted in the blood of others, I knew what needed to be done.

So I <u>trained</u>. Nothing half-shot this time. The day I escaped with my life because of ill-received eminence stemming from currency, my plan had never been more clear. Easier to swallow, I ate the whole of the idea.

Time to track down the others.

Let's be smart about it. Host another lavish family function full of tree branches carrying the fruits of our collective delusions. Some roots there to pluck as well. The servants whose families never harmed a soul were given time off weeks in advance. Training runs for the new staff whose families have skeletons in the closet. Staff, whose families proved treacherous to humanity. It was simple. Only took me five months to get the PhD in chemistry needed to understand precisely how to make the perfect gas for vengeance's sake. It was silent, colourless, odourless, quick. I watched them all dance and laugh the night away until they fell into permanent slumber. Sat alone in the sealed, glass champagne room for eight hours. Watching. Making sure not a single soul left that dance floor. To my sweet, sweet relief, none had earned the gift of spirit that my sibling held. The World needs not to worry about Droûx blood rising here again.

85% of them off the list! Party of the year! My lifeless clone—*easy currency for me, damn my privilege*—found among the 'Wreckage Of Droûx' as the media crowned it. I was gone in the wind. The other 15% weren't easy to remove from existence. No matter.

Do the work. One by one.

In their homes—*bashing in Uncle Deryn's head, his piano taking the paint job, fresh coat*—On vacations—*lovely pool, cousin, let's take you and your family for a long nighttime swim*—UnderCity's bowels—*scattering like the new age crevents they are. Fine. Leave um some off-market eKtons and lure um directly in the middle of a fucking drug deal. Murder returns with the instinct to survive. Nature, take your course. Smile at the news report the next* _day._

It didn't matter where they hid, even after the remaining 8% got wind of their family members dying out so ominously. Seedy business dealings and overtakes, rings of illegal drugs harming the masses, babies made and left to starve—I rectified them all. All the Droûx handiwork history conveniently forgotten. I repaid the debts my family owed to the affected members of society. The World was a million ziccolights safer now. The work almost done.

There was only one left.

She was inspired by Callisto's travels while embarking on journeys of her own.

My dear sibling.

My baby sister…

She's just like I remember. **POP!** "That gift you have. It's always been special. Like… your soul is releasing on the outside, touching the World. It's beautiful, sis. Truly."

"Then why are we here, brother?" _She asked me with those big, reddening eyes._ "On top of this mountain. You hunted me to the very end."

I bowed to my dear sister—a show of respect for what's to come. "I've never taken my eyes off anyone since the day my mission became true. I offer you an official challenge. **POP!** Combat to resolve our issue."

"You're the one with the issue. I have no quarrel with you."

"I wish I could trust you won't take after our forefathers, sissy. But the family must die."

"And what of you?! The Executor of our will! Are you the only one left to bathe in the sunlight? Or will you script your demise shortly after mine?"

"My fate remains in the stars, sissy. I think it calls me to continue enacting true justice on those undeserving of their breaths. I'm not sure I have the stomach anymore. Not after you." **POP!**

"Then <u>trust</u> me, <u>brother</u>. _She pulled on my sleeves as though tugging at my heart._ You're the only heart I've known in our family to care enough to reach me. Understand me. Understand me now, brother. I can help you." *Her smile weakened me. We were kids all over again.* "We can thrive together. Like when we were children."

I thought we could possibly make it work. *—Maybe we can—*

POP! "I can't trust you! ***POP!*** *Argh, don't cry, pussy. I no longer have use for my tears. Seal them away. This is it. Man up! Don't let her stop your mission.* I wish I had your inner power. So I could know in my soul exactly what was."

"Power is overrated, my dear brother. It's the value you put out that <u>receives</u>."

POP! "Though you walk with your soul on your side, you are still human. ***POP!*** Accept my challenge. ***POP!*** <u>Please</u>, sister. *Don't shake your head. Don't.* Please! *This has to happen.* PLEASE!"

And so written in blood. My will be done...

... ...
....
....

<pre>
          BROTHER VENGEANCE (V.O.)
     Memories still echo into the
     present. They thought a
     courtroom could hold my rage.
</pre>

"Bloodlines be damned!" *I told them.* "How much pain can a family be responsible for? Is it not true that your science shows that there's a 68% chance of a son taking after his father's ill vices, a 64% chance a daughter or enby takes after either parent's delinquencies, as well as a 51% chance of a binary doing the same?"

That stuffy, rotten pig in suit approached me as though he's already won. "Well, ah-huh, Mr. Droûx, let's wrap this up. By that ordinance, and I won't make the mistake of calling that your hunch—In your philosophy, I can tell that you <u>believe</u>."

POP! *Why is he coming near me? Scumbag attorneys—*

"But, ah-huh, by that ordinance, wouldn't you then have to agree that <u>you</u>—"

Dirty, crooked finger—

"—would then have to be eliminated?"

"I'm not done cleaning smuggy fucks like you off the World's plate."

"Ah-huh, fuck you, Mr. Droûx."

"Your Honoeerrrrr?!" *My squealing, fucking weasel counsel sang. Put some stiff in your back!*

Stuffy lawyer patted my cuckold attorney's shoulder. "Sorry, your Honour! It's been a long week. I accept my court charge and recant my statement, apologising to Mr. Droûx. It's troubling, your record, Mr. Droûx."

Yeah, yeah, piece of shit. **POP!** "I've seen your records! **POP!** *And my piss ant attorney, stand straight! Let him get away with that? Callisto's fuckin' rollin'.*

"Alright, I think that's enough for the jury to deliberate. *Obtuse Judge.* Does the defendant's Counsel have any closing statements?"

"Hi, yes, your Honour, my client Mr. Droûx is invoking his right to make a closing statement, as a member of the World, before the World Committee ziccographically—"

Look at them. **POP!** *<u>—The seven heads of our World's judgement, hovering in shadows, they coerced— Wide streaming my life, are you? What secrets do they hide?—</u>*

"—before the great lands of the, **er-hem-hem**, excuse me, sorry—"

Say it.

"—before the great lands of the Celtic Welsh—"

"CYHYRAETH!"

"Oh!"

 Drops his fucking papers, the pansy.

"A-huh, your Honour, who let The CyRaeths in here?!"

POP! POP! POP! *The gaveling madman irks me...*

"Order in the Court! Audience, no more interruptions, or

you're out of here!"

"Honour, Brothers." *They don't know the meaning of the message. I'll die on my word.*

"His followers—please, gentlepeople—right, well, **er-hem-hem**, um, before Great Britain and Greater United Europe, and of course, before all-of-you-here-today-That's it."

"Very well. Mr. Droûx, go on."

Fuck you, judge. "I'm here to help the deserving. Not all of us want to help one another. There's not enough room for everyone in this World. *POP!* This rich soil can provide for those who deserve it. Return power to the people. It's already happening. *Listen to their pathetic murmurs. Peculiar piss theorists! Good in the desert to keep you runnin' away from dry, but it's still PISS. POP! Unevolved, loathing cowards! POP!*

"Stay on topic, Mr. Droûx."

"I am always on topic. Look at us! Our speed, strength, and mental capacity far exceed ANYTHING humans thought capable decades prior. *POP!* Why should <u>we</u> hate <u>Peculiars?</u> If I would've known how bad things would get, maybe I would've left my sissy alive... She was a damn fine example of evolution. If she could control her spirit, Peculiars Worldwide could learn to do the same. We out-advanced the machines, rewriting what our ancestors <u>thought</u> would happen to us—"

"—Knowledge—" *POP!*

"—We THINK THINK THINK THINK FUCK the FEELING—" *POP!*

POP! "—I feel the violence raging in my bones. *POP!* Willing to unearth itself onto the masses, *POP!* that shit on the innocent's doorstep, sometimes going further. *POP!* The violence was already here. *POP!* Hiding. I'm just making sure it's spread solely on the UNdeserving."

"**Er-hem-hem,** Mr. Droûx, hey-please, let's wrap up, k? T-thank you, thank you."

"My sister... If she didn't die, the evil of Droûx would spread. At least that's what I thought. My younger self was naive enough to believe their family was the sole purpose for the World's damages. But evil still exists outside our influence. *POP!*

It still spreads… even in some of yous. *Look at them. **POP!** Tell me who. **POP!** I'll kill him. If his heart's not right… Him and his family will PAY!* ***POP!*** *Is it Red Shirt in the second row? Or Mr. Blue-pressed Suit? Yellow Hat? Who wears a yellow hat, anyway?* Mini Skirt *with PUMpsss… who's the evil, I'll kill 'im, I'll kill 'im,* I'll kill 'im. Whose family breeds evil? Send them to me. Send me your uncles. Nephews. Couzinz. Your best friend's father was a rapist? I'll see ya at your best friend's funeral. That Margaret at the park beats her son when it's convenient—*always? Like my nanny. **POP!*** Give me her address."

"Uh, your Honour— let's, uh—er-hem-hem—"

"RACISTS PIECES OF SHIT, SENDUM! ***POP!*** GET OFF MEH! ***POP!*** *FUCKING GUARDS!* ANIMALS! *PROTECTING eeeeevil. Some of them are, too.* NEIGHBORS! *Ugh, my fucking knee, you fuckin—fuck* SHIT—*dragging me like a Gyaads humutt!* Callisto is <u>DEAD.</u> But the spirit lives ON in you! You! And you! YOU, YOU, YOU!!!" ***POP! POP! POP! POP! POP!***

Her Revival


```
          MS. DROÛX (V.O.)
      He nearly killed her, leaving
      her for dead.
```


Had he gone a little further, he would have succeeded. Shortcomings of a man. No patience. At least not when it matters most. Not with her.

The girl with ambition.

Me.

He cut my throat. He slit my wrist. Smothered me in my own puke & blood. I bled for seven hours. Without my soul, I should have died in three. He hoped his brutality would take me sooner. My guttural instinct? I would not let my body die! My one desire? Live like I've never lived before. Live for what's better! I had seen the other side. I had stared evil directly into his eyes. Now, my bloodshot eyes gaze into the sky for what should've been my final moments on this Earth. My life meant nothing. I will turn that into something! My hatred is never stronger than my dedication.

Seems my soul agreed.

Before then, my research across the Seven Regions led me to the many possibilities of the soul. Becoming a citizen in three regions, I gained residency with some of the finest scientific minds in the toddler field of espírituology, including its founder, Dr. Clemencia Verónica Estrada.

Living a double life was exhilarating. Exhausting. I questioned every day whether I should let the World's most extraordinary mind know of my secret. Was it worth the risk? Of course it was. Our love affair sprinted from the moment we gave in. Her smile was <u>everything</u>. In our early twenties, minds of soul and science—we needed each other. Our worlds were lonely.

Limonada de Cocos cooled our throats while we watched families along the beach. Beautiful children played so peacefully, laughter in the air, and memories made for years to come. It was heaven on Earth—Our Heaven. Colombia became our home for five years. Not even the SCIA training on top of Castillo San Felipe Dos could make me feel safe. Five years of unnerving safety. On the sixth, everything changed.

You came in through the fortress, same way as I, and every other citizen or tourist. Working on the docks, overtime at that cigar shop. I watched. You're not the only one shielded by currency, dear brother. You bided your time so I could feel just safe enough.

You showed patience.

I left Dr. Estrada there one somber, simmering night. I couldn't tell if it was the beautiful tropical climate or the spirit inside me boiling, but my fever tantrumed as I left the love of my life that night on Calle 38.

Antarctica was home for a while until a friend told me of a new ship of journeyfolk seeking work. I escaped on the Sub Service—or so you thought. I made my actual flee through a connect's unofficial service running through the defunct Drake Passage. Region to region, you followed. Persistent in your delusions. Your quest for power over fates, not yours, left you wasting away a life of potential. With all that anger, all that dedication, you could have created something majestic on your own. The same currency you used to chase me could have bought you anything in this World! I guess you were starving more than I. Your powerful delusion caught up to me, finally. Well done, brother.

'The power of my inner soul' —*as you so often called it*— was barely done. Scraping pieces of knowledge of the soul's inner strength. Its manifestation as light controlled by our externals. It healed my wounds slowly… painful, searing skin reforming over time. Four hours from your departure, my dear brother, I could walk again. More like dragging myself. Even if I died, you still wouldn't have won. My body could have risen into its undead lifeform, also segregated from our society. Your head could have been on my platter. After all…

You didn't show patience. With me. Not at the end.

MS. DROÛX (V.O.)
Let's sum up your devolution.

You killed your only loving little sister, emboldened by your convictions, assured of your impunity, making judgements on us all before they finally caught you, you-son-of-a-<u>bitch</u>. The punchline? Now, you sit in this orb of misery. Your soul floats with light, just as mine. Except yours didn't manifest while you were still breathing.

I'm happy The Light brought your soul to me to satisfy the needs of a greater calling.

"Do you feel in charge now? Are you enlarged by your boast?"

These tears, salty as they feel, are the last tears I'll ever spill. For you, for anyone, for anything. There is no more time for tears.

When they found me, I was crawling for my dear life at the brink of death. Where you thought no one would find me... They saw my shimmering essence, purely by chance, halfway down the mountain, and they brought me in. The damage you had done was irreversible, despite my accelerated healing factor. The Light replaced a majority of my flesh and bones. 85% bionic. At least some of my more human qualities no longer burdened me. Next step was to train hard. By the power of Callisto, I was destined to unlock the secrets of my soul.

'No one names their fucking kid Andy anymore because of them' The Andryex. Society's voices, always trigger-happy for a chance to rip apart what's not understood. Trying to swallow and breathe simultaneously felt like an impossible task. I was once a supreme figure where I—We—came. Now, I was yet another thing that needed to go away.

Blé taught me her mantra. *'I have it. I claim it. It is mine.'*

I trained harder.

I have it. I claim it. It is mine.

Getting used to my new artificial intelligence and senses, I ate everything I could to strengthen the human part of me that lingered. I needed to keep up with the machine in me. And I was no longer bothered by childish, human things, like good or bad. It all tasted like fuel for my mission. To be part of the Andryex meant overcoming futile human notions known to me since birth.

I have it. I claim it. It is mine.

I slept for ten hours straight, an extra two on weekends. Not because I needed to. I trained my body to be alert even in my sleep phase because I would never sleep another second with my guard down.

I have it. I claim it. It is mine.

Giving prayer to Callisto for the strength to do what need be done and the perception to manage my appetites accordingly so I didn't suffer as my brother did. Patience in Her Light.

I have it. I claim it. It is mine.

I went on a mission to obtain what she asked, the prominent Madame. The means to build something incredible beyond my understanding. Across the World, I collected seven artifacts that could contain one's spirit. And retrieved one power Source to contain them all. When I returned, I delivered the means to bring back The One True Light.

Did Madame Blé thank me for my service, then toss me aside?

No.

She asked one crucial question.

'Why are you here today?'

Many answers pleaded to rush forth. It was either the human side of me, still experiencing perpetual uncertainty, or the machine side that interfaced regularly with the Internet, feeding me thoughts within a second.

I answered.

"To live a longer life, you must let things pass through you."

HISTORY / HER REVIVAL

Chapter XXXX

MS. DROÛX (V.O.)
Here we are today. Bound by blood.
Reborn. United by Her design. For
Her glorious purpose.

FADE IN:

EXT. LOT - NIGHT

Ms. Droûx holds up a glass orb in her
palm: the latest version of the Vyktrex
Core. Her eyes twinkle as she examines
it. Four diamond-shaped edges SHOOT from
it.

GREEN SPIRIT seeps from each tip and
floats into the air. The silky, natural
luster shines stronger. Its fluid streams
combine, forming a swirling spirit ball.

Ms. Droûx's eyes FLASH SCARLET RED.
Unleashes a beam of light—

—that washes over the green spirit ball.
Red spirit encircles the green.

                    MS. DROÛX
          Madame Blé, bring us home.

                MADAME BLÉ (O.S.)
          Callisto BELIEVED—

Madame Blé waltzes in. Places The Source
into a slot at the top end of one of the
caskets.

                 MADAME BLÉ
          —that WE, as humans, are better
          than we allow ourselves to be.
          WE are the answer to many problems,
          yet constantly get in our own
          way! So, she studied and gathered
          every resource she needed to help
          aid her in creating a better WORLD
          for us ALL.

The green and red spirit ball floats
towards the center of the lot. Its bright
light reflected off—

Blockbuster shades. Jamari pulls them
down, his mouth a pinch ajar.

Madame Blé, front and center of the lot.

                MADAME BLÉ (CONT'D)
          Because of your precious votes,
          those with high spirit levels
          have had enough energy for two
          revivals. Making Callisto's Light
          stronger than ever!

The crowd cheers *like she scored the
winning point in a rugby match.*

The green/red spirit ball drops slowly

towards the earth.

>   MADAME BLÉ (CONT'D)
>   Remember those who made the
>   greatest sacrifice to allow us
>   victory tonight.

SHAWK! A stake shoots out of the ground
and remains upright.

SHAWK SHAWK SHAWK! Several others follow
suit, lined up along the lot's edges.

Ms. Droûx's eyes flash red, sending a wave
of her spirit across each stake.

White ziccolit screens light up on the
top of every stake.

On each of the screens, a face fades in.
The faces are in various states of
lifelessness. Heads hang, mouths open for
some, and eyes are closed or half-open.
(taking portraits of the dead can prove
rather difficult; do not judge, only
embrace)

On one of the screens, a boy's face fades
in. His eyes are closed, his head is
tilted back, and his mouth droops open. A
name appears in white ziccolights under
it: Trilbledy Williams.

>   MADAME BLÉ (CONT'D)
>   Show your respects. Remember them
>   as they were when they exhibited
>   the most remarkable courage in
>   Her Light. For Her purpose. To
>   bring Her home.

Madame Blé nods to the members circling
her.

All the Callisto's Light members in the lot step back. Stop. Raise one of their hands over their head as though needing assistance to rise. Their other hand meets the raised, palm to palm— *a handshake to self.*

>   MADAME BLÉ (CONT'D)
> We came here on a whim. However, something drove us through these roads, telling us that the fixtures were not sturdy. Came to find that the Damned were left to rot in their misery. We, The Light, provided a solution. Help the Damned harboring their fears overcome themselves.

Madame Blé spreads her hands apart.

>   MADAME BLÉ (CONT'D)
> The sacrifice of those chosen spirits will not be in vain.

The green/red spirit ball seeps through the soil. Disappears into the earth.

>   MADAME BLÉ (CONT'D)
> With their power, we create life.

The soil rumbles and boils. Rises like fresh dough.

>   MADAME BLÉ (CONT'D)
> Rise again, renewed warrior of The Light!

A hand launches from under the earth and grabs towards the night sky.

Madame Blé's smile expands.

Ms. Droûx's scowl curls further.

An upper torso sticks halfway out of the ground. He shakes out his perky blond locks full of dirt and pulls the rest of his smooth, athletic frame onto the surface. Lifts his head. His piercing green eyes stare straight ahead.

> MADAME BLÉ (CONT'D)
> Give your Vengeance avenger his due respect! Welcome him to The Light!

The members filling the square's outline ALL DROP their cloaks, baring all. Only Ms. Droûx, Madame Blé, Jamari, and about ten others not in the lineup remain in their cloaks.

BY THE BUSHES OVER AMY'S SHOULDER

> AMY
> You've gotta be fucking kidding me…

BACK IN THE LOT

Jamari watches with a dropped jaw.

> JAMARI
> (whispers)
> You've gotta be fucking jokin' mate…

The freshly risen man, VENGEANCE, marvels over each of his hands. He runs a hand down his glistening abs. Smiles. Licks his lips.

> VENGEANCE
> That spirit form… so limiting…

> MADAME BLÉ
> Take your time, child.

Vengeance flinches at her voice.

> MADAME BLÉ (CONT'D)
> It might take a moment for you
> to compose yourself within your
> new body.

He eyes the others around him as though noticing them for the first time. Uses one hand at a time to bring himself to a knee. Bows.

> VENGEANCE
> Madame. Respectfully, fuck is
> this? An orgy?

BEHIND THE BUSHES, SWEAT DRIPS DOWN AMY'S FACE

She licks some away. Her arm trembles as it itches her chest.

> AMY
> They're all here. Some from
> Endfield… some from Jadesfeld…
> This is—

> (soft laugh)
> They've checked in clinical.
> They're all signing into this
> shit. And Droûx… with aura? Fuck.

Her flinching eyes hit the dirt.

> AMY (CONT'D)
> Mary J. Waana, send a message to
> Gma. Possible danger, need to
> talk.

Communication systems down.

                    AMY
          What?

BACK IN THE LOT

Ms. Droûx approaches Vengeance's rear,
her hands clasped in front of her. She
bows.

                  MS. DROÛX
          Welcome home, brother.

Vengeance faces her with a blank stare.
Smooths his hair back and out of his
face.

DIVES at her—hands choking—

—an unbothered Ms. Droûx.

Several hooded members grab him, unable
to hold him back.

                  MS. DROÛX
          It's okay. Let him have his moment.

Vengeance lets go of her. Panting.
Smirks.

                  VENGEANCE
                  (laughs)
          BWAAAAAAA, SISTER!

He leaps onto her with a bear hug.

Madame Blé opens her arms to the crowd.

                  MADAME BLÉ
          Brother and sister. United again,
          flesh to flesh. All in Callisto's
          Light.

The crowd claps and cheers.

                    VENGEANCE
          It's been too long.

                    MS. DROÛX
          Not long enough.

Ms. Droûx pulls away and walks past him.

                    MS. DROÛX (CONT'D)

          The   Light   appreciates   your
          fulfilling your duties. We still
          have some souls to mend.

                    VENGEANCE
          Graahh, I'm tired of the pony
          show. How many more of these lost
          souls do I have to torment?

                    MS. DROÛX
          It's not torment, brother. It's
          enlightenment for the Damned.

                    VENGEANCE
          Porn is porn, sis.

Madame Blé strides up to him.

                    MADAME BLÉ
          Thank you for your service. We
          are all grateful for what you
          have done for these communities.

                    VENGEANCE
          Sure thing, Madame. With respect,
          where's the grub?

                    MS. DROÛX
          Right now, Brother Vengeance?

                    VENGEANCE

> (to Blé)
> It's been ages, Madame. Man's gotta eat!

Madame Blé nods to one of her members. They beckon Vengeance to follow them.

Vengeance winks at Ms. Droûx.

> VENGEANCE
> Catch up later, sissy.

Jogs after the member, who is already halfway down the lit path leading into the woods.

Jamari tips to the side, avoiding collision with Vengeance and watches him run for supper.

> MADAME BLÉ
> Hungry souls feast the best!

Laughs from the gallery.

The spurt, now three feet eleven inches, tugs at Madame Blé's cloak.

> SPURT
> **Arg-guk! Arhg-gak-gak!**

> MADAME BLÉ
> Soon, my love.

> (to gallery)
> Hearts are suffering. Now, it is time to witness Her—

> JAMARI (O.S.)
> Ight, nuffs-a-nuff, mates.

Jamari pulls his hood off, dodges the curious hands of the spurt, and steps up to Madame Blé.

                    JAMARI
          This is wild. Madame, with all
          due respect, what the hell is
          this about? You told me we were
          helping people, not damning them.

Madame Blé places a hand on his shoulder.

                    MADAME BLÉ
          This is helping them.

She turns him to face the rest of the
members.

                    MADAME BLÉ (CONT'D)
          Every one of them has vowed to
          help these communities find the
          power within themselves. We find
          those who can harness the strength
          of their spirit, unlike any other.

                    JAMARI
          And what about the so-called
          Damned?

                    MADAME BLÉ
          Brother Vengeance is commissioned
          to unravel the darkest things
          crawling inside of those who can
          no longer live to fight for
          themselves. To help prepare them
          for Her imminent return. These
          towns, these communities, are in
          pain. They needed us. Needed the
          will of Callisto to pull them
          from the depths of insanity and
          sorrow. She will help them. She
          will help you.

She turns him to face Ms. Droûx. Closes her eyes.

Ms. Droûx's eyes GLOW RED.

Jamari DROPS. His unconscious body quakes.

Madame Blé puts her hands together.

                    MADAME BLÉ (CONT'D)
          Put him up for the sixth chair.

Three hooded members lift Jamari.

                    HOODED MEMBER ?
               Heavy lad.

Madame Blé turns to the others.

                    MADAME BLÉ
          We lost Emildade this morning.
          Rest her soul. Mr. Wyst will take
          her place. All in Callisto's
          Light. Only then does one truly
          shine.

The earth rumbles. Two large mounds of dirt rise in the lot's middle.

Ms. Droûx walks over to the rising mounds. Waves a hand.

A red flash of spirit escapes her and washes over the mounds, pushing the dirt off to reveal two sparkling glass caskets.

Madame Blé skips over. She runs her hands over the smooth glass. The five-foot spurt mimics her.

                    MADAME BLÉ

It is time.

                    SPURT
YAAAAAAAA-ahk!

The glass MELTS from the middle of each chamber top, sizzling down the sides midway, then ceases. A mist rises out of the open caskets.

Hooded members place Jamari in one casket. Glass **crackles** and creeps back up the edges on both sides, rebuilding and sealing the casket shut once more.

Madame Blé and Ms. Droûx peer over their new captive.

Jamari's eyes open. Pounds and screams his protests from inside his entrapment, all muffled sounds.

                    JAMARI
What—fucks—do—my spirit?!

                    MS. DROÛX
No worries, child. It's merely been suppressed. Your spirit gleams with power. You've always been our chosen second.

                    JAMARI
Why?! Why—doing this?!

                    MADAME BLÉ
You want answers, Mr. Wyst? You have brought them to us. She is already here.

Madame Blé points out—

TOWARDS THE BUSHES.

Amy's eyes go wide.

Several hooded members surrounded her from behind.

Chapter Twenty-Four

Rise Of Vengeance

*O**k. Okay. Droûx is with aura. Is Blé?* Amy slapped her sweaty hands together and shook them out, still crouched on bouncing forefeet. **Gasped**. *What are they doing to Jamari? Is this part of the show? Why are they whispering now? Fuck. What are they— I've gotta get in there. OK, I can do it. Need to get the jump on Droûx. Environment is key. There's about... great, over forty— maybe more. Most, if any, won't be fighters. I'll have to knock some out with a blow or two. Blé could be with aura, too, so I have to keep an eye on her. Her lackey's a fucking <u>bot</u>—language— <u>Andryex</u> <u>with</u> <u>aura</u>, fuck me. OK, two-on-one odds. Not the best. Can I even use my aura to fight?*

Amy closed her eyes. *Gma, answer your bloody call—Fuck, the one time—*

GASPED—

She falls back with eyes on Madame Blé's finger— pointed in her direction.

"The fuck?" She threw on The Singer's Mask. Cocked her fists and balanced herself, one hand pressed into the dirt.

"Don't be alarmed, child." An elderly man stooped feet behind her.

Behind him, a dozen hooded figures closed in. They opened their arms.

"Rise and serve The Light."
"Rise and serve The Light."
"Rise and serve The Light."

"Come. Rise with us, Chosen One." The old man hooked her arm with a smile. Two more hooded members held her other arm and shoulders.

"Fuck—off!" The Singer delivered a headbutt to the old man, downed another member with a high knee, barely escaped the third's clutches, and downed him with three lightning jabs to the face.

The Singer dashed through the bushes.

SHIT—FUCK—so much for the element of surprise—FUCKING—FUCK—OW—SHIT—

She sprinted into the lot, stumbling to a stop.

"Stop! Let him go!" The Singer pointed at the glass casket containing Jamari.

Madame Blé beckoned her with open arms. "We welcome a new soul. One who Mr. Wyst has deemed worthy beyond belief."

"Relax." Ms. Droûx marched towards The Singer. "You've been selected for greatness. Your words. Your song. Your power of spirit. You believe in Callisto's Light, don't you?"

"I don't believe in whatever this is. Let him go." The Singer raised her fists. "A fair wager. You're familiar? I beat you; you let him go."

Ms. Droûx stifled a laugh. "There's something unhinged about you." Her amused face reverted to her natural, stoic essence. "I'd love to beat it out."

"C'mon then! First to pin for three-counts wins."

"Ah, wrestling. Very well, this won't take long, girl." Ms. Droûx nodded over to Madame Blé.

Madame Blé returned her nod. She faced her members. "We have entertainment. Quick."

The members moved in at once, tightening the space around the soon-to-be combatants. Some, still naked, all members created three lines of rows around the *prize fight.*

A naked woman moaned into the night air. "In Her Light, we find a way." She expanded her arms as she looked at the moon.

A man followed her lead. "In Her Light, we resolve dispute!"

The Singer lifted her eyes from his genitals. *He needs to put that thing away. They're all just—I can't do this. Wait, that's my old neighbor. Ew. Focus, Devine.*

The Singer and Ms. Droûx circled each other, feet out of reach of one another.

The Singer dragged her feet across the crunching earth. Maaura Style, she placed her left forearm on the back of her right one.

Ms. Droûx stopped in the center, hands clasped in front of her.

What is she doing? The Singer rushed forth on light feet. She delivered a sidekick to her opponent's leg and stepped back out of reach.

Ms. Droûx hadn't budged.

Come on, let's see it. The Singer's foot swung and rechecked her opponent's leg.

Ms. Droûx stepped towards her, hands still clasped.

That's it. Let's piss her off. The Singer swung a high kick— CONNECTED with Ms. Droûx's barely moved face leg pushing against it to no avail.

Ms. Droûx grabbed the leg and <u>squeezed</u>. She lifted her opponent.

"AH— OW— *fucking*—OH fuck—"

The Singer's body flew high— landed face-first in the dirt. She flipped over and scampered back on her ass.

The still Droûx stared down at her. "You'll want to hit a little harder, dear. Use that youthful spirit within you. Now get up."

Bitch! The Singer rose. *I'll show her.* The Singer threw a wild flurry of punches— pulled back— left jab—right hook— curled into herself with her left forearm on her right, Maaura Style. She pushed up with a right uppercut and swung her left hip into the *rock of a* woman. Aimed her left elbow and swung back—

—Into the woman's waiting hand. "I am The Light, and I am here to fulfill Callisto's grand legacy." Ms. Droûx squeezed her elbow.

"You're insane!" The Singer's right elbow SPED—

—stopped by the woman's—*hard as a krhyzo*—forearm. "Sanity isn't the question." Ms. Droûx sent lefts and rights to block more incoming blows.

The Singer pushed forward, stomped, danced her feet onto

the woman's feet each time— buckled back— delivered more leg checks.

Ms. Droûx took her stomps, bending back to avoid fists. "Are you even trying to pin me?" She spun, grabbed The Singer's arm, and WRUNG it around the wrong end— HEADBUTTED her.

"Shi—" The Singer stumbled back. *What the fuck is she on? Dalestone's dre—***CRACK** as a flying elbow came down on her skull.

The Singer shook her cobwebs loose— failed to block two more blows of random limb— buckled to a knee. *Shit, wait.*

The right arm on top of her left, Maaura style, The Singer leapt up—

Ms. Droûx caught her arms—

—WITH HER OWN VERSION OF MAAURA STYLE, crossed right arm over left. Ms. Droûx's eyes scanned her opponent's arms. "Interesting style." Her *fucking elephant* grip brought her opponent to her knees. "Can't seem to find anything about its origins. Internet isn't always reliable. Dr. Estrada and I frequently wondered about the secret spiritual societies undisclo—"

The Singer pushed back the *robotic* woman before dipping her legs underneath her— hands on the ground, leg sweep skidded the dirt— missed—

Ms. Droûx KICKED her stomach—

"OOOF!" The Singer held her belly— *No*— raised her arms in defense as—

Ms. Droûx's legs were around her head.

click-click

What's that?

Ms. Droûx rode on her shoulders and squeezed her legs against the resisting force of the girl's persistent arms.

The Singer buckled to a knee, straining from the pressure of her head being crushed.

Ms. Droûx's Andryex legs STRETCHED LONGER THAN NORMAL— HOOKED UNDER HER OPPONENT'S

STRUGGLING ARMS.

The Singer's body flipped— head—neck—back—smashed flat on the ground. "Fuck!"

"Shall I pin you now?" Ms. Droûx stepped away. She wiped the dirt off her gloves.

Fucking cunt. The Singer growled and hit a small button under her mask's chin. Her modulated scream echoed as She ran for her target—TACKLED the woman, a panther, onto her meat, with a crunching SPLAT on the ground *Urrrghhhh—that hurt.*

The Singer growled and sat up on her opponent's torso. SMASHED down a left fist—SMASHED a right—came down with a DOUBLE ELBOW—

Into the woman's face. Ms. Droûx ate each blow with a head jerk that always pivoted right back on her target's mask. Ate and STOPPED a HOOK with her forehead and PUSHED BACK— standstill between her murderous face and the unwavering fist. Ms. Droûx's blank eyes stared into the mask. "Why aren't you pinning me, <u>dear</u>?"

Rain trickled over them.

"Come now, Droûx." Madame Blé waved the rain away as the rows of nudity opened up to accommodate her stroll towards the match. "Can't we be done with this game?" She wiped the wetness from her face and placed her hands on her hips.

The now six-foot spurt cheered the fight on.

Madame Blé shook her head. "Teenagers."

"AHHHH!" The Singer launched a left UPPERCUT— threw a right—

BLOCKED by the mad-eyed Droûx. "Enough." Her palms cracked backwards at an unnatural angle and ensnared her opponent's fidgeting wrists. Her arms SPREAD EAGLE—

—The Singer fell towards her—

Their heads SMASHED TOGETHER.

Ms. Droûx's SCARLET RED AURA ENCLOSED HANDS interlocked with The Singer's— swung her around in a furious waltz. Let go—

A portion of the crowd parted like the seas as The Singer's body FLEW past them—

—and dumped on the wet ground like trash by the bushes.

"Wretched." Ms. Droûx wiped her muddy hands on her cloak. "I can tell by how you fight that you've been sheltered."

The Singer crawled towards her. Rose on trembling knees. *Piece of shit.* Her modulated **SHRILL** of a **HOWL ECHOED— small waves of sound visible in the air—** *mistake—* CLUTCHED her throat and fell to her knees. *Aura... Ace... I need you to be stronger.*

The crowd dispersed, letting their bionic champion through.

It's not working. Plan extreme. Swallow the light. Sacrifice your consciousness, Devine. And pray you're not killed in your coma. A minor fever flushed across her forehead. *Spread the warmth.*

Inside her mask, Amy blinked. *C'mon!* She thumped her chest. **SCREAMED**. Blinked. Slapped herself repeatedly. *C'mon, c'mon.* Blinked. **"COME ON!"**

"Urg. That thing's as dreadful as Dalestone." Ms. Droûx grabbed The Singer's Mask and ripped off half the mask. She flicked her hand to the side, the mask half rolling off her fingertips. For the first time since they'd met, the woman showed genuine shock. "<u>You</u>?"

The Singer brought her hands up to her face— *Come on, Ace! Where—*

Ms. Droûx flushed her hands away. Ripped off the other half of the mask. "<u>Amy Devine</u>."

Now or never. We can do this. Amy wiped her face clean of the turbulent rainfall. **"COME ON!"** Screamed to the sky. Panted. **"AAAAH-urr-up—"** Her eyes started to close...

As a shadow on the ground in front of her grew three times as tall.

Ms. Droûx skated backwards.

The cult members gasped, hollered in fear, and recoiled, cowering at *whatever the sight was,* just as Amy's eyes closed.

I can... still hear them. I'm not unconscious. Amy raised herself on her fists, getting to one knee. Then on both.

Madame Blé dropped to her knees. "She really is The One."

"You BITCH!" Amy's body seized up in a vicious fit, drool flying out of her mouth, arms twitching at her sides. She fell over, still seizing on the ground. Stopped, her eyes wide and mouth frothing.

Amy jumped and punched—

Ms. Droûx caught her fist with an aura-enclosed hand. Her eyes went red.

Amy fell to her knees from the snapshot of light.

"Stay." Ms. Droûx's aura-enclosed hand palmed Amy's head, stifling her attempts to rise.

Amy's blurred vision spiraled as it cleared up slightly, the peripherals still too fuzzy.

Madame Blé crept up beside her. The old woman's cracked lips touched her ear. "I knew you would spite me when one of my devotees from the JPD saw you exchange info with those foreign detectives. I <u>never</u> <u>dreamed</u> you and the mysterious Singer could be one-and-the-same. Full of spirit. That's a bonus."

Amy spat blood at Madame Blé's feet. "I knew from the day we spoke who you <u>really</u> were."

Red snapshot of light ate her vision.

Ms. Droûx forced Amy's body to stand and locked both arms behind her back. "She's a tough one to quell."

"We have our seventh chair-***chair-chair-chair-chair-chair***!" Madame said.

Amy shook the ringing voice out of her head. *What did she do to me? Those flashes of aura... I can't even sense mine right now.*

Ms. Droûx pushed the resisting Amy forward with ease. "I don't know why I couldn't read it before. Yes." She leaned into Amy's twitching ear. "Something inside her. That spirit is stronger. Easier read now."

"You hold a gift of divinity," Madame Blé said, walking alongside *the sacrifice*. "That does not make you one. However, I can raise a Divinity. Now—" She turned to face the members all around the lot. "Let us take the time to remember those who helped bring us to this momentous moment in our history."

Amy struggled against her captor, tripping over her feet as she's forced to march towards the remaining casket. *They're all watching. Detectives. Neighbors. That's my childhood dentist. Whole fucking town.* Amy watched her own feet drag through the wet blades, dirt caking her sneakers. *I... I'm trapped again. Such a fucking idiot.* Closed her eyes. *I'm sorry, Gma. I'm—* Out of breath, her eyes wandered to the now glowing wooden stakes lined along the edges of the lot that Blé was now praying to.

Between each, white screens with images crossfade showing different people, dressed to the nines, while posed in odd positions with their names underneath their photos in bright yellow ziccolights:

A set of eyeballs on a woman's charred face stared into space.

A man's head, slit throat, hung to the side.

A couple, Cheshire cat smiles on their faces, and identical holes in the sides of their heads.

"Memento mori. Remember our fallen heroes. Those who took the oath to do whatever it takes to restore Her glory." Madame Blé pointed back at Amy. "The woman you see before you has walked amongst our ranks, lying through her teeth about her intentions. She came to us with the false desire of connection." Blé marched towards Amy. " I can tell you who she really is."

Wait... it can't be...

On one of the screens: Marmi. She wasn't visibly hurt compared to others, but her head hung forward, a vacant expression peering down. Her face wore frustration— *no, determination. The last look she had before she...* "NO!"

Fading in on a different screen, a boy's tilted head seemed to look up at the night sky. His image crossfaded with another photo of him, this one with his eyes rolled back and looking straight ahead. His name lit up in ziccolights under his portrait: Trilbledy "Trinks" Williams.

— *"What's a bird without its voice?"* —

"No." Amy shook her head. "No, he was just a boy!" She turned her head to Madame Blé. "How could you?!"

Madame Blé nodded. "Young Trilbledy was a terrible accident. He took the place of his brother, unknowingly to us. His suffering led him to believe that he was the one who possessed the external power of his spirit. Tragic. We left the brother alone as the family had already lost too much. Trinks recognized his sacrifice would bring Callisto back. Ensuring no youth would ever succumb to a curse like Saint Cloudy again. We honour his courage in Her Light."

The six-foot-five spurt danced around Amy. Its claws swiped and scratched Amy's cheek, leaving four deep cuts.

"No!" Madame Blé scolded. "No, bad boy! Go grow in slumber!" She shot a finger out. "Callisto will need you at your strongest, my child."

"Ar-gi, ar-gi, shunackle, shunackle..." The spurt soured off, jumped, and dove into the earth, leaving a crater behind. Its digging sounds and vocal protest burrowed deep below.

The march of shame came to an end at the foot of the opening glass casket. "How could you?!" Amy shouted at Blé. "I trusted you! You helped me—" Amy looked down at her feet. "How could you?"

Madame Blé came up to her with the look of a disappointed mother. "I offered you salvation and a seat at my family's table." She gestured to all the members, who watched in silence. "And you spat in our faces. Looking for a reason to destroy all we built as a community."

"You're full of shit, always have been. My home let you in and you sic your lap dog's brother to torture the minds of innocent people. Some nerve—"

"You have. Mr. Pudersmitt's nowhere to be found. Mali almost didn't go through with her birth because of you. Infecting the minds of others with your lust... Swear her in, please."

A hooded figure moved over to them, removing her hood: Celestia. She made a cross symbol across her forehead and made one across Amy's.

Amy woke herself up from the shock of the reveal. "You, too? You can't be this dense. She's manipulating you!"

Celestia looked her dead in the eyes. "It's all in Her light."

"Adored members!" Madame Blé said to the crowd. "Please acknowledge your newly anointed leader after my time is done! Madame Celestia!"

The Light members around the lot raised their hands to the skies. "We acknowledge you, Madame Celestia!"

Madame Celestia raised her fists to them. "I am humbled. And once my time comes to lead this great family, I will do so with pride. For all I have sacrificed will walk with me in power as we all walk alongside Her!"

Cheers roared through the night.

Amy's head spun on them all. "You're all monsters! Every last one of you!"

Ms. Droûx HEADBUTTED Amy's skull from behind. Tossed the limp girl's body into the open glass casket. The glass edges **crackled** back together—sealed shut.

Amy shook out her cobwebs and banged on the glass. "Let me out of here you sick piece of shit!"

Madame Blé leaned over, peering straight down at her *captive.* "As I told my members, there were only two paths for you. This is the least favourable path, and you chose it. Congratulations, Amy. It turns out Callisto's One Big Fault exists after all. When my members asked me if I believed you would choose the other path and join us, I told them I was not sure, even though it is my sworn duty to believe in all the children of Callisto. My truth is that I did not believe in you. I am ashamed of my feelings."

"We absolve you, our Madame!" the Light members declared in unison. "For all you do is in Her Light. She speaks through you as you speak through us."

Madame Blé's teary eyes left her members and stared back at Amy within her glass box. "In the past, my conflictions had gained me a sore reputation that I had to eliminate. I was either too hard or too soft when dealing with viable solutions. So I tried a different approach with you. As I told you before, never force, only encourage. You chose this path, Amy. We thank you for it. I thank you for it. You are the bravest soul I have met in a long time." She walked away, out of Amy's sight, leaving only Droûx and her glare behind.

Amy shivered as the temperature dropped inside the casket. She flinched as Blé's voice echoed on the outside.

"Callisto's return will fulfill the rapture! For all who are living or decaying with life will be united as One!"

Inside the casket, a silver mist spritzed from the corners and surrounded Amy. She **SNEEZED**.

A snapshot of red aura ate her vision, and her small world got bent by vertigo, a high-pitched hum traveling through her ears.

Droûx's voice warped all around her. "This is the way towards your long-sought-after redemption. Everything you are will be with Her."

Outside her *cell,* more members closed in, ogling her in turn before scurrying off.

"Our Chosen One. Incredible..."

"See the light! The answer to our prayers!"

"Her Light will return..."

"Are we sure..."

"Her Eminence! She'll be here. Finally!

The muffled sounds of glee, awe, shock, wonder, and anxiety continued.

Madame Blé's voice echoed. **"Her sacrifice is necessary."**

A symphony of murmurs filled the night air. Their soulless eyes poured over their *sacrifice.*

"NO!" Amy banged on the glass. "Let me the fuck out!" She cleared her hoarse voice. Itched her neck, thighs, chest, everywhere, mind tricking matter into belief. She readjusted her body within the tight space, sending painful tickles down her spine. She massaged the choking feeling in her neck and coughed. Pounded a fist into the glass. "No." Sunk into the *bed's* softness, the finality of the situation filled her mind. *So sleepy...*

I'm so... it's okay... okay... Her eyes fluttered.

Madame Blé's ringing voice shrilled against the glass, words in and out of earshot. "Callisto calls on you all—stand—feet—towards unveiling the light. Start them up."

Silence.

No.

Silver haze filled the entirety of the casket's interior.

Amy's chest heaved in and out. She closed her eyes. *NO.* Her eyelids twitched. Eyes shot open and zipped side to side. "NO!" *This is not gonna end this way. Please— I'll kill them all. I'll...* Her eyes slowly closed. Opened slowly.

Madame Blé's face pressed against the glass from the outside. Her eyes penetrated Amy's. "Your power. Your essence. Will echo within Her... Your voice will go on." She moved away. "Finally! Our Chosen One! Here to bring The Light and Callisto... Home."

Amy banged the sides of her *cage.* Her brown cheeks pushed against the glass, growing a red flush. *I won't quit...* Her ears jerked—

"You sure? This One's the last? The main source is cracking."

"I have it. I claim it. It is mine," *Madame Blé answered.*

How can she do this? I trusted her, even if it was only to get her to trust me... This is my fault. It was— No. It can't be right. I'm more than a— pawn.

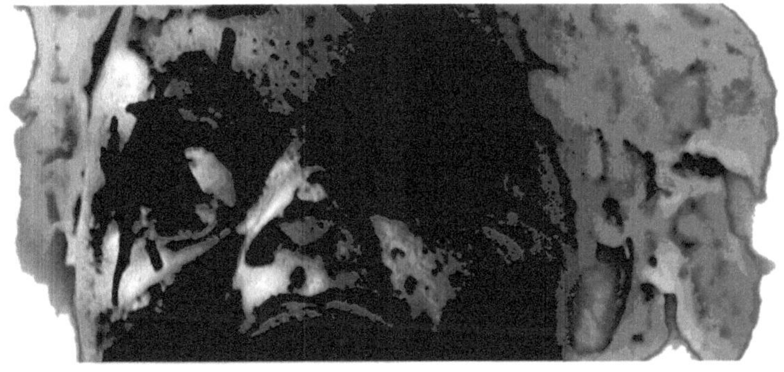

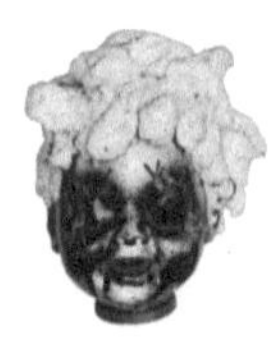

.

.

.

.

.

.

.

"*NO.*"

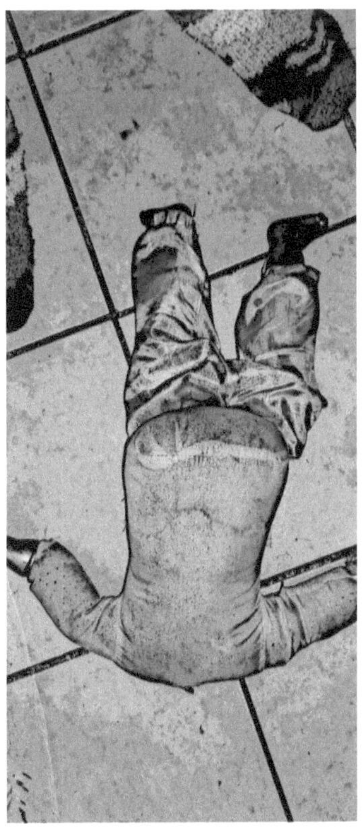

Fuck! "I can do it. I can do it... Shit, I can't breathe—I can't—FUCK, LEMME OUT OF HERE!" A seizure erupted over Amy's body as her eyes rolled back. *No.* Her eyes rolled back down to her hands.

Her WHITE AURA PULLED away from her skin— *as though siphoned by vacuumbeetles*— Silver shimmers STRIPPED from the aura's whites.

Scatting of words filled the space around Amy. **"I have it. I claim it. It is mine. I have it. I claim it. It is mine. I have it. I claim it. It is mine. I have it. I claim it. It is mine."**

"**Madame, she's scaling! The Source is overheating!**"
"**Leave it!**"

Demora... I'm sorry I failed you.

I shouldn't have ratted my Mum out publicly like that. Not like that. Not like this.

"Jamari?" Amy tried to turn her head, but it lay slightly left. *My throat's so dry. So hot.* Her face was lathered in sweat.
"**She's at 70%! The boy's <u>only</u> at 50!**"
"**Highest it's been!**"
"**She's draining more power than he!**"

Gma...

"**Oooh, sissy, what did I miss?**" The face of Vengeance with a sausage in his mouth pushed against the glass. "She cookin' yet?" He pushed away. "I don't remember her being on the list. What's this one done, anyway?" His obscured body dipped off.

"**Will you step back from the seventh chair? She's The One, brother.**"

No. Not like this—shit. Amy grabbed the glass and clawed at the smooth surface.

"**What's she done, sis?**"

"**There—no stability—meaning in this manufac— world— we—reated. That's why—must—find—own meaning that justifi—every breath we take.**"
"**She's at 72%!**"
"**Are we bringing Her Light or buying Her mercy?!**"
"**You spit that Celtic death rattle all the time!**"
"**You can't—**"

I CAN DO IT! Amy pushed against the glass. "I can do it. I can break this. Even if I pass out... Don't... Ace, don't you fucking give up—"

The glass **CRACKED** under her finger pressure.

Amy PUSHED *with everything I have! DON'T you—* "Don't you fucking quit!" *EVER!*

Amy blinked.

"You really want to do this now, brother?"

Amy frothed at the mouth. *Hang on, Jamari... Don't go yet. Hold on... hold...* Amy's eyelids kissed as her head went limp, though one of her hands remained suspended inches from the glass covering.

"It's all in Her—"

CLONG Stzriiiiiiip-ook!

"Not my granddaughter, you IN-SECT!"

TWik-tinkletinkle-twACKt

Craaacck-ack-ack-ack

Crick— KSSSHHHHK!

Through almost kissed eyelids, in between fine hairs...

Cra... cracks... in the ce... ceil... ceiling...

Shattered glass fell— SUSPENDED in mid air, small crackles of black light BLACK LIGHT electrified over each piece. The glass siphoned upwards towards the sky.

—The arms of a faceless woman with long aubergine-colored hair reach into a crib—

Mother's lifting me again. Do you know the ache of a forgotten mother? Lost in time. Whether by choice. Arguments ago. By nature's design? By captivity's cruel infrastructure of—

"You did so well." *Gma's voice echoed through the white space around me.*

Blurred vision, earned as Rezna's face came into full view. "Didn't require saving, did you? I'm proud of you."

"How... how did you find me?"

"I don't know. Someone's aura kept pinging in this direction. Wasn't yours, but it felt like yours."

"Droûx."

"No. She hides it well, but I felt hers the moment I arrived. We must find her."

"The Spiritualist!"

"Where did she come from?"

"She's a graceful mad bat."

"The shadows love her. Look! There she is!"

"WILL YOU SEIZE HER?!" The voice of Blé ripped through the air.

"I'll be back." Rezna laid Amy on the ground and marched away.

Amy turned on her side, face to drenched grass. COUGHED UP remnants of *the five Urhzunian donuts I scoffed down a half hour ago. My head's on fire. Getting cold.* Through blurred vision—*GMA*— pummeled two hooded *crooks* to the ground. Amy shook her head and raised herself on an elbow, eyes on her grandmother's back.

Three cloaks rushed Rezna—SMASHED INTO EACH OTHER—REZNA'S AFTERIMAGE peered down on them before vanishing.

"Your lack of aura's depth ends your journey here." Rezna appeared behind them. Grabbed the backs of the outer men's collars—SMASHED them into the middle woman's head— Dropped the bloody conjoined triplet of human heads.

Amy leaned into Rezna's coming arms.

Rezna caressed her face, moving the hair out of it. "Can you stand?"

"I can try."

Rezna smiled. "We always do."

"I can't let you leave, Ma'am." Brother Vengeance approached them from the rear, massaging his bothersome jaw. "Hell of a right you got there. My sis got some explaining to do. I don't know your record, but I've gotta ask you to stay put. May I offer you a challenge?"

Rezna smirked. "Ah. New murder to inspire."

Vengeance bowed. "With that, we will—"

Rezna grabbed his shoulders—RIPPED him in half, his right side gaining his head in the divorce. In two blurred motions, Rezna cast her arms to her sides like a chef, *the butchery done.*

The discarded puppet of Vengeance's bionic halves fell to either side.

Rezna returned to Amy. "Stay hidden. Gather your reserves

and <u>kill if too close</u>.”

I never thought we'd use that one. “Okay.” Amy shifted her weight with her grandmother's help and got to a sitting position.

Rezna entered the *battlefield,* facing a line of members of The Light, ready to square off with her. Others prayed on their knees.

Amy's eyes dragged up and down the lot. “Where's Droûx?”

Madame Blé fell to her knees in the center of the battlefield. “It's all in Callisto's Light. It's all in Callisto's Light. It's all in Callisto's Light. It's all in Callisto's Light. It's all in Callisto's Light.” Her trance carried through the winds.

Nobody likes me...

Amy frowned on her knees. Pushed off her thighs and ran on wobbly legs.

Nobody likes me... but that's okay.

She collapsed on top of Jamari's casket and peered inside—

Jamari **BANGED** his token against the glass. **CRACK. CRACK CRACK.** He groaned and fell back—jumped up—BASHED his head against the glass with a **BANG**, further splitting the cracks. “I don't fucking like y'all anyway.” **BANG!** “Man, I DON'T—” **BANG!** His eyes grew a RAGING RED— “like—” **BANG!** Blood trickled down his forehead. “Y'ALL—” **BANG!** His mouth, wide, his red aura growing inside of it. “ANYWAY!”

His aura BURST from every inch of his being— the casket's interior scorched with the red light—His **SCREAM**—

Amy dipped off to the side, shut her eyes and shielded her ears.

His **scream** died out. His blinding light diminished.

Amy pulled herself back on top of his coffin. She smashed her fists over and over. *I'm too weak. Please, hang in there, J.* She studied the casket's exterior.

Jamari's aura siphoned on the insides of his enclosure, leading up to a hole over his head.

She followed the trail to the top end of the casket. A pocket held Droûx's glowing orb with Jamari's red aura building inside it. *About 92% filled.*

Amy put her hands on it—her body FLEW back—spine **SMACKED** on the ground.

She shook out her scorched fingers. "GMA!" Her raspy voice let out. She massaged her burning throat. *I don't CARE!* "GMA! Someone! HELP!" She took labored steps forward and threw herself over Jamari's *tomb* again. "HELP!" Banged her fists on it with increasing fury.

Jamari's chest jerked up as he seized.

"NO!" Amy raised her fists above her head.

A glint of white light grew in her pupils. She **SCREAMED.**

Hands caught her arms. "I got you." Demora SMASHED into the glass casket, her upper half falling inside. She lifted Jamari out of it. "Ugh." Threw his body on the ground.

Amy crouched over him and checked his pulse. **Sighed.** "He's still alive."

"Jolly," Demora said.

"RISE MY CHILD! HER MIGHT NEEDS YOU!" Madame Blé's shrill cry broke the air.

Earth erupted from the crater in the middle of the field—the spurt in the mix. He crashed onto the surface. "TARGGAAAAAAA!" Multiple vine-whipping limbs flailed down on the battlefield. Vines twisted and merged into hulking arms for the *nine-foot-five!* beast and SMACKED praying members off their feet or knees. The creature charged towards Rezna.

"What the fuck is that?" Demora's eyes squinted as she helped Amy to her feet. "I'll go help her with it. You—"

"I've got this." Amy flexed her fists. "My aura's recovering." Her eyes fell back on her Gma's fierce battle with the spurt. "Handle <u>that</u>."

Demora looked down on Jamari.

"Thank you," Amy said. "He—"

"Didn't know." Demora nodded. "I got you. Always." She rushed off to the battlefield.

Amy grabbed her ribs, chest and finally, her shoulder.

"None of that feels good." She rolled her shoulders. "Droûx. Where the fuck are you?" She bent over Jamari. "Hang tight, J."

She picked up his fallen token.

—*Click-click*—

The sound behind her legs. Maybe a weakness. Her eyes trailed up.

Half of The Singer's mask rocked as rain poured onto it. The puffy back swellboo slithered from its cracked edges and felt along the wet ground.

—Higher power sources may cause swellboo to bend and disrupt electrical fields—

Amy walked over and picked up the mask half. Her eyes searched the field.

Madame Blé scurried off the lot and ran between the glass towers, following the path through the woods. One by one, the red lights on each tower dimmed to nothing as she passed them.

Amy's eyes narrowed. "Not today, bitch."

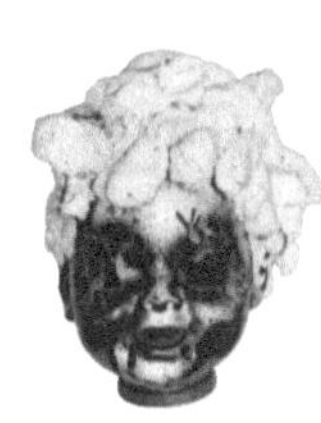

Chapter Twenty-Five

You're nothing without us.

allisto's Haven. Amy shivered with chattering teeth as she scanned the *shitty little cottage town full of schemers, abusers, and unworthy pieces of Dalestone's maggot-filled shit.* She kicked nearby bushes. *Where's the trap? Wait till I find her.* Her eyes locked onto the largest cottage in The Light's dark and dreary town.

The rainfall eased.

Amy took her eyes off the clouds in the dark sky and wiped her face. The howling air sent shivers up her spine. She rolled her shoulders. Scanned the trees above. *I know she's here. Why so easy? I can feel her energy a little. That's an improvement. Finally. Still foggy, though. I can feel Demo and Gma from here. So much energy around. If only my aura could focus on one. Come on, Ace.* She grabbed her chest, uttering a grunt with every step. Clutched her migraine. *My fucking head, fuck. Shan-fucking-Hiska.* Took several deep breaths and trudged ahead.

Crunch.

Huh?

BOP!

Amy opened her eyes. Raised her cheek off the gritty, cool earth. Arms splayed at her sides, she struggled to move them for a moment before regaining control. A dull pain pulsed at the back of her skull. The damp ground's weight pressed against her chest, soaking through to her skin and making it difficult to breathe. She rose on numb hands. Held her head. *That didn't help.* Holding her bloody ear, She rolled onto her back.

Large hands yoked her up to—

A smiling, cloaked figure. The man pulled his hood back. His large hands helped her stand straight.

Her fuzzy vision focused on the massive figure before her. *I've seen you be—*

His thick foot KICKED her stomach, sending her feet away into some bushes between two cottages. "The Light bears reward again."

That voice. Her eyes widened. *The pirate.*

"Anything's possible in The Light." *Milard* the pirate chuckled. He opened his cloak, a stylized CL buckle revealed on a hunter's belt. "Now's the time, my pretty. Thought you'd be closer to death by now."

Amy swung a weak fist—caught by his massive palm.

"Oh-ho-ho. You've lost far too much spirit to be fighting ol' Milard." His hand squeezed her trapped one.

Amy cried out, falling to a knee in the high bushes. She twisted her knee in the dirt as her fist pushed against his palm and the massive weight behind it. Her eyes shot darts into his. "Those kids. All those people you violated."

Milard's eyes widened. "How'd you—" He peeped his surroundings. "There's time. While the night's still ours." He unbuckled his pants with his free hand and pushed her down.

"You piece of shit!" Amy's hands thumped against his

chest as he lowered his weight onto her.

His hand squeezed her throat. Caressed her cheek with his other hand. "Shh. You're weak, darling. Let ol' Mila—"

GASPED. His eyes bulged, staring into hers. He released his grip and sat up on top of her. Looked down at his belly. Blood pooled out as his flesh TORE from crotch to chin. The guts from his barely halved carcass rushed out. He fell over.

With the bright moonlight shining down behind, a silhouette stood over Amy.

"Useless predator. One more issue resolved in Her Light." Ms. Droûx kicked over the deceased. "That's never allowed. Especially in Callisto's Light."

Amy got to her feet and scampered out the bushes. "Oh, you do have a heart."

"Here I was laying a trap for you only to end up saving you." Ms. Droûx smirked. "If I'd known he was amongst our ranks... if I'd known who he was... he would have never made it here tonight." She stalked towards Amy. "Your future is with us. Your spirit holds the key to Her great revival." She opened her hands, ready to embrace. "You're an anomaly. An exemplary one. We promise to bring you back after the great deed is complete. You saw what we did for my brother. Let us help each other bring peace to our World. True peace."

"Peace?" Amy spat blood. "My Gma told me true peace can't exist with people like you, whose aura is off balance." *Her eyes are always scanning.* She studied the woman's legs. *Where's the weak point?*

"Silly girl." Ms. Droûx chuckled. Her mouth curled in its usual manner. "You dare place your <u>aura</u> over Callisto? You don't deserve the breath."

Her breaths are shorter. So you DO get tired. Amy charged at her. *Underneath all that artificial mess... her 15%. ..* She delivered two LIGHTNING KICKS before spinning— *She's just a woman*— to jab the woman's ribs.

"**Ah-ssss!**" Retracted her throbbing fingers from the *ribs of steel.*

Eyes on fire, Ms. Droûx's waistline TWISTED like a deranged noodle. She grabbed Amy's shoulders—

OH SHIT. Lifted in the air, Amy's body flailed to get out of the bionic clutches. Trickling rain blinded her as She faced the sky. *She's too strong.*

Ms. Droûx raised a knee, balancing Amy's spine over it—

Amy reached down and grabbed the innards of her captor's nose— YANKED.

"You stupid— Ms. Droûx THRUSTED Amy's back towards her knee—

Amy FORCED herself to roll— landed stomach first into the *artificial* knee— **click-click**— and crumpled onto the ground.

There it is again. Amy ate STOMPS. *That clicking behind her leg.* Amy turned over—arms crossed, left on the top right, Maaura Style—and caught her abuser's foot. PUSHED against the *elephant-level weight.* Up on one knee, she twisted it—**click-click**—only to eat a foot to the face that tossed her several feet away.

No time. Amy's fists hammered the ground and spun around.

Ms. Droûx, over her, delivered a gut punch, face **slap**, face punch, and knee strike- a flurry of blows— *miss— miss—* **THWACK**— *miss— Ow! — hitting with 60% accuracy.*

55%

40%

38— She's always calculating. So can I. Amy spun her leg— smacked the woman's face.

Ms. Droûx ate it and pushed the young woman back. Threw a HAMMERFIST at her chest—

Tried to drain MY aura— Amy's arms crossed— CAUGHT the blow within her right palm—Maaura

Style. *Something's not right. This hold is off. What did Gma say?* Took a PUNCH to the chest but held on. Amy grabbed her opponent's other arm with her left. Dropped—her legs split, sloshed and skidded across the mud. She dipped back, right leg sweeping under Droûx's knee, bringing her down— Amy spun her left leg over—and sat atop her opponent.

Teeth grit, Amy's hands illuminated WHITE AURA. *Fuck yes!* Squeezed her grip on both struggling fists. "Let me show you—" EYES FLASHING WHITE "true power of aura." Her body grew a white outline of her aura. Silver flame-like aura strands danced on the edges.

"This again." Ms. Droûx struggled against the grip on her crossed arms over her chest. Her bionic arms SEARED under the grip, skeletal metal peeking through on the skin of her fingers and back of her hands—both MANGLED under the grip. Her eyeballs ran up, and the whites of her eyes FLASHED, BLINDING RED— released a SNAPSHOT OF LIGHT.

Amy blinked. Blinked again. Shook her head. *No vision.* She shielded her closed eyes. Opened one of them— **PUNCH! SLAP! SWOOP!**

Amy's body tossed to the side like a broken ragdoll.

Ow. I can still hear. She slid to her knees with her hands, using the wet dirt as leverage. *This is how she disabled Jamari.* A tremendous wind from a missed blow flew over her head. *Come on, Ace, wake back up, let's give her a show.* Amy opened her hot, glowing white eyes. They dimmed. *50% vision. If I can get to HER eyes*—withdrew her stomach from a missed punch—*maybe*— her right knee met the knee of the Andryex. *Ow-fuck!* Dodged two more fists—*Any moment...* "Fuck!"—grabbed her throbbing knee. Hands flew up to block another kick—*WAIT*—She spun—hand shifted in and out of her pocket— her back elbow countered a headbutt— She twirled around Droûx's rear—Jamari's TOKEN CLUTCHED in hand—SLAMMED it into the bionic woman's spine. *Gotcha.*

It's effective!

Ace!

"**ARGH!**" Ms. Droûx craned her back *with a smile?* "Great to feel pain again. It's been a while." Teary-eyed, she chuckled. Her arms EXTENDED TWICE AS LONG, mechanical parts exposed, and stretched behind her to locate the foreign object in her back.

Amy's knee UPPERCUT her jaw. Delivered another. And *ONE MORE.*

Ms. Droûx's body stood upright. Her spaghetti arms hit the ground and cartwheeled her away.

This is ridiculous.

We've got her on the run. Don't let up!

Amy pursued. *I appreciate the backseat driving, Ace, but I've got it from here!* Dashed after her spiraling-on-elongated-arms opponent.

Ah, don't shut me out now! We're kicking ass!

Ms. Droûx continued her retreat, one arm still focused on her spine, without missing a step in her cartwheel getaway. Threw a long left—

Careful—

Amy dodged— the arm RECOILED and wrapped around her waist. "Ah, fuck! Shit—"

Ms. Droûx tossed her into the ground, creating a small crater. Lifted— smashed her into the ground again, enlarging the crater.

Amy's hands grew white— her aura hands CRUSHED into the robotic arm as its owner barreled towards her.

Watch it!

Ms. Droûx's right arm went for the choke—

Amy interlocked her fingers and squeezed— Yelled in AGONY—

—as the hand squeezed back.

Amy pulled the lengthy arm towards her.

—Jamari's feet shuffle on the disco floor— **YOU'LL NEVER FIIIIIIND'—**

Amy shuffled her feet, *Jamari-style*, and side-stepped— yanked the robotic arm over her shoulder. *Let's prove our weight.* She spun— HER ENTIRE ARM ENCASED IN HER WHITE AURA— CHOPPED DOWN— RIPPED the mechanical arm in two. **OOF**— Amy's head bounced back from a straight punch.

Ms. Droûx's *good* arm went for her neck—

Amy's hands flew up to her neck just as the Andryex's bionic arm tightened its grasp around it.

Amy's feet left the ground—

Her body reeled in close to the mad eyes of Droûx.

One of Amy's hands reached around and snatched the token from the hole in Andryex's back.

"You will submit!" Ms. Droûx threw her to the ground, arm still around her neck. She lifted a foot over Amy's head.

Amy THRASHED the RETRIEVED TOKEN into the back of the woman's knee.

"Bloody—" Ms. Droûx scurried away with mechanical **clicks. Click-click—**

Click-click-click-click-click-click Stopped a few yards away and checked her knee's nape. She pulled on the token—**SCREAMED** a mix of human cries and whirring echoes— got it out and FLUNG it—

Amy's head flinched—the token whizzed past. She marched over. "It's over, Droûx."

Ms. Droûx's body twitched, electricity sparking from her wounded leg and her back. She steadied on her stable knee and threw a wild punch.

Amy blocked and kicked her nose, sending her crashing onto a cottage's porch. Amy sped forth, YANKED her up—

Amy blinked. *Wha—*

Ms. Droûx's body flew back first against a tree and landed with a **SMACK** into the wet ground some yards away. Her arm and half-arm grew shorter, then retracted into her torso. She slithered in short bursts like a speeding slug toward Amy.

Amy stopped her in her tracks with a KICK to the face. Dropped an elbow on her neck.

"You'll never win." Ms. Droûx's neck CRACKED at an unnatural angle. "More of us are on the rise." Her eyes grew red. "The Light will never die."

Amy slapped a hand over the woman's eyes. "Tired of your tricks." She slipped a forearm under her head to put the resisting Andryex in a chokehold. Their eyes burned into one another.

"NOT MY SIS!"

Amy SWALLOWED HARD. Jolted to her feet.

A GREEN AURA— *VENGEANCE*— moved like syrup over her face, forcing itself inside her mouth, nose, and ears.

Amy fell to her knees.

Everything around her disappeared as the world around her darkened. Grey clouds zoomed past her. Only the earth beneath her feet remained.

Amy's head **WHIRRED**—ROTATED—360— NONSTOP.

Two upside-down corpses dropped in front of her. Their arms grazed the wet earth as they swayed. Decaying patches of skin peeled on their bloody faces. Their blank, grey eyes watched Amy. Their noodle bodies spun, moving closer to her with every turn.

They stopped nose to nose with Amy.

The undead Demora and Rezna smiled.

"You can't save us, dear. Die with us."

"You can't save us, dear. Die with us."

BLINDING RED LIGHT ATE Amy's vision.

"You had a lovely voice," Ms. Droûx's voice echoed. Her glowing red eyes grew large above the dark atmosphere and dimmed to normal. **"Your fight's over,"** echoed the mixed voice of Droûx, Demora, and Rezna.

Gma. Demo.

"OOF!" Amy held her stomach. "NO—" Her body launched. **BRACK!** Her teeth ate dirt. *Feels like my fucking spine and chest got broken at the same time.*

Get up! We're drained, but we're still in this!

Our aura's done, Ace. I'm done. How can—

You can! Thrive! Survive! You've got this.

Amy's head whiplashed from two more invisible, vicious blows to the head.

HAHAHAHAHA HAHAHAHAHAHAHAHA

DOZENS OF LAUGHING REZNA AND DEMORA HEADS CIRCLED HER.

"Stop." Amy clawed the sides of her head. "Stop stop stop stop stop! **STOP!**"

Watch it!

Her arms rushed up to stop the pair of bionic arms trying to twist her head around. The mechanical arm stub sparked into her face.

"One way or another, girl, you <u>will</u> come to The Light."

HAHAHAHAHAHAHAHAHAHAHAHA

The Rezna and Demora heads looped in and out of sight.

Amy discarded her stomach's contents over the arm around her neck. **SPLAT!** Her face hit the cold, wet dirt, warmed by her puke. Pressure rose at the back of her neck. She blinked her bulging eyes. Her hands held onto the invisible weight squeezing her neck.

Amy blinked.

Enough. Amy's eyes GLOWED WHITE. She pushed off the ground—twisted her body—and tackled the massive weight holding her to the ground. Pushed away and gained her balance several feet back.

Thump Thump Thump Thump Thump Thump

Amy crouched as the footsteps approached. She dug in her pocket and pulled out her mask-half.

Thump Thump Thump—
Amy turned around and shoved the mask-half—

—onto Droûx's face. The Andryex's head seized with violent spasms.

The World returned around Amy, the night's black sky above her in the village of Callisto's Haven.

On her ass, Ms. Droûx's head spun out of sorts as the puffy swellboo from the mask-half on her face felt the air around it. Her undamaged arm elongated and grabbed a nearby cottage's rail to balance herself. LAUNCHED her own body into the air at Amy.

Dove down— Exchanged a flurry of hands with Amy in the middle of the village.

"When will you stop?" Amy's hoarseness came out. *Sound as motivation.* "AH! Hi-yaa!" She sent a HIGH-KICK.

Blocked. The uncovered half of Droûx's face closed in near Amy's. "I've trained in the dark for longer than you've pissed." She HIGH-KICKED—

Blocked.

Amy HIGH-KICKED—KICKED— KICKED— KICKED— KICKED.

Ms. Droûx HIGH-KICKED—KICKED— KICKED— KICKED— KICKED.

Their kicks met each other, but neither budged.

Amy—SPINNING BACK KICK—

Ms. Droûx—SPINNING BACK KICK—

Amy blinked. Her *missed* foot on the ground. "Huh?"

Ms. Droûx's foot—LANDED across her face.

SPLAT! Amy scurried off her ass to a hand and knee, balanced pose on the ground. *Calculating <u>cunt</u>.* Shook her body out. *Alright.* She stood tall and bounced on the balls of her feet. *Way without way, huh? Wait—*

Ms. Droûx rushed towards her.

Amy placed her RIGHT FOREARM ON TOP OF HER LEFT FOREARM, locked in Maaura Style-*Major.*

Dominant forearm on top. My right over my left. Got it now. Let's intercept those fists.

The undead heads of Demora and Rezna spun around her head.

Sorry, ladies, can't do this right now.

Ms. Droûx SMASHED her forehead into Amy's.

Amy's forehead held her back, eyes boring into hers.

In between them, Amy's Maaura lock held Droûx's arms in place.

Ms. Droûx stretched her slightly disjointed leg out, electricity sparking loose. "You may have given me extra elasticity in my knee joint... you <u>stupid</u> CUNT! Get this <u>thing</u> off my face!"

"e-YA!" Amy HEADBUTTED her back. CHOPPED her leg.

Ms. Droûx's head sat at an angle, tilted to the sky, with her eyes still locked on her rival. She **GROWLED**. Charged with LIGHTNING SPEED BLOWS—

Their blows met with perfect harmony.

POOM   POOM   POOM   POOM POOM

BLOCK   BLOCK   BLOCK   BLOCK BLOCK   POOM   POOM   POOM POOM   POOM

BLOCK   BLOCK   BLOCK   BLOCK BLOCK

The bent-neck Ms. Droûx threw a flying SHARP JAB—

Perfect—

—but her elongated arm landed under Amy's armpit.

Amy—Maaura Style-Major lock between them—her left hand clutched the Andryex's half-arm, her right fist squeezed the elongated arm—

Ms. Droûx twirled around Amy, her arms coiling around and trapping Amy inside.

Amy squeezed the arms harder.

Ms. Droûx's arms squeezed Amy's body into hers.

Teeth grinding from the suffocating clutch, Amy stepped onto the woman's foot. Pulled her arms back in turn, still holding on with her grip crushing the arms— SMASHED the bionic woman in the face with left and rights—

SPARKS flew as Ms. Droûx's arms TREMBLED. Blood seeped through her cloak.

Amy KICKED– SMASHED *her tibia on her stable leg*—

The mechanical arms around her loosened their grip— and dragged onto the ground.

Ms. Droûx buckled— and fell into Amy's arms. Swellboo from the mask-half whipped around as her body spasmed.

Amy hooked Droûx's neck under her arm. YANKED it while KICKING her VICIOUSLY from behind. Her torso ate the elbows that flew into it. Teeth grinded.

Ms. Droûx pulled out of the headlock. Her head dragged against the ground. Rose—swayed on its ELONGATED NECK.

The undead Rezna and Demora heads bounced around Amy.

You're nothing without us.

You're nothing without us.

Shut it. Amy bounced back on her feet. "Read somewhere your lot had a bit of an elasticity issue with your necks." Her smirk turned upside down. "Time's up."

Ms. Droûx SCRAPED the mask-half off of her face, bringing some of her flesh and mechanics along with it. She tossed it aside. Shot a clawed hand out—inches from Amy—

Amy's GLOWING WHITE AURA HANDS grabbed the woman's arm before it reached.

Ms. Droûx tried to yank away, frustrated at each failed attempt.

Amy tightened her grip. Circuitry and flesh crackled

under it.

Ms. Droûx's eyes GREW SCARLET.

Amy blinked.

Amy, EYES GLOWING WHITE HOT, sat on top of Droûx. Her fists pounded into the woman's face. Out of breath, she grabbed her rival's arms and pulled— RIPPED OFF BOTH OF THE ANDRYEX'S ARMS.

Amy spun on the struggling torso and grabbed her opponent's flailing legs.

Ms. Droûx's torso JERKED UP—CHOMPED into Amy's shoulder.

Amy **SCRE**-CLAMPED her teeth together— RIPPED the legs off her opponent and tossed them. ELBOWED the head biting into her—spun around again—CHOKED the throat of the seething limbless flailing Andryex with her glowing white aura hands.

Ms. Droûx's eyes dimmed to normal.

Amy SLAMMED her onto the ground, still choking her. Again. Again. Again.

The Andryex gasped for air, her raspy breath mixed with looping **whirs**.

"One, two, three, look who's pinned," Amy's voice growled. Her hands <u>crushed</u> the throat further— *I'm still holding back. After all she's done. They've done. I can do it. Pull the trigger, Devine. She doesn't deserve the breath.*

The undead Rezna and Demora heads laughed behind Amy's head.

Kill her! Kill her! Kill her! Kill her!
Kill her! Kill her! Kill her! Kill her!

Droûx's eyes bulged from her crackling mesh of human flesh and circuitry. Her mouth spat blood between choking gargles.

I can't. Amy's glowing eyes dimmed, scrutinizing her downed bionic foe. *Not again.*

"Life is more than PINS, girl!" Ms. Droûx bared her bloody teeth. "You can't finish this."

"I <u>CAN</u>." CLAWED fingers CLAMPED into Ms. Droûx's face—caved in her eyes, nose, and mouth. The hand retracted, leaving a gaping hole behind.

Amy scooted off and away from the sputtering faceless Andryex.

Ms. Droûx's body twitched in erratic spasms. A steady hum stuttered out, followed by a broken rhythm of sputtering, failing circuits. Steam rose with a soft hiss as a metallic groan escaped from deep within the mechanical core. The head slowed its side-to-side beats against the ground. "Your time will come..." Her head came to a **crackling** stop, with Droûx's final glare fixed on the one standing above her.

Chapter Twenty-Six

Last Resort

Demora stood over them and surveyed the mangle of bloody machine and flesh all over and inside her clenched fist. Flung it away from her body. "Bloody bot."

"Language." Amy took her best friend's hand.

"I'll pay penance later." Demo's smirk left as she tried to pull Amy to her feet, but her friend failed to rise. "Are you alr—"

Amy waved her off. "Gimme a second." She sat on the ground. "Is Gma—"

"She's solid. Whatever that Franken-spurt was, it was no match for two of us. Rez is subduing that thing till the Dets arrive with some way to contain it. Cult had a distraction going on in Endfield during their ritualistic nonsense. Met Rezna there. I was searching for Blé." Her eyes shifted ahead. "One left." Demora wiped her hands on her pants and booked it.

"Hold on—" Amy stumbled to her feet.

Demora grabbed the handles on the main cottage's front doors.

"Demo, wait!"

Demo swung the doors half-open—

The GREEN AURA OF BROTHER VENGEANCE flushed her face.

"Get the f—" Demora struggled against the aura invading her orifices.

Amy ran to her side, with undead Rezna and Demora heads behind her.

You'll never save her.

You'll never save her.

"Just GO!" Demora said, eyes GLOWING PINK as she held her head. "DON'T let <u>her</u> get away!"

Amy readied her Maaura Style. Her fingertips illuminated, and her arms outlined with her aura. BLINDING CIRCLE OF AURA swirled clockwise in front of her shield stance.

At the ready, Host.

Amy grabbed the vertical slants. Pulled the creaking doors open.

A FIREBALL hit her Maaura shield, pushing her back, but her shield's force evaporated the flames. *That's boiling* hot. Amy pressed forth.

Another fireball shot at her— ate by her shield.

Madame Blé stood on a stage behind the grand altar, across the room, with several rows of seats between her and Amy. "This altar was crafted on a crisply hewn block of Dalestone."

Several hooded members crept from the shadows behind her. A dozen bodies filled the stage. "In Her Light. In Her Light. In Her Light. In Her Light. In Her Light."

"Thank you, Droûx, for your courage." Madame Blé's hands rose from behind the altar. Both ENGULFED in RAGING FLAMES. "Your essence lives on."

Amy rushed ahead.

"STOP!" Madame Blé cast a hand out—a trail of FLAMES SHOT into the space Amy nearly stepped into between the congregation seats and the stage. Her other engulfed hand waved menacingly above her head.

"It's over, Blé!"

"<u>MADAME</u> BLÉ."

"Come in, easy. No one else has to get hurt."

"I beg to differ." Demora stepped in beside Amy, her raging pink eyes focused on Blé. "Steal me and then toss me like trash. **WHY?!**" Her shaky eyes stayed on the old woman.

"In Her Light. In Her Light. In Her Light." The members never ceased their chant.

"You weren't enough, girl." Madame Blé shook her head. **"Tsk, tsk, tsk.** Your output wasn't enough. However, your friend…" She smiled at Amy. "She's The One." Her crystal-grey eyes *of madness* glared. "You <u>will</u> fulfill your duty."

"In Her Light. In Her Light. In Her Light."

Demora raised her arms. "ENOUGH!"

VENGEANCE GREEN—DROÛX RED—AURAS ENGULFED Demora's head.

Madame Blé shot a fireball—

Amy pushed the floundering Demora out of the way—ATE the fiery blast with her shoulder.

The siblings' tag-teaming auras flushed across Demora's body—spread her limbs eagle wide—her LEG ON FIRE, Demora screamed FURY—her body YANKED BACKWARDS in midair—auras circling her—and launched out— the DOORS SLAMMED behind them.

"In Her Light. In Her Light. In Her Light."

Madame Blé cackled like a giddy schoolgirl and twirled in her spot. "Let the pit of despair bring her to The Light!" Her hands shot down—

Amy jumped back as a RUSH OF FLAMES devoured the floor space.

Chipped—CRACKED—parts of the floor CAVED IN.

Waves of flames splashed the sides of the building and surfed behind Amy, cutting off her only exit.

"In Her Light. In Her Light. In Her Light."

A ring of fiery death surrounded Amy.

A burning pit stood between her and Blé.

"It's all in Callisto's Light," Madame Blé whispered. "It's all in Callisto's Light."

"In Her Light. In Her Light. In Her Light."

Amy **coughed** blood and staggered back, falling to her knees. She hurled a puke-blood mixture onto the floor.

"My, my. My Droûx did a number on you. Rest her soul."

Amy glared at Blé. Threw her hands out.

Nothing escaped them. *Ace?*

"You do not believe. Do you accept Her Light?"

"Never," Amy snarled.

"In Her Light. In Her Light. In Her Light."

"KNEEL." Madame Blé's unblinking eyes stared into Amy's soul. "It's all in Callisto's Light." The fire around her hands ran up her sleeves— down her torso— RAGED over her ENTIRE BODY, except for the head. She opened her arms out to her followers.

Her hooded members kneeled around her.

"In Her Light. In Her Light. In Her Light."

She grabbed one of them by the cloak with an unflamed hand. "It's all in Her Light." She THRUSTED the member INTO THE BURNING PIT between the stage and Amy.

"ScaAAAAAAAAAAAAAAAH   HEEEEEELP HEEwEE—"

Amy's eyes of terror stayed on the flailing arms in the sunken *Hell.*

"It's all in Callisto's Light." Madame Blé grabbed another whimpering member. Yanked her forward—

"In Her Light. In Her Light. In Her Light."

"STOP! What are you doing?!" Amy paced behind the fiery barrier. *Fucking insane!*

CREAK.

She stepped back as more of the floor crumbled.

Madame Blé's eyes narrowed on her.

No. "No, wait—" Eyes raced across the floor. *Floor's hollow—*

"In Her Light. In Her Light. In Her Light."

Madame Blé TOSSED the whimpering woman into the pit.

"AAAAAAAAAAAAAAAAAAAA!"

Grabbed another shaking member.

"HOW MANY HAVE TO SUFFER FOR YOUR BELIEFS?!" Amy clutched her throat.

"ALL!" Blé TOSSED the member. Grabbed another.

"Jus—" Amy clawed at her head. "Wait-wa-wa-wait! STOP! I'll join!"

"In Her Light. In Her Light. In Her Light."

Madame Blé yanked the member she grabbed back away from the pit, knocking off the young lad's hood.

The sobbing lad kneeled beside her.

"I'll join, but please stop this!" Amy charged forward as much as She could without walking into the wall of flames raging around the pit.

"You don't believe." Madame Blé peered into the face of an elderly woman who prayed opposite the sobbing lad. "It's all in Callisto's Light, my child."

The woman nodded. "I'd die for you and Her Light, my Madame."

The elderly woman YELPED—kicked into her fiery grave.

"NOOooo-**hurech**—" Coughed. Amy held her stomach and her throat. Her short breaths echoed. Her heavy eyes fell over the charred remains that reached towards her from inside the pit. Eyes of fire found the gallery on stage. "Push HER!" She pointed to them all, her hoarse voice's volume defying its weakness. "Don't let her kill you off! You are not her weapon!"

"It's all in Callisto's Light." Madame Blé tossed another member. "It's all in Her Light." Then another.

Amy turned away as the sobbing lad **HOLLERED** his way into the blazing grave. She clutched her chest, coughed up more blood, and wiped the persistent sweat from her forehead. She squeezed her stomach and pinched her nose, the smell of burning flesh rising from the barbeque. "STOP, I SAID I'LL JOIN!"

"Madame, please—"

Another member tossed.

"It's all in Callisto's Light." Madame Blé nodded down at the searing flesh.

"STOP THIS SHIIIIIT!" Amy slammed her feet—

The floor PITCHED at an angle.

Lopsided, Amy fell to one side.

"Join us." Madame Blé tossed a hand out.

A glass orb with moon symbols fell to Amy's feet.

Amy picked it up.

Inside, a reddish-brown pill.

Amy twisted the top half of the orb off. Tipped the pill into her palm.

"Take it," Madame Blé said. "You will wake once She has risen again. We will bring you back. Be a part of something grand, child of Callisto." She spread her flame-flickering arms like a hungry serpent across the building. Her arms acted as flamethrowers in every direction, unmoved by the parts of the interior falling around her.

In the pit, a charred corpse ceased its movement, its hand gripping the stage.

"You're never too important to see the world around you." Amy stared at the pill. She gestured around, dodging the falling debris. "Is this really <u>Her</u> vision?"

Madame Blé readied another scared member for the toss. "It's all in Callisto's Light."

Amy wiped her tears. Bit her tongue. *I can't do this.*

"It's all in Her Light." Madame Blé, madder eyes, tossed the member. "CHOOSE! Callisto's will must be done! It will!"

Amy's blank eyes stared at the many members still available for sacrifice. *It's all in Her Light. It's all in Her Light.* Her fists clenched <u>TIGHT</u>.

You won't get through to her.

I know.

We're outta gas. Oh— Your temperature's rising. Are you alright? Uh, Host? Host?

I'll do what I do best. Amy **YAWNED**. Stretched. "Welp, if it's <u>Her</u> vision." Her trembling hand teased the pill near her mouth. "Doubt she was real, anyway." Shrugged. "We'll see." Put the pill in her mouth— *and underneath the tongue.* Blinked. Blinked. Blinked.

"You—" Madame Blé banged her hands on the altar, caving it in. "<u>DARE</u> hesitate for Her revival! <u>DARE</u> speak of which you do not believe??? You ungrateful, incessant, parasitical swine of a degenerate failure in Her Light! You ARE Her One Big Fault, but you will be corrected! CATTLE! You will be <u>cattle</u>— ANYONE will be <u>cattle</u> to fulfill Her Light!" She grabbed a terrified woman—

—Who pulled her hood off. "PLEASE, MADAME—"

Amy blinked.

Madame Blé smiled at the cowering member in her hands. Brushed her hair. "It's all in Her—"

"<u>SHE</u> HAS NO <u>PURPOSE</u>!" Amy's eyes GLARED BRIGHT WHITE—BURSTED INTO <u>ORANGE</u>—Narrowed on target. She shot a clawed hand out—her SILVER-CLOUDY WHITE aura flew to the altar—

—and CHOKED MADAME BLÉ'S THROAT. The ever-burning old woman grabbed Amy's aura stream— cried out as a **sizzle** deterred her hands.

A white and silver blanket of Amy's aura swept past the altar. It engulfed the screaming members and flushed them onto one side of the cottage. The aura blanket burst through the wall, carrying The Light members with it.

Amy's glaring orange eyes never left the altar. Never left Blé. Her nose flinched. Her mouth stirred at every choking utterance of Blé's. Her *protective* aura spanked away the alarming amounts of falling debris. "You just couldn't stop yourself." Amy's outstretched clawed hand curled inward, her fingers almost touching her palm. Her face twitched from the smell of death in her nostrils.

"Ack—" Blood dribbled out of Blé's mouth. She choked up more. **Croaks** escaped between gasps for air.

The <u>Light</u> got her tongue. Amy's aura expanded, holding the raging inferno at bay. "How many have to suffer for your beliefs?"

Madame Blé's bloody lip curled up. "A—"

Wha—Amy's eyes widened—She DUCKED—

A GARGOYLE SOARED THROUGH THE FRACTURED CEILING—**screeching**— **CRIED**—

—as it POUNCED on top of Madame Blé.

Amy's aura balled itself around Amy's body.

The building CAVED IN.

INSIDE HER AURA BALL, Amy dashed through *MELTING?* wood. She TACKLED through one—two—three blocks of smouldering debris— BROKE through to the outside—

DASHED OUTSIDE— FLAMES TRAILING BEHIND HER, and CAUGHT AROUND HER— the flames EXTINGUISHED around her aura ball.

Amy stopped, dropped, and rolled within her solid, shimmering, silver aura sphere.

Her orange eyes dimmed to natural. She collapsed on her knee—then her butt. She faced the wreckage's inferno. *All this for what?* With staggered breaths, she peered around at the other perfect cottages unaffected by the decadence. *Fever's back...*

Amy fell onto her back.

Blinked.

"Hey." Demora limped and hovered from above. "There she goes."

Amy sat up. "How long was I out?" She held her head.

Demora stooped and threw her arms around her best friend. "You're a star." Her chin snuggled on Amy's shoulder. "Is she...?"

Amy sighed. Nodded. "The terror twins? Where—"

"Done for. A gargoyle swooped in. Snatched them whole."

"It got Blé, too. It only confirms what we know. The evil

shall pass."

"I'm sorry I wasn't here sooner." Demora sat beside her, edged up on her elbows. "We should've been side by side throughout. Worked together. I'm sorry I left you. I..."

"I shouldn't have pushed you out of the Prison Games. But Demo, you can't just run off anymore when the world crashes. I'm your friend, but I can't be there for a ghost. Promise me we'll stay together, act together from now on, and I promise you I'll never do anything like that again. I'll restore your trust in me."

"I promise. You and me against the World. No more running."

They smiled at each other.

BOOM! POOSH!

All around them, other cottages in the Haven burst into flames, all linked to the Haven Church.

"Oh." Demora shrugged. Dek and I may have set some firestarters last night."

"Dek?"

"Pudersmitt."

They watched the smaller blaze of the main cottage's remnants grow as the other fires field it. Demo tapped Amy's arm. "Gang's all here."

Behind them, *Gma*, shades on, hair out of whack and barely held together by her headwrap, approached, sporting a nasty limp. "You girls, alright?"

"Yeah," Demora said, raising an eyebrow. "Are you?"

"Peachy."

Amy jumped to her feet and hugged Rezna for dear life.

Rezna smiled. "Of all the things I thought of that woman... never did I..." She huffed out hot air. "Curses."

"Who could have? You were more than great. You always are."

"I'm human." Rezna groaned, holding her back. "Shows, doesn't it?" She frowned as Amy moved past her.

Fucking— Amy stormed towards the crowd of blue cloaks, wandering into the village.

Now, wait a minute.

Hush. They did this. Bloody IDIOTS!

Listen to your aura. We're a team, remember?

As she neared, the crowd backed up. Amy paused her march.

They're scared.

They better be. Amy crept towards them. *I've had enough of this town and the next over.* Her nostrils flared.

The crowd backed further away.

But one man stood forward, leading the crowd, still wearing his cyan cloak of The Light. Detective Sellers brushed back his white hair, maintaining eye contact with Amy for a few seconds before *shamefully staring at the earth between them.* "The uh, the JPD rounded up all residents who are members with... the cult to uh, offer our sincerest apologies for what's happened here and are ashamed of what we did."

Amy glared into them. "Yet you still wear their cloaks."

The detective raised his eyebrows, looking down and shiftly removed the cloak, dropping in on the ground.

"No matter." Amy's right eye watered.

—Trinks jumps into a hero pose with the toothiest smile—

"What's a bird without its voice?"

Amy stared at nothing. Letting her tear fall down her cheek. "Doesn't matter. Damage is done." She looked Detective Sellers in the eye. "Am I still only Jimmy's pet project?"

"Forgive us!" A man in the front row dropped to his knees. "We gave her everything! She told us she'd bring Callisto back to heal the World."

"She did!" Another woman walked up from rows behind. "I gave her my family heirlooms."

"She made us vote!" Another voice yelled from the crowd. "Said it was necessary!"

"Gave'er muh two passed cuzins." An old, gruff man near the edge of the crowd came forth. "Had their spirits in heiligjars fuh over seventy years. Won't get um back, but thank you." He got on his knees, hands locked. "Thank you for saving us."

"Yes, thank you!" The heirloom woman said. "Praise our saviours!" She got on her knees. "Our Trinity!"

"Thank you, Trinity!"

"Our Trinity! Thank you!"

"We owe you our lives, great Trinity!"

"Our salvation all along—"

"**ENOUGH!**" Amy's shoulders squared as her chest heaved with such force that her saliva spat out of her slightly open mouth. Her eyes BURNED ORANGE. Her cloud-white aura grew around her body, dancing around her like a flame against an unseen wind. Silver flickers of her aura shot off from all angles and vanished into the night sky.

The crowd's shaky eyes gawked at her. Shaking from head to toe. Deers in headlights as their bodies leaned back slowly, but they were frozen otherwise.

—Trinks jumps on quiet feet—Takes a hero pose—flashes his toothy smile—

I'm not Blé. I'm not Droûx. They aren't me. Amy's aura faded. Her eyes dimmed to normal. She shook her head. "What's a bird without <u>her</u> voice?" She looked at her hands. At the scar on the back of her right hand. Stared into the crowd. "I'll ask you all the same question I asked Blé. How many have to suffer for your beliefs?"

The many eyes of the crowd found their feet. Others shook their heads. Some exchanged somber stares with their neighbor.

Amy clenched her fists. "If you need us, you know where to find us. <u>Good</u> <u>night</u>."

Amy glided through the body of bowed heads and shuffling feet as the crowd split like the parting seas to accommodate her. She glanced back.

Rezna and Demora's stunned but satisfied faces followed her. Nodded their approval.

Amy's face softened.

Past the crowd, her body loosened as she neared the end of the village.

Jamari, E'oné, Ms. JellyRoll Ling, Mr. Pudersmitt Stoicism and Professor Graves cruised towards her.

"Cleaned up your messy town for ya." Jamari smiled.

"You had me. I thought you were doing another bit like your Vegas stunt last year."

"No freaky Andryex or preggos in my art from now on." Off his sister's look. "Not that anything's <u>wrong</u> with that." He nodded at Amy. "So… you <u>are</u> familiar with my work."

"Please." She chuckled, patting his shoulder.

Jamari held her hand. "I'm sorry I told Blé your masked alias had spirit. Aura. I felt it first time we met in Enfield Square. When you sang."

Amy nodded. "It's okay. It's not your fault. <u>Any</u> of it."

He gave a slow, *knowing* nod.

"Thank you for saving my brother." E'oné hugged Amy.

"Oh." Amy hugged back. "Thank you all for helping my unstable little town." Cracked her neck. "Or towns."

E'oné pulled back. Looked at Demora. "You too. Thanks."

Demora bowed her head. "Don't worry about it."

"Seems like some real freaky-deeky going on for sure out in these parts," Mr. Stoicism said.

"Shut up, 9," Demora *warned*. "Where's Ms. Mopey?" Off Amy's confused look, "Kassandra. She helped with the cleanup."

Kass…

"Are we still not allowed to exchange names?" Ms. JellyRoll asked.

Professor Graves shrugged with a big smile. "I'll leave that up to your lot."

Mr. Stoicism/*Number 9* offered his hand to Amy. "Deklance Pudersmitt."

Amy took his hand. "Amy." Eyebrow raised. "Devine."

"Akila Ling." Ms. JellyRoll bowed and shook her hand next.

"Kassandra. Owens." Kass rolled her eyes with a teeny smirk. "Jamari and E'oné Wyst. Everyone knows Demora. I-forgot-her-name-Graves—Are we all acquainted now?"

Amy laughed. "I'd love to chat more." Held her head. "But I need to lie down. For days. Weeks, maybe."

"Yes, let's get Ms. Sleepyhead home." Demora's hands guided Amy's shoulders forward. "Come on, now. Catch you rebels later." She smirked at the lot of them.

"Rest peacefully, girls." Graves gave both a warm touch on the shoulders. Her eyes met Rezna's. "Well."

Rezna stood in front of her. "Well." Moved on.

As they got further away, Amy turned to Rezna. "Is everything alright, Gma?"

Rezna's sharp stare remained ahead. Silent.

Until next time on— *Not just yet.*

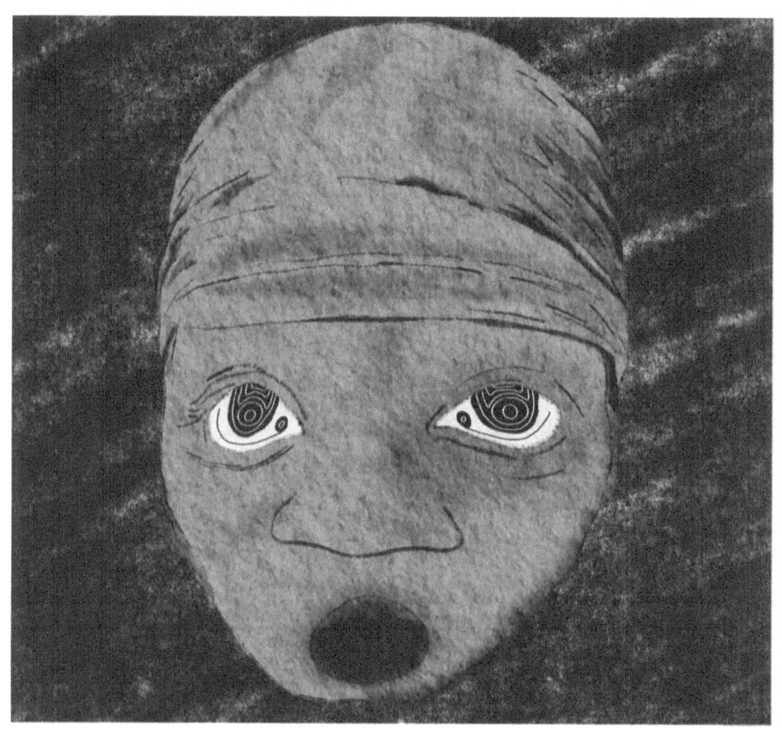

"You have another visitor."

A small frame walked from far away.

In seconds, Trilbledy "Trinks" Williams smiled in front of Amy. "Can you give my folks a message for me?"

27

Note To Self

'*You're only as destructive as your mentality.*' Life's a horror film I'm desperately drawn into but constantly running away from. I can't figure out my dread of leaving this blue stone without some purpose fulfilled. I can't imagine not seeing my loved ones again. The past couple of weeks taught me that.

This should have never happened.

I stepped outside for the first time in a long time, not scared of my shadow or reflection. I would've welcomed death two months ago in this very room as a courtesy or as karma for my hypocrisy.

However, I reneged on my former vow, as Gma reneged on her separation from the public. Yesterday, she performed the last exorcisms for those troubled by the vengeful curse. I could only stomach two of those experiences. I'll get better with it. A new turn for my dear grandmother, who now flows through the streets, ever annoyed, as Rezna Devine, Chief Mortician, Surgeon of Death. She quite likes that last bit a lot.

The fact is, shit like this is unavoidable without the growth of the people.

An underground lab under that entire fucking lot. All signed, sealed, and commissioned by the Mayors of Jadesfeld and New Enfield without a bat of the eye. All in Her fucking Light. Collecting souls and trying to combine them into one body. What were they thinking? Even an Andryex shell can't sustain that much aura. All those people they fooled. I wonder when folks will start thinking for themselves, though this issue is as old as humanity. Joint Commissioners for J-Feld and NewEn confiscated what remained of The Light: 54 prototype android vessels, 11 "birthing" chambers, 8 of those soul capture devices *(Vyktrex Core)*, a shattered 'Source' and the remains of Ms. Droûx. Her model wasn't as sophisticated as the current gen of Andryex, but there was tech inside her parts, mainly the head, whose origins couldn't be worked out.

Death. There it was, lying right in front of me once again. Though we've courted thousands of hours over the past year, still, you remain a mysterious disease inside and around me. Death is in my bloodline. Ruined it. With only me and Gma here to show for it. Death, you haunt my wicked brain with the vicious visions you've left behind. My core rots at your desire.

—Ms. Droûx's body twitches in erratic spasms—a soft hiss of steam rises—a metallic groan—her head beats side-to-side on the ground—

Sometimes, I think about how she should have been saved and not manipulated. But the hurt in her heart became irreversible. That's what I tell myself.

Hm, what's this?

JPD's official report. Off-market blood transfusion from Droûx to Blé. They weren't sisters, but they sure went the extra mile to become blood sisters. Interesting. Somehow, it helped Blé wield the fire she produced. Protected her from its burn. But how did she produce it in the first place? I'll have to research those flames. Find out what type it was.

Dets don't know squat about spirit, and it shows in their report versus Blé's. Blé wrote her reports like movie scripts. Truly lived in her fantasies. She was tracking me. She knew I went to Euyrkm. How? Who told?

There's nothing more on her transfusion from Droûx. One thing's for certain: The transfusion attached a part of Droûx's aura to Blé, but Droûx still maintained her aura's color. It may be possible to detach your aura without losing its color after all. Guess I'll have to study the Founder of Espírituology, Dr. Clemencia Verónica Estrada. Connect her understanding with mine. Maybe get my orange back.

Gargoyles. Raw energy fills their belly. They go wild for it, sometimes forgetting their own safety; Gargoyles linger around unsettled, disruptive spirits.

So why didn't the gargoyle go for me?

Whatever path Droûx and Blé were on has been shut down by the new leader of Callisto's Light: Vyolai, the sister of my classmate Vyaila. Once released from the hospital, she gave full accounts of all the cult's activities for the past five years that she's been a part of their ranks. After reuniting with their Gyaad sisters, Vyolai chose to lead The Light in a new direction. One that values the importance of each other while acknowledging Callisto's dedication to expanding the knowledge and depth behind aura.

The Gyaads sure know how to throw a reunion party. I was just happy to be invited, even after the fifth shot of their way-too-strong beverage. They said I was safe within their sister circle for eternity. Not entirely sure what that means, but the parting gift intrigues me.

—Amy studies the metallic ocean-green crystallization tracing over the scar on the back of her right hand—

*—Vyolai opens her mouth, "**Oooooooooeeeeaaaa**"—*

—Amy smiles through clenched teeth—

Thank the stars for Demora for the translations. I'm still working on understanding the Gyaad's language. I had to ask why they infused Dalestone in my hand if it's supposed to be toxic to aura. Her answer surprised me. 'Sometimes what we perceive as a threat makes us ignorant of the benefits.' We'll see how this goes. I'll trust her word. Getting better at that, too.

I must admit I'm super glad Vyaila chose to stray from her pack. She said it best: *'I have my own story to complete. Here.'* Seeing her say goodbye to her sister was difficult because I could tell neither wanted to leave the other ever again—not after this.

Vyolai also gave me some of The Light's off the book paperwork—and this.

A 9th Vyktrex Core. She slipped it out before the count. To think I only nicked a chip from Droûx's head. Like the old jigsaws from the Games, it seems to be missing its counterpart. Really don't want to break in JPD again, but... time will tell.

—Silver haze fills the entirety of the casket's interior— Amy bangs on the glass— Her WHITE AURA PULLS away from her skin— VACUUMBEETLES! — Silver shimmers STRIP from the aura's whites—

Why didn't I see it before? Vacuumbeetles. Able to suck in energy from external sources in order to use that energy to melt their shedding exoskeletons in order to create nests and escape their predators. They simulate a shadow effect that covers their tracks.

If I can somehow use excess energy... and mimic my shadow... I could create black light. It's only seen in curses. I'd have to do it without giving up any of my aura while using the external energy as my own. The only question is how are vacuumbeetles able to siphon other aura energy without overheating themselves?

Will I be able to?

I'll keep fulfilling my promise to Jonathan Jones. To Trilbledy 'Trinks' Williams. I went to see his folks the other day to do just that.

—Amy sits across from the parents and the twin brother of the Williams family—

I recited every word. Just how he wanted. Every word.

— "I'm a little lost, but it's okay. That's how it has to be. I'll find my way. Just like you'll find yours now without me. But I'm only gone physically. Mama, remember my song?!"

—tears fall from the mother's eyes—

—Amy holds back her own—hums and sings:

"I will fly away with you today

I'll spend the whole day, too

It's our spirits meshed forevermore

So Mama—"'

— "I love you," Amy and the woman finish at the same time—

—The flood of a woman fell into Amy's embrace—the teary-eyed spouse nods from behind—the parents hold each other—Trinks' twin cries through his laughter—

—Amy takes the mother's incoming hand and smiles. "Sorry for the theatrics. He wanted me to stay it—"

—Just like that," the mother finishes. "I'm so glad his star has only grown."

My brain's still picking apart the Prison Games. Shout-out to the students who make me want to push myself further daily...

Jamari Wyst, the Midnight Inferno: The kid who refuses to be stomped out or made a muppet of.

E'oné Wyst: A fashion icon and one smart, tough firecracker. Still going through the online shops she recommended. Her style is unmatched.

Vyaila: I'll be fluent in your language in under a year. Maybe. I'm trying. All we can do, right?

Deklance Pudersmitt: A bit of a snob sometimes, yet soft inside. Guess he's got a big heart when he's not being too annoying.

Akila Ling: A hell of a woman whose homeland I won't visit anytime soon until they catch that Dragon and Phoenix. In the meantime, I'll inspire myself to build up half your poise.

Vedessia: Whose bubbly laughter vibrates the walls of my... brain. Apparently, a hell of a fighter. I hope I get to see it soon.

Hideko Ang: **blech**. This isn't over, you little brain full of farts. Challenge accepted. Got your number, kiddo.

Kassandra Owens: Why do you hate me so much? Do you? You've lost so much, and you wear mystery in comfort. I'm not sure where our paths lead. But I hope it's any path but head-to-head.

Demora Corbyn-McDonald: Always there to tip the odds and remind me of who I am. After all these years, I'm still figuring you out. Your decision to stay with Gma and I for a while will help me accomplish that. Would you have killed Jamari? We don't have to find out.

Then there's me: Amy Devine. I got a book full of shit I can't believe I've drafted. If I published, they'd imprison me.

—Amy laughs at her desk—another laugh echoes around her—

I'll continue the UnderCity therapy solely because it's diabolical to think <u>no</u> one can beat that bloody game, even if it's the phenomenal boxing legend Atzra[2] Rutt[1] in ziccolit form. I'm going to beat it.

Callisto's Light became so focused on a symbol to worship that they forgot their why. They forgot the heart of the message lies with the people. Seeing so many fall under ill persuasion gives me fuel to turn their misguided message into one that can actually benefit the people. I don't know about this inknowledge business. Perhaps there is some weight to seeing yourself in others. It all has to start within.

I may never regain my aura's true light. I had to say it over a billion times in my head before I let it sink in. I acted as if my aura was lost when, in reality, it had just changed. *— Amy raises a palm— a cloud white aura ball bursts to life over it, silver flickers around it—* This new development is quite tasty, though. Plenty of research ahead to monitor it and find a way to weigh the output of this tinge of strength I've gained. My aura needs me to believe in it, and I can't fulfill that if I don't have the original faith: Faith in myself. That's what I'm after. Always.

—Amy's pen lingers over the page—

I should stop writing here for today. *Hm.*

Who can I be honest with if I can't be honest with myself?

I have to admit. Not everything played out as it seems... my apologies, journal...

Before this story began, I racked myself a little Criminal Class B charge I never saw coming. I wasn't myself. Demora ignored me. Gma, always on my back. Jimmy was busy cleaning up the mess Cloudy left behind.

And this motherfucker just had to ruin two lives in his single, pathetic one.

It was a few days after Cloudy. The first time I had stepped outside since.

Damn, crevent stood over her with his unbuckled pants, enjoying the thrill from her quivering. Giving himself a pre-jack before pouncing on her somewhere in the depths of Alleycat Ave. Possibly the reason my unconscious, snoring carcass found itself there so many cold nights... attracted to chaos... in lust with setting order... seeking another predator...

I'd never seen anything like it before that night. Rape was a myth that only existed in a past world that I was not a part of. It's like ever since murder reintroduced itself to society, all the other depraved activities targeting innocents also came to light. Even ol' Perry never got this far, as the spotlight backfired for him before he could live out his disgusting child-preying fantasies.

And here was another predator. Taking advantage of that innocent woman.

I'll never understand why some need to impose themselves on others. I pray for the unwilling parties to gain the strength to do what I did. Do whatever it takes to STOP the advantage-takers. Perhaps not go as far as I did. It changes you.

All I could think—what if it was a child?

The thing is, all of us once thrived as carefree children. When did our innocence stop mattering?

Maybe it was the doll's voice in my head...

—Amy stares at her reflection in the mirror—Her reflection smiles back—laughs—

Or possibly my ambitions. Maybe I just had enough. Seen enough.

—Her reflection bows to her—

I pummeled his face into the pavement right down to the steel boundary between the 'Surface World' and the UnderCity. That was after I kicked his genitals somewhere inside of him. I needed to ensure that chest of his, which he beat so proudly over his victim, caught some dents in it. So he can remember the reward for his abusive nature. Remember the symphony caused by his monstrous tendencies. The cracking of his ribs and other bones—*music to my ears.*

—Amy sits on top of a man's torso—SLAMS rights and lefts into him—

—his chest CAVES in—his face DENTS from a blow—

I wasn't thinking. Just feeling.

— Amy sits in a pool of blood beside the body—

—Jimmy rushes onto the scene—stops and stares at the mess she lies in—

—Amy places her hands up, waiting to be cuffed—

Ended up in a dark room. How typical. Here came newly crowned Knightship Burt...

—"What the hell did I tell you, Ms. Devine?! Stay in the shadows!" He leans in with the hottest of breaths, and his scruffy 'stache tickles my cheek. "You should be fed to Mickelspiff. Some penitentiary time'll teach you about discipline." He pulls back. "Next time. One more slip-up, and you're heading straight in, no deals. Only nightmares." —

So, my Criminal Class B murder charge became a Class C Civil. Scrubbing cams. **Scoff.** Look what influence buys you. Vengeance was right about that. Ol' Burt won't admit it, but he's way out of his depths when it comes to 'Peculiar' activity. No worries, Burt. My victim's mangled face in my dreams and nightmares will tighten the leash. I'll never be free of the torture that murder bestows upon me. I'll never be the same…

And of course, that all only led up to—

HER.

—Madame Blé's crazed eyes full of judgement—Through clenched teeth, "You will be **cattle***—ANYONE will be* **cattle***—to fulfill Her Light!"—*

Passion's ember became a blaze for her. One, she got swallowed in.

"SHE HAS NO PURPOSE." Amy's GLARING ORANGE EYES narrow on target—her clawed hand outstretched—Silver-white aura enclosed around her—her aura stream—

—CHOKES MADAME BLÉ'S THROAT—

—Madame Blé's sizzling hand retracts, unable to escape—

"You just couldn't stop yourself." Amy's outstretched hand closes the gap between fingers—almost a fist. "Obessive, ignorant bitch." —

—"Ack—" Blé couldn't breathe all that much—

Amy's head cocks to the side. The Light's got her tongue.

"How many have to suffer for your beliefs?" —her hand SQUEEZES.

Madame Blé's bloody lip curled up. "A—" Her eyes roll up—her struggling body ceases its struggle—

Gonna make sure every breath of life is out of this self-righteous—

The old woman's body went limp.

Is she dea—Wha— Amy DUCKED—

I can't confirm who got her first, the gargoyle or I. I can't help but smile at the fact that she's gone. *Have I truly gone mad? Have I?*

No time for all these diagnoses. Already got a nasty blink and SUTBAA to worry about.

The best thing to do is to get to know my Self.

—Amy's laughter fills her bedroom—a crack splits her reflection—

—Amy watches the crack in her wall mirror's reflection grow—

Although I'm not sure what the next test holds, one thing is for certain.

—Ace, cloud white form, walks out from behind her. Stands at her side—

—Their eyes GLOW ORANGE—

"I'm devoted to ME."

27

About the Author

Hailing from the depths of NYC, W.K. Phoenix has lived a life full of intrigue. The horrific and supernatural have always fallen onto his radar, leading him to record these instances of inspiration. Although ignoring the writing craft for some time, inevitably, the stories and characters that roamed in his mind would spill out into reality. Now the Phoenix universe is here to stay...

Please take the time to leave a review after reading!
Thank you!

You can connect with me on:
https://linktr.ee/wkphoenix
https://twitter.com/wkPhoenixLegacy
https://www.facebook.com/wkPhoenixLegacy
https://www.instagram.com/wkphoenix
https://www.amazon.com/author/wkphoenix
https://www.goodreads.com/author/show/21979218.W_K_
Phoenix
https://linktr.ee/Wbjr

Subscribe to my newsletter:
https://wkphoenix.wixsite.com/waynebaptistejr/contact

Also by **W.K. Phoenix**

Peculiar Cases Of Something Devine:

The Prison Games

(Gravity Of Devotion Book 2, Part 1)

"If you have a mind, you can create a prison." - Graves

*Amy Devine has fallen into a game...
I should be dead. Instead, I'm trapped in a nightmare—a prison with strangers, a cryptic teacher, and my best friend Demora—who I'm not even sure I can fully trust after what happened recently...
This prison is getting worse. The walls shift, reality fractures, and we're forced into twisted psychological games designed to strip us down to our core. Sanity is a fragile thing here, and mine is slipping fast.*

Something is wrong—something inside me. The only way out is to unlock the shadow of my aura and face whatever has been festering within me... before it takes control.

Let the Prison Games begin.

ii

ALSO BY W.K. PHOENIX (CON'T)

Peculiar Cases Of Something Devine:

Something That My Head Had Said

(Book 1)

What would you do if your small-but-actually medium-sized town was murder-free for decades…

… until they just stumbled on a double homicide…

… and you're afraid of death?

Amy Devine was just fine ignoring that. With the start of her Intermissionary school year and training with Gma nightly, there was no time to worry about the "problems of common folk". She needed to be the strongest she could be in order to tackle the dark forces when they may come. She only needs to master the newest aura technique, but that proves a lot more difficult than she anticipated; especially since Gma isn't giving her the necessary information she needs. After all, aura and soul are one. But when Amy finds herself literally thrown into the middle of the investigation, she can no longer ignore the madness happening around her…

… and inside of her.

"What's it gonna take to make you crack?"

COMING

Peculiar Cases Of Something Devine:

******

(Book 3)

?

Follow for updates and more...